T

SILENT

DAUGHTER

BY PHILIP ANTHONY SMITH

GET A **FREE BOOK** BY VISITING:

WWW.PHILIPANTHONYSMITH.COM

INSTAGRAM: @PHILIPSMITHFICTION
FACEBOOK: PHILIPSMITHFICTION
COPYRIGHT © 2025 PHILIP ANTHONY SMITH

CONTENTS

PROLOGUE 1

PART ONE

THE RELEASE 10
THE FRIENDS 18
THE LOVEBIRDS 27
THE BURDEN... 39
THE GATES.. 48
THE PARK 58
THE INTERVIEW 68
THE PROMISE 76
THE THIRST 86

PART TWO

THE WORD... 98
THE CANDLE 110
THE OUTING.. 120
THE BITCH 131
THE DRESS 141
THE HANGOVER... 152
THE INQUISITION 162
THE HOSPITAL 171
THE TUB...182
THE DATE 193
THE PANTRY 205
THE HOMECOMING 217
THE PARTY.. 228

PART THREE

THE LAKE	243
THE RESIGNATION	255
THE BREAK	267
THE PAINTING	278
THE SWAN	290
THE ROSE	301
THE SWING	313
THE DIG	325

PART FOUR

THE ACCIDENT	336
THE PUNISHMENT	347
THE SHAME	359
THE FUNDRAISER	372
THE BARGAIN	383
THE GOODBYES	395

PART FIVE

THE STRANGER	409
THE TUNNELS	421
THE NIGHTCAP	430
THE TRUTH	441
THE SCREAMING	451
THE PIER	451

EPILOGUE	471

PROLOGUE

ROBYN - BEFORE

Out of all the exclusive shops in Manchester's jewellery quarter, Baker and Roberts was one of the most luxurious. Plush leather seats. Crystal chandeliers. The delicate scents of leather and rose pushed around the room by the crisp air conditioning. A fragile piano concerto started to drift down from the overhead speakers, cutting through the noise, so I subtly bobbed my head along as the melody grew stronger. The lighting was warm, welcoming and low, casting a glow across all of the sprawling, immaculately clean glass cabinets housing treasures that a girl like me could only dream of owning.

As for the staff, well, they weren't exactly run off their feet.

To my left, an older man browsed the wristwatches, inspecting each one with a keen eye. From what I could gather, he'd created two piles: one he was intending to purchase and another that he'd rejected. I didn't know much about timepieces, but it was clear even to me that his 'keeper' pile was already into six figures, and he was showing no signs of stopping. To my right, there was a young couple, maybe five years older than me, giggling to each other while the man draped necklace after necklace over her neck. I tried eavesdropping, trying to work out whether it was his wife's birthday or even their anniversary, but regardless of the occasion, they seemed to be having the time of their lives.

Then, there was little old me: Robyn.

Like most twenty-one-year-olds, I had my insecurities, but I didn't scrub up half bad. I was wearing my best boots and a little black dress, made slightly damp by the Mancunian drizzle. My tatty jacket had taken the brunt of the downpour when I pulled it over my head as I ran into the store to protect my curls, and thankfully, the wave of chestnut hair over my right eye had survived, just thick enough to obscure the heart-shaped birthmark on my cheekbone. To my friends' collective irritation, the rest of my caramel skin was always glowing, blemish-free and baby soft, and I was never one for false eyelashes or heavy makeup either. In all honesty, I didn't know where they found the bloody time.

I suppose my defining feature was my tattoos. Mum disapproved, obviously, but I started getting them shortly after my eighteenth birthday, and it's safe to say that I got a little carried away. I had the makings of a sleeve on my left arm, stopping just after the elbow. They were pretty meaningless: line drawings of flowers and birds, wrapping around my forearm in a messy collage. I also had a large rose tattooed on my right hip, but I mostly kept that one covered up when I could. I was pretty sure the so-called 'artist' was half-cut when he did it.

I checked my phone. Still no word from Ellie. Typical.

"Is anything catching your eye?" the sales assistant asked me.

"Oh, I don't know! Can't I just take them all?" I joked, locking my phone.

She looked me up and down briefly. "If you'd like!"

Every ring, bracelet and necklace in the cabinet winked at me, desperate to be chosen. I had the time, so I pressed my palms against the glass to take a closer look, and the gems within sparkled as I rocked my head left and right to catch the glimmers. Although I couldn't afford a single thing in that cabinet, not by a long shot, the hopeful woman behind the counter didn't know that. To keep up the pretence, I slipped out a few dramatic 'ums' and 'aahs,' even stroking my chin to add authenticity, then pointed at one of the more extravagant pieces.

"Can I see that one?" I asked, tapping the glass with my fingernail.

"Fantastic choice!" she cheered.

Sally, the poor sales assistant who'd spent the better part of forty-five minutes parading every piece, flashed me a professional smile and licked her lips with fervour at the prospect of finally concluding the sale. Little did she know that all I wanted to do was kill a bit of time, maybe snap a few pictures for *The Gram* to keep up appearances, and then make up some excuse as to why I wasn't going to be completing the purchase when my friend showed up. Her name badge tilted as she ducked to fetch my selection, and as soon as she retrieved it, I popped my fake *Louis Vuitton* bag on the counter and slipped my prize onto my index finger. It was gorgeous. I extended my arm so I could watch it twinkle in the downlights.

"It really is a beautiful piece." She let out an exasperated sigh. "You have fantastic taste."

"Thank you!" I gushed, pulling out my phone to take photographs like a paparazzo on overdrive.

Oh my God. It was to die for.

From what little I remembered of Sally's sales patter, it was a twenty-two-carat gold band, like the dozen or so on either side of it. However, it was only when it was on my finger that, rather peculiarly, I noticed it wasn't a perfect circle. In fact, it had a strange and distinctive wave to it, like it was hundreds of years old with a history of its own. For a moment, I lowered my phone and wondered how many hands it had been on before, how many women had coveted it, and how the hell it had ended up on a finger like mine. I sucked in a breath when I spun it around my knuckle to unveil the real showstopper: the giant diamond embedded in it.

Fuck. I was in love.

"Hey, do you want to know what the best part is?" Sally chimed in.

I peered up and nodded keenly.

"Check the inside of the band," she said, almost with a measure of pride.

With a puzzled expression on my face, I slid it from my finger and looked inside, and lo and behold, there was a tiny ruby embedded within.

"It's a Kozlov. The designer always places a jewel inside that only you'd ever know about. Isn't that delightful?" she asked, raising her eyebrows.

"It *is* delightful!" I gasped in agreement.

"What do you think, then? Shall I box it up for you?"

Here it comes.

"Tell me—how much is it again?" I asked, slipping it back on for another shot.

"Just nine thousand!"

I swallowed hard, almost breaking character. "Right!"

"It's worth every penny, don't you think?"

Before I had a chance to conjure a believable justification to get me off the hook, I spotted what looked like the manager glaring at me out of the corner of my eye. Without thinking about it, I swivelled my head to the left to send a disarming look his way, but it dropped from my face when he seemed to see straight through my act. My upper lip immediately started sweating when I vaguely recognised him from one of my window-shopping trips a few weeks before, so I quickly averted my eyes before he put two and two together.

"Is something wrong?" Sally asked, leaning in.

"Nope," I dismissed, clearing my throat. "Not at all."

I already knew the jig was up when I heard him stomping over.

"Sally, this young lady is a time-waster, so wrap this up and deal with actual paying customers," the man announced with contempt.

"What? How dare you!" I exclaimed as believably as I could.

"You didn't think I'd remember, did you?" he said, turning to me. "I spent over an hour going through our entire stock only for you to tell me that you left your purse in your other trousers."

I stifled a chuckle. Looking back, it was one of my feebler excuses.

"Oh, you think this is funny, do you?" he remarked.

I chuckled. "A little, yes."

"Well, we're running a business, so get the hell out of here."

"Fine, I'll—"

"And take your fake bag, bogus designer gear and grubby boots with you."

"*Grubby*?" I repeated, aghast.

He dipped his head, folding his arms over his chest.

"Unbelievable!" I snapped before turning on my heels.

"Er—Miss?" he asked searchingly. "Aren't we forgetting something?"

I looked down at my hand and saw that the ring was still firmly positioned around my digit. I tugged, but my fingers had swollen due to embarrassment and refused to give it up. By the time I reached the counter again, it had barely budged a millimetre, so I continued struggling as the manager held out his hand expectantly for me to return it.

"Now, please," he urged.

"Can't you see I'm trying? Keep your bloody wig on."

Miraculously, the band gave way at long last, so I slammed it on the counter and met the manager's gaze with a wry grin, but something was wrong. His smarmy expression had vanished, replaced with one of total horror. It took me a split second to realise that he wasn't looking at me at all, but over my shoulder, so I followed his eye line, and his change of demeanour instantly made sense.

"Oh, fuck," I muttered.

The rest happened in the blink of an eye.

Someone was storming towards us, head to toe in black, face mask to match. Before I knew it, I was shoved out of the way and thrown on the floor, crab-walking away as they smashed the cabinet with a pipe. Glass became airborne. Alarms sounded. The staff backed into the wall with their hands up in surrender. I could do nothing but watch as the assailant stuffed their pockets with the treasures I'd been ogling only seconds before.

Then, something happened that I couldn't explain.

The thief stopped in their tracks and bent over to pick up the jewel that I'd been trying on from the shards on the floor. They took a single step towards me, stared at me for a breath, and then carefully put it in their pocket.

"This is *mine*," they spat.

Before I could respond, they were already sprinting for the exit. Behind the counter, the manager slammed a panic button, and I watched helplessly as steel shutters descended in the doorway, locking me inside a split second after the robber had slipped through the opening. I stayed still for a moment to get my bearings before I grabbed my bag and got back on my feet, clutching my elbow, waiting to observe what happened next. The manager reached for the phone and dialled three numbers, holding it to his ear as the line began to trill.

"Police! Please!" he said down the line. "I'm calling from Baker and Roberts on St Ann's Square—we've been robbed!"

"Sorry, but can I leave?" I asked Sally, hardly registering what I'd said. "I have somewhere to be."

"No—they escaped!" the manager barked down the line, turning his stare on me. "But we have their accomplice trapped in the store."

"*Accomplice?*" I gasped.

PART ONE

"LOST"

SIX YEARS LATER

1

THE RELEASE

ROBYN

Guilty. Can you believe it? To be honest, even after spending over half a decade locked up for a crime that I didn't commit, I couldn't believe it either.

The court case was a farce, where every corner of my life was dragged into the light over the course of four long days. I was innocent, simply in the wrong place at the wrong time, but that didn't matter to the prosecution. In fact, they threw everything but the kitchen sink at me, twisting every fact to fit their narrative. At first, the duty solicitor was pretty hopeful, especially considering that I hadn't broken a single law, and he was confident that the case would either be tossed out at best or end in a community order at worst.

He couldn't have been more wrong.

On day one, every single comment, caption and private message that I'd ever typed online became public record. Everything was carefully scrutinised and misconstrued to paint me as some kind of criminal mastermind, to the point where even I almost accepted their lies. Suddenly, the selfies taken inside Baker and Roberts were attempts to get photographs of camera placements. My long, drawn-out conversations with staff members were reconnaissance. My social media feed, filled with snaps of fake designer bags and clothes, was evidence of the proceeds. And the worst part? It was the tip of the iceberg.

As predicted, day two wasn't any better because the prosecution had the nerve to share my bank statements in open court. The jury heard that I'd been overdrawn for most of my adult life, so I had no legitimate reason to be in Baker and Roberts in the first place. As I didn't have a job to speak of, only caring for my mum, I was berated on the stand for what felt like hours about how I planned to even pay for anything. In spite of arguing until I was blue in the face that I was only there for a spot of window shopping and to meet a friend, it still didn't fly. At the end of the day, the jury was left thinking I was some scruff who was only out to make a fast buck.

By day three, I had a break from the stand because my character witnesses were called, but they were a bust, too. Half of them couldn't even be bothered to make an appearance, and the ones who did only made my situation worse. There was a particularly embarrassing moment when one of my so-called friends couldn't even recall my last name, so all the testimony that came after that was understandably ignored by the jury.

I understood why most of them didn't leap to my defence, but Ellie? I thought my best friend would've at least shown her face, even after how we'd left things.

Besides, she could've told them that I was waiting for her, and just her statement alone would've cleared my name. But she never returned my calls, or my solicitor's, for that matter.

Then, on day four, the final nail was hammered into the coffin.

My gut turned to stone when they dragged a trolley into the courtroom, an old television mounted on top, and that grainy CCTV footage that it played would stick with me until the day I died. It was of the robber, taking a moment between the carnage to talk to me. My solicitor argued that it was a random act by someone I'd never met, but the manager lied on the stand that the robber used my name when we spoke. The only thing that was more damning than that testimony and the footage was how I choked up when I was questioned about it under oath.

I was sentenced the day after.

Six miserable years.

But against all odds, I survived it, and I was finally getting out.

The discharge office was a ten-by-ten room, furnished with a long desk across the middle, and rows of shelving behind filled with brown paper bags. Sitting at the desk was a grumpy-looking officer, sporting a thick layer of stubble on his cheeks and propping his head with his hand. His eyes were bloodshot and unfocused, like he'd had a liquid lunch, and he didn't look at all pleased to see me. In fact, he barely lifted his eyes from the computer screen six inches away from his face.

I cleared my throat and stepped forward.

"Name?" the officer grunted without looking up.

"Robyn."

He sighed. "Your full name, please."

"Robyn Fletcher," I enunciated. "With a Y."

As though it caused him great physical pain, he removed his chin from his palm and started tapping away at the computer. My heart fluttered when he paused, his forehead creasing as he leaned back to interlock his fingers behind his head. Panic gripped me for a beat when I thought there'd been some massive clerical error and that I'd be swiftly escorted back to my cell, but the silence was broken by the ancient printer beside him clunking to life. He wheeled his chair over to whip the printout from the tray, then stuffed it in a brown envelope.

"Well, Miss Fletcher, it looks like your stay with us is officially over," he announced.

Relief hit me like a smack in the face.

"Thank fuck for that," I mouthed.

"Here are the possessions that you had when you were incarcerated here," he continued as he robotically emptied an oversized paper bag in front of me.

I looked down in humiliation as he dropped a few coppers on the counter, an uncharged mobile phone, a bracelet with my name engraved on it, a set of old keys, and a hot-pink makeup bag that I couldn't even remember the contents of. I rapidly scooped all of the items into my prison-issued plastic bag with the rest of my belongings, and then he proceeded to hand me my old leather jacket, along with a padded envelope with my prisoner number stamped on the front.

"What's this?" I asked, lifting it off the counter.

"That's your discharge pack," he replied.

"Okay?" I said, raising an eyebrow as I pulled on my jacket.

"On behalf of HMP Styal, we hope not to see you again. If you need any support after your release, there are some useful telephone numbers in the pack I've given you," he said, like he was reading from a script.

"Er—thanks," I uttered.

"You're free to leave," he said as he pointed behind me.

"Wait, that's it?" I asked in bemusement.

"Uh-huh," he grunted before returning his jaw to the safety of his hand.

I turned around and stumbled out of the room, almost bumping right into the guard who was still waiting for me in the corridor. Without a word, she marched over to the steel door on the exterior wall and unlocked it before taking a step back, gesturing me through. I reached out for the handle, but something stopped me, and I immediately pulled my hand back.

"Well? What are you waiting for?" she asked.

What *was* I waiting for?

I'd pictured getting out as some glittering prize and the light at the end of a very long, dark tunnel, but as I stood there with a plastic bag of junk, it didn't feel like freedom at all. If anything, it felt like starting a race six laps behind everyone else, with a lead weight on my back and my ankles strapped together. On the other side of that door, there were no officers telling me when to eat or sleep, and no bars keeping me penned in. Out there, every wrong step would be mine alone, and for the first time, I wasn't sure if I was ready for that.

When I first dreamt of my release, I imagined the warmth of the sun as I victoriously sauntered through the open prison gates, brandishing my middle finger over my shoulder to the place that confined me for so long. I pictured my friends lit up in joy with their arms held out, beckoning me over. One of them even had the foresight to bring a couple of beers, and we'd all share a cold one to toast my return to independence. Then, I'd be handed a pair of *Gucci* sunglasses as I hopped over a convertible car door into the passenger seat, and we'd all speed off to rejoice in my homecoming.

But it was bullshit, wasn't it?

There was no one waiting for me on the other side of that door, and why would they be? Deep down, my self-obsessed friends couldn't give a toss whether I lived or died. Case in point: I hadn't enjoyed a single visitor, taken a two-minute call, or even received a lousy letter from any of them in six years, so the notion that they'd mix with a convict now, innocent or otherwise, was absurd. In reality, the only person on earth who'd be caught dead waiting for me was Mum, but she was gone now, and I was almost glad that she wouldn't be there to witness the same walk of shame through the prison gates that she once made.

"I have got other places to be, you know?" the guard prompted.

"What am I meant to do out there?" I mumbled.

"I don't know, do I?" She pushed the door open. "Get a coffee, or something."

I peered through the doorway as the cold daylight stabbed into my eyes. As predicted, the whole place was devoid of life as far as the eye could see, apart from a man in a green jumpsuit, picking up litter in the corner of the car park. There was no sunshine, no rainbows and no welcome party: just drab buildings, grey skies and the drizzle soaking into the concrete. I looked over my shoulder at the guard, begging for one last instruction, and she begrudgingly obliged as she shoved me into the unknown like she was pushing me out of a plane without a parachute.

"Wait, I—" I began.

She didn't give me the opportunity to finish. The door was promptly slammed behind me—the full stop to my sentence.

The wind spat rain in my face as I turned back around to face the great unknown. Feeling almost naked in my too-thin jacket, I tugged the fabric closer around me and began walking towards the gates that ominously sprang open. Six years gone, and this was what my twenties amounted to: a plastic bag of junk, a criminal record, and a face I just about recognised in the mirror. Once I'd made my way through, I hastily took the envelope I was given out of my pocket to find a grand total of forty-six pounds inside and a few nauseatingly positive-looking pamphlets.

"The Sofia Blackthorn Foundation," I read with an incredulous laugh. "What a fucking joke."

I heard the gates ominously whirring behind me, so I turned back around to take one last look at the cage closing that had thrown me onto the streets. Feeling totally adrift, I trudged over to the mucky-looking bus stop outside the prison and then plonked myself down on the rain-beaten bench. The world spread out in front of me like a blank canvas, with the sprawling opportunities that it brought. However, at twenty-seven years old, with only forty-six quid in my pocket and the clothes on my back, it felt a hell of a lot smaller than it was.

There was a colourful, illuminated advert next to me, ramming some expensive perfume down my neck. It featured an impossibly skinny woman, elegantly clad in red silk as she suggestively sprayed her neck with an ornate bottle, and it brought back all the bitterness I'd buried over the years.

I decided it was time Ellie gave me some answers.

2

THE FRIENDS

ROBYN - BEFORE

Although I considered myself entirely straight, especially after ruling out a brief experimentation phase in my late teens, I still often found myself in Manchester's Gay Village on a Friday night. Out of all the bars, The Topaz Tipple was a firm favourite of mine, and I knew that once I was settled in, I'd be pickling a few vital organs for fun into the small hours of Saturday morning. There was something much less intimidating about drinking there because, as you can imagine, most of the blokes partying weren't in the least bit interested in me, and the women were a hell of a lot more respectful and far less handsy. Besides, it was fun, vibrant, and a welcome distraction from the humdrum reality of my situation.

The real reason I chose Canal Street itself was simpler: I always went out alone.

It wasn't through choice but necessity because I literally had no one to go out drinking with. It'd started gradually: Kirsty moved down to Coventry for university, Amy did a gap year, which turned into five, and slowly but surely, the rest of my friends drifted away in similar ways until we'd all lost touch. It didn't help that I hadn't gone to university myself, mainly because we couldn't afford it, but also because Mum required round-the-clock care following her accident. After what we'd been through, there was no doubt in my mind that her affliction was pure evil, and it clearly wasn't content in eventually taking my mother's life as she knew it from her. It had to snatch my youth along with it.

I took another sip of the Cosmopolitan I was nursing to remind myself that Friday night was *my* night. Like every week, I was determined not to spend it wallowing in self-pity, even though I was staring down the barrel of another six days of attending to my mother's every need. To be honest, I was grateful for the diversion when the latest gaggle of screaming girls burst into the joint, so I swivelled around on my stool to watch them giggling and joking as they boogied across the dancefloor. They were regulars at The Topaz Tipple too, yet they usually had a couple of cocktails apiece before taking their high-pitched voices and no-fucks-given attitude to somewhere a little livelier.

As usual, the ringleader splintered off from the pack and began stumbling over to order some drinks. She was a stereotypical hot blonde with an evident weakness for massive false eyelashes, skin-tight minidresses, and singing '*Girls Just Want to Have Fun*' at the top of her lungs. When she drunkenly arrived beside me, her shoulder accidentally bumped mine, spilling a dash of my bright-red cocktail onto my white dress. I moved my glass away to stop further spillage as she turned to me with an apologetic expression on her face, grabbing my arm with both hands.

"Oh my God!" she drawled. "I'm so sorry, babe!"

"It's fine, honestly," I grumbled, swiping some of the liquid off my thigh.

"No—let me get you another!" she said before leaning over the counter. "Barman!"

I opened my mouth to object, but buttoned it back up again. In truth, I'd been waiting for an opportunity to speak to her for ages.

"You're Ellie Fairfax, right?" I asked, grabbing some tissues to soak up the stain.

"I am," she admitted, furrowing her brow. "Have we met before?"

"No, not that I can remember." I shook my head. "I think I follow you on Instagram."

Her eyes lit up. "Oh, really?"

Ellie had one of those fashionable and mindful wellness profiles. It was packed with artsy shots of flat whites in back-street coffee shops in Manchester, the occasional contrived image of her at a shooting range in tight leggings, and pictures of super-food salads that weren't fit for human consumption. Although she had over twenty thousand followers who ate her content right up, I was seemingly the only one who didn't. In fact, the only reason I was even on that list in the first place was because she'd tagged herself in The Topaz Tipple a few times, and I got nosy. I couldn't help wondering what her health-conscious fans would think of her getting pissed up on a Friday night and then probably savaging a greasy kebab afterwards.

"Yeah! I loved the post about green juice curing cancer!" I said as convincingly as possible. "Real inspirational stuff."

"Right! I'm trying to spread awareness!" she announced with pomposity. "All this shit we put in our bodies, it isn't right, is it?"

I smiled. "Well, you're doing a great job."

"Hey, I didn't catch your name?" she said, suddenly interested in me.

"Robyn."

"What are you drinking?"

"Er—a Cosmo," I replied.

Ellie closed one eye and spun around, counting each of her party on her fingers before turning to the barman who'd arrived to take her request.

"Five Cosmopolitans," she instructed. "And make it snappy."

"Coming right up," he said, shooting me a look to criticise Ellie's lack of manners.

"What do you do?" Ellie asked me.

"Er—I work in fashion," I said, the lie rolling off my tongue.

"Really? That's so cool." She grinned. "Where do you work?"

"I can't say," I mustered, playing with my hair. "I've got to keep it on the down low."

Ellie's eyes widened into saucers as if I'd revealed I worked for MI6.

"*Chanel?*" she asked, sitting down and resting her chin on her hand.

I allowed the silence to answer for me.

"Dior?"

"Honestly, I can't—"

"It's not *Cartier*, is it?" she interrupted.

I flashed her a knowing smile, hoping that it would be enough to put an end to her incessant guessing game.

"I can neither confirm nor deny," I added for effect.

"Shit!" she let out. "Bitch, I think you're my new best friend."

"It's nothing really, I just—"

"Girls!" she squealed over her shoulder. "Come and meet Robyn!"

* * *

Sweet Mary and Joseph. Those girls drank like they didn't want to live.

I didn't know how they were still standing after a few rounds of increasingly potent cocktails, followed by even more, then a tray of garishly coloured shots, and finally topped off with a batch of tequilas. I had a two-drink maximum most nights, chiefly because I couldn't justify spending a fortune on overpriced drinks when we had so little to begin with, but also because the mere thought of a hangover was enough to turn my stomach. With that in mind, it was pretty handy that the girls were so mindlessly plastered that they didn't notice me switching glasses with their empties to avoid getting soused myself, so unlike them, I was still in control of my faculties.

After spending a few hours with Ellie and the girls, it was becoming abundantly clear to me that each of them was more brainless than the last. Kait worked in sales and marketing, which was a fancy way of saying she utilised her massive fake knockers to convince weak men to buy whatever crap she was peddling that week. She'd spent the night snapping selfies, whereas Sydney kept yammering on to me about some huge deal she was on the precipice of closing, like I gave a toss, and I only realised that she worked in property when she went as far as to ram one of her listings in my face on her phone. Allisyn, the most conservatively dressed of the group, was an alleged influencer like Ellie, and pretty much forced me on pain of death to follow her after bizarrely taking the time to tell me how unusual the spelling of her name was.

Despite being one of the most obnoxious groups of young women I'd ever met, there was something stopping me from leaving. To tell the truth, I didn't know why I pretended to be like them when I wasn't, but just being in their orbit made me feel almost normal, and I even found myself admiring the fact that they didn't have a care in the world. They simply sauntered around like money grew on trees and that nothing mattered beyond where they'd get their latest picture to impress their followers with. It seemed a much simpler existence than mine.

"Robyn! You haven't passed out in there, have you?" Sydney slurred through the cubicle door.

"No," I muttered. "I'm just finishing up."

"Get out here!" she barked, banging on the door.

Much to my annoyance, they had this strange habit of all visiting the loos together, and I was dragged there every time one of the girls heard nature's call. Given how much they'd put away, the trips were constant, so I was having a breather on the heavily graffitied toilet with my knickers around my ankles for appearances' sake, counting tiles. When I emerged from the cubicle, the girls were in front of the large mirror above the bank of washbasins, drunkenly fixing their hair and makeup for the umpteenth time that evening, so I strode over to the sink to the left of them to wash my hands.

Just as I turned the tap, I heard an exaggerated sniffing noise coming from their direction, so I awkwardly bobbed my head around to see what was going on. To my horror, it looked like Allisyn was chopping up some white powder with her dad's credit card in full view of the other occupants, right there on the side of a sink. I started mentally preparing a list of excuses as to why I wouldn't be able to partake, yet it was made entirely redundant a few beats later when Kait hoovered up every particle.

"You fucking bitch!" Allisyn cried out, shoving Kait's back.

"What?" Kait replied, shaking her head violently.

"Was that the last of the damned coke?"

Kait nodded almost involuntarily.

"For fuck's sake," Allisyn groaned. "I was saving that for Robyn!"

"I'm good, actually," I pointed out, juddering my head.

"Don't be silly," she said dismissively, nudging Ellie. "Can you see if your contact can drop any off?"

"You mean her boyfriend?" Kait and Sydney said almost in unison.

"Piss off!" Ellie snapped before shaking her head in laughter. "I'll text him, okay?"

"Hey, aren't we calling it a night soon?" I chimed in. "It's almost midnight."

My words hung in the air, everyone giving me dirty looks like I'd suggested we should take a taxi down to the nearest monastery and become nuns.

"Or not," I added.

After a brief text message exchange in the toilets, Allisyn calmed down, and before I knew it, we were waiting out in the cold for Ellie's supposed dealer to arrive. Sydney immediately lit a cigarette as soon as we hit the open air, and I had to listen to the rest of the girls berating her for maintaining a nicotine habit, despite their eyes looking like piss-holes in the snow. I started to feel like I'd made a massive mistake in allowing myself to be near them, so I was trying to formulate a passable excuse so I could leave, when a new Range Rover with blacked-out windows pulled over on the kerb in front of us.

"Finally!" Ellie announced before sauntering over, whipping her hips left and right like she was gracing a catwalk.

With Ellie's back turned, I thought it was the perfect moment to say my goodbyes, but when the car window wound down and I recognised the driver, I pressed my lips back together. Without taking my eyes off him, I bumped Sydney's arm with the back of my hand to get her attention and leaned in slightly before pointing over to the fancy vehicle parked a few metres away from us.

"Who's that?" I asked, numb.

"Lucas," she replied, shaking her head. "He's a piece of shit."

"What's his last name?"

"Blackthorn," she added. "Have you met him before?"

"No," I mumbled.

The name cut into my mind like a shard of glass.

Perhaps meeting Ellie and her friends wasn't a mistake at all.

Maybe it was *fate*.

3

THE LOVEBIRDS

ROBYN

It was raining sideways by the time I arrived at Ellie's apartment building, so I had my shabby jacket pulled over my head to shield me from the volley as I jabbed the buzzer with my thumb. On the bus ride into Manchester city centre, it did occur to me that it had been six years since the last time I'd visited her, so it was entirely possible that she could have long since moved. However, when I saw the slip of paper with her name scrawled on it, punctuated by the juvenile love heart in place of the dot above the 'I' in her name, I knew my trip wasn't in vain.

"For Christ's sake, come on!" I barked into the intercom. "I'm getting piss-wet through here!"

Although I didn't know Ellie that well, I never thought to ask how she could afford an apartment in central Manchester to begin with, let alone one in the heart of the Northern Quarter overlooking Canal Street where we first met. She lived a stone's throw away from the city's best bars and clubs, and although the noise alone would drive most people to madness, it didn't bother her most of the time because she was usually drinking herself into oblivion with the rest of the reprobates. The thing that I was most jealous about was that her building had a complimentary gym in the basement. Not that she ever needed to use it because she was one of those people with an annoyingly fast metabolism.

Lucky bitch.

"Ellie! It's Robyn. Answer the bloody door!" I shouted at the speaker in the hope that she'd hear me.

There was a strange crackle as if someone were on the other end of the line, so I pressed my forehead against the panel in defeat.

"Please," I added. "I've got nowhere else to go."

To my surprise, the door buzzed and unlocked, so I put my weight against it to push it open. Ellie's apartment was on the fourth floor, and the residents in that building considered themselves far too important to debase themselves by traipsing up a set of stairs, so I strode over to the lift and pressed the button to call it. After a few moments of humming, it pinged as it arrived, and an impossibly good-looking couple decked out in gym wear sauntered out of it, looking down on me like I was some weather-beaten rodent who'd tottered through the front door uninvited. I allowed them to pass before I stepped inside, then hit the button for Ellie's floor.

As it whirred into action, I leaned against the handrail, peering into the mirror beside me and trying to pull a thick piece of hair to cover my birthmark. My hair was wet through and wouldn't play ball, so I ended up defeatedly combing it back with my fingernails instead. Once I was on her floor, I wasted no time and marched down the short corridor to her flat and bashed on the letterbox with the heel of my hand.

"What are you doing here, Robyn?" I heard Ellie's voice meekly coming through the door.

"We need to talk," I replied.

"I'm a little… indisposed right now. Can you come back later?"

"Open the damn door, El!" I pleaded.

"Fine," she snapped. "Give me a minute."

I stepped back from the door with my hands on my hips. I waited almost a whole minute until my patience wore thin, then lunged forward to smash on the door again, but it swung open before I got the chance. Ellie retreated, propping herself up against the wall and tugging a loosely tied silk robe around herself that scarcely went beyond her thighs. The shade was perfectly paired with her vermilion-coloured nail varnish, which matched her lipstick, smudged well into her cheek. Her golden-blonde hair was all over the place as though she'd been dragged through a hedge backwards, and one of her false eyelashes was hanging on by a thread.

"What the fuck was all that about?" I asked as I strode in.

"Like I said, I was busy," she retorted.

"It's been six years, El. The least you can do is open the door for me."

"Well, you're here now, aren't you?"

I exhaled through my nose sharply. "I am."

"Well?" She threw her hands up. "What is it?"

I parted my lips to speak, but I quickly realised what had been going on when I heard heavy footsteps coming from Ellie's bedroom, and my heart almost burst through my ribcage when a devilishly handsome man stumbled through the doorway.

It was Lucas. Lucas Blackthorn.

Although he was a little older, I instantly recognised him not only from the image that was plastered all over the hideously positive leaflet from my discharge pack, but also because his smug little face was forever seared into my memory. He was midway through putting his *Ralph Lauren* T-shirt on as he approached Ellie, delaying pulling it down long enough for both of us to see his washboard abs. Once it was on, he slid his hand around her hips, then planted an amorous kiss on her lips as if I wasn't in the room with them.

I couldn't believe that Lucas and Ellie were still in touch after so many years. To tell the truth, they had a rocky connection to say the least, but it was plain to see that their association had evolved far beyond the casual arrangement they had before I was banged up. He flashed me an awkward grin for a moment, obviously embarrassed that I'd forced my way inside whilst he was getting his end away. However, after a moment of scrutinising my appearance, a strange flicker formed in his eyes, and then the colour drained from his face as though he'd seen a ghost.

Shit. He *did* recognise me. How could he not?

"Hey, it's Robyn, isn't it?" he asked with a furrowed brow.

I hugged my chest and nodded.

"I haven't seen you in ages. What happened to you?"

"Prison," Ellie interjected, as flat as a pancake.

"Ouch," he mouthed.

"Ellie!" I exclaimed.

"What?" she said defensively. "It's the truth, isn't it?"

"Well, it's nice to meet you… again," Lucas said to me, offering his hand.

"You too," I mumbled as I begrudgingly shook it.

After a split second of staring, he thankfully seemed to lose interest in me. He ran his fingers through his dishevelled, black hair before grabbing his pair of tan *Berluti* shoes from the floor to put them on. I let out a sigh of relief as I shot Ellie a sideways glance, but she ignored me in favour of keeping her eyes on him with a flirtatious smirk curling the corners of her lips.

"You don't have to leave, you know," she told him as if I didn't exist.

"I know, but I need to get going anyway." He smiled, tying his shoelaces.

"Another drug delivery, perhaps?" I said under my breath.

"What was that?" he asked, wincing.

"Nothing," I dismissed.

"Listen, I'll call you later, okay, babe?" he said to Ellie, getting up to kiss her neck.

"You'd better!" she gushed, playfully batting him on the shoulder.

"I will!" he responded with a laugh before turning to me. "See you around, Robyn."

"*Adios*," I said as casually as I could.

Lucas pushed past me with a clumsy sneer, and as soon as he stepped into the lift, Ellie rapidly fluttered her lashes at me. It was evident that she was trying to goad me into giving her some forced compliment about who I'd seen stumbling out of her boudoir, but I couldn't bring myself to stroke her ego. I turned around to close the door behind him while shaking my head in contempt.

"You clearly have something to say, so why don't you stop beating around the bush and come out with it?" she asked.

"Okay then," I said flatly, turning to face her. "Are you for real?"

"What?" she said with confusion.

"I've been gone for years, and the first thing you want to discuss is your sex life?"

Without muttering a word, Ellie rolled her eyes and turned on her heel before flouncing straight through to the kitchen. By the time I'd followed her inside, she was brushing some of the designer shopping bags sitting on the dining table out of the way with her arm and then setting two wine glasses in their place. She poured us both a hefty measure, but I declined, pushing my glass away as I perched on the edge of one of the chairs. She shrugged, shooting me a look that said 'more for me' as she drank like she was dying of thirst.

"Some people never change, do they?" I asked.

"What's that supposed to mean?" she demanded, almost offended.

"I don't know—all this designer gear strewn on your dining table, in bed with that piece of shit, and now you're cracking open a bottle of wine when it's not even lunchtime?"

"He's not a piece of shit," she mocked. "Don't forget that I've known him longer than I've known you."

"And here's me thinking he was just your drug dealer," I remarked.

"Oh, Robyn, he was never *just* my drug dealer," she corrected, narrowing her eyes.

"Well, you could've both fooled me."

"He's one of the most eligible bachelors in Manchester, and his family is filthy-fucking-rich," she boasted.

"So what? Is he your boyfriend now or something?" I asked probingly.

"*Boyfriend?*" she scoffed. "Yes, we're courting with the intention of marrying in the spring."

A deep sigh escaped me before I could stop it, so I instinctively went for my glass, taking a gulp as I carefully considered what I was there to ask her. My first sip of alcohol after six years of abstaining was nothing short of a taste sensation.

"So, come on then. Why didn't you show up to the hearing?" I asked matter-of-factly.

She blew out a puff of air. "I don't know."

"I *needed* you, Ellie, and you couldn't even be bothered to show up? What the fuck?"

"Listen, for what it's worth, I wanted to. I did, but—"

"But what?" I interrupted.

"I mean—armed robbery? What the hell did you get mixed up in, Robyn?"

"I didn't do it!" I said firmly. "For a start, I was waiting for you! What did you think happened, huh? I got bored and decided to hold up the place?"

"Well, you got convicted of it, didn't you?"

"And in your eyes, that automatically means I'm guilty?"

Ellie grimaced, which I took to mean she did think I was indeed responsible.

"How could you think I was even capable of that?" I exclaimed.

"It wasn't only that, though, was it? Everyone found out that you're broke and—"

"So what?" I interjected.

"You were *lying* to us, Robyn. You made everyone believe that you had this high-flying lifestyle, working in fashion, but it was all bullshit, wasn't it?"

I picked up my glass and drained every drop. "Listen, I've made mistakes, okay?" I started.

"I'll say," she murmured.

"But I had nothing to do with what happened in the jeweller's," I continued. "You have to believe that."

"I don't know what to believe."

"Believe *me*."

Ellie allowed my words to hang without response as she crossed her legs and peered out of the window reflectively.

"I just need—" I paused to take a breath. "I need a favour."

"A favour?" she asked, crinkling her forehead. "What?"

"Can I stay here a few nights while I get back on my feet?"

Ellie's eyes widened, and she reached for the wine again to top up her glass, leaving mine unfilled.

"Can't you try one of the other girls?" she asked as delicately as she could muster.

"They wouldn't give me the time of day," I muttered.

"Sydney might have some apartments available," she suggested.

"Yeah, right! I can't afford any of those."

"What about your parents?"

I deflated a little. "Still dead."

"Shit—sorry." She shifted around in her seat. "There must be someone else, though!"

"You were my best friend, Ellie. If you turn me down, then I have nowhere else to go."

She grimaced. "Best friend? *Really*? We barely knew each other when you got sentenced."

I buried my head in my hands. "Please. I'm on the bones of my arse here."

"Surely the prison can help you find somewhere. They won't have tossed you back out onto the street without at least something."

I inhaled deeply through my nose before I heatedly grabbed the discharge pack and slammed it between our glasses.

"They gave me a bunch of useless leaflets and forty-six quid," I announced, aloof.

"Wow," she gasped.

"And I spent a fiver of that getting here," I added.

"But wait!" she said, almost excitedly. "What about this?"

Ellie plucked one of the leaflets from the stack, the one entitled 'The Sofia Blackthorn Foundation,' and then tapped on it with her fingertip.

"This is Lucas' family. They can help you!" she explained.

"Absolutely not," I dismissed. "Over my dead body."

"No, Robyn! This is perfect!"

"What are you harping on about?"

"Lucas is always moaning that they don't have enough staff on the estate. He could get you a job in the kitchens or something."

"You want me to *work* for them?" I tittered. "You've got to be kidding."

"What choice do you have? Besides, they even provide accommodation."

"No, I can't," I said, throwing my head back. "I've got a criminal record, El. They wouldn't touch me with a bargepole."

"Are you joking?" she scoffed.

"What?"

"Half of that family probably has a record!" She chortled. "Besides, just don't tell them, dummy."

I knew precisely what Ellie was plotting when she reached for her phone, so I tried to yank it from her grasp, but she moved it out of my reach before managing to fire a text message off.

"What the hell have you done now?" I asked, my jaw agape.

"Solving your problem."

"El! No!" I yelled.

Her phone chimed a minute later, and a smile broke out on her face.

"There you go, all done," she said victoriously. "Lucas said to call round at the house later, isn't that great?"

I instantly felt sick, staring down at the leaflet still in my grasp. "I don't know what to—"

"You don't have to thank me, honey!" she drawled. "What are friends for, anyway?"

I grabbed Ellie's glass and took a swig to calm my nerves.

"Make yourself at home while I grab a shower, and then I'll drop you off after, okay?"

"Er—yeah." I bobbed my head. "Sure."

"This will be good for you." She placed a hand on mine. "I promise."

She jumped out of her seat and left the room, leaving me transfixed on the portrait of the Blackthorns on the front of the leaflet. I hadn't told the truth to Ellie—I knew exactly who they were. In fact, after seeing Lucas at the roadside on the night that I met her, I made it my mission to find out absolutely everything about them. I thought that six years locked away would've been long enough to put them from my mind, but all roads seemed to lead back to the Blackthorns, and somehow, I was right back where I left off.

I couldn't think of anything worse than stepping into their home, in their employ.

Mum was probably turning in her grave about me even contemplating it.

Yet, it was *exactly* where I needed to be.

4

THE BURDEN

ROBYN - BEFORE

After quite a bit of practice, I'd become pretty good at sneaking back into our tiny two-bedroomed flat in Salford in the small hours, even after a heavy night out with Ellie and her merry band of drunken troublemakers. It hadn't escaped my notice that my usual Friday night respite from looking after Mum had leaked into Saturday evening, and on occasion, Sunday. But I was just enjoying it while it lasted. It was only a matter of time before I inevitably made a mistake and gave up the game, or one of them realised that I hadn't prised open my purse once to pay for a single round.

It went without saying that Mum didn't know how I was spending my evenings. Although my body was well and truly broken after such a heavy weekend of binge drinking, I still always made sure that I was up and ready for when she woke up. She needed me, and I was the only one there for her, so it didn't sit right with me to allow my quarter-life crisis to get in the way of her care.

The memory of the day I got the news was seared into my mind forever.

I'd been sitting one of my final exams at college, totally unaware that Mum was lying unconscious at Salford Royal Infirmary, fighting for her life after being run down by a drunk driver in the streets of Manchester. One of my tutors had pulled me from the sports hall and delicately explained to me that Mum was awaiting emergency spinal surgery in a desperate bid to save her life, so I had no option but to drop what I was doing and go to be at her bedside. She may have escaped the ordeal with her life, but a dozen surgeries and about a thousand hours of physiotherapy later, we were told that she'd never walk again.

Even though I was studying fashion and textile design, I genuinely didn't have any idea of what I wanted to do with my life after I left. However, it definitely wasn't becoming strong enough to lift my mother in and out of bed every day. It wasn't learning how to insert a catheter or dealing with the emotional toll that all of that brought, either. The first year was rough, *really* rough, and to be honest, I thought that we wouldn't make it. But after the initial shock wore off, we eventually got over the sheer indignity and depression of it, and I quickly forgot that my life was headed anywhere else at all.

Before I even thought about entering our flat, I took a deep breath in an attempt to steady my drunken hands for long enough to get the key in the lock, then slowly slid it into the chamber. Once I began to turn the key, I put some weight behind the door until it clicked, then pushed my way inside, careful not to let it bang against the shoe cabinet fitted directly behind it. After I made it past the doormat, I remained motionless for a moment, trying to listen out to hear if Mum was snoring away in bed and if the coast was clear, but to my horror, I heard the television blaring instead. Feeling like I'd been caught out, I quietly kicked off my heels and tiptoed through to the kitchen to grab a glass of water, hoping it would dilute the stench of vodka emanating from my mouth on the off chance that she was still awake.

"Robyn?" I heard her call as soon as my hand clasped the tap. "Is that you?"

Shit.

I half-filled my glass and strode through to the living room after a few gulps, doing my best to walk in a straight line. Mum was inexplicably sitting in her wheelchair, clearly half-asleep in front of the late-night reruns of some sitcom from way before my time.

There were times when I barely recognised her from the woman who raised me. Given her Jamaican heritage, her skin was much darker than mine, dry and cracked, and filled with pockmarks. She used to wear braids, but ever since her accident, she favoured a durag instead to keep the frizz under control. The only thing that was the same was her eyes: warm, welcoming, and mostly brown with little specks of gold near the pupils. Considering her condition, it wasn't much of a surprise that her arms were a lot bulkier since the accident, but her legs were nothing more than withered sticks, usually kept underneath a blanket to keep them warm.

Already suffering the sting of guilt for leaving her alone for so long, I took a cursory glance at the clock and saw that it was almost 3 am. Yet, instead of the face of thunder I was expecting when I turned back, she had a strange grin on her face, which made me narrow my eyes in bewilderment.

"Mum? How the hell did you get out of bed?" I asked.

"I'm not a total invalid!" she joked. "I couldn't sleep, so I pulled myself into the chair."

"You could've hurt yourself," I muttered. "What are you even doing up?"

"Never mind me, what are *you* doing up?" she repeated back to me with an arched eyebrow.

I rubbed my neck. "Er—I was just meeting with some friends."

"Did you meet them in a bar, perhaps?" she probed with a wicked smile.

"Why do you ask?"

"Because I can smell the booze on your breath from here!"

Well, that was me rumbled.

It reminded me of when I'd get blackout drunk in some random field with my friends when I wasn't even of legal drinking age, and I'd stumble back in at some ungodly hour, thinking that I could get away with it. Mum was still on her feet back then, so she'd give me the bollocking of a lifetime, and I'd promise never to do it again. But, of course, I had forgotten all about it by the following weekend.

"Listen, I won't see them again, okay?" I said, rushing to her side. "I promise."

"You bloody will!" she responded, craning her neck to face me.

"What?" I gasped in shock.

"I think it's absolutely fantastic you've finally got someone to go out with."

"But what about you?"

"Me?" she said, breaking eye contact. "I'm fine."

"You are not fine, Mum."

"I am, and I refuse to allow you to spend every waking moment looking after me in these four walls any longer."

"I like looking after you!"

"Don't bullshit a bullshitter!" she chuckled. "We'll get some help around the place if we have to."

"We can't afford that," I objected, tightening the blanket around her legs.

"Come on then, who are they?"

I rocked back onto my ankles. "My friends?"

She nodded keenly.

"They're just a group of girls I met at that bar I go to sometimes."

"Do these girls have names?" she asked, struggling to lean forward in her chair.

"Ellie, Kait, Sydney and Allisyn."

"Are they nice?"

I instinctively shook my head whilst muttering, "Yeah."

Mum leaned back again with a grin on her face, letting out a little wistful exhale through her nose whilst bobbing her head left and right. However, after a few moments, her face turned, and her bottom lip started quivering, so I stretched over, stacking my hands over hers.

"What is it?" I murmured.

"Nothing," she dismissed with a teary smile.

"Mum?" I demanded, widening my eyes.

She stayed silent for a time, peering at the television with glazed-over eyes. "It's just—I'm going to be gone one day, and it makes me happy to know—"

"Will you stop saying stuff like that, please?" I interrupted.

"It's grim, but it's the truth. I need to know that you're going to be okay without me."

"No," I dismissed. "I don't want to think about that."

"I know you don't, love, but we have to."

I felt a tear rolling down my cheek, and Mum promptly turned around and then reached out to wipe it away with her thumb.

"Oh, Robyn," she uttered, her voice breaking. "I'm so sorry."

"For what?"

"This," she said, gesturing around the room. "You never asked for any of it."

"It wasn't your fault, Mum," I murmured. "It was an accident."

"I know it was, but why should you have to pay for it?" she asked. "It's not fair."

I dropped back onto my shins with a defeated groan. "We'll get through it. We always do."

That seemed to give her great comfort.

"I'm just—" she began before clearing her throat. "I'm just so proud of you, you know?"

The word 'proud' hurt more than it should've. Would she really be proud if she knew that I'd befriended four binge-drinking trollops, who spent their evenings bitching about their other friends and getting high as kites? Would she be full of pride if she found out that I'd lied through my teeth to worm my way into that friendship group in the first place? And above all else, would she be pleased that I was mostly continuing it in an effort to get closer to the Blackthorns, of all people? No, she wouldn't be proud of me. She'd be utterly disgusted.

"Thanks, Mum," I said in spite of myself. "Come on, I'll get you to bed. You must be shattered."

I released the brake of her chair and pushed myself up, but she immediately slammed her hands on the tyres to stop me.

"Don't bloody wheel me off! I'm not finished talking!"

I yawned. "Can't it wait until morning?"

"God, I'm such a burden, aren't I?" she remarked, rolling her eyes.

I sighed deeply. "You aren't a burden, okay?"

"Oh yeah?" she jested. "Tell me, how are you going to get me in bed again?"

"I'll lift you up, like always," I said, shrugging.

She let her droll grin do the talking.

I rocked my head incredulously. "You're in an odd mood tonight."

I continued to field questions about my evening on the short trip through to Mum's bedroom, and after I got her safely tucked up in bed, the inquisition continued. While I didn't have any illness to speak of, my eyelids were getting heavier by the second, yet Mum was still absolutely wired, hanging on every word as I regaled her with the heavily redacted tales of my sly nights out. She seemed to be living vicariously through my stories, and although it was nice to see her smile for the first time in weeks, it was becoming apparent that I wasn't going to be able to stay awake much longer.

"Anyway, it's late. You'd better get some rest," I said, yawning.

"What are you going to do?" she asked.

"Get in bed. I'm knackered."

"By the way, I think we're out of that Prega-what's-it."

"Pregabalin," I corrected.

"That's the one."

"I'll call the doctor in the morning," I said, giving her a kiss on the forehead. "Night, Mum."

"Night, love." She smiled.

I pushed myself off the floor, turned off the lamp, and shut the door behind me. I could still hear the television blaring in the living room, so I went inside to try to find the remote to turn it off. I eventually discovered it strewn on the floor beside the fireplace, so I squatted down and hit the red button. I placed it on top of the mantelpiece and picked up the photograph displayed in the centre.

There were almost a dozen people featured on it, but my eye was drawn to Mum, a few faces to the left. It was taken about a year before her accident, back when she still had a job and the use of her legs. She was wearing a black and white tunic, tied around the waist with a white ribbon, and standing beside others who were all dressed the same. In the centre of the frame was the Blackthorn family, arms wrapped around each other and toothy grins as if butter wouldn't melt.

Mum was a proud woman, so she never asked for help, even from me. Yet surely, if she told the Blackthorns what had become of her after she stopped working on their estate, they would jump at the chance to help us. With their endless wealth, they could drag us out of this cesspit. They could put an end to our misery because they had the kind of money that could make any problem disappear.

I just needed to get close enough to them to make it happen.

5

THE GATES

ROBYN

Despite the weather being bone dry, it was still bitterly cold, even more so considering that Ellie was insistent that we kept the roof of her soft-top convertible down for the drive out to the Blackthorn Estate. We pulled outside of a set of nondescript wrought-iron gates, and she peered into the mirror at once, fixing her windswept hair. I stared down the dark road, presumably leading to the main house. I squinted my eyes, trying to make out a single building through the thick treeline beside the road, but all I saw was darkness. Ellie had taken immense pleasure in telling me how disgustingly moneyed they were on the ride over, as though her association with them was something to brag about. However, it wasn't the imposing, dramatic entrance that she'd described. It was just some rusted gates in the middle of nowhere.

"Wait—is this it?" I asked, scrunching up my face.

"Uh-huh," she hummed while reapplying her red lipstick.

"I thought you said they were mega-rich? This looks like some grotty cut-through."

"Oh, honey!" she drawled. "You've never been to a place like this before, have you?"

"That remains to be seen," I mumbled. "What are we even waiting for, anyway?"

"Harris to get off his lazy arse and open the gates," she uttered back.

"Who the hell is Harris?" I asked, my cheeks flushing.

"The gamekeeper."

"Gamekeeper?" A stiff chuckle escaped my lips. "You're kidding, right?"

Ellie threw her arms down in defeat and turned to me, almost appearing like she was annoyed by my list of sensible questions.

"Listen, these people—they've been wealthy since the dawn of time."

"So, what?" I argued.

"So, when we go through those gates, please *try* and act like you belong there, okay?" she instructed. "No stupid questions. No snide remarks."

"Fine," I snapped. "I'll behave."

"I think this is him," she said as she turned the key in the ignition again.

I peered over to the entrance, and sure enough, Harris was dragging open the gates so we could drive through. He must've been allergic to any fabric other than tweed because he was decked out from head to toe in it. In fact, he looked like he'd just stepped out of a cover spread of *Posh Twats Weekly,* even down to the fitted waistcoat with the gold pocket watch hanging from it. Without even acknowledging his presence, Ellie slowly negotiated her way through the tight opening, and I turned my head from his stalwart gaze as we passed through. Once we were clear, he closed the gates behind us, and we hit the cobbled road beyond it. She accelerated, the car jolting from side to side along the uneven track.

"Do you know him?" I asked.

"Who?"

"*Mr Tweedy* back there."

"No," she dismissed. "I don't fraternise with the help."

"Delightful," I commented.

"Don't be so immature. You get what I mean."

I sighed, feeling my nerves getting the better of me. "Are you sure I can't crash on your couch for a few nights?"

"Trust me: this is better. You want to rebuild your life, don't you?" she asked, shamelessly quoting the leaflet.

I pulled a face. "Why are you so adamant that I do this?"

"Sorry?"

"I don't know—it's just all happening so quickly."

She sighed defeatedly. "I'm just trying to help, Robyn."

"I guess."

After thirty seconds or so, the road opened up, the treeline thinned out, and my heart was in the pit of my stomach again when I saw the house in the distance. Ellie's description was bang on the money: it was astounding. The main house was built from sandstone, with immaculately preened ivy crawling up the walls around the leaded windows. The grand oak doors sat atop some stone steps, with the Blackthorn emblem carved into the rock above. My jaw dropped when I saw a few peacocks strolling across the lawn, brazenly grazing on the flawlessly kept grass and totally unperturbed by Ellie's extravagant motor rumbling past them. We stopped at the side of the indulgent water feature in the middle of the circular driveway, and Ellie turned the engine off as she turned to gauge my reaction.

"Well, what do you think?" she asked.

"They're going to let me live here?" I asked, sceptical.

"God no!" she exclaimed. "The servants' quarters are around the back."

"Servants' quarters?" I scoffed. "What century is this?"

Ellie exhaled sharply. "Robyn? You need to drop the attitude."

"Excuse me?"

"I've stuck my neck out to sort this for you!"

"I know you have, but—"

"And all you've done is take the piss."

I shrank in defeat. "I'm sorry."

"Besides, the Blackthorns don't suffer fools gladly. Trust me on that one."

I opened my mouth to say something sarcastic, but thought better of it. Ellie stepped out of her car, and I followed her, but we barely made it a few feet up the driveway before the doors swung open. Lucas glided down the stairs to meet us, and much to my annoyance, he rushed to pluck Ellie off her feet, spinning her in the air for a few moments whilst I felt like a spare part standing beside them. After they'd finished their adolescent canoodling, he approached me with his hands in his pockets. I couldn't help but spot the dusting of white powder clinging to the stubble around his nose. He seemed to notice me gawping because he pressed his thumb into his nostril, inhaled deeply, and wiped away the surviving remnants.

"Well, what do you think of the old digs?" he asked me with a bright smile.

Ellie's glare could've cut glass.

"It's incredible!" I said as enthusiastically as I could.

"I've already spoken to Dad, and he's agreed to take you on until you find your footing again."

"Oh—fantastic!" I said as Ellie shot me another stern look. "Thank you."

"You can cook, right?" He arched an eyebrow.

"A little."

"Well, that's good because the last one could only just make cheese on toast."

"Right!" I cackled.

"Where is your dad, anyway?" Ellie interjected, fiddling with her fingernails.

"He's in his study," he said, nodding skyward. "Fair warning: he's in a fucking terrible mood."

"Because of me?" I asked.

"God, no. He's a grumpy old fart in general these days," he said with an eye roll. "Have you got any bags?"

"Nope. Just the clothes on my back!" I announced, tugging my jacket around me.

"You should stay in the house tonight. I'll get Martha to make up a room in the morning."

"Wait—she's staying in the fucking house?" Ellie exclaimed, striding forward.

"Yeah, what's the problem?" he asked.

"Nothing," she dismissed quickly. "I just thought she'd be staying with the rest of the staff."

"It's only temporary and there's plenty of room," he replied before turning to me. "You cool with that?"

"Err—yeah, sure," I responded, kicking at the gravel.

Ellie bolted her arms around her chest, inexplicably pissed off that I was going to be staying under the same roof as her unbearable boyfriend. Despite her sorting this whole thing out for me, I was still pretty annoyed at her for not showing up for me at my hearing, and I'd be lying if I said it didn't feel good to get one up on her for a change. However, she had absolutely nothing to worry about. I'd rather be caught dead than anywhere near Lucas bloody Blackthorn.

"When will I see you again, anyway?" Ellie asked Lucas, hands on her hips.

He smirked. "I can call round tomorrow night and—"

"I'm not some booty call, you know?" she interrupted.

"Fine," he said, stepping forward. "How about we have dinner tomorrow? My treat."

Her scowl eased. "It's a date," she gushed, almost forgetting she was green with envy not five seconds before.

Lucas pulled her in for another kiss, but Ellie went for his ear instead, shooting daggers at me as she whispered something into his ear. They separated a moment later, an awkward silence following it until Lucas clapped his hands together and turned back to me.

"Come on then, Robyn," he announced. "I'll take you through."

Out of obligation, Ellie offered a half-hearted hug, which I begrudgingly accepted, and then I followed Lucas up the steps. I turned back around to wave Ellie off, but she was already back in the car and almost halfway down the drive before we even got to the top. Eager to show me inside, Lucas beckoned me inside as I watched her speed down the driveway, so I spun around when she was out of sight and let out a quiet gasp once I saw the interior.

I'd expected the inside to be in keeping with the outside, but to my surprise, I was wrong. Instead, it was bright and modern: polished marble floors, brilliant-white walls, and the smell of fresh paint still lingering in the air. There were a few sparse photographs and pieces of art hanging from the walls, but other than that, it was very minimalist—classy even, and I couldn't believe that I'd be spending the night there after the twelve-by-four cell I'd been sleeping in previously.

"What did Ellie whisper to you?" I asked as we approached the stairs.

He frowned. "I don't remember."

"You don't remember? It was five seconds ago."

Lucas couldn't stop the cynical laugh. "You know El, right? Always marking her territory."

"Right," I said, wrinkling my brow.

"Anyway, you can take the room upstairs at the end of the hall," he announced over his shoulder. "It's been empty for ages, anyway."

"Great. Thanks."

"I think Dad will want a word with you before you settle down for the evening."

"Seriously?" I winced. "I look like shit."

"He won't care. Just don't say anything to antagonise him any further, okay?"

I rubbed my neck. "I won't."

"Before you head up," Lucas started, turning to face me. "I need to warn you about something."

I sniggered. "I know the script. Don't piss off Daddy."

"No, not that," he said, leaning on the bannister. "I gave him a fake last name."

I blinked. "And why did you do that?"

"Well, if he searches your real name, it's going to come up with your record, yeah?"

A lump formed in my throat. "Yes."

"He doesn't know you've been in prison, so keep it that way."

"What if he finds out?"

"He won't. Not unless you tell him."

The lump grew bigger. "Listen, I don't feel comfortable—"

"You need this, don't you?" he interrupted.

I bobbed my head.

"Then just keep your mouth shut, and everything will be fine."

"Why are you helping me?" I asked, narrowing my eyes. "After everything."

He dragged his hair back with a single hand. "I'm just doing Ellie a favour. Let's leave it at that."

I lifted a shoulder in agreement. "Works for me."

"He'll be in his study," he said, glancing at the ceiling. "It's up the stairs, third door on the right."

"Wait, you aren't coming with me?"

"Hell no!" he exclaimed. "I've had enough of him for one evening."

With that, Lucas abandoned me in the lobby and started walking down one of the sprawling corridors with his hands back in his pockets.

Oh, God. What the fuck was I doing?

Getting a job here legitimately was one thing, but under false pretences? That was dodgy, to say the least, maybe even dangerous. I told myself that I had a choice, that I could take off into the night, jump the gate, and forget the Blackthorns ever existed. But I didn't—I needed this job and a roof over my head. I mean, what the hell else was I going to do? Spend the night beneath a bus-stop canopy? In a shop doorway?

Against my better judgement, I peered up the staircase and then grabbed the handrail before pulling myself up the first step. It bent round onto the landing, and I counted the doors until I spotted the one for the study, which was ajar with a thin shaft of light seeping through the crack. I gingerly took an uncertain step, smoothed out my jacket, and then tapped on it with bated breath.

I was more nervous than I had ever been in my life.

Absolutely everything hinged on his accepting me for who I was.

If he didn't, well, I had no idea what I'd do or where I'd go next.

"Enter," I heard a gruff voice say inside.

6

THE PARK

ROBYN – BEFORE

The bus coughed and spluttered up the hill, brakes screaming as it finally wheezed to a stop outside Heaton Park. On a number of occasions, I thought it might've given up the ghost altogether and left me stranded with a yoga mat under my arm like some budget *Bridget Jones*, but it thankfully made the climb, so I squeezed past the standing passengers to alight onto the pavement.

I caught a whiff of something strange as soon as I hit the fresh air. To me, it smelled like the faint tang of disinfectant concealing lingering body odour, and to my horror, I quickly realised that it was the mat tucked tightly against my ribcage. I'd borrowed it from Sandra downstairs in a mad panic that morning, and not only was she nice enough to give it to me, but she'd also agreed to check in on Mum whilst I humiliated myself exercising in public with girls I only vaguely liked. Still, regardless of the context, it was nice to be out in the park for a change instead of being stuck in the flat. No matter how much I sneered at the joggers with their protein shakes and the middle-aged couples doing 'mindful walking' like they'd just invented putting one foot in front of the other, I couldn't pass those gates without thinking about Mum.

Back when I was knee-high to a grasshopper, it was our place. I remembered catching the bus in, probably the exact one that I'd just stepped off, and then she'd sit me on the swings and push until her arms were about to drop off. After I eventually gave in, we'd split a bag of chips on the benches by the boating lake, vinegar soaking through the paper into our laps while we made funny faces at the geese honking for scraps. Sometimes, we'd do the long walk around the grounds, her pointing out squirrels hiding in the trees, explaining the statues, and making up fake backstories for the ridiculous old hall at the top of the hill. Back then, it felt huge, magical, like we had all the time in the world.

It wasn't the same without her.

To my disgust, a group of shirtless teenage boys wolf-whistled as I walked past them, ogling me over their shoulders at my worn yoga shorts like I was a piece of meat. I gritted my teeth and stuck up my middle finger when I caught their eyes, and they quickly averted their gazes and started kicking a football on the grass instead. When I turned back around, I almost ran square into Kait, who was waiting on the path with her arms outstretched, her silicone chest packed into a tight crop-top.

"Robyn!" she shrieked.

"Hey!" I winced, giving her a half-arsed hug. "It's a nice day for it."

"Isn't it!" she said before the smile dropped from her face. "Do you need to get changed?"

"No." I looked down at myself, raising an eyebrow. "Why?"

"No reason," she dismissed, beckoning me to follow her. "Come on, we're just getting set up."

"Set up what?" I muttered in confusion.

Allisyn and Sydney were already there, and they'd staked out a spot near the pond like they owned the place. To my horror, Allisyn was setting up a tripod and clipping her phone in, adjusting the angle to catch the best bit of the grey sky. Sydney was sitting cross-legged in the frame, clasping her fingers and thumbs together and flicking her hair back and forth like she was auditioning for a shampoo advert, pouting like her life depended on it.

No Ellie, though. Typical.

"Robyn!" Allisyn squealed the second she clocked me. "You made it!"

"Yeah," I said, dropping the mat onto the damp grass. "The bus in was a nightmare."

"The... bus?" she asked, disgust curling her lips. "Eww."

"Oh, yeah, er—my car's in the garage at the moment."

She threw her head back in relief. "Right! Of course!"

"Are we starting, or what? I'm in the zone, here," Sydney groaned, performing a pose that would've landed me in the hospital.

"We have to wait for her majesty, don't we?" Allisyn rolled her eyes.

"Is she coming?" I asked.

"Yeah, but you know El, right? Always fashionably late."

I snorted. "What about Lucas?"

"Lucas?" Allisyn sniggered. "Why the hell would *he* be coming?"

I let my shoulders sag. "I don't know, I thought he might want to join in."

Allisyn and Kait giggled like I'd just made a hilarious joke.

"Sweetie, the only yoga Lucas does is when he's bending down for another line," Kait chimed in.

"Right," I said, clutching my mat tighter. "Forget I said anything."

Kait exchanged a weird look with Allisyn and nodded at me, like she was daring Allisyn to speak. When Allisyn didn't immediately pipe up, Kait took the reins, moving closer with her hands pressed together.

"I'm glad we've got you on your own because we need to have a chat," Kait announced.

My heart dropped. Had they realised that I'd been lying to them?

"What about?" I asked, tugging some hair over my birthmark.

"Your socials," she said, holding a pitying smile.

A breath of relief broke free. "My—what?"

"Your feed! It's tragic," she stated, holding her hands up. "No offence, honey."

"None taken," I said into the ground.

Her eyes went straight past me and landed on my phone poking out of my bag. "Do you mind?"

"Go for it."

I unlocked my phone and gave it to her, and Kait quickly joined her side as they tapped away at the screen like they were about to diagnose me with something terminal. I rubbed my arm as I waited for their report, occasionally glancing at Sydney in the corner of my eye as she continued to turn herself into a human pretzel.

"I mean, babe, you've got to be consistent. Stories every day, reels twice a week, grid posts that actually mean something," Allisyn listed with her fingers.

"I've been a bit busy at work and—"

"What's your aesthetic?" Kait cut in.

"Aesthetic?" I knitted my brows together. "What the hell does that mean when it's at home?"

"I thought you worked in fashion?" she asked, scrunching up her face.

I managed a nod, praying there wouldn't be a follow-up question.

"Then why don't you post about that?"

"Kait! It's all hush-hush, remember?" Allisyn added, putting a finger to her lips.

"Oh yeah," I deadpanned. "Top secret."

"The pics of jewellery and clothes are great," Kait began, turning my phone to me with a picture of some takeaway I'd posted months before. "But pizza? What in the world were you thinking?"

"Oh, come on!" I threw my hands in the air. "Who the hell doesn't like pizza?"

"It's hardly aspirational, is it? You got what, ten likes?" Allisyn chimed in.

I had to bite my tongue before telling her the only thing aspirational about her was the way she managed to spell her own name without autocorrect.

"It was my birthday," I explained.

"Still," Allisyn said, face full of sympathy. "You shouldn't be eating that shit, anyway. A moment on the lips…"

"A lifetime on the hips," Kait finished for her.

Before I could fire back or maybe even go into a rant about how I'd witnessed them both snorting Class A off a toilet seat the week before, Ellie arrived at long last. She looked like a celebrity trying to evade the public eye, marching over the grass in a baggy black jumper, hood tugged over her head, oversized sunglasses obscuring her eyes. The girls all lined up to receive her like she was royalty, but when she took her glasses from her head, we all let out a collective gasp.

The bruise.

Her left eye was twice its usual size, ringed in purple and black. The white was red and bloodshot, and the lids were tender and puffy. She could see us gawking at it and quickly put the glasses back on before dumping her bag beside the tripod. My gaze scanned over the girls. They did everything they could to avoid eye contact with Ellie, shuffling around on the spot and trading glances. Like me, they wanted to ask how she got it, but unlike me, none of them had the courage.

"Christ, El, what the hell happened?" I asked.

"I had a fight with a doorframe," she said breezily. "It won."

The other girls didn't buy it, but they didn't call her out either.

"Maybe we should do this another—"

"No," she interrupted, slinging her mat on the grass with unnecessary force. "Let's get this over with."

So, we did 'yoga.' In all fairness, I wasn't a fan.

Given that Ellie had a shiner, she opted to remain mostly behind the camera, barking orders at us from afar. To my surprise, she was seemingly fluent in Sanskrit, shouting out the names of poses like anyone else knew what the hell she was talking about. In truth, none of them gave a monkey's about yoga; they were too busy plumping their backsides for the camera, touching up their makeup, and squealing whenever someone managed to hold a pose that looked 'fire.' Much to the other girls' quiet amusement, I managed about one and a half downward dogs before I keeled sideways and almost landed in Kait's lap, which is when Ellie yelled, "Cut!"

"Sorry," I announced, brushing grass off my shorts. "I'm clearly not as limber as I thought."

"You looked like a dying swan," Sydney snorted.

"I felt like one, too." I giggled.

"I think we got what we needed," Ellie announced, looming over me.

"Seriously?"

"Yeah," she said, barely looking up from Sydney's phone. "I can edit out the bits when you fell flat on your face."

"Appreciate it," I grunted.

"Let me have a look," Allisyn interjected, running to Ellie's side.

"It looks pretty good," Ellie remarked, turning the phone to her.

"Urgh," she grumbled. "I look so fat. Delete that clip."

Ellie cocked her head. "Honey, no, you don't."

"I do! Cut it!"

"No, the light looks good there!"

"Why are you so bothered? You aren't even in the shot!"

"We haven't got much footage," Ellie started, nodding over to me. "Thank *her* for that."

They continued their juvenile argument, but I heard something that instantly diverted my attention. An engine was roaring in the distance, and a moment later, a black car was shooting up the verge, tyres spitting mud, skidding all over the shop. I batted Ellie's arm without turning away, and before any of us clocked the licence plate, the door swung open. Lucas stormed out, so I instantly turned my back, walking over to my bag in the hope he wouldn't spot me there, watching what was about to unfold over my shoulder.

"Ellie!" he bellowed, barrelling over. "Get in the car."

She froze, the colour draining from her face.

"What are you doing?" Kait yelled, standing between them. "You can't drive that monstrosity here!"

"I can do as I bloody well please," he spat before turning back to Ellie. "Get in the car."

"No," she said, hugging her chest.

"Get in the damned car!"

"No! I'm not going back there! Not until *he* apologises!"

Everyone in the park was now staring at the spectacle, holding their phones and snapping pictures as Lucas reached for Ellie's arm. He wrapped his fingers around her forearm and tried to yank her towards him, but she resisted. After a short struggle, Kait and Sydney jumped in to try to pry her from his grip. He only released her when he saw the growing crowd.

"People are watching," Ellie snarled. "Compose yourself, will you?"

"I will when you get in the car," Lucas warned. "Last chance."

Obviously wanting it to be over, Ellie turned on her heel and stormed over to me to grab her bag from beside the tripod. I put my hand on her arm as she reached down for it, and she quickly spun her head to meet my gaze.

"Did he do *that* to you?" I whispered, glaring at her eye.

"No, of course not," she denied.

"El, if he's willing to do that, then he's—"

"It wasn't him, okay?" she said, slumping her shoulders. "It was his dad."

I thought I'd misheard her. "His… dad?"

She gave a slight nod. "We disagreed about the current whereabouts of his favourite child."

"Lucas?" I arched an eyebrow.

"No," she said, shaking her head. "Sofia," she mouthed.

"Come on!" Lucas growled, wrenching the passenger door open. "We haven't got all day."

And, without uttering another word, she got in the car, just like that.

"Put your fucking phones away!" Lucas snarled at the ogling crowd. "Do you even know who my father is? He'll fucking bury you if this shit ends up online."

Lucas jumped behind the steering wheel, and in the blink of an eye, they were reversing out of the park. I got back onto my feet and joined the rest of the girls, with grass stains on my arse and the taste of bile in my mouth. No one spoke for a minute or two until what we'd seen finally sank in.

"Fuck. Poor Ellie," I remarked.

"Oh, please," Allisyn replied. "She knew what she was getting into with that family."

"Does it happen a lot?"

Her face stayed blank, saying it all.

"We should call someone," I suggested.

"No point," Kait mumbled.

"You can't be serious? You saw her eye, right?"

"Daddy will make it all go away," Sydney cut in. "He always does."

7

THE INTERVIEW

ROBYN

I peered through the crack in Mr Blackthorn's study door, and I could see him standing by the partly open window, holding a clay pipe in his hand and blowing out tobacco smoke into the fresh air. Although he was in his early fifties, he was as wickedly good-looking as his son, with his silver hair slicked back and a bushy, grey moustache to match. He was a little overdressed for 10 pm, still inexplicably wearing a brown, houndstooth suit jacket with an immaculately pressed shirt, topped off with a racing-green tie, giving the impression that he was about to pop out to a meeting.

"Come in!" he bellowed when I didn't immediately enter.

I took a deep breath and pushed the door open.

His study was intimidating. For a start, it had escaped the modernisations of the foyer, and each wall was clad in aged oak panelling, save the back wall that was dominated by a huge bookcase filled with dusty tomes and trinkets. There was an impossibly polished mahogany desk in the centre, littered with paperwork and opened letters. The windows afforded a view of the driveway, where he likely watched and heard my arrival ten minutes before. He didn't acknowledge my presence until I cleared my throat, which is when he finally turned to face me with an indifferent expression. Yet, after a few seconds of staring at me, his jaw dropped, exactly like his son's did in Ellie's flat.

"Hi," I said, feeling my cheeks blush. "I'm here about the job."

"Robyn Marsden, correct?" he asked after snapping out of his stare.

I gave a short nod.

"It's a pleasure to meet you, Robyn," he gushed, holding out his hand.

"Likewise," I said, shaking it gently.

"I like getting to know everyone in our employ," he explained, releasing his grip. "It's a habit of mine."

"Well, I can't thank you enough for the opportunity, Mr Blackthorn."

"My son tells me you are a dab hand in the kitchen. Is that true?"

"Yes, I did a few cooking courses when I was—"

"In college?" he interrupted.

In truth, most of what I knew about cooking I'd picked up inside from a greasy kitchen where we churned out shepherd's pie for two hundred inmates at a time. It wasn't glamorous, but it had kept me sane and given me something to focus on. However, there was no way in hell that I could tell him that my signature dish came with a side of razor wire and a strip search. So, I swallowed the lump in my throat, kept my eyes on the polished desk, and forced another polite nod.

"Excellent!" he roared. "We could certainly do with some fresh ideas down there. I don't mind telling you it's been a little stagnant as of late."

"Well, I'll do my best."

After a second of introspection, Mr Blackthorn groaned as he sat down behind his desk and then gestured for me to sit across from him. I meekly tottered over and lowered myself onto the chair, folding my hands across my lap. He sized me up for a long second, rocking his head slightly, for just long enough for it to become incredibly awkward.

"Tell me, what do you know about my family?" he asked.

Bollocks, had we just slid into a job interview?

"Erm—not much to tell you the truth," I admitted.

Mr Blackthorn pointed at an oil portrait hung on the wall. "Do you know who he is?"

I looked up at the portrait, and I thought it was of Mr Blackthorn at first. He had the same tight brow, scraped-back hair and even the same dress sense. The man's name was inscribed on a small, brass plaque underneath, but to my dismay, I was too far away to read it.

"Sorry, no," I murmured.

"My great-grandfather," he announced. "Ethelbert Blackthorn."

"He looks like he was a snappy dresser," I said, instantly cringing.

"And for bloody good reason! He built some of the biggest garment factories that Manchester had ever seen."

"Wow!" I said as eagerly as I could.

"Were you aware that British troops wore Blackthorn uniforms during the war?"

"No." I smiled. "I didn't."

"Those were the days…" Mr Blackthorn sighed wistfully. "Nowadays, we don't even make a stitch of clothing over here. It's all imported rubbish with our name stamped on the back."

I opened my mouth to speak, but I almost yawned, so I forced it shut.

"Do you have any brothers or sisters?" he asked to fill the silence.

"Nope. It's just me."

"And your parents? Do they live in Manchester?"

I rubbed my neck. "I never knew my father, and Mum, well—she died a few years ago."

"Christ," he said, leaning back slightly. "So sorry to bring that up."

"It's fine." I waved my hand in the air. "Like I said, it was a long time ago."

Mr Blackthorn's gaze raked over me, and it gave me the creeps. I instinctively readjusted the chunk of hair covering my birthmark before covering my midriff with my arms.

"Lucas warned me, but I still wasn't expecting you to look *so* much like her," he admitted.

The hairs on my neck rose to attention. "Who?"

"It doesn't matter," he said. "Tell me, have you spoken to Martha yet? Has she prepared a room for you?"

"No—Lucas said I should stay in the house for tonight, and he'd sort everything out in the morning."

"Perfect!" he said, clasping his hands together. "Well, you have a big day tomorrow."

"I have the job?"

"Of course! We can't very well throw you onto the street at this ungodly hour, can we?"

I closed my eyes in relief. "Thank you, Mr Blackthorn."

"You're welcome. If you need anything, please give me a shout. I don't sleep much these days anyway."

"I will," I said, standing up from my seat. "Have a nice evening."

He gave me that searching look again. "Good night, Robyn Marsden."

I turned on my heels at once and made for the door before softly closing it behind me, taking a moment in the hallway to decompress. Mr Blackthorn wasn't at all what I expected. Between the horrible stories I'd heard and Lucas's warning, I was expecting some kind of monster, but that didn't seem to be the case. From first impressions, he was welcoming, if not a little eccentric, and dare I say it: nice. In fact, I almost felt a little guilty about concealing my chequered past from him, as he seemed like he would've actually understood if I'd told him the truth.

Muffled giggling from one of the bedrooms startled me, so I looked up and down the hallway again before making my way to the end and to my bed for the night. The sconces buzzed as I breezed past, stretching my shadow as I crept beyond the endless bedrooms on either side. I kept repeating Lucas's instructions in my head, the room at the end of the hall, but to my bemusement, there were two. I tried the door on my right, but it was sealed shut, so I turned to my left. That door was locked too, yet the key was in the handle, so I turned it and pushed my way inside.

"Fuck me," I uttered as I stepped over the threshold.

I felt like I had just wandered onto the set of *Downton Abbey*. Just like Mr Blackthorn's office, the décor didn't seem to match the rest of the house at all. The walls were decorated with old-fashioned wallpaper and wood panelling, and there was a thick layer of dust on every surface, as if I were the first person to enter it in years. Despite it being one of the most grandiose bedrooms I had ever stepped into, it was normal in every other sense of the word, with various wardrobes and chests of drawers, and a four-poster bed slap-bang in the middle of the back wall.

"*Creepy*," I sang under my breath.

I placed both hands on the bed and put my weight on it, bouncing up and down like I was giving it chest compressions. I'd spent the last six years sleeping on a paper-thin mattress on top of a slab of steel, so it almost felt alien to me. I perched on the edge, scanning the room, and it was only when I glanced up that I spotted what looked like a painting directly facing me and beside the door I'd entered through. It was obscured by a thin, cotton sheet, and I knew that I wouldn't be able to sleep a wink if I didn't unearth whatever was underneath. I stood back up again and tottered over to lift the corner.

As I peeled the cotton back, I realised that it was a Victorian-style oil painting of a young woman, posing in some gardens. The detail in the painting was phenomenal; I could almost make out every stitch of her ornate dress and the intricate pattern of the fabric that'd been painstakingly brushed by hand. I pulled the sheet back a little further, and I saw her reddish curls resting over her shoulders, with her hands clasped in her lap, clutching a single black rose. Letting curiosity get the better of me, I made the decision to pull on the sheet so the whole thing would drop, and suddenly, the entire painting was visible.

"What the actual fuck?" I gasped, clutching my chest.

It wasn't some random woman in the painting.

It was *me*. Or at least she looked *like* me.

While the woman in the painting had dyed red hair and marginally paler skin, we could've quite easily been mistaken for sisters. Unlike me, she had no tattoos to speak of, and she had a slightly larger frame and different facial features, but I was still taken aback by how uncanny the resemblance was. It was in the eyes: emerald-green following me around the room like a reflection. I reached out, running my fingertips over the canvas as I tilted my head down, which is when I saw a small plaque screwed into the gilded frame, engraved with a name.

"Sofia Blackthorn," I whispered.

Suddenly, all the strange looks from Lucas and Mr Blackthorn made sense. Did Lucas know what he was doing all along? Was this some twisted prank to watch me squirm? The longer I stared, the harder it was to convince myself it was only paint. My pulse thudded in my ears, and goosebumps prickled down my arms despite the heat trapped in the old room. I swore I heard a floorboard creak in the hallway, so I whipped my head around, but the corridor was silent again. When I looked back, Sofia's painted eyes were still on me, pinned in place, and I almost heard Mum's voice from beyond the grave.

Stay away from them, Robyn.

This wasn't just a spare room.

It was a shrine.

8

THE PROMISE

ROBYN – BEFORE

Getting Mum to the supermarket was a full-blown military operation. For a start, there was the chair: heavy as hell and temperamental with its squeaky wheels that caught on every bloody doorframe. Next, we had the lift for our block to contend with, which was twelve inches wider than the chair and always two inches deep in last night's second-hand lager. Once we made it out onto the street and to the bus stop, we'd have to cross our fingers for a driver willing to get the ramp out. Most of them just grumbled like we couldn't hear or saw the chair and didn't stop at all.

Then, there was Mum herself. She'd insist until she was blue in the face that she didn't need to go anywhere in the first place, arms tight over her chest like a defiant toddler, and scowling into the distance as if the mere suggestion of going out into the world was an insult. She wasn't all wrong. It was far easier to go on my own or even have the groceries delivered, but delivery slots cost money that we didn't have. Besides, she needed reminding sometimes that there was more to life than watching crap TV in our two-bed flat in Salford.

"We'll be quick," I promised, as I pushed the chair off the bus on its back wheels.

"You say that every time," she complained, glaring at the blanket tucked over her knees. "I'm missing *Taggart*."

"Mum, there hasn't been a new episode for fifteen years. I'm sure there'll be a re-run."

"What do we even need, anyway?"

"Just bits and bobs," I said, checking the list written on the back of my hand. "Bread, milk, maybe some chicken if it's on offer. That's it."

"We both know we'll end up traipsing round for hours while you compare prices."

"Nope. I've got it down to a fine art now," I lied, forcing a smile. "The whole shebang should take about ten minutes."

By the time we made it to the entrance, I was sweating like I'd run a marathon. Mum wasn't much better, fiddling with the collar of her cardigan like she was being strangled by it. The security guard offered to help us inside as we approached, but I shook my head and lifted the chair over the threshold into the foyer by sheer force of will alone.

"Are you okay?" I asked after all four wheels were back on the ground again.

"Wonderful," she muttered. "Just wonderful."

"Can you please just lighten up?" I asked, rolling my eyes.

"I told you. You should've left me at home where I'm comfortable."

"Is it not nice to get out once in a while?"

"It's a bloody trip to the supermarket, not a day at the seaside."

We were reminded that we weren't at the beach when the blast of air conditioning made both of us shiver as we bowled inside. I grabbed a basket and slung it over one arm, pushing Mum along with the other. It felt clumsy and lopsided, exactly like everything else in my life those days. The fluorescent lights hummed overhead, glaring down on aisles stacked high with tins, packets, and special offers that, on closer inspection, weren't even discounted.

"I'm sorry, okay?" Mum said over her shoulder. "I just hate people seeing you like this."

My face tightened. "Like what?"

"Pushing your decrepit mother around."

"Mum, no one is even looking at us."

"They are!"

"You're just being paranoid," I protested, tossing a few packs of instant noodles into the basket.

"That's what you think," she said, nodding down the makeup aisle. "Look at these two, for instance, I'll bet you anything that we'll get a dirty look in about three seconds flat."

I glanced where she'd pointed, and panic gripped me when I spotted who she was talking about. It wasn't the whole gang, thankfully, just Kait and Allisyn, swiping lip gloss samples onto the backs of their hands and cackling to each other. I instantly pulled my hood over my head and ducked behind the end of the aisle. What the hell were they doing there, anyway? They wouldn't usually be caught dead in a place like that, let alone smear off-brand makeup onto their precious, plump lips.

"Robyn?" Mum craned her neck. "What's up?"

"Nothing," I said too quickly.

"It sure doesn't look like nothing." Mum followed my gaze, straining to see. "Do you know those girls?"

"Yes," I said, pushing her down the next aisle.

Her lips twitched. "Friends?"

"Sort of," I dodged, tugging her chair back the other way. "Look, it doesn't matter. Let's just grab what we need and get out of here, okay?"

Anyone else would've gone straight over, introduced their mother, and probably had a chat before carrying on with their shopping, but not me. I couldn't. The instant that they clapped eyes on me with Mum in her chair, juggling a discount-store basket full of basics, the stupid web of lies I'd built would come crashing down. Mum frowned but let me steer her toward the dairy section. My pulse hammered as I kept checking over my shoulder, praying Kait's self-diagnosed lactose intolerance hadn't disappeared, and she found herself thirsty all of a sudden. It turned into a bizarre game of hide and seek, ducking my head and shoving Mum's chair toward the tills before anyone could notice.

* * *

By some divine miracle, we got what we needed and made it back onto the bus without being recognised. It wasn't until we got home that Mum turned to me, her eyes sharper than usual, pinning me down like I was the one in the chair. It went without saying that I didn't want to discuss what had happened, but I could already tell by the way she had her arms firmly locked over her chest that she wasn't going to let it go without a fight.

"Are we going to talk about it?" she said with a sternness I hadn't heard for a while.

"No," I said, stuffing the loaf into the bread bin. "I'd rather not."

"Come on, Robyn," she groaned. "Why didn't you stop to say hello?"

"Didn't feel like it."

"That's rubbish and you know it. You saw them and bolted."

My eyes rolled into the back of my head as I peered at the heavens for strength.

"They're not my friends, okay?" I admitted. "Not really, anyway."

"Who were they, then?"

"Kait and Allisyn," I said after turning to her.

"Two of the girls you've been going out drinking with?"

I winced. "Mum, I—"

"What were you so afraid of them seeing?"

Her question hung heavy in the air. I opened my mouth to spew more lies, but Mum jumped in with an explanation before me.

"You didn't want to introduce me, did you?" she added.

I froze, gripping the handle of the fridge. "No, that's not true."

She started prodding her leg with a single finger. "It is."

"Mum—"

"You're ashamed of me, aren't you?"

The words sliced through me.

"No! That's not it." I dropped the milk onto the counter and spun around, heat rushing to my cheeks. "Don't say that, okay?"

"Then what is it?" she said, tears forming in her eyes. "Because from where I was sitting, you couldn't get away fast enough."

I cracked. Even though I knew the reality wasn't any more comforting than her theory, at least it had the benefit of being true. Hell, it would've been much easier just to stay silent and let her believe that I was embarrassed by her, but I wasn't that cruel. The lies, the pressure, the weight of keeping up appearances—it all tumbled out before I could stop it.

"I've been lying to them," I blurted out.

Mum narrowed her eyes. "What about?"

"No. It's stupid."

"Tell me!"

"Okay," I said in defeat. "I told them I work in fashion, that I've got this big career. I made them believe I was someone else. Someone who wasn't stuck—"

"Pushing their disabled mother around town?" she suggested.

I managed a nod, and it was met with silence. Mum wiped a single tear that had trickled down her cheek with her sleeve, then started trying to rotate herself around in the chair to leave the kitchen.

"Mum, wait. I didn't mean it, I'm—"

She stopped dead. "Why?"

I left it hanging, sinking against the counter and drumming my fingers on the cupboard doors. "I'll tell you, only if you promise not to overreact."

"Why, Robyn?" she asked firmly.

"Because of Lucas."

Her expression hardened instantly. "Lucas… Blackthorn?"

I nodded, shame burning my throat. "They know him."

"So, what?"

"If I get close to the Blackthorns, then maybe…"

"What?" she barked.

I steadied my chest. "Then maybe they'll agree to help us," I continued.

Mum closed her eyes like she'd been bracing for this. When she opened them again, there was no softness left.

"Robyn Fletcher, listen to me very carefully," she started, clenching her fist. "You need to stay away from them."

"What? Why?"

"My room. Top of the wardrobe," she said, teeth gritted. "The black shoebox."

I scowled but did what she asked. I wandered into her room and got onto my tiptoes to run my hands through the dust on the top of her wardrobe. My fingertips felt the edge of a box, and I managed to shimmy it towards me before I could grab it with both hands. I dropped it onto her bed and opened it. Inside was a bundle of photographs, yellowing around the edges, and a handful of trinkets that smelled faintly of old polish. A staff badge with Jada Fletcher printed on it. A folded apron embroidered with the Blackthorn crest. A menu from some long-forgotten estate dinner.

"Have you found it?" she yelled from the kitchen.

With some trepidation, I went back inside and placed it on her lap, and she started rifling through, hands trembling, before she selected a photo from the stack and handed it to me. It was a picture of the Blackthorn family, not unlike the one on our mantel, but more recent. I spotted my mum three people to the left and pulled the photo closer to me to inspect it as she cleared her throat to speak.

"I worked in the Blackthorn kitchens for almost twenty years," she began. "It was the only job I could get after prison."

"I know," I mumbled. "I remember."

"That picture was taken a few weeks before my injury. Do you see the man at the end?"

I moved my eyes across the image and saw the man standing a metre or so away from Mum. He was head-to-toe decked out in tweed, with a shotgun slung over his shoulder, staring at my mum with a haunting expression on his face.

"Who is he?" I asked.

"Harris," she mumbled. "The gamekeeper."

"Why are you showing me—"

"He's the one who found me after the accident," she said.

"Wait—it happened on the Blackthorn Estate?"

She tipped her head.

"I thought it was a drunk driver? In fact, you *told* me it was."

"It wasn't," she admitted. "I lied."

"Why?"

Mum's gaze moved to the corner of the room as she swiped her eyes with the back of her hand.

"Mr Blackthorn gave me a choice. Keep quiet about the accident and leave with a payout, or go to the police and be labelled a liar."

"You took the money?"

Her silence gave me the answer.

"Oh, Mum!" I cried out.

"We needed it, okay? I couldn't work anymore, and I wanted you to stay at college."

"What happened to it?"

"I spent most of it buying this fleapit, didn't I?" She snorted bitterly. "And the rest went on all the physiotherapy that didn't do a damned bit of good."

I tossed the photograph on the sideboard with the intention of going to my room to clear my head, but Mum reached out for my arm and gripped it tightly before I made it to the door.

"Someone in that family hit me, Robyn," she said, her voice sharp.

I gasped. "Who?"

"I don't know, but I do know that they're dangerous." She tightened her grip. "They all are."

"In that case, we need to tell someone!"

"No, you just need to promise me that you'll stay well away from them. No more Ellie, no more Kait, and definitely no more Lucas."

"But if we go to the police and—"

"Swear to me!" she shouted, her nails digging into my arm.

I ran my eyes along the line of people pictured in the photograph, and anger rose up in my throat. One of those faces was responsible for crippling my mother. One of them was responsible for ruining our lives. Mum wanted to protect me, and if the roles were reversed, I'd be doing the exact same thing. However, I didn't know if I could leave it be. They owed us. They owed *me*. And they were the only people with the means to drag us out of the shit situation they put us in.

"Robyn?" she prompted.

"I swear," I mumbled.

I already knew that it was a lie.

9

THE THIRST

ROBYN

I couldn't sleep.

It didn't matter how plush and comfortable the mattress was, or how utterly exhausted I felt; I was simply incapable of drifting off. My eerie double was trapped in the oil painting at the foot of the bed, almost relishing in my failure, her emerald-green eyes following me around the bed as I tossed and turned. I was cursing my decision to stay. In fact, I would've gladly taken the shop doorway or a bus-stop bench after all, and it was only the fear of waking up Harris with the gates that was keeping me put. It all got too much, and I couldn't stand Sofia's haunting gaze brushing over me any more, so I jumped out of bed in just my underwear to hang the sheet back up.

"Good fucking night," I said, tossing it over the frame.

The fact that the Blackthorn men must've noticed my resemblance to Sofia the second they clapped eyes on me knotted my insides. I mean, if she were dead like I suspected, who the hell would want someone who's the spit of her knocking about? I may have lied through my teeth and concealed my past to land a job there in the first place, but what they were doing was far more sinister. Weirder than that, I had never seen a photograph of her, not in Mum's shoebox, the leaflet from the prison, or anywhere for that matter. It was as if she didn't even exist.

I dived back into bed. As I was staring up at the ceiling rose, feeling my eyes becoming heavy at last, the old house let out a jarring crack and a creak, which instantly startled me back fully awake. Out of frustration, I decided to clamber out of bed again to nip into the en suite for a glass of water. The bathroom was in a similar vein to the bedroom, somewhat archaic, with exposed beams and a claw-foot bath in the centre of the room. Strangely, there were two sinks, each with a curved, navy-blue cabinet underneath, so I searched each of them for a clean glass. When I came up empty-handed, I opted to scoop some water into my mouth with my hand, but as soon as I turned one of the copper-coloured taps on, the old pipework started violently rattling underneath.

"Shit, shit, shit!" I uttered as I quickly turned the tap off.

The very last thing I needed was to wake up my unsettling new employers on my first night in their home, so I mindlessly grabbed a robe from the back of the door and decided to go in search of the kitchen instead. The hallway was eerie, lit only by a skinny column of moonlight bleeding in through one of the windows. I held my breath as I tiptoed past Mr Blackthorn's study to the staircase and made my way down. Each marble step was almost ice-cold, sucking the warmth from the soles of my feet. After checking that the coast was clear, I took one of the corridors at random in search of the kitchen.

Thankfully, it didn't take too many wrong turns before I found what I was looking for. The kitchen floor was composed of stone slabs, and I could feel my bare feet picking up every particle of dust as I stepped over it. I spotted a sink in the corner, so I grabbed a glass from one of the cupboards and then proceeded to fill it to the top as I kept checking over my shoulder for fellow insomniacs. I downed the first measure at once, wiping what I'd missed from my chin before filling it up again. There was a small wooden table in the middle of the room, so I set my glass down and decided to have a minute there before I took myself back off to bed.

Like Sofia's room and Mr Blackthorn's study, the kitchens had escaped the refit, and it felt like something from a period piece, if anything. The back wall was almost all timber shelves, filled to capacity with wicker baskets brimming with fresh produce and vegetables. Right beside them was a giant hearth with two ancient-looking stoves installed in it, and to the left of them, the door to the pantry. The rest of the kitchen was essentially worktops and other storage, far more than what I thought was necessary for one family, but like everything else on the Blackthorn Estate, they prided themselves on having everything in excess.

I took a sip, but my quiet moment was cut short when I heard clattering out in the hallway.

"Hello?" I said softly. "Is there anybody there?"

There was silence for a few beats, followed by what sounded like a woman wailing.

I abandoned my glass and darted over to the door, peering through the crack into the corridor. There was a woman outside, probably slightly older than me, wearing nothing but a pair of black French knickers and her jet-black hair stuffed into a slumber net. I started to think she was pissed out of her skull when she started bumping into things willy-nilly, and when she began incoherently mumbling something under her breath, I was almost sure of it. Given that she was blocking the only route back to my room, I decided to delicately approach her with my hands raised in surrender, hoping that I wouldn't frighten her.

"Don't freak out," I announced, my arms shaking. "Do you need some help?"

The woman stopped dead in her tracks, violently swivelling her head left and right as if she couldn't see me walking towards her. I went still too, craning my neck in the hope of catching her eye.

"I've just got a job here, and I was thirsty and—"

"Camilla Cavendish-Bowes!" she sang bitterly. "That snooty bitch! I'll fucking kill her!"

I took a few more steps. "Sorry—did you say kill?"

"She thinks she's *so* sexy with her perfect ass and fake tits!" she spat. "I could look like her if I paid for it like she does!"

"What the fuck is going on?" I muttered to myself, shrinking slightly but still creeping towards her.

"And that fiancé of hers! How the hell did a skank like her convince a man like him to get down on one knee?"

"Hello? Can you hear me?" I said tenderly.

"She doesn't deserve him! He should be with *me*—everyone thinks it!"

"Just calm down, okay?" I said, inching over.

I was in touching distance, so I reached out to put a comforting hand on her shoulder. However, the instant our skin made contact, all hell broke loose. She crawled backwards in a frenzy, screaming her lungs out and thrashing her arms. I narrowly avoided being hit, but after a few seconds, she seemed to snap out of whatever trance she was in. She rubbed her narrowed eyes, bobbing her head from side to side, undoubtedly clueless about how she got there in the first place.

"Sofia?" she asked in disbelief. "Is that you?"

"No." I scowled. "Robyn."

The woman realised that she was almost buck-naked in front of a perfect stranger, so she covered her bare chest with her arms and got back onto her feet, shivering slightly. I flashed her an awkward smile before peering at the ground, and we stood there for a few seconds before she decided to speak again.

"How on God's green earth did I get here?" she asked.

"No idea." I shrugged. "I was just getting something to drink and saw you walking down the hall."

"What was I doing, exactly?"

"I don't know—bumping into stuff and mumbling to yourself."

"Oh, for crying out loud!" she let out, smiling.

"What?"

"I must've been sleepwalking again. It happens from time to time."

I giggled, my nerves getting the better of me. "That's what that was?"

Without answering my question, the woman opened the door closest to her and grabbed a tablecloth from the small room to wrap around herself. Once she had her dignity back, she shut the door again and then stepped a little closer to me.

"I didn't say anything undignified, did I?" she asked, awkwardly baring her teeth.

"Er—it sounded like you were having a nightmare or something," I explained.

"What about?"

"I'm not sure, but it sounded like you wanted to kill someone," I uttered.

She gasped. "Who?"

"Camilla… something, something."

"Cavendish-Bowes?" she suggested.

"That's the one."

"Well, that's new," she remarked, rolling her eyes. "Camilla is a dear friend of mine—I'd never want to hurt her."

I chuckled awkwardly, wanting more than anything to end the uncomfortable exchange and retreat to the safety of my room. However, she looked like she wanted to continue our chat rather than let me retire.

"You're the new girl—Marsden, isn't it?" she asked.

"I am," I mumbled.

"Penelope Blackthorn," she introduced herself. "My little brother told me about you earlier."

"Well, he's got a big mouth," I quipped.

"Quite!" She chortled. "He was right about one thing, though: you're the spitting image of Sofia."

"Yeah—I've been getting that a lot," I remarked.

"Although now I'm thinking about it, she had freckles but no birthmark. Not to mention the crazy red hair."

I relaxed a little. "To be honest, I thought the same thing when I saw her portrait."

"Portrait?" she asked with a furrowed brow. "Which portrait?"

"The big one in her room."

Penelope's face dropped, and the sheet almost went with it until she gripped it tightly, closing the distance between us.

"You've been in her room?" she asked with a flicker of anger.

"Yes, Lucas said it was okay to stay in there tonight," I explained, jutting my neck back. "Is there a problem?"

"No one has been in that room for years! Hell, Mother barely even allows the staff to go in there!"

"But why?" I asked, cocking my head.

"Penelope!" a booming voice interrupted from down the hall.

I looked over Penelope's shoulder, and my heart was in my throat when I saw an older woman storming down the hall, with one of the staff wearing a black and white tunic in tow. I knew exactly who she was the instant I saw her: Lucinda Blackthorn, the only member of the family who couldn't bring herself to smile in the picture featured on the leaflet from my discharge pack. She was wearing a silk dressing gown in off-white and a pair of glittery slippers, with her platinum-blonde hair set in a neat bob. As soon as they arrived at my side, Lucinda pulled Penelope's neck into her shoulder for a hug and then turned to face me with unfathomable fury in her eyes.

"How *dare* you wear that robe!" she spat. "Who the hell do you think you are?"

I peered down and saw the letters 'S' and 'B' monogrammed onto the bust in ornate stitching.

"I'm sorry, I was getting a glass of water and—"

"I don't care what you were doing!" she interrupted. "Take it off! At once!"

I laughed initially, presuming that she was joking, but as the wrath on her face only deepened, I knew that she was being serious. She held her hand out expectantly, so I did the only thing I could. I undid the tie from my waist, slowly removed it from my shoulders and held it out to her. I hardly had a second to digest what was happening when she whipped it out of my hand. I quivered, holding my chest for warmth as she looked me up and down with disgust, clicking her tongue and shaking her head.

"You know, my husband told me you were a dead ringer for Sofia, but a skinny, common street rat like you couldn't hold a candle to her."

"I'm so sorry, please—"

"Get this whelp out of my sight, Martha," she hissed.

With that, Lucinda clutched Penelope and led her down the hallway, quickly disappearing from view. I turned to Martha, who'd popped into the cupboard to get me a sheet of my own, and I wrapped it around myself as she averted her eyes from my half-naked body. She was quite thin and had a pasty complexion to match, with her auburn hair, streaked with grey, scraped back into a tight ponytail.

"Follow me," Martha instructed before turning on her heels.

"What the hell was that about?" I asked as I followed her, drying my eyes with the corner of the sheet.

"Lucinda Blackthorn is the lady of this house, and it is not our place to question her," she said over her shoulder before stopping. "Do I make myself clear?"

"Yes," I said with a sniffle.

"Good." She continued walking.

"I just—"

"What?" she snapped.

"She looked at me like she *hated* me."

"Tell me, what exactly were you doing in Sofia's room?" she asked firmly. "It's strictly off-limits."

"Trying to get to sleep."

"And who told you that was acceptable?"

"Lucas."

"Well, Lucas must've been playing one of his legendary practical jokes. No one is to enter that room without express permission from Mrs Blackthorn. Is that understood?"

"I'm sorry," I began nervously. "I didn't know."

"Well, you do now."

I waited a few more steps before speaking again.

"I'm not being fired, am I?"

"No." Martha stopped dead. "Not tonight."

"Oh," I said, releasing a sigh of relief. "I can't tell you how much I need this job."

"Come. I have your quarters ready."

I was led through a service entrance in the kitchen, and across the courtyard towards a separate building beside the main house, then shown through the doors. It was clearly the servants' quarters, dark and damp, and hadn't seen a paintbrush for decades. My room bore a startling resemblance to the cell where I had spent six years of my life, only furnished with a single bed, a small wardrobe, a bedside table, and a dingy-looking sink in the corner. There was one window, a tad wider than my shoulders, fitted with a ragged curtain doing a terrible job of blocking the moonlight. The walls were exposed brick, with erratically placed nails hanging out of the mortar where things had been previously hung, and dangling off one of them was a black and white tunic, exactly like Mum used to wear.

"Be in the kitchen at 6 am for your induction," Martha ordered. "And not a minute later."

"Six?" I swallowed after checking the time. "Perfect."

"Get some sleep," she instructed before slamming the door behind her.

Get some sleep? Was she for real?

To my surprise, my meagre belongings had already been collected from Sofia's room and were folded in a neat pile on the bed. Still reeling from the indignity I'd been forced to suffer, I grabbed my clothes and began hanging them up in the wardrobe so I could turn in. I went through them one by one until I got to my jacket at the bottom of the pile, but when I picked it up, I felt a foreign object sitting in one of the pockets. After sifting through them, I realised it was some kind of ring, so I held it up to the pillar of light pouring in through the window.

A gold band, slightly deformed, with a huge diamond sitting proudly in the centre.

I sucked in a breath, turning it over in my hands, and a tiny ruby winked back at me.

"What the fuck?"

PART TWO

"HOME"

FOUR WEEKS LATER

10

THE WORD

ROBYN

Scrub. Scrub. Scrub. After a month on the Blackthorn Estate, I was starting to discover how things worked. Shit rolls downhill, and my hands were outstretched to catch it. For example, Martha had tasked me with cleaning the dining room that morning, so I was on my knees, scouring the porcelain tiles with a battered brush that was older than me. I could still taste the toothpaste when I started, and I'd been at it over an hour at that point, under strict instructions only to stop when I could see my own reflection in them. Even worse, she laughed her arse off when I asked where the mop was kept and claimed that a brush, a bucket of hot water and a shot of white vinegar were all I needed.

I begged to differ.

The other girls, Elena and Catherine, were a few rungs up the ladder from me. They worked in the kitchen too, but the length of their service meant they could deflect Martha's more demeaning requests onto me. Besides, Elena was Spanish, so there was a language barrier to contend with, and she had a dodgy leg, so she could scarcely move around the kitchen unassisted most days. Catherine wore one of those wrist guards like she had carpal tunnel or something, and she made a strange groaning noise every time she was forced to bend down. I was convinced that they were putting it on, and I was only bitter about it because I didn't think of it first.

Then there was Martha herself: the self-proclaimed ruler of the roost. She predated the rest of the staff by at least two decades and mostly wandered around the manor with her hands glued behind her back, supervising her dutiful minions. Not only did she have a direct line to Lucinda, but she had a real mean streak of her own. Like the other girls, I quickly learned that it was better to just put up and shut up, complete the tasks as soon as possible, and hope the next demand wasn't to freshen Lucinda's chamber pot.

The twine I was hiding beneath my collar tugged at my hair, so I placed the brush down to readjust it. It was threaded through the ring that I'd found in my jacket pocket on my first night, so I glanced over my shoulder to check the room was clear before staring into the diamond like a magpie. How the hell it ended up in my possession after all these years was totally beyond me, and who put it there was even more of a mystery. However, I knew that I couldn't hand it in or leave it unattended in my room. I'd have to keep it close until I discovered who left it there and why.

"Where's Martha?" I heard someone grunt behind me.

I quickly stuffed the ring back down my tunic before looking over my shoulder to see Harris, our grim gamekeeper, standing in a wet patch near the doorway where I'd already cleaned. To my horror, not only did he have muddy boots on, but he was also clutching three or four dead pheasants by the feet that were dripping blood onto my newly immaculate floor. I let out an exasperated groan and dumped the brush back in the bucket. He seemed to realise his faux pas when he looked down at his feet.

"Sorry," he mumbled.

"Have you tried the kitchen?" I asked.

He gave a slight nod.

"Check the library. Lucinda should be due for her first gin and tonic any minute."

To my surprise, a little smile curled the corner of his lips. "Ta."

He left the way he came in, so I rushed over to clear up the mess he'd left before Martha spotted it. I didn't dare look to see if he'd left a trail in the hall.

Luckily, I'd only seen Harris a handful of times since Ellie first drove me through the gates, which was a good thing because his whole vibe frightened the life out of me. He'd appear in the kitchen every few days with a shotgun propped on his shoulder, dragging in some poor creature that he'd shot dead at the crack of dawn to be prepared for dinner that evening. On top of that, he always looked at me strangely, like he vaguely recognised me. Given that he'd once known my mother, I was worried he'd eventually make the connection between us, and it would be game over. Yet, so far, so good.

After what felt like forever, I'd finished cleaning. My knees were screaming as they creaked back into an upright position, so I bent down to rub them before stepping back to admire my handiwork. I was certain that Martha would find fault with it, but still, I was pretty pleased. I wiped my filthy hands on my tunic and took my time to go back to the kitchen, bucket in hand. Once I stepped inside, I saw Elena and Catherine running around like headless chickens, juggling multiple pans on the stove as they prepared breakfast. I went over to the corner of the room to empty the bucket in the sink and rolled my eyes when I heard our fearless leader clearing her throat behind me.

"Harris was looking for you," I said over my shoulder as she materialised behind me.

"Dealt with," she grunted. "Is the dining room floor finished?"

"Spotless," I said, tipping the murky water down the plughole.

"Did you polish the table?"

"To within an inch of its life."

"And what about Mrs Blackthorn's breakfast?"

I paused to check the time. "I was just about to—"

"For God's sake, Robyn!" she spat. "What are you playing at?"

"I'm going as fast—"

As soon as I dropped the bucket, Martha shoved a tray into my grasp. It was loaded with a black coffee, some avocado toast with a perfectly poached egg sitting on top, doused in black pepper.

"Now, please," she added.

"Righto," I mumbled, trudging through the kitchen to reverse out of the door into the corridor.

It went without saying that Lucinda was the last person I wanted to see, especially given that she defrocked me in the middle of the hallway on my first night. To tell the truth, I'd only survived the weeks that followed by avoiding her at all costs, but that couldn't last forever if I planned to keep my job. With a sigh, I lumbered up the stairs, hoping that her black coffee, which was rattling against the saucer with every step, didn't plummet onto the marble floor. Her bedroom door was slightly open, so I tapped on it lightly and then stepped back, trying my best to look professional.

"Come in," I heard Lucinda's hoarse voice call out.

I braced myself and used my elbow to push the door open, then stepped inside. She was sitting up in bed, still in her nightgown and engrossed in a battered book, so I swivelled my head around to see where I could place the tray. There was an elaborate dressing table in the window, so I started walking over to it with the intention of setting it down, but Lucinda quickly cleared her throat, rooting me to the spot.

"Not there!" she ordered.

I inhaled deeply through my nose. "Where would you like it, then, Mrs Blackthorn?"

She peered over her glasses. "Next to me."

"Sorry, I—"

"Tell me, why the hell would I want my breakfast over there when I'm visibly still in bed?"

I bit my tongue.

"Idiot."

Winning her over was going to be a lot more difficult than I thought.

Doing my best to fix my frown, I emptied the tray onto the table next to her, and she whisked the cup of coffee off it without even muttering a word of gratitude.

"Can I get you anything else?" I asked.

She shot me a contemptuous look in lieu of words, rapidly becoming more annoyed the longer I stayed. It would've been best just to leave there and then, but I was desperate to find some common ground, so I did the unthinkable: I spoke to her like I was a human being.

"What are you reading?" I added.

"A cautionary tale," she mumbled.

"Oh, I love books like that!" I announced. "What's it about?"

"A maid who asks far too many questions," she grumbled back.

A thin chuckle escaped me before I could stop it. "Okay, I'll—"

"Do you want to know how it ends?"

The answer was obvious.

She smirked. "I didn't think so."

I narrowed my eyes, finding myself wondering what Mrs Blackthorn would look like with a perfectly poached egg slapped against her forehead.

"Will that be all, madam?" I asked, digging my fingernails into my palm.

"For now," she said before turning back to her book.

I made for the door and delicately closed it behind me, wondering how I was going to endure this hell. What the fuck was her problem, anyway? Fine, she caught me wearing her daughter's gown in the dead of night, but that in itself didn't warrant her scorn towards me, surely? Whatever it was, I needed to go back to giving her a wide berth. I'd hardly been there five minutes and I'd already somehow managed to piss off half of the house.

"Miss Marsden!" Mr Blackthorn announced heartily behind me.

I sucked in a breath before turning around. "Good morning, Mr Blackthorn."

"How are we this fine day?" he asked.

Well, somebody was in a good mood.

"Grand," I uttered back. "You?"

"Marvellous! Just marvellous!"

"Can I get you anything? I'm just heading back to the kitchen."

"God, no," he replied, patting his stomach. "I haven't eaten breakfast in over a decade. An old armed forces habit."

"A coffee, then?"

"No, but I do need a word with you. Do you have a minute?"

"I think Martha is expecting me, and I don't want her to think I'm slacking off."

A shiver shot down my spine when his face turned to stone. "It wasn't a request."

I felt my throat close up. "What was I thinking?" I asked gawkily. "Of course I do."

His grin returned. "Splendid! Come on in!"

Was it the conversation I'd been dreading?

In truth, I was a shitty maid and an even worse cook, so it wasn't beyond the realms of imagination that I was being given the brush-off for something as simple as that. However, the look in Mr Blackthorn's eyes told me it was something more sinister. Had Lucas blabbed that I'd been in prison? Did his wife instruct him to fire me after what happened? Was it the ring I'd found? Or all of the above?

"Please, sit down," he instructed, pulling out a chair.

I complied, holding my hands together to steady them. "What's all this about?"

"It's a little awkward, but we do need to have a chat about your first month here."

Here it comes.

Mr Blackthorn produced a small red envelope with the Blackthorn crest printed on it from his jacket pocket and handed it over to me.

"What's this?" I uttered.

"Your wages," he explained. "I can only apologise for how long it's taken."

"Oh!" I blurted out, relief washing over me. "Thank you."

"I've only just been made aware we didn't have your bank details."

"I'm kind of... between bank accounts at the moment," I said, scratching my jaw. "Cash is fine."

"Fine, but I'll be having a frank discussion with Martha after we've finished."

"That's not necessary, Mr Blackthorn. I honestly forgot all about it."

"Good," he said, getting out of his chair to glance through the window. "Then there's the small matter of what happened on your first night here."

My heart rate shot up again. "What do you mean?"

"Penelope only told me yesterday," he explained as he began pacing the room. "I can only apologise for how you were treated."

"Mrs Blackthorn was upset. It was just a misunderstanding."

"And why didn't you come to me?"

I paused. "I'm new. I didn't want to make waves."

"Still," he said, stopping behind me. "It was utterly unacceptable."

"It's fine. Besides, I had a sheet and—"

Every muscle in my body seized.

I didn't realise what was happening at first until I turned my head to the side and saw Mr Blackthorn's hands resting on my shoulders. They lingered for a split second, as if he was giving me a chance to protest. When I didn't, he dug his thumbs in, making little circles at the base of my neck, wrapping his clammy fingers over my collarbones.

He paused again. "Is everything okay?"

I nodded quickly, gnashing my teeth together.

"Relax, then," he continued, pressing his body against the back of the chair. "I want you to feel safe here."

"I—I do," I croaked.

His touch deepened. "Does that feel nice?"

"Uh-huh," I grunted, impulsively arching my neck.

"Did you know I was in the Royal Navy?"

I rattled my head.

"I was, for several years. It's where I learned this."

"It's, erm, great," I said, leaning forward.

"Listen, if *anything* like that happens again, you need to come to me directly, okay?" he said, the scent of scotch heating the back of my neck.

"Err—yeah," I said, hunching my back. "Anyway, I'd better return to—"

Before I could finish, his hands shifted position again.

Paralysed, I watched in horror as his fingers slid down the front of my tunic. His grip softened. His fingers spread. I could only just hear him speaking over the sound of blood rushing around in my eardrums.

"I mean, being paraded around the house like that in your underwear?" he said softly. "I can only imagine how it must've looked."

"How it… looked?" I stammered.

"I bet you felt so vulnerable. Tell me, did anyone see you?"

"No, I—" I choked.

The very tip of his finger touched the top of my bra. I decided enough was enough.

Without thinking, I abruptly reached over for the photograph that was sitting on his desk to serve as a diversion. To my horror, I hadn't realised that it was a photograph of him and Sofia from many years ago until I picked it up. However, the distraction worked, and he backed off almost on reflex.

"Is this your daughter, Mr Blackthorn?" I asked, adjusting my tunic.

"Yes," he sullenly replied, returning to his chair. "That's our Sofia."

"She's beautiful," I commented.

"She was," he mused as he removed the photograph from my grasp.

"Was?" I echoed. "What happened to her?"

Mr Blackthorn took the photograph with him to the window and started peering out of it reflectively.

"She—she died. Seven years ago, now."

"Oh, God," I said, throwing my hands in my lap. "I'm so sorry."

"Don't be. You weren't to know."

"How did it happen?" I asked before realising my faux pas. "If you don't mind me asking."

"She was murdered," he deadpanned.

"Shit," I said without meaning to, catching him off guard. "Why?"

"I spent a fortune in pursuit of an answer to that question," he explained, shaking his head bitterly. "But we still don't know."

"That must be incredibly difficult."

"It is," he sniffled. "It hit my wife the hardest. I think a part of her is still living in the hope that Sofia is going to walk through those doors one day as though nothing ever happened. That's why her bedroom has been turned into that damned tomb."

I swallowed. "Well, people deal with grief in different ways, don't they?"

"That they do," he mumbled before snapping out of his sullen mood. "Sorry, I shouldn't be offloading on you like this."

"No—it's fine," I said before getting out of my chair. "Anyway, I'd better go back. Martha probably has a search party out."

"Of course, of course," he said as he returned the photograph to his desk. "She runs a tight ship."

"She does." I laughed uneasily. "Have a pleasant day, Mr Blackthorn."

"You, too," he muttered.

I couldn't get out of the room fast enough. The instant the door closed, I stumbled back into the wall, clutching the ring around my neck for comfort. What in the living hell was that? Was it an unspoken rule that the help had to allow him to have his wicked way with them, just to keep their jobs? Did he do that to the rest of the girls? Did he do it to Mum?

She tried telling me what they were like.

Why the fuck didn't I listen to her?

11

THE CANDLE

ROBYN – BEFORE

I sucked in a deep breath, pursed my lips, then blew out with all my might. However, much to Mum's amusement, the candle just wouldn't go out. She cackled as she held the thickly frosted cupcake closer to my mouth, and after another try, the flame was finally extinguished. I tilted my head back as I watched the tiny whisper of smoke float up into the heavens, then looked back at Mum, who'd leaned out of her chair to place the cake on the table and started clapping in celebration.

God, I hated the eighteenth of July.

Most girls celebrating their twenty-first birthday would probably be with their mates, out celebrating till dawn, but not me. Don't get me wrong, I'd always enjoyed them when I was younger. At first, it was with sweets and toys, and then with booze and music when I was older, yet ever since Mum's injury, I just couldn't bring myself to switch off. It marked another year gone, another year trapped in our squalid little flat without two pennies to rub together—a further reminder of what we'd lost and would never get back.

I couldn't help but wonder what Ellie and the girls were up to. Even though it was difficult to admit, I missed them. I yearned for the distraction, for the escapism, and for a few hours where I could forget the crushing weight of responsibility on my shoulders. But it had been weeks since Mum barred me from seeing them, and the only contact I had with them was when Sydney posted a picture of some random girl on our group chat, and the rest of them savagely laid into her outfit choice. Given that Mum had been riding my back ever since she found out they were connected to the Blackthorns, sneaking out to see them was virtually impossible.

Still, it wasn't all bad. I'd popped out to the shops that morning to buy my own cake, and Mum had fished an old candle out of the cutlery drawer to stick in it. It was a half-melted number one from two birthdays before, but it did the job. Mum had insisted that we get dressed up for the occasion, so I was wearing my nicest dress that I'd got on sale. To top things off, she'd pushed the boat out and used part of her disability allowance to order us a rare takeaway. Although I kicked up a fuss and was already working out how we'd cut the forty quid she'd spent on it from next week's budget, I'd be lying if I said I wasn't glad of the break from behind the stove.

"Come on! Are you making a wish, or what?" she asked.

"A wish?" I grumbled. "It's a bit childish, don't you think?"

"Don't be a stick in the mud and humour me!"

"Christ…" I muttered, closing my eyes.

Let's be honest, there were a million things to wish for, maybe for a cake that didn't come with a yellow sticker because it was a day past its shelf-life, or for a lacklustre birthday meal that wasn't going to be delivered in a sweaty, plastic bag. If I were feeling particularly courageous, I could've asked for five minutes' respite from the relentless care of my mother, or even for her injury to heal altogether. Yet, I didn't wish for any of those things—I didn't wish for anything. I only went through the motions, just like everything else in my life.

"Done," I announced.

"What did you wish for?"

"I can't tell you that, can I?" I chuckled. "It won't come true if I do."

"Twenty-one. I don't believe it!" she pondered, wheeling herself over to the rack to grab some plates.

"I know!" I smiled.

"God, it only seems like yesterday when you were sucking on a bottle."

"I might need to again if this damned takeaway doesn't turn up soon," I remarked, peering up at the clock.

"Remember: all good things come to those who wait…"

"I should've just cooked. That chicken in the fridge is about to turn and—"

"For crying out loud!" She chortled. "Enough of the damn chicken, Robyn! Live a little!"

I wanted to go into a spontaneous lecture about how we didn't have the money to be throwing good food in the bin, but I kept shtum. However, Mum seemed to spot my mood change and sighed in defeat, fiddling with the cupcake in front of her.

"Listen, I get it, okay?" she began, arching her neck to catch my gaze. "We should be out celebrating at some fancy restaurant, not stuck here."

"Mum, come on. You know I don't care about that," I explained.

"Then what's the matter, love?"

"Honestly?" I mumbled.

She nodded brightly.

"I'm just hungry!" I deflected. "Besides, you know I'm a sucker for a greasy takeaway."

With a hearty laugh, Mum rolled over to the cutlery drawer to grab some utensils. I ran my fingers through my hair while her back was turned and took a sip of the tepid prosecco I'd found in the back of the cupboard earlier that evening. I needed to try and snap myself out of the funk I was in, or I risked making the whole evening ten times worse. She was struggling to reach out of her chair, so I set the glass down and lifted my bum off the seat.

"Mum, I can get those," I suggested.

"Sit that backside down!" she ordered over her shoulder. "I'm not totally useless yet."

She returned a second later to lay out our place settings, then returned to her side of the table.

"What did we do for your eighteenth? Do you remember?" she asked.

"Barely. Kirsty and Amy managed to get that bottle of vodka, didn't they?"

"How could I forget? I spent all night holding your hair back while you chucked it back up."

"Those were the days, weren't they?" I rolled my eyes. "It seems like a lifetime ago now."

"Maybe it wasn't your eighteenth I was thinking of. What did we do the year after?"

I quickly peered at the floor. It didn't surprise me that she didn't remember what we did that night. I'd turned nineteen a few weeks after she'd been discharged from the hospital, so between the chaos of her returning home and adjusting to the changes, neither of us even mentioned it.

Luckily, the doorbell rang before I had to answer her question.

"Finally!" I exclaimed, leaping out of my chair.

I rushed through to the front door and undid the chain to open it. The delivery driver was waiting outside with a helmet on, visor down, holding out a steamed-up bag of slimy food at arm's length. I gratefully received it before grabbing the money that Mum had left on the side.

"How much?" I asked.

"Thirty-eight seventy," he mumbled.

"Here," I said, handing over two twenties. "Can I have the change?"

He grumbled, counting out some coins from his pocket before dropping them in my palm. "Enjoy."

I closed the door and ripped the bag open on the way back to the kitchen, then set it on the table to start sorting through the oily containers.

"Bastards! I think they've forgotten the prawn crackers," I announced.

"Robyn?" Mum murmured, chin on chest.

"False alarm—they're here!" I proclaimed, raising them in the air like a trophy.

"You—you promised me," she stuttered.

I slid the bag out of the way and saw that Mum was clutching my phone to her chest.

"Give it back," I instructed, holding out my hand.

"Your friend Ellie just sent you a picture. It looks like they're all at some fancy nightclub."

I blinked. "So? Nothing to do with me."

"She's invited you to go along."

I held out my hand again, and Mum begrudgingly gave me my device back. Lo and behold, there was a message waiting from Ellie with an address for some club in Manchester, along with a contrived photograph of the whole gang downing shots at the bar.

"Lucas is with them," she pointed out.

I plonked myself down on my chair. "Mum, I—"

"You told me you were going to cut contact. The Blackthorns, they're—"

"Dangerous," I added, finishing her sentence with an eye roll. "So, you keep saying."

"I'm serious, Robyn. You don't even know the half of it."

"But Mum, they're my only friends!" I argued. "What am I meant to do? Just cut them out?"

"Yes!" she spat. "People like that—they don't have friends. Just people they can use."

"The Blackthorns help people, Mum! They have a charity for Christ's sake!"

"Open your eyes, Robyn!" Mum shouted, rocking her head in doubt. "It's all make-believe!"

"Make-believe?" I sneered. "Do you even hear yourself?"

"How can you even question it after what they did to me?" she asked, gesturing to her chair.

For obvious reasons, I'd been holding back my true motives from Mum. However, right there, with the candle still smoking and her looking at me like a lost child, my inhibitions gave way. I was doing a good thing. The *right* thing. I wasn't planning to blackmail or hurt anyone. I just wanted the Blackthorns to step up and take responsibility for the damage they'd caused.

All in all, some home truths were long overdue.

"Precisely!" I shot back. "They owe you for what happened!"

"No, they don't," she dismissed.

"They do! And with their money, they can sort all of this out."

She narrowed her eyes. "Sort what out, exactly?"

"Come on, Mum, look around! We can't carry on living like this."

"We'll manage. We always do," she grunted.

"Think about it: we could move somewhere bigger, not up three flights of stairs. Maybe even get someone to help out around the house and replace your manky chair."

"We're fine the way we are!"

I drew in air slowly, desperate to stop the words leaving my lips, but I couldn't.

"I am not fucking fine!" I yelled. "All I do is wake up and look after you. Day after day. Week after week. I can't—I can't carry on like this."

"But you said you liked looking after—"

"I know what I said," I bit back. "Anyway, it's not all about the Blackthorns. The girls—they distract me. It's a few hours a week where I don't have to be me."

Mum's jaw dropped. That was the moment I should've felt a stab of guilt, but I didn't. She needed to know what I was wrestling with on a daily basis. Without making eye contact, she took the brake off her chair and rotated around to point herself at the door, then placed her open palm on the table.

"Listen, you're an adult," she began, picking at the wood grain. "You can do as you please."

"I know, and I—"

"And I can't stop you from seeing them," she continued. "But please, for my sanity, just do as I asked."

I dropped my gaze to the table. "I can't."

She braced herself. "What's the big plan then, huh? Enlighten me?"

"I'm going to get close to them," I said, raising my head. "I'm going to find out what really happened to you, and then I'm going to convince them to make things right again."

Mum's nose wrinkled as she fought back tears, her bottom lip quivering as she reached between her thigh and the chair to produce a pink envelope.

"I was going to give you this after we'd eaten," she said, her voice brittle. "You may as well have it now."

With that, she left the card in my hand and gracelessly turned around in our tiny kitchen to wheel into the living room, leaving me alone with the untouched takeaway. I wiped away a tear before I ripped the envelope open, and a pound coin and two ten-pound notes fell out, folded into the shape of love hearts. The front had a puppy wearing a party hat with birthday cake all over its face and paws, with the caption, "Have a *paw-some* birthday!" written on the front. I had no idea how she managed to get it. She must've begged one of the neighbours to pick it up for her.

Robyn. You're the best daughter anybody could ask for. Happy Birthday, sweetheart. Love, Mum.

The television was already blaring by the time I finished reading the message. I grabbed my phone from the table and strode out of the flat before I could change my mind, telling myself I was doing it to continue my plan of getting closer to the Blackthorns, but it was bullshit. In truth, I wanted nothing more than to spend my birthday drinking myself numb, in the company of some drug-addled slappers whom I half-despised, just to feel alive again.

I didn't know it at the time, but it was the point of no return.

It was the beginning of my downfall, and it would cost me what little I had left.

12

THE OUTING

ROBYN

Sweet, sweet freedom.

I'd almost forgotten that there was a whole world outside of the Blackthorn Estate. It felt so good to be out in the open air, out of that ill-fitting tunic, and blowing my first wage packet on whatever mad whim took me as I traipsed around the streets of Manchester, loaded with shopping bags like a packhorse. Martha nearly had a heart attack when I asked her for the day off, and she only agreed to it when I pointed out that the Blackthorns were all off the estate themselves, on various errands. Above all else, the biggest relief was having the monkey off my back and not having to look over my shoulder for once.

It went without saying that technology had moved on while I was in prison, so I decided that it was high time that I retired my trusty old phone, the cracked and temperamental antique, and moved into the twenty-first century with something fancy. I was perched on a concrete bench outside the shop, stuffing a sausage roll into my mouth with one hand and setting up my new mobile with the other. The pigeons had formed a queue in front of me, inexplicably organised by size, cooing and creeping over whenever a stray piece of pastry hit the ground.

"I've told you—you can scavenge when I've finished," I said to the flock.

Most of them weirdly seemed to understand, but the largest one broke rank and stepped forward.

"Cheeky little shit, aren't you?" I said, tearing off a corner of the pastry. "Here."

I threw the scrap into the line, and they all pounced on it, hacking it to pieces with their beaks. Before I knew it, a dozen others showed up, so I ended up throwing the last half of my lunch a few metres away, just to keep them away from my new trainers. After the commotion died down, I felt a tap on my shoulder, so I instinctively rotated my head slightly before turning back to my phone.

"Sorry," I uttered. "No change on me."

"I'm not some beggar, Robyn," a voice drawled.

I fully turned around, and I saw Penelope Blackthorn standing there, elbows laden with oversized designer shopping bags, wearing a smile as sharp as a blade. I straightened my back and started batting the crumbs off my top, hovering over the bench for a beat before she gestured for me to remain seated. She peered down at the space next to me in disgust, but finally decided to plonk herself down when she decided it was clean enough to park her behind.

"Miss Blackthorn, I had no idea it was you!" I exclaimed, subtly sliding the ring from my finger and placing it in my pocket.

"Relax," she said, bumping her shoulder into mine. "And please, call me Penelope."

"What are you doing here?"

"A spot of shopping. My wardrobe was looking a little dated." She peered down at my bags. "I see you're doing the same."

"Yeah—I thought it was time to get some clothes that aren't a tunic or pyjamas."

Without asking, the cheeky cow reached into one of my bags and unfurled the folded pair of jeans I had just bought with her finger and thumb, holding them in the air like they were roadkill.

"How quaint," she said, dropping them back in the bag with a face that disagreed with her comment.

"Anyway," I said, gathering my purchases. "I was just about to head home and—"

"So soon? It's barely midday."

"Yeah, well, I'm back to being skint again!" I laughed. "If I spend another penny, I won't even be able to afford the bus ticket."

Penelope pulled a face like she didn't understand a single syllable of what I just said. "Right."

"Well, it was nice seeing you," I said, standing up to leave.

"I can always give you a lift, if you'd like?"

I stopped and turned back around. "A lift? Are you sure?"

"Uh-huh," she grunted in agreement. "I have a few more things to pick up, and I could use a second opinion."

My mouth opened, poised to tell her that I'd rather crawl across broken glass than accept a lift from her. But as the bags felt even heavier in my grip, I buttoned it back up again to reevaluate.

"I'd like that." I smiled.

"Wonderful!" she cheered. "I've not had a shopping partner in ages!"

With that, she leapt off the bench and started flouncing down the street, leaving her bags still on the ground.

"Penelope, your—"

"Would you mind grabbing those for me?" she interrupted. "They've been cutting into my hands."

Regret filled me up. "Sure."

* * *

On the short walk over towards St Ann's Square, I realised that the apple doesn't fall far from the tree. Penelope was basically a mini-Lucinda, only without the crow's feet, alcohol problem and halitosis. She flounced through the lunchtime crowd, not sparing a single thought for me trudging behind her, feeling like my arms were about to fall out of their sockets. We must have visited a dozen jewellers, scouring every window display for the perfect necklace she could wear for some big dinner on the weekend, but everything was either not shiny enough, not grand enough, or simply too cheap.

"Sorry to be a killjoy, but Martha is expecting me for dinner service," I called after Penelope, who was already making her way to the next window display. "I really need to make tracks."

"Don't be so fatuous," she spat over her shoulder. "She's hardly likely to reprimand you when you were out with me, is she?"

"I suppose not," I said, readjusting my grip on the bags to allow some blood into my fingers.

"Besides, we have one last place to check. They've never let me down before."

"Where?"

"Baker and Roberts," she announced. "It's heaven!"

The air left my lungs. I ended up dropping a few of the bags onto the pavement in shock, and Penelope spun round, racing over to rescue them.

"Careful!" she hissed. "They're very expensive!"

"Maybe I should just get the bus back," I suggested, taking the bags back from her. "I'll bring your stuff back with me."

"Nonsense! I can't have you riding the peasant wagon with all that in tow, can I?"

"It's just…"

"What?"

I looked over her shoulder and saw Baker and Roberts a few hundred metres away, the sound of the security shutters falling still echoing in my head. It had been well over six years since my life was changed forever within those walls. If the manager and Sally were still employed there, they wouldn't recognise me, surely? It was a gamble stepping foot in there, but it was even more of a risk to tell Penelope the truth of why I couldn't.

"Well?" she prompted.

"Nothing," I dismissed. "Let's hunt this necklace down, shall we?"

I felt like I was entering the jaws of death when I followed Penelope into the store. I posted up at the entrance, lowering the bags onto the carpet as she pranced around, browsing each of the cabinets in turn with a shit-eating grin. I thought she was going to leave me be, but after a minute or so of perusing, she beckoned me over, so I abandoned the bags and trudged to her side.

"*This* is the place. We're sure to find something appropriate here."

I quickly scanned the display. "How about this one?" I said, pointing to one at random.

"Rose gold? You can't be serious."

"Okay then, that one," I said, aiming my finger at the necklace next to it.

"Hmm," she pondered. "That isn't a terrible suggestion."

"Penelope Blackthorn!" I heard a voice boom across the room.

My chest seized. It was the manager.

"Michael! How the devil are you?" she drawled.

"All the better for seeing you here!" he yelled, almost taking out another customer as he rushed over. "How long has it been?"

"Too long!" she said, offering her cheek.

He leaned forward and gave her a peck, then, to my horror, turned his attention to me.

"Don't I know you from somewhere?"

My heart skipped a beat. "No, I don't think so."

"No, I do! I never forget a face!"

I tugged at the hair covering my birthmark as his narrowed eyes slid over me. After a moment, they widened, and he stepped back with a grim expression on his face. Did he remember me from the robbery, or from when he lied on the stand and got me sent down for a crime I didn't commit? It didn't matter. To put it bluntly, I was fucked either way.

"I know exactly who you are," he uttered.

My eyes flitted to Penelope as I lifted my hands in surrender. "I'm sorry, I—"

He ploughed into me without warning, wrapping his arms around my back before holding me by the shoulders at arm's length.

"Sofia!" he bellowed. "I swear I heard that you were missing!"

"She *is* missing, Michael," Penelope chimed in, placing her hand on his arm. "This is one of our staff."

He slowly released his grip and turned to her. "Oh, Miss Blackthorn, I'm so sorry."

"Don't be silly," she responded. "I agree with you— the resemblance is uncanny."

I flashed him a lopsided smile as he took one last glance at me.

"Tell me, do you have any other pieces in the back?" Penelope asked him. "I don't think these will cut the mustard."

"Certainly," he said with a little bow. "What sort of thing are you looking for?"

"Something *extraordinary*. I need to upstage my friend, Camilla."

"Miss Cavendish-Bowes?" he suggested.

"Yes," she uttered, her eyes rolling back.

Ah. So that wasn't just sleepwalking chat.

"She was in last week with her intended, actually," Michael explained.

Penelope scoffed. "She can hardly afford anything from here, can she?"

"On the contrary, they were picking out their wedding bands," he delicately corrected.

"Genuinely?" She clutched her chest. "Hmm. Good for them."

"Thinking about it, she was looking at some of our more extravagant pieces. I can fish them out, if you'd like?"

"I won't be caught dead wearing her cast-offs."

Michael leaned in. "I think it was more of a budgetary issue," he whispered.

Penelope's eyes lit up again. "Then what are you waiting for?" she drawled. "Let's see them!"

"Splendid!" he blurted. "I'll just be a moment."

The manager left us by the cabinet, so I took a breath and leaned my hands on the glass.

"Are you okay?" she asked, arching her neck slightly. "You look a little pale."

"I'm fine," I snapped back. "I just don't like being manhandled."

"Manhandled," she parroted, shaking her head.

"What?" I uttered back.

"It's nothing—just Sofia used to use words like that too," she explained, almost with a touch of sadness in her voice.

"Sorry," I said, lifting myself back up. "Were you close?"

"Not as close as I'd have liked."

"Did you two not go shopping together?"

"God, no. She was a hermit—barely left the estate."

"What happened to her?"

Penelope's eyebrows shot up before she started peering into the cabinet again. "That entirely depends on who you ask."

"I'm asking you," I said out of reflex.

"Why are you so interested?"

"I just am."

She shrugged. "There isn't much to the story. One day she was there, gone the next."

"Why, though? You must know if someone wanted to hurt her."

Penelope squared her shoulders in front of me and ran her tongue over her bottom lip.

"Do you want the truth?" she asked.

I nodded keenly.

"She was an ungrateful, spiteful, little witch!" she spat. "It's not a surprise that someone decided to put her out of her misery."

"But you seemed like—"

"I mean, she won the lottery when Mum and Dad adopted her," she interrupted. "But she wasn't content with that, was she? No. She had to try to force Lucas and me out!"

"Force you out?" I pulled a face. "Of what?"

"The family!" she announced. "She clung onto Dad like they were joined at the hip. Constantly whispering into his ear and manipulating him."

"He seems like he really misses her," I pointed out.

"Of course he does! Everyone knows *she* was his favourite. It was utterly pathetic."

My lips parted, but I literally had nothing left to say.

"And you know what else?" she added.

"What?" I murmured.

"I'm *glad* she's dead."

My arms broke out in goosebumps.

"Here we are!" Michael announced, returning with a velvet tray of necklaces in each hand. "I'm sure one of these will be perfect!"

Penelope broke her scowl before turning to him. "Marvellous! I'm sure they will!"

I slowly backed away, returning to the bags as my imagination ran wild. Penelope wasn't capable of doing anything to her sister, was she? As far as I was concerned, the whole family was batshit crazy, so it wasn't unthinkable that she and Lucas orchestrated their sister's disappearance out of some perceived slight. One thing I knew for sure was that I felt sorry for Sofia. If she earned the disdain of a horrible, vacuous woman like Penelope, she couldn't have been half bad.

"We have a winner!" Penelope declared, prancing around the shop floor.

"Great," I deadpanned.

13

THE BITCH

ROBYN — BEFORE

After spending ten of the twenty-one quid Mum left me in my birthday card on a taxi, I arrived at the address Ellie had sent and began tottering over to the entrance. I hadn't visited Palacio on Deansgate before, mainly because the entrance fee alone would've cleaned me out most nights, and that was before I even tasted a single drink. It was an old building, maybe a bank or a municipal building once upon a time, but it had been totally retrofitted since then. The carved, stone pillars were underlit with pink neon spotlights, a buzzing neon sign fitted between them, and the windows were entirely blacked out. There was a queue running as far as the eye could see, filled with hopeful clubbers dancing in the wintry air to the thumping bass pouring into the street.

I swallowed on my approach to the red carpet, the dirty looks from the queue bouncing off me as I kept my eyes locked on the entrance. There was a tall but skinny man with a full face of makeup chatting with the bouncers, with a headset on and holding a clipboard. I started preparing my arguments to let me inside, mumbling them under my breath as I walked over, but he traced every inch of me and blocked my path as soon as I tried.

"Honey, did you not see the queue?" he asked, shaking his head.

"But my friends are already in there," I argued. "They'll be on the guest list."

He rolled his eyes. "Name?"

"Ellie Fairfax."

He half-heartedly scanned the list and shook his head. "Nope."

I exhaled through my nose. "Try Lucas Blackthorn."

"Sweetie, he's here every Saturday night." He cackled. "Back of the line."

I peered down the endless queue. I was about to bite the bullet and trudge to the end when I heard someone shouting my name.

"Robyn!" Sydney squealed. "You made it!"

Before I even had a chance to turn around fully, she had her arms wrapped around me, depositing a bit of cigarette ash on the shoulder of my frayed coat as she pulled me in close. She was wearing a particularly skimpy number that evening: a mirror-finish, silver dress that struggled to conceal her backside and a pair of six-inch heels that made my ankles hurt just by looking at them. She stank to high heaven of expensive perfume, tobacco smoke and vodka, and was inexplicably covered in glitter like she'd just been blasted by a confetti cannon. It was only when she released me that I realised how woefully underdressed I was for the occasion, sporting my discount dress, ragged jacket and scuffed wedges.

"Everyone's inside!" she howled. "Ellie's going to lose her freaking mind!"

"They aren't going to let me in," I explained. "Not on the list."

Sydney pouted, turning her attention to the doorman who was holding up his clipboard like a shield.

"Come on, you miserable sod! It's her birthday!" she barked.

"She's not on the list. Besides, we have a dress code, and—"

"You remember who we're with, right?" she interrupted.

He glanced at the bouncer beside him. "Yes."

"And how do you think he'll react when I tell him that you didn't let our friend in?"

"Well, I don't think he'd be happy," he muttered.

"What was that?" Sydney got in his face.

"I said, I don't think he'd be happy," he repeated louder.

"Exactly, so are you going to let her in, or what?"

Begrudgingly, the doorman stepped to one side, and Sydney grabbed me by the hand to drag me past him. I was compelled to shoot a wink his way as the line erupted into a chorus of complaint beside him, just before we descended into the darkness of the club.

I couldn't hear myself think once we got inside. Mirrored walls. Crushed velvet seats. Tiny glass tables like islands surrounding the sea of bodies pulsing with the music. The crowd parted, and I spotted the rest of the gang at the rear, sitting in a booth with enough empty glassware in front of them to warrant a risk assessment. Kait was sitting on the end with her legs crossed at an angle that defied physics. Allisyn was on the other side, trying to create some volume in her hair using her phone as a mirror. Ellie was between them, chugging champagne directly from the bottle and blankly staring into space.

"It's the birthday bitch!" Kait announced, leading the other girls to whoop in celebration.

"Where the hell have you been?" Ellie asked, offering the bottle at arm's length. "I sent you like six texts."

"Sorry," I said, reaching over to accept the bottle. "I couldn't get a taxi."

"Luckily, we're just getting started!" Allisyn turned to the group. "Isn't that right, ladies?"

The collective scream they let out was even more deafening than the music.

"How did you even know it was my birthday?" I asked as I plonked myself onto the seat.

"Allisyn told us!" Sydney chimed in.

"It's my superpower," Allisyn announced, her eyes twinkling with mischief.

"Don't believe a word she says," Kait said in my ear. "She checked the date on your pizza post."

"Do you have to ruin everything?" Allisyn asked, scowling at her.

"Give her the present! Give her the present!" Sydney repeated like an impatient toddler.

"Wait, you got me something?" I asked.

"Yeah, we all clubbed together and got you this," Ellie said, pulling out a small jewellery box from her clutch.

The box was made from black leather, with a hot-pink bow tying it together. Wasting no time, I ripped it apart and flicked the lid. There was a delicate bracelet staring back at me, with a small, gold plate engraved with my name. I would've had to save up for a whole year to afford something like that, and it went without saying that it beat the lukewarm takeaway and twenty-one quid that Mum got me hands down.

"You guys!" I gushed. "You shouldn't have!"

"It's nothing!" Ellie said, reaching over Kait to show her wrist. "We've all got them."

All of a sudden, everyone crowded around me and put their wrists together to show me the matching bracelets we now all owned, like we were the *Famous Five*. Is this what it was like to have friends? Or to be in some sort of cult?

"Where have you been, anyway?" Allisyn asked. "Hot date?"

"I wish!" I threw my head back. "Just had dinner with Mum."

"Mum?" she asked, arching an eyebrow.

"Yeah, I do have one." I mocked, laughing. "What's the big deal?"

"Nothing—you've just never mentioned her before."

"Hey! You should've brought her along!" Sydney added.

"Yeah, right!" I chuckled. "Nightclubs—not her scene."

"Hey, handsome!" Allisyn hollered at a random clubber. "Will you take a picture of us?"

The stranger took the phone from Allisyn as we all crammed up like sardines in the frame. Sydney had her face pressed against my left cheek, and Kait was flattened on my right, all grinning at the camera with their drinks raised in the air. Ellie and Allisyn stood on the chair to get behind us, wrapping their arms around us so tightly that I could hardly breathe.

"Say, 'birthday bitch!'" Ellie sang.

"Birthday bitch!" we all repeated, grinning as the flash went off.

My smile faded as my eyes adjusted, and I saw Lucas approaching from the toilet door behind our amateur photographer. He had an entourage of his own: four men with tattooed biceps thicker than their thighs and skin-tight tops. I turned to Allisyn and Sydney to ask who they were, but they were already out of their seats, sprinting at the two taller men with their arms outstretched. Ellie followed a beat later, giving a brief nod of recognition to Lucas before chatting with the boys and pointing over at me. Kait remained seated with me, pulling out a small mirror to touch up her makeup.

"Hey, do you want one?" Kait asked in my ear.

For a heartbeat, I thought she was offering one of the blokes standing in front of me until I swivelled my head and saw she was holding out a little pink tablet, with a tiny, cartoon duck etched into the surface.

"No thanks." I lifted a hand. "I'm good."

"But it's your birthday!"

I winced. "What even is it?"

"Ecstasy," she said before pulling a face. "I think."

"You think?" I scoffed. "Honestly, I'm alright."

"Come on! It'll loosen you up."

"I don't do stuff like that. Besides, I need to keep a clear head for tomorrow."

"Why, what's happening tomorrow?"

Suddenly, my mind was taken to Salford, to a grimy little flat in a crumbling block, and to Mum sitting alone in it. She was probably exactly where I left her, languishing in front of some godawful show, making herself sick with worry about where I was. I could almost hear her telling me to say no. Come home. Lose their numbers. Forget all about them. Yet, at twenty-one years old, I'd already said no to so much. Not only stupid things like a tiny pill with a duck etched on it, but things that mattered. Freedom. Independence. Love.

No more. What harm could it do?

"Fuck it," I snapped, holding out my hand. "Give it here."

Kait excitedly dropped it into my palm, and I tossed it in my mouth, washing it down with a random drink from the table. She did the same, then rubbed my shoulders with childlike glee as she pulled me out of the booth by my hands. She raced ahead, sultrily beckoning everyone to accompany her to the dance floor, but Lucas held back, signalling that he was going to the bar first. I tried to follow the rest of the group, but the blood turned to ice in my veins when I felt fingers wrapping around my arm to stop me.

"You're the birthday girl, aren't you?" Lucas shouted in my ear.

"Yeah," I yelled back. "Robyn."

"Buy you a drink?"

"Er—sure."

To my horror, he threw his arm over my shoulders and began escorting me to the bar as Ellie glowered in our direction. A barmaid appeared to take his order the instant we arrived, leaning in to hear it.

"Give me a bottle of *Dom P*," he instructed. "And two glasses."

She smiled and strode over to the chiller.

"Have I met you before?" he asked, narrowing his eyes.

"You might've spotted me when you tore up Heaton Park with your Range Rover."

He chortled. "Shit, you were there?"

I nodded, cringing.

"Oh boy, did I get in trouble for that one!" He chuckled. "Dad went off his nut."

"What was it over? Some argument about your sister?"

Lucas raised an eyebrow. "Who told you that?"

"Ellie," I said after a pause.

His face softened again. "I don't remember, but probably. She's all anyone talks about."

"Siblings, am I right?" I remarked.

"They're a fucking nightmare," he announced before peering at me weirdly. "You look like her, you know?"

"Who?"

"My sister Sofia. It's a bit unnerving, actually."

I turned away for a few seconds as I flattened a curl against my birthmark automatically. When I spun back, he had his phone out, scrolling through some group chat that was abuzz with activity.

"Speaking of family, I think you've met my mum," I announced, flinching at my own ham-fistedness.

"Your mum?" he mumbled, eyes locked on his phone.

"Yeah, she used to work at your—"

"Hey, can you hurry up? I'm dying of thirst over here!" he bellowed over the bar before turning back. "Sorry—the service here is shocking."

"It's okay," I said, gripping the counter. "Like I was saying, she used to work in the kitchens."

"Kitchens?"

"At your estate."

Lucas put his phone away. "What's her name?"

I opened my mouth to speak again, but Ellie had materialised between us, dragging her hands down Lucas' chest to stake her claim.

"What are you two chatting about?" she asked, giving me the stink eye.

"Nothing," I said quickly. "Just family."

"Fuck me! Are you picking the bloody grapes yourself?" Lucas bellowed to the barmaid.

She rushed back over with the bottle of champagne, and Lucas popped the cork, misting half of the queue.

After the foam had calmed down, he tried to fill the two flutes she'd left on the bar but ended up getting more on the counter than in the glasses. Ellie downed the one closest to me, dropped it on the ground like a threat, then crunched the surviving parts with the heel of her shoe. I nervously took a sip of the second as she grabbed Lucas by the belt buckle and all but dragged him to the dance floor.

I felt strange when I began to follow them. I didn't know whether it was the booze, the pill, or nothing more than the anxiety, but my heart started beating out of my sternum. Then came a rush. Energy. Colours were brighter—the music crisper. I physically felt my pupils widen when I spotted Ellie, waving me over as she whispered something in the lone Bicep-boy's ear. He grinned like a Cheshire cat as he approached me, not even bothering with a hello before sliding his hands over my hips. Under normal circumstances, feeling a stranger's fingers inching over my arse would've resulted in them getting a fresh slap to the face.

But not that time.

That time, I didn't care.

14

THE DRESS

ROBYN

For the most part, life on the Blackthorn Estate was mundane. Given the sheer size of it, it required constant upkeep, and unfortunately for me, cleaning. In reality, most of the missions that Martha sent me on were a fool's errand—dusting rooms that no one had set foot in for years. Case in point: I was making the bed in one of the guest rooms, which could easily have been last cleaned by my mum if the thick layer of dust over everything was anything to go by. But I couldn't grumble. It was a chance to be alone in my thoughts, listen to a bit of music on the new phone I'd bought, and avoid any awkward run-ins with my benevolent employers.

Thankfully, Mr Blackthorn largely remained in his study, barking down his phone and stomping around on the floor so hard that I could hear it on the other side of the house. His meals were brought to his office door on a tray, and every time it fell to me to deliver them, I essentially dumped them and ran after the whole massage incident. Thinking about his hands snaking over my collarbones made my skin crawl, yet I didn't dare tell anyone. It was my word against his, and I already knew how that would go.

Weirdly, I'd never seen Mr Blackthorn interact with his wife, even in passing, and I wondered if he even realised that Lucinda was living under the same roof as him at all. They ate alone, slept in different rooms, and from what I could gather, led entirely independent lives. Maybe that's what married life was really like for people like them: the wife drinking herself to oblivion night and day, whilst the husband gropes the staff.

The door swung open, so I quickly whipped the earphones out. Lucas reversed in, with a laptop under his arm and a box of tissues in the other. It took all of two seconds to put two and two together, so I already had disgust written on my face when he spotted me standing on the other side of the bed.

"Shit," he said, a smile breaking out on his face. "I thought this room was empty."

"Well, it's not," I remarked, tightening the sheet around the mattress.

"What are you even doing in here?" he said, subtly moving the tissues behind his back. "I'm the only one who ever comes in here."

I looked down at the mattress and fought the urge to heave. "Just doing as I'm told."

Lucas didn't speak for a moment, so I stopped what I was doing and looked at him.

"Ellie has been asking about you."

"Honestly?" I arched an eyebrow. "What did she say?"

"Mostly if we've sacked you yet," he jested.

"Funny," I retorted, going back to the sheet. "Well, there's always tomorrow."

"What even happened between you two, anyway? I asked her and she wouldn't say."

"We just lost touch."

"Prison will do that."

I glanced over his shoulder and then shot him a look of thunder. "Keep your voice down, will you?"

"Relax!" he exclaimed. "It's just us."

Not wanting to take the conversation further, I shook my head and started stuffing one of the pillowcases in silence.

"I never thanked you, by the way," he added, stretching his neck closer to get my attention.

I dropped the pillow and patted it flat. "For what?"

"For not telling Ellie about us."

"Us?" I chortled. "There is no *us*."

"That isn't entirely true, is it? We both know you had the hots for me."

I blinked slowly. "Lucas, can I tell you something?"

"Go ahead," he said, hugging his laptop to his chest.

"Even if you were the last man on earth, I would—"

"No, no," he interrupted. "I understand. Forget I said anything."

I failed to hide the shudder as my cheeks wobbled left and right.

"Anyway, I've got some... matters to attend to," he said, lifting the laptop slightly. "I'll see you around, yeah?"

I candidly raised my eyebrows in response, and he scarpered out of the room as I put my earphones back in. I spotted the time, and it dawned on me that I'd spent the better part of an hour making that bed, so I finished up before Martha lost her rag and came looking for me. I wafted the quilt in the air to straighten it in the cover, neatly tucked it into the sides of the bed like she'd shown me on my so-called induction, and then flattened some of the bigger creases with the palm of my hand. After I was satisfied, I grabbed the wash basket and left the room, closing the door behind me.

"Robyn!" I heard Lucinda screech from down the hall. Oh no.

"Yes, Mrs Blackthorn?" I asked after turning to face her.

"Take those blasted things out of your ears!" she ordered.

I reluctantly removed my earbuds and tucked them down my tunic. "Sorry."

"Tell me, did your mother not teach you any manners?"

I kept my eyes locked on hers, teeth cutting into my tongue. "It won't happen again, Mrs Blackthorn."

Lucinda rattled her head and exhaled. "What are you doing up here, anyway?"

"I was just changing the beds in the guest room."

"And have you finished?"

I placed the basket on my hip and tucked some hair behind my ear. "Yeah, I was just about to head back to the kitchen and grab a bite to eat before dinner service."

"That can wait. I need your help with something. Leave the basket."

"Okay, well I'd better tell—"

"Now!" she added before flouncing down the hall. Great. What now?

I inhaled deeply as I dropped the basket and then reluctantly followed her through the hallways, scarcely able to keep up with her pace as she stormed towards her chambers. Whatever she had in store for me, I knew that it wasn't good. I mean, in all the time that I'd worked there, the only things she'd ever asked me for were something from the kitchen or for me to get the hell out of her way. Still, as futile as it was, it was a chance to undo the awful first impression I made on her.

We arrived, and she stopped abruptly at her door, turning to me to scan me from head to toe.

"Are those your only clothes?" she asked, frowning.

"My uniform?" I tugged at my tunic.

"Yes," she snapped. "What else would I be talking about?"

"No, of course not."

She took a step closer. "Penelope said you went shopping together."

"We did," I gulped.

"She said you have a keen eye for fashion. Is that true?"

I couldn't hide the smirk. "Er…"

She almost looked disgusted. "I knew it was a long shot."

"On the contrary, Mrs Blackthorn, I know quite a bit," I said to shut her up. "I did a course in college."

"Hmm." Her eyes widened. "Truthfully?"

"Yep." I smiled. "What's the matter? Do you need some tips?"

"Something like that."

Lucinda opened the door and stepped inside, gesturing to the three dresses laid out on her bed. I didn't need any expertise in fashion to know that the garments displayed must've cost a fortune. Closest to the headboard was an elegant ivory number, maybe a *Zimmermann*. It was made from satin, long and flowing, with a deep slit in one of the legs. The next was undoubtedly an *Elie Saab*, blood-red and off the shoulder, and so revealing that even I'd feel uncomfortable wearing it. The last option was black silk, with a ruffled bust and lacy detail around the edging, sophisticated and understated. I didn't recognise the style. It looked custom-made.

"Wow! They're gorgeous," I remarked.

"Richie and I have been invited to a benefit tonight, and I can't decide which to wear," she announced.

"Oh!" I said, placing a finger on my chin. "What's the vibe?"

"Vibe?" She arched an eyebrow. "What on earth do you mean?"

"Well, is it more of a party atmosphere, or a classy dinner?"

"Classy," she said firmly. "Definitely classy."

"If it were me, I'd go with the black," I suggested, running my finger and thumb along the hem. "It's beautiful."

Lucinda came to my side and stroked the fabric. "I don't know—black washes me out."

"Trust me. Black is timeless."

"And you're sure it won't look like I've just been to a funeral?"

"Are you kidding?" I exclaimed. "You'll be the star of the show!"

"Hmm," she mumbled. "I was leaning towards the red."

"God, no!" I said out of reflex, forgetting where I was standing. "The red one is trashy."

Lucinda's jaw dropped slightly. "*Trashy?*"

Shit. I could've kicked myself. That was the most normal conversation I'd ever had with Lucinda, and I'd derailed it within seconds because I couldn't keep my big mouth shut.

"Mrs Blackthorn, I'm so sorry, I just—"

"Calm down, will you? You're right." She sighed. "An old mutton like me can't very well go out dressed as lamb."

"I didn't mean it like that."

"No, I appreciate you being honest. Christ, that's in short supply around here."

I narrowed my eyes, unable to resist the urge to pry. "What do you mean?"

Lucinda burst into cynical laughter before perching on the edge of the bed. She began sizing me up, obviously debating whether to make me privy to something or not.

"You've spoken to my husband before, haven't you?" she asked.

"Yes, of course."

"Alone?"

I nodded, toying with my tunic. "Once or twice."

"Did he mention why he spends hours on end at that ghastly boating lake?"

"No. To tell you the truth, he mostly just gave me a history lesson on the Blackthorns gone by."

Lucinda rolled her eyes and reached for the stagnant gin and tonic on her bedside table.

"He thinks I don't know, but I do," she remarked as she took a sip.

My pulse hammered. "Know what?"

"About his pathetic dalliances." She took a swig. "I bet he has a different tart for every day of the week."

"Well, I wouldn't know anything about that, Mrs Blackthorn."

My face was straight, professional even. But inside, I was screaming, praying that she wouldn't ask me the question I could almost see balancing on her lips.

"He hasn't tried it on with you, has he?" she asked, widening her eyes.

The back of my neck started prickling. "No, of course not."

"Because if he has—"

"He hasn't," I insisted.

She downed the rest of her drink. "Maybe I'm just paranoid."

As much as I hated her, I could see how much pain she was in. It was written on every line in her face. I mean, she'd lost a daughter, married a scumbag, and just those two facts alone explained why there were always a couple of empty glasses beside her bed. She wasn't wrong, either, but I wasn't stupid enough to tell her the truth. She would've only blamed me.

"Listen," I began, taking a step forward. "Can I speak freely?"

"Please do."

"What you two have been through—it's enough to drive anyone to madness."

"And what do you think you know about that?" she said, tone sharp.

"Enough," I replied. "Perhaps you should talk to him about it."

"Pfft," she dismissed. "We haven't had a proper conversation in years. Ever since Sofia."

"Then it's long overdue. Why don't you speak to him after you've been out tonight? I'm sure you'll be able to patch things up."

Lucinda raised her eyebrows in agreement before turning back to the dress.

"You're certain about the black?" she asked.

"Positive."

"In that case, can you take it down to Martha to be pressed?"

"Absolutely, Mrs Blackthorn."

"And Robyn?"

"Yes?"

"Thank you." She rubbed her neck. "I needed that."

Feeling quite happy with myself, I bent down to fold the dress in half to carry it downstairs. But as I angled my torso down, the ring around my neck came loose and fell out in full view of Lucinda. I tried to tuck it back in. It was too late. She reached out and gripped it, pulling the string tight. I instinctively grabbed it myself, and her arm began trembling as her teeth gritted.

"Where did you get this?" she hissed, yanking it closer.

"Mrs Blackthorn, you're hurting me!" I yelped.

"Where!" she bellowed.

"I found it!"

"You *found* it?" she barked. "*Where* did you find it?"

"In my jacket pocket on my first night!"

She tugged the twine tighter. "Liar!"

"Mrs Blackthorn, I swear! I'm telling you the truth!"

The string yielded to the pressure and pinged, sending me sprawling backwards and leaving the ring in Lucinda's palm. I was expecting a fist, a foot or a tepid gin and tonic to the face, but she remained motionless on the bed, peering down at the ring with a sudden calm washing over her.

"This was my mother-in-law's," she explained. "I'd recognise it anywhere."

"I didn't steal it! I promise!" I pleaded.

"I know you didn't," she said, turning her gaze to me. "You couldn't have."

"Then why did you—"

"Richie gave it to Sofia," she uttered. "She was wearing it the night she was murdered."

15

THE HANGOVER

ROBYN — BEFORE

I hadn't even opened my eyes when the splitting headache hit me like a freight train. The night before came in flashes. The pill. The drink. The dancing. Then, nothing but a blur. How the hell did I get home?

Without warning, a slice of daylight crept through the curtains, burning through my eyelids, so I grabbed the quilt and pulled it over my head. It didn't help, and a whimper slipped out, my lips cracking as I smacked them together. I badly needed water, so I reached out of the duvet, hoping that I'd been sensible enough to leave a glass there the night before, but when my hand didn't land on my bedside table, I was thrown into an instant panic.

Then came a weary groan from the mass lying beside me.

My eyes broke open, and I popped my head out of the mess of covers. I wasn't at home at all, but in a hotel room. The back wall was panelled with thin slats of oak with a television fitted in the centre, hovering above a long desk. There was a wardrobe next to it, doors open and entirely empty apart from the coat hangers. With a wince, I turned my head and saw one of the Bicep-boys still fast asleep beside me, stomach-down with his gelled hair glued to his forehead and drool drying in the corner of his mouth. The springs creaked when I shifted my weight, so I immediately froze, but it was too late. His blue, bloodshot eyes were already open, clearly trying to remember who I was and whether he should be pleased about it or not.

"Oh. You're still here," he pointed out, voice hoarse.

"Apparently."

I did a quick inventory while he dragged his arm over the side of the bed to scour the floor for his phone. Thankfully, my dress was still on, so was my underwear, and my wedges were dumped by the door next to my jacket in a sad heap. The bracelet the girls had given me had pressed a dent into my skin where I had slept on it, leaving an imprint of the gold plate just below my wrist. My hair was frizzy and pointing in all directions, so I flattened it out as I hopped out of bed to get my shoes. Bicep-boy sat up in bed, scratching his jaw before he brought his ear to his shoulder, and his neck let out a jarring crack.

"Do you, er, remember much?" he asked.

"Bits and pieces. Mostly dancing with the girls then—" I almost retched when I remembered the fishbowls. "Not much else."

"You were absolutely off your face," he said with a small grin. "We all were."

"We didn't... you know, did we?"

"No," he said quickly. "You were basically unconscious the minute your head hit the pillow—I'm not some creep."

Relief rose and fell in one breath. "Thank God."

"No offence taken," he remarked.

I gave him a thin smile. "It's not that. I just don't 'do' one-night stands."

"Good," he replied. "Me either."

"Sure," I uttered, struggling with my shoes.

"By the way, you kept calling me BB in front of Lucas."

I squirmed. "Did I?"

"Yeah. What does it mean?"

I wanted the ground to swallow me whole.

"Bicep-boy," I admitted.

He dropped back onto the pillow in laughter. "Seriously?"

"I'm so sorry." I shut my eyes. "Honestly, I'm mortified."

"Don't be, it suits me. I might even change my *Insta* handle to it."

I gave up trying to tug my shoes on and sank back onto the bed in defeat. "Did he say anything else about me?"

"Who? Lucas?"

I nodded sharply.

"I don't think so," he said, a flicker of jealousy in his eyes. "You aren't sweet on him, are you?"

"God, no!" I dismissed. "Just curious."

"To be honest, he was a little preoccupied with El."

"No change there," I muttered.

"They had that screaming row at the end of the night, don't you remember?"

I vaguely recalled Ellie dousing him with a drink, but the context was still fuzzy. "Not really."

He rolled over again, dangling his arm over the side, only to find a half-empty bottle of beer sitting under the bed. To my horror, he lifted it to his lips to drink some, but thankfully, he thought better of it. Although he wasn't my type and a little rough around the edges, he wasn't *totally* unattractive. Like mine, his left arm was covered in tattoos, but mostly mythological creatures that my banging head couldn't conjure the names of. He smelled like pepper and cedarwood, which was pleasant at first until it began to make my stomach turn.

"By the way, where the hell am I?" I asked, glancing through the half-closed blinds.

He pointed at the window. "*The Hilton*."

"Why the hell didn't I go home?" I asked.

"You were in a bit of a state, and you wouldn't tell anyone your address for the taxi."

At least I didn't blow my cover. "Listen, you haven't got any water, have you? I'm spitting feathers here."

"Check the desk. Next to the chips you didn't finish."

I walked over and sure enough, there was a half-drunk bottle of bubbly water sitting next to some scrunched-up, vinegar-soaked newspaper. I grabbed the bottle, taking a polite sip, but nearly coughed a lung out when I spotted the time displayed on the radio on the dresser.

Half eleven.

"Fuck!" I exclaimed, rushing over to jam my feet in my wedges.

"Whoa," he said, levering up on an elbow. "You alright?"

"I've got to go," I snapped back. "I've left my mum on her own."

"She'll be fine!" he drawled. "I can make us a late breakfast?"

"She's not bloody fine!" The words tore out sharper than I intended. "I should've just gone home."

He looked slightly offended, tugging the quilt over his midriff. "Look, I can run you back if you're in a rush. My car's downstairs."

"Thanks, but I'll get a taxi," I uttered, grabbing my jacket.

My phone slid out, so I scooped it up off the floor to check it. There wasn't a single missed call or even a text. Why wouldn't she ring me? Had something happened? I opened our thread and sent her a quick text.

> *I'm so sorry, Mum. I'm on my way. x*

"Anyway, I had fun last night," he said in my ear after suddenly materialising beside me.

"Me too," I uttered out of reflex, fumbling with my jacket buttons.

"Can I call you later?" he blurted out. "Just to check you got home okay."

I stopped dead. The idea of him calling me felt a little absurd, but also quite sweet.

"You haven't got my number," I pointed out.

"I do," he said, waving his cracked phone. "You gave it to me. It's just missing a name."

"And they say romance is dead," I remarked. "Robyn."

"Aubrey," he said, tapping his chest.

"Aubrey?" I chortled. "Seriously?"

"Yeah, why?" he asked, confused.

"I think I prefer BB."

He grinned. "Call me what you like."

"Listen, I really need to—"

"Yeah, sorry," he interrupted, opening the door for me.

The hallway was dimly lit and classy, with laminated notices and fire alarm call points every few metres. He walked me to the lift in bare feet and pressed the button to call it. It arrived a second later, and the doors rattled open, so I rushed inside and repeatedly bashed the button for the ground floor with the pad of my thumb.

"Nice meeting you!" he said through the closing doors.

"You, too," I said as they clunked shut.

I peered into the mirrored glass as I descended. My eyes were crusty with yesterday's mascara. Lipstick was smeared into my cheek and, rather embarrassingly, on my teeth. My bargain-bin dress was somehow torn at the thigh, and one of my beige wedges had been stained luminous green by some garish cocktail Kait had forced down our necks. How BB saw all that and still wanted to stay in touch was beyond me, but I'd be lying if I said it didn't make me feel good about myself.

The lift pinged, so I raced outside, crossing the road to climb into one of the taxis waiting in the rank.

"Where to, love?" the cabbie asked.

"Salford," I said. "Please hurry."

* * *

I held my breath as the taxi made the final turn into the courtyard of our block, only releasing it when I saw that everything appeared normal. I posted my last ten-pound note through the little plastic window and jumped out of the cab, clutching my jacket around my sides to keep the cold out. I didn't bother with the lift; it was only working half the time anyway, and the state of it would've had me retching, so I took the stairs. I arrived at our floor and rushed over to our door to slide the key in it, but as soon as I touched it, it gave way and creaked open. There was nothing but silence inside. No telly. No kettle. No hum. Just the sound of my own heartbeat thumping away in my neck.

"Mum?" I shouted.

"We're in here!" I heard a strange voice call.

I ran for the bedroom.

Mum was on the floor, slumped beside the bed with her eyes firmly shut, one arm tangled in the duvet as if she'd tried to pull herself up and missed. Her durag was skew-whiff, and a handful of hair had matted to her forehead over a split near her temple. Our downstairs neighbour, Sandra, was down at her side, tightly clutching her hand. For a moment, I didn't move. Then, before I knew it, I was on my knees, carpet burning my shins, hands on Mum's shoulders, trying to shake her awake.

"Mum? Can you hear me?" I asked frantically.

"I only popped by to check if she wanted anything from the shops! I used my spare key and found her like this!" Sandra explained.

My chest heaved. "Mum? Just say something, okay?"

I noticed she was clutching the birthday card I'd abandoned on the kitchen side the night before, so I took it from her grasp and tossed it on the bed.

"Have you called an ambulance?" I asked.

"About fifteen minutes ago, they're on their way."

"Robyn?" Mum croaked from the ground.

"Mum!" I said, diving down. "I'm here, I'm here."

"Where were you?"

"I was just—"

"I needed you, and you weren't here."

"I know—God, I'm so sorry. Just hold on, help is coming, okay?"

Mum's eyes drooped again when we heard boots stomping into the flat. Two paramedics strode into the bedroom, one of them delicately dragging me away as the other began listening to Mum's chest and feeling for her pulse.

"Are you family?" the female paramedic asked, holding me by the elbows.

"Yes," I said shakily, unable to take my eyes off Mum.

"My name's Becky, and this is Dan."

"Just help her, will you?" I exclaimed.

"We are, but I need you to tell me what happened."

"I think she's fallen and taken a knock to the head," Sandra cut in. "I found her."

"Is she on any medication?"

"Yes," I muttered.

"What?"

"Loads—she had a spinal cord injury years ago. She's paralysed from the waist down."

Becky glanced over at Dan, who gave her a nod of recognition before running his stethoscope over Mum's chest.

"When did it happen?" Becky asked.

"I don't know," I murmured.

"Well, when did you last speak to her?"

"Maybe eight last night."

"And she's been like this ever since?"

"I don't know!" I admitted, throwing my hands in the air.

Becky paused. "Are you her sole carer?"

"Yes," I mumbled.

"And you left her on her own?"

I didn't answer. I just bowed my head.

"I think we'd better take her in," Dan said from the ground. "Her pulse is very weak."

Becky gave me a filthy look before turning on her heel to drag a gurney into our tiny flat, and I helplessly watched as they hoisted her up onto it and wheeled her out. Sandra raced ahead to call the lift, but I lagged behind, numbly following until I felt my phone buzzing in my pocket. There was an unknown number flashing up on the screen, and I'd already hit answer before I realised what I was doing.

"Hello?" I groaned.

"Hey, it's BB! Did you make it home in one piece, then?"

I paused, taking the phone from my ear.

"Don't call me again," I said down the line before hanging up.

It was my fault.

If the worst happened, I'd never forgive myself.

16

THE INQUISITION

ROBYN

Mr Blackthorn's study smelled of leather, pipe smoke, and power. It always did, but waiting for him to arrive made it a hundred times more potent, like the panelled walls and fusty décor themselves were closing in on me. Lucinda was sitting bolt upright opposite the desk, her manicured nails drumming out a rhythm onto the mahogany, each beat sounding like a gunshot in my ears. She'd roped Penelope in for muscle, who was standing in the corner of the room, scraping her nails with a brass letter opener. The article in question was sitting twelve inches away from me on the desk, delicately glinting in the late-afternoon sunlight like it was mocking me, with a few strands of string still clinging to it.

That fucking ring.

I didn't believe in witches, the supernatural, or any of that nonsense, but even I was beginning to think there was a curse on it. I mean, how else could I explain it? My whole world fell apart every time I touched the damned thing. Even worse, the fact that Sofia was supposedly wearing it when she was murdered only confirmed my fears. How the hell did it end up in my jacket? Or in that jewellery store six years ago? Those were the questions that Mr Blackthorn was surely going to ask when he eventually arrived. I didn't have the answers.

On the bright side, I wasn't in cuffs, not yet anyway, but that didn't help my predicament. Lucinda had locked the door after she'd dragged me in there by the scruff of the neck in a mad rage twenty minutes before, and the key was nestled safely in the front of her bra. With no other option, I glanced desirously at the window, wondering if I'd survive the fall if I jumped out. If I'd managed to get over there before she yanked me back inside, maybe I could've used the trellis to climb down, and hopefully, be in the wind before she even made it downstairs.

"You're joking, right?" Lucinda asked, almost reading my mind.

"What?" I said, shrugging my shoulders.

"Even if you landed down there without breaking your legs, Harris would pick you off before you even made it to the gates."

"Charming," I remarked.

Lucinda's jaw tensed. "If I were you, Robyn, I'd spend this time getting your story straight. Not devising ludicrous escape plans."

"Mrs Blackthorn," I began, letting out a shaky exhale. "I've told you a hundred times: I haven't done anything wrong."

"Well, I'll let Richie be the judge of that."

My knee started jerking involuntarily, so I placed my hand on it to try to stop it, yet it only got worse. If they called the police, I'd be well and truly fucked. Not only would it look like I'd been chasing that ring around, but all the lies I'd told to land this job in the first place would also come to light. They'd find out who I was. Who I was before. They might even piece together why I accepted the job in the first place.

"For the love of God, stop that incessant twitching!" Lucinda snapped.

"Sorry," I uttered, my knee freezing mid-bounce.

"If you are indeed telling the truth, you have nothing to worry about, do you?" Penelope spoke up.

I looked Lucinda dead in the eyes, carefully considering what I was about to ask. "You haven't called the police, have you?"

"The police?" she asked, arching an eyebrow.

I juddered my head.

"Not yet. We prefer to deal with matters like this *in-house*."

Short-lived relief rose through me until I started pondering what she meant by 'in-house.'

These people had guns, and I knew from Mum's stories that the family had no qualms about using violence to get what they wanted. On top of that, they had the money and connections to make somebody like me disappear from the face of the earth. One whistle out of that window and Harris would come running with his shotgun, and I'd be dragged to some distant corner of their land and buried in a shallow grave before dinnertime.

"Are you sure you haven't got it wrong, Mother?" Penelope whispered in her ear, replacing the letter opener on the desk.

"It was around her damned neck!" Lucinda exclaimed over her shoulder. "How on earth could I have got it wrong?"

"Stranger things have happened." She lifted her hands. "She might be telling the truth."

"I am," I interjected, barely making a sound.

"Quiet!" Lucinda hissed, slamming her hand on the table.

"Seriously, it's just some old ring, and you've got it back. Just give her the sack and send her packing," Penelope suggested.

"No! Please, Mrs Blackthorn! I can't tell you how much I need this job!" I pleaded.

"I will *not* let it go!" Lucinda boomed. "This was Sofia's ring, and I need to know where she got it."

"I told you," I murmured, burying my head in my hands. "I found it in my damn pocket."

Lucinda bared her teeth. "No, there's something you're not telling us. I can feel it."

Before either of us spoke again, the sound of tyres crunching against the driveway filled the room, so Lucinda stopped her drumming and walked over to the window to see who it was. I knew it was Mr Blackthorn when a sinister smile cracked her scowl.

"He's here," she announced.

"Mrs Blackthorn, please! I'd never steal from you, I promise!" I begged.

"Do not speak unless spoken to," she instructed, turning to me. "Understand?"

I made myself small in my chair, giving her an uneasy nod, even though the idea of being berated by them both in silence made me want to hurl myself out of the window again.

A car door slammed, footsteps chomped on the gravel, then a moment later, he arrived out in the hall. Lucinda unlocked the door for him before he reached it, and he swept in, jacket unbuttoned, clay pipe lit and still clamped between his teeth. He looked flushed, either from the short run up to his study or from barking down the phone again. Lucinda closed the door behind him and stood with Penelope in the corner of the room as he placed his pipe on the stand to pick up the ring instead.

"You dragged me all the way back from Manchester for some ring?" he asked her.

"It's not just *some* ring. It was your mother's."

"And what," he began, pointedly nodding to me, "she's supposed to have stolen it?"

"You gave that ring to Sofia," she said, bitterness seeping out of her eyes. "And I found it tied around the maid's bloody neck."

Mr Blackthorn stared at it, his face unreadable. His eyes flicked once to me, then back to the ring. Finally, he moved it between his thumb and forefinger, turning it so the hidden ruby caught the sunlight.

"Is that true?" he said to me, his tone dangerously calm. "You had this?"

"Yes," I said, as quiet as a mouse.

"Look at me when I'm speaking to you!" he roared.

I reluctantly raised my head. "Sorry, I just—"

"Did you steal it from somewhere?"

"No."

"Then where did you find it?"

I slumped back into my seat, shaking my head to avoid repeating myself.

"Well?" he demanded.

"She said she found it in her jacket pocket," Penelope answered for me.

I shrugged, letting out a dry chuckle. "It's true."

"Very convenient," Lucinda scoffed.

"Silence!" he ordered her, voice like ice. "Let her speak for herself."

My eyes flitted to Mr Blackthorn before I leaned forward, hands clasped in prayer with my elbows on my knees.

"Listen, it was my first night here, okay? I left my jacket in Sofia's room, and someone moved it down to the quarters. When I picked it up, the ring was sitting in the pocket."

"Who moved the jacket?" he asked.

"Beats me," I muttered.

"Martha moved it," Lucinda cut in again. "After this one was found skulking around the corridors in the dead of night!"

He rubbed his temples. "And have you asked Martha about it?"

"Why on earth would I do that?"

"To confirm Robyn's story."

"She's lying! I don't need to bloody confirm it!"

He picked up the ring and took it over to the portrait of Ethelbert before pulling the frame away from the wall. There was a safe housed underneath, and he shot the Blackthorn women a look to avert their eyes before he quickly tapped in a code to lock it inside.

"Well, we have it back," he said over his shoulder. "That's all that matters."

"Wait, you *believe* her?" Lucinda gasped.

"It doesn't matter what I believe," he said, turning to face her. "But for the record, I do."

A breath escaped my lips.

"*Your* daughter was wearing that ring the night she was taken from you, and you're not in the least bit interested in where Robyn got it?" she argued.

He slammed the portrait closed again and then turned to me, gritting his teeth.

"Leave us," he said quietly.

"Mr Blackthorn, I—"

"Now!" he bellowed.

I didn't need to be asked a third time. I leapt out of the seat and rushed past Lucinda, dodging her daggers as I scuttled back into the corridor. Penelope followed, pacing on the spot with her hands on her hips as the door slammed behind her. Without warning, a muffled argument erupted inside the study, both of them screaming at each other at the top of their lungs as I rested the back of my head on the wall to allow a single tear to escape my eye.

"Are you lying?" Penelope asked.

"No."

"Are you?" she repeated.

"No!" I said without a flicker of doubt.

"Listen, Mother hasn't been the same since Sofia. If you know something, then—"

"I don't," I cut in.

"Just go back to the kitchens, okay? Let her sleep on it and apologise tomorrow."

"Apologise? Me?"

"Trust me. It's simpler that way."

Before I could very loudly explain to Penelope how utterly ridiculous her request was, Lucinda burst through the door, stumbling into the hall while clutching a red handprint on her right cheek. She almost blew right by until she noticed we were still standing there, then shoved Penelope out of the way to step so close to me that I could taste the gin on her tonsils.

"Are you happy now?" she asked, her voice flat.

"Did—did he hit you?" I stammered.

"This?" She snorted. "This is nothing."

"God, I'm sorry," I uttered.

"Not as sorry as you're going to be."

My eyes narrowed. "What's that supposed to mean?"

"You're hiding something, and I'm going to find out what."

"Mrs Blackthorn, please—"

I didn't get a chance to finish because she cleared her nose and spat the contents in my face.

I recoiled in disgust, almost cracking my head open on the wall as she grabbed Penelope by the wrist and dragged her away. I lifted my arm and wiped it away with my sleeve before Mr Blackthorn emerged in the doorway, looking me up and down with what resembled pity in his eyes. I fled down the hall, wiping tears back as I ran, wanting to put as much distance between me and those people as possible.

Lucinda had me in her crosshairs.

It was only a matter of time before she pulled the trigger.

17

THE HOSPITAL

ROBYN – BEFORE

Salford Royal's Accident and Emergency department was far too bright and way too cold for my liking. The curtain around us didn't close all the way. I could see a bit of the corridor and a pair of trainers going past every few seconds as the nurses struggled to keep everyone comfortable. To be honest, I probably should've been in a bed myself because the raging hangover I woke up with in Bicep-boy's hotel room was showing no signs of relenting. The faint smell of bleach and the flickering fluorescent lights didn't help, but I needed to be there when Mum woke up, regardless of how much I wanted to go home for a greasy fry-up and a catnap. I tried not to think about it. Instead, I kept my eyes locked on the monitors, resisted the urge to check my phone, and tortured myself about the last twelve hours and all the stupid choices I'd made during them.

The only thing worse than the hangover was the guilt. It was debilitating.

I played with the bracelet on my wrist and had the sudden urge to rip it clean off. I mean, my reasons were innocent enough: I just wanted one night of fun, to celebrate my twenty-first in style, and maybe, if I was lucky, forget who I was for a few hours. But fate is cruel, so the moment I decided to be selfish, I was instantly and brutally reminded that I wasn't allowed to have any of those things.

God, Mum.

If I had the chance to undo it all, I would. She was propped up in a hospital bed beside me, muttering gibberish in her sleep, the bruise tucked away in her hairline already blooming purple. Her chest was a tangle of wires and tubes, leading to various machines monitoring her vitals on the back wall. I kept picturing her alone in our grimy flat, desperately trying to reach for the phone or shout for help. Was she scared? Did she think it was the end? The most disgusting part was the thought that she was going through that ordeal when I was just up the road, drinking myself stupid without a care in the world.

I'd been telling myself that I was doing it for her, to get justice for what happened to her at the hands of the Blackthorns, but I was lying to myself. The truth was, I'd been seduced into that lifestyle: the binge drinking, the rampant self-indulgence, and now, the drug taking. In fact, everything that mattered to me before I met Ellie and her clique had fallen by the wayside. Even worse, what happened to Mum in that flat wasn't even the beginning of my neglect. It was simply the cherry on the cake.

"Robyn?" she groaned, eyes still half-shut.

I grabbed her hand. "I'm right here, Mum."

She swallowed. "What time is it?"

"Er—just after four."

"In the afternoon?"

My brow wrinkled. "Yeah."

She winced when she tried to turn her head. "Great."

"Try not to move, okay?" I warned, moving my hand further up her arm. "You're in the hospital."

"The hospital? Why?"

"You had a fall, Mum. Don't you remember?"

Mum squinted as she took in her surroundings, then wearily lifted a hand to her temple. The confusion seemed to have cleared when she opened her eyes again, so I filled her cup from the jug of water and held it to her lips. She took a few sips before shaking her head and coughing violently.

"What the hell happened?" I asked.

She gave me a look. "I could ask you the same."

"I went out." I shrugged.

"To that nightclub?"

I was too tired to come up with a lie, so I stayed quiet and gave a weary nod.

"Was Lucas still there?" she asked, peering down.

"Yes," I said quickly. I watched her heart rate shoot up on the display.

"Did you speak to him?" she asked.

"A little," I admitted.

Mum opened her mouth to speak, but a jolt of agony took all the air from her lungs, so she grabbed her head with both hands instead.

"My head is killing," she groaned, shutting her eyes.

"How did it happen?"

"Isn't it obvious?" she scoffed through the pain. "Like you said: I fell."

"How, though?"

Before we could get any further, a doctor peeled back the curtain and stepped inside. He was in his early thirties, wearing a set of battered trainers and a badge pinned to his blue scrubs that said Dr Khan. He eyeballed Mum's vitals for a minute as he rubbed his neat, jet-black beard, then did the light-in-the-eyes business before pressing along her scalp and jaw with careful fingers.

"Okay, Jada," he began, making sporadic eye contact. "How are you feeling?"

"Terrible," Mum uttered. "I'm in agony."

"I'll get the nurse to swing by with some more painkillers," he said, turning to me. "Has anyone been through the scans with you both yet?"

I leaned forward. "Not yet."

"Well, the good news is there's no bleed on the brain."

I released a breath. "Thank God."

"But it does show that there's a minor non-displaced skull fracture along the parietal bone."

"A skull fracture?" I gasped.

"Don't panic, it's not as serious as it sounds." He smiled. "There's no need to operate, and it should be fully healed on its own within a few weeks."

Mum grabbed my hand. "Can we go home, then?"

"Under normal circumstances, yes. But given your mobility—"

"For fuck's sake," Mum grumbled.

"Nothing major, okay? We'd like to keep you for a few days for observations. A week at most."

"Oh, just fantastic," Mum said sarcastically, dropping my hand.

"I'll come and check on you both later, okay?"

Mum griped under her breath, so I took the reins. "Thanks, Doc."

"No worries. Buzz if the pain gets any worse," he said before creating an opening in the curtain. "Robyn, can I have a word with you in private?"

My eyes flicked to Mum before I turned back. "Sure."

The doctor beckoned me to follow and took me down the corridor, stopping at the coffee machine. He fed a few coins into the slot before making a selection, then swivelled his head to me.

"Do you want one?" he asked.

"No," I mumbled, waving a hand. "I'm good."

"So, the paramedic said Jada was alone at the time of the fall. Is that true?"

"Yeah, I'd just popped out," I explained, fiddling with my bracelet.

"Overnight?"

I felt my cheeks flush. "Yes."

Dr Khan stacked his arms across his stomach as the machine began to spit brown sludge into a cup. "I'm not here to give you a lecture, okay?"

"Honestly, I've learned my lesson. It was my birthday and—"

"But I do have some other concerns," he continued.

"What concerns?"

The machine finished, so he grabbed it and took a sip before placing it on the side.

"You care for your mum full-time, don't you?"

"Yeah."

"And you don't have any help?"

"Nope," I said, raising my eyebrows. "Just me."

"So, no one else has access to your flat?"

"Well, the downstairs neighbour has a key for emergencies, but other than her, no."

Dr Khan huffed and leaned against the machine. "How are things at home in general?"

"Fine," I said, tilting my head.

"No arguments?"

I took a step back. "What are you getting at?"

"I'm not accusing you of anything, but I don't think your mother fell."

My skin prickled. "What do you mean?"

"Well, the working theory is that she hit her head on the bedside table, yeah?"

I nodded.

"And she hasn't said otherwise?"

"No. She's still a little hazy."

"Medically, there's no way she could've hit it with enough force to cause those injuries."

"No, she said she fell!" I laughed nervously. "She wouldn't lie about it. Not to me, anyway."

"Robyn, I've been working in A&E since I got my licence, and I've seen my fair share of falls. This isn't one of them."

"What do you think happened, then?"

"Well, unless the nightstand was made of pure concrete, her injuries are more consistent with her being struck by something."

A lump formed in my throat. "Something? Like what?"

"I don't know, but it had to be heavy."

My heart jackhammered. Who in their right mind would want to hurt Mum? For a start, she didn't have any friends, let alone enemies. Secondly, it was plain to see by our front door that we had nothing to steal. Worst of all, there was no evidence of a break-in, so if someone had been in our flat, she must've let them in.

"Look, it's plain to see you've got a lot on your plate, but I just thought you should know," Dr Khan explained, grabbing his cup from the side.

"Right," I uttered, barely registering what he'd said.

His hand found my arm. "Listen, we've got people you can speak to. Both of you. God only knows how difficult your situation is."

"We'll be fine," I dismissed, batting away his hand. "I'll speak to her."

"Okay," he said, narrowing his eyes slightly. "Well, good luck. Give me a shout if you need anything, okay?"

"Will do," I murmured.

Dr Khan left me by the machine and walked into another room, so I went back into the ward and shuffled through the small gap in the curtain. Mum had put her glasses on and was scowling at her old Nokia at arm's length, tapping on the screen. Was she lying to me? Or did she really not remember what had happened?

"You didn't answer my question from earlier," I announced, dropping onto the chair.

She glanced at me and then went back to her phone. "What question?"

"How did you fall?"

"It was stupid. I tried pulling myself into bed and slipped."

"You've done that a thousand times, Mum. You've never once fallen before."

"Robyn, I was upset!" she shot back. "I wasn't paying attention."

I crossed my legs. "Where did you hit your head?"

"Christ, Robyn!" She chortled, placing her phone down by her side. "What's with the third degree?"

"Just answer the question."

"Right here," she said, pointing to her bruise.

I leaned back, shaking my head incredulously. Mum just rolled her eyes like I was being domineering.

"I cracked it on the nightstand, okay?" she said matter-of-factly. "Just drop it."

"Truthfully?" I widened my eyes.

"Yes, why?"

"The doctor seems to think otherwise."

Mum started toying with her gown. "What did he say?"

"He thinks someone hit you with something."

"Don't be absurd!" she dismissed. "I fell. It's embarrassing, but it happened. Case closed."

Mum's phone started vibrating, and she rushed to grab it from the mess of sheets, but accidentally knocked it onto the floor instead. She almost leapt out of the bed to stop me from picking it up, and when I finally grabbed it from underneath the mattress, I realised why.

"Who the hell is 'RB?" I asked, peering at the name on the screen.

"No one," she said, reaching out. "Give it here."

"Not a chance," I said before clutching it to my shoulder.

Mum dropped her arms in frustration and stared into space.

"Mum?" I prompted.

"Bloody hell!" she snapped. "Richard Blackthorn, alright?"

It felt like the floor gave way. "Why is he calling you?"

"Well, he's probably returning one of my many calls."

I paused to calm myself. "You called him? When?"

"Last night."

"Why?"

"Robyn, just give me the damned phone, okay?" she said, holding out her hand.

I begrudgingly placed it in her palm, and she abruptly cancelled the call.

"I was calling him to tell Lucas to leave you alone."

"You *what?*" I shouted.

"I'm just trying to keep you safe, Robyn! I didn't know what else to do!"

I scoffed, leaning back until the penny dropped and I shot forward again, the sneer falling from my face.

"He was in our flat, wasn't he?" I asked.

"What? Of course not," she said, her voice weak.

"He was, and he hit you, didn't he?"

"Robyn? No."

"Just tell me the truth, Mum!"

"Christ! How many times are you going to make me say it?" she yelled. "I fell getting into bed. That's it."

Mum had a look on her face that I hadn't seen before. She *was* lying to me. Richard Blackthorn had been in our flat, and he'd tried caving her skull in, but why? Did it have something to do with her accident all those years ago? Was it because I'd been sniffing around? For what reason was he calling her? Why wasn't she telling me the truth?

Suddenly, it was as if all the air was sucked out of the room. Heat rose through me like wildfire. Without a word, I stood up and burst through the curtain. The toilet was in the hall, so I sprinted through the door and dropped to my knees in the closest cubicle. What came out of my mouth didn't look like vomit. It was thick and black, sticking to the porcelain like tar.

And in that moment, the plan shifted.

With my head still hanging over the toilet, I pulled out my phone and sent Ellie a text.

> *OMG! I had so much fun last night, girlie! How are you feeling? x*

> *I'm hanging out of my arse! How did it go with Bicep-boy? x*

> *Really good! In fact, we were wondering if you wanted to come on a double date with us. x*

> *I love that! I'll text Lucas right now! x*

> *Can't wait. x*

I wasn't going to cosy up to the Blackthorns anymore. I wasn't going to go to them, cap in hand, either. I was going to uncover the truth at all costs and *take* what was rightfully ours. Mum was right, they were dangerous, but I had nothing but time, anger, and a mother with a cracked skull left.

It made *me* dangerous.

18

THE TUB

ROBYN

The house felt different after what happened in Mr Blackthorn's study. It was quieter. Darker. Greyer. As though even the walls themselves had stopped their incessant cracking and creaking out of respect for my situation. In many ways, the encounter hadn't changed a thing—I already knew my days were numbered. However, I'd always envisaged that I'd simply be shown the door once they discovered the truth of my past, or that I'd be escorted out of it in cuffs. It never crossed my mind that Mum wasn't exaggerating about them, and that I might never leave the grounds at all.

One of the worst days of my life was finally over, so I left the house through the service entrance and then began trudging over the gravel. I barely got halfway across the courtyard when the sound of a car engine roaring to life startled me. I turned around just in time to see Lucinda standing beside the Jaguar on the driveway, her body draped in red silk, hair curled to within an inch of its life, and her eyes burning into mine.

I was right. The red dress *did* look trashy.

"Get in," Mr Blackthorn shouted through the window, glancing in my direction. "We'll be late."

Begrudgingly, Lucinda stepped into the car, and they sped off down the driveway a moment later, leaving nothing but a haze of dust behind.

As I stood in the courtyard, wearing my soiled tunic and my knees straining to hold me up, I couldn't help but feel like there was no justice in the world. I mean, how was it that a dreadful woman like her got to go to some fancy dinner? Live in a house like this? Be waited on hand and foot by people like me? She hadn't worked a single day in her life and never would. She'd spend the rest of her days flouncing around that house, half-drunk, and treating everyone she bumped into like the shit on her shoe. It rubbed me the wrong way.

The wind picked up, so I hugged my chest and rushed to my quarters. I wanted nothing more than to get into the grotty communal shower, possibly scald a layer of skin off, and then barricade myself in my room with my earphones glued in my ears. I tried the shower room first, but nearly broke my nose when I tried walking through a locked door. I held my ear to the doorframe and heard running water, so I banged on the door with the heel of my hand before stepping back.

"*Ocupado*!" I heard Elena shout.

"How long are you going to be?" I yelled back.

"A saber!"

"What?"

"Who knows?"

Fantastic. I'd just have to settle for a whore's bath at the sink instead.

I walked down the dingy hall towards my room. To my surprise, the door was wide open, with a pair of battered heels poking out from behind it. At first, I thought Penelope was having one of her night terrors and had wandered into the wrong room, but when I stormed inside, I realised it was Martha. She was on all fours, inexplicably wearing Lucinda's ivory dress, with her head underneath the bed and dragging her hands across the floor.

"Er—what the hell are you doing?" I asked, tapping her feet with mine.

"Looking for something," she uttered without getting up.

"For what, exactly?"

Martha grumbled, reversed out from underneath the bed, and then batted the dust off her borrowed dress as she got back onto her feet.

"For anything else you've 'found,'" she announced.

"I've never stolen a thing in my life," I spat.

"Strange," she remarked, tilting her head. "That's not what Mrs Blackthorn told me before she left."

"It was a misunderstanding. It was in my jacket pocket and—"

"Save your breath," she cut in. "I don't believe a damned word of your cock and bull story."

The single thread of patience I still had snapped.

"Oh, fuck off, will you?" I barked.

She gasped. "Excuse me?"

"I don't have to explain myself to you! You're the help—just like me."

"I've been with the Blackthorn family for over twenty years, you jumped-up little—"

"And that gives you some kind of power over me?" I interrupted.

"Of course it does!"

I backed up into the wall, shaking my head. "Okay then, *Columbo*, do your little search. I've got nothing to hide."

Martha raised her eyebrows in agreement, then shamelessly set about turning my room over. Elena appeared in the doorway, a towel wrapped around herself, discreetly rolling her eyes as Martha opened every drawer, searched every crevice, and even went as far as to rip the sheets from my bed. As expected, she found nothing, but still continued to scan the room like she'd missed something. It didn't faze me. Hell, it happened on a weekly basis back in the clink.

"Are you satisfied?" I asked.

"For now," she said, taking one last peek in the wardrobe.

"Listen, it was a mix-up, okay? You know what *she* is like."

The way that Elena sucked her teeth and hobbled down the hall to her room told me that I'd crossed the line. Martha got in my grill, raising her hand to grab me by my collar before thinking better of it.

"Mrs Blackthorn is the lady of this house! You'd do well to show her a little gratitude!" she hissed.

"For what?" I grinned despite myself.

"This job! I worked my fingers to the bone to get where I am, I didn't just swan in here, looking like you, and have it handed to me on a platter!"

"What on earth are you talking about? 'Looking like me?'"

Martha exhaled through her nose and took a step back. "*He* gave you the ring, didn't he?"

"Who?"

"Mr Blackthorn! Who else do you think?"

I backed into the wall. "Of course not."

She bit her bottom lip, waving her finger in the air. "Don't think I don't see what you're doing."

"I'm not doing anything, Martha," I said with a sigh. "You're imagining things."

"Yeah, right! Batting your eyelashes. Sticking your chest out. It might work on him, but it doesn't fly with me!"

I narrowed my eyes. Why the hell would my likeness to Sofia give me an advantage? For a start, I was sure it was the sole reason that I'd been mistreated by Lucinda since I arrived there. Secondly, the way that Mr Blackthorn's gaze raked over me whenever I bumped into him made my skin crawl. In fact, I locked my door every night and hardly slept a wink since he put his hands on me, so the notion that I was somehow trying to seduce him was ludicrous.

In spite of all that, I already knew I wasn't going to convince her otherwise, so I changed tack. She was right: between us, she did have all the power, so I did exactly what she accused me of. I batted my eyelashes and clasped my hands together in prayer, preparing to gobble down a big fat slice of humble pie.

"Look, I'm sorry for what I said, okay?" I said, bowing my head slightly. "I've had a terrible day, and I shouldn't have taken it out on you."

"It was totally unacceptable! I mean, to *swear* at me. I have a good mind to—"

"Please don't give me the sack," I interrupted, taking a step forward. "It won't happen again."

Her scowl softened slightly. "Well, see to it that it doesn't!"

"I will! I will!" I repeated, relaxing slightly.

Martha rolled her eyes as she swivelled her head, then made her way over to the mirror to check herself out. I came up behind her and locked eyes with her in the reflection as she fixed her hair.

"You look nice, by the way," I said.

A look of disbelief cracked her face. "I do?"

"Like a million quid! That dress isn't a *Zimmermann*, is it?"

Martha looked shocked. "It is! I borrowed it from Mrs Blackthorn."

"Well, it definitely suits you!" I stepped forward to touch the fabric. "Who's the lucky bloke?"

"No one," she explained. "If you must know, I'm going to the benefit to assist Mrs Blackthorn."

"Wow! Go you!" I cheered before walking over to the wardrobe to grab my nightdress.

"Er, Robyn, what are you doing, exactly?" she asked.

"I was going to get a shower and an early night," I replied, unknotting the tie around my waist. "I'm off the clock, aren't I?"

"You most certainly are not! Mrs Blackthorn's chambers still need to be turned down!"

"Turned down?" I asked, arching an eyebrow. "Can't one of the others do it?"

"They've done enough! They were busy scrubbing the kitchen whilst you were slacking off in Mr Blackthorn's study."

I fought the urge to swear at her again.

"Of course. I'll do it right away," I said, cupping my hands together on my front.

"And take her dirty washing away."

"I will."

"And be sure to—"

"Martha, I've got it," I interjected. "You just have a lovely evening, alright?"

"I will," she said, lingering in the doorway, slightly confused. "Thank you."

The grin tumbled off my face the instant the door was closed. It made me feel sick to suck up to Martha, but I was on the thinnest of ice with Lucinda, so the last thing I needed was to be fighting a war on two fronts. Besides, it couldn't hurt to have an ally the next time 'the lady of the house' tried laying into me.

***

The heavens had opened whilst I was inside, so I shielded my hair with my hands as I jogged across the courtyard to the service entrance, but I found the door locked. Without any other option, I ran around the perimeter of the house to the main doors, stopping to see Harris leaning into the window of Martha's beaten-up jalopy before it began chugging down the driveway. I met his gaze, but the rain had seriously kicked it up a notch, so I rushed inside, already soaked through.

"This fucking day…" I grumbled as I began to climb the stairs.

Lucinda's door was slightly ajar, and I instinctively knocked as I pushed it open. The last of the rejected dresses was still on the bed, scrunched up into a pile by the headboard, almost touching the four empty glasses collecting condensation on the nightstand. The clothes that she was wearing earlier were in a pile on the floor, almost like she'd dissolved on the spot, with her frilly knickers wide open on top, laid out like some kind of bear trap.

"Urgh," I muttered. "Filthy bitch."

With a wince, I squatted down and scooped up the pile, grabbed the black dress from the bed, and then carried them out to the wheeled laundry basket left in the middle of the hall, which was when I noticed something.

Sofia's door. The key in the lock.

I knew I wasn't going to get another opportunity like it. Martha was out, the rest of the staff were in the quarters, and the Blackthorns were probably already too drunk to even remember I existed. So, with a quick glance over my shoulder to check if the coast was clear, I stepped over, unlocked it, and shuffled inside.

I'd forgotten how beautiful that room was. Although it wasn't exactly to my taste, there was a time when I'd kill to stay in a room like that. Drawers filled with expensive underwear. Wardrobes buckling with designer dresses. A dressing table, stocked to the gills with anything a girl could ask for. And then, the bed. I mean—the bed alone. I couldn't help myself. I dumped Lucinda's dirty washing onto the floor and leapt onto the mattress, feeling every muscle moan in ecstasy as my body melted into it.

Then, an idea popped into my head which was impossible to ignore.

I pictured Mr Blackthorn's hands sliding over my shoulders. Lucinda's spit running down my face. Martha's utter disdain towards me. How powerless I was.

So, without thinking too much about it, I sauntered into the bathroom and peeled my tunic off, letting it slide down to the tiles. Next, I walked over to the bath and turned the taps, the pipes coughing like a smoker until the flow steadied into a stream. As it began to fill up, I removed my underwear and walked over to the sinks, picking up the brightly coloured bottles in turn to take a sniff. The purple one was lavender, my favourite, so I took it over to the bath and poured a healthy measure into the water. After swishing the water around with my hands until there was a thick layer of bubbles on the surface, I stepped in before I could talk myself out of it.

The heat climbed my shins to my thighs as I lowered myself down, then to my stomach, and I let out a little moan as it closed over my ribs. I'd always hated the shower, even more so when I was in prison. Besides, there was something so self-indulgent about soaking in the tub for thirty minutes, and I hadn't realised how much I missed it. I was happier than a pig in shit, so I sank until the water kissed my ears and dipped my whole head underneath the waterline, emerging a few seconds later to flatten my hair back out.

That's when I heard something. Not the pipes. Not the rain beating against the window. Not the house settling.

It was someone in the bedroom.

I jumped out of the bath, grabbing a towel from the side to wrap around myself, then crept to the door. I could just about hear the floorboards softly creaking over the sound of water dripping onto the tiles, so I pressed my ear against the wood and stopped breathing. It sounded like the drawers being opened, followed by the wardrobe doors, then, to my horror, the sound of the bathroom doorknob being turned from the other side.

I quickly threw on the latch before taking a step back, covering my mouth as it started to rattle wildly. Whoever it was, they were intent on breaking into the room, and without any other exit, I had no choice but to announce my presence.

"Hello?" I called out. "Martha?"

The doorknob went still.

I didn't move a muscle for the next five minutes. I could've sworn that I heard the bedroom door open and shut, but I was too terrified to go and check. It was only when I started shivering in the cold that I braved it, armed with a glass bottle of bubble bath, yet I found the room was exactly how I'd left it. Wasting no time, I threw my damp tunic back on as the tub emptied, but as I flattened the creases out, I felt something lodged in the pocket.

It was the fucking ring.

19

THE DATE

ROBYN – BEFORE

True to form, Ellie went out of her way to pick a venue where you needed a small mortgage just to sit down. Even from the outside, The Glasshouse screamed posh nosh, conceited customers and complicated cocktails. They didn't even bother to print the prices on the menu—only ingredients, all of which required Googling to know what the hell you were ordering. A violinist played tortured covers of club bangers in the corner while servers drifted about like ghosts, dropping minuscule plates of food in front of ungrateful faces. I was the first to arrive, so I pressed my hand against the window, peering at muggy Spinningfields below.

Sorry, Mum.

In the week since her fall, it had been frosty between us, to say the least. She still hadn't admitted that it was anything other than an accident, and I stopped pressing her on the issue. It was far simpler to just come to an unspoken agreement that neither of us would mention it, so the brief daily visits mostly entailed tedious small talk about hospital food and inane conversations she'd overheard. As awful as it sounds, Mum being stuck there had its advantages. For one, she had professional, round-the-clock care, which was far better than me making it up as I went along. It also afforded me the opportunity to come and go as I pleased, which meant I could attend my fabled double date without fear of being ticked off. I'd be lying if I said I wasn't anxious about it. I'd felt far braver when I suggested it, but it was way too late to back out now.

My nerves shot up a gear when I spotted a taxi mounting the kerb below. Lucas was the first to jump out, spitting on the pavement and scraping his hair back with his hands. Ellie emerged a moment later, scowling and waving her arms as if they were already mid-row. For a second, I was adamant that he was going to give her a smack, but he pulled back at the last instant. Instead, he shook his head in disgust and stormed into the entrance, with Ellie trailing a few metres behind him. I grabbed the menu and buried my nose in it, too fearful to make eye contact with them as they entered.

"Earth to Robyn!" Ellie said, flapping her hand in front of my face when she arrived at my side.

"Shit, sorry!" I tittered, getting up to give her a hug. "I was miles away."

"Well?" she said, giving me a little twirl.

She was red-lipped, blonde hair immaculately curled, and wearing a dress that probably required a team of people to get into. Lucas stood behind her, black shirt and jacket, no tie, and donning a superficial smirk that never reached his eyes. He didn't greet me. He only flicked his gaze over me, down then up, like he was hoping I'd be gone when he looked again.

"You look gorgeous, as per," I said, clutching my bag tight to my hip.

"Bitch, I know," she jested, taking her seat.

Lucas remained standing. I had the almost irresistible urge to leap onto his front and begin clawing his eyes out, but thankfully, I managed to control myself.

"Hey, Lucas," I said, trying to catch his eye. "How are you?"

"Fine," he muttered, sitting across from Ellie. "Have you ordered drinks yet?"

"No, I—"

I let out a little yelp when two slabs of meat wrapped around my torso. It was Bicep-boy in the flesh, sporting a sparkly shirt fighting for its life over his chest, the tightest jeans I'd ever seen, and a watch the size of a biscuit. He released me to allow me to turn around, then hugged me again like we'd done it a thousand times, arms locked around my back, woody aftershave lightly stinging my nostrils. I panicked when I saw his lips on an intercept course with mine, but just managed to turn my cheek before they made contact.

"How are you?" he asked in my ear.

"Oh, yeah. Living the dream," I let out, squirming out of his grip. "Sorry about that whole business on the phone."

"It's fine, I understand. How is your mum, anyway? Out of the hospital yet?"

"Your mum's in the hospital?" Ellie cut in.

"Don't worry, she's fine." I glanced upwards, trying to keep track of which lies I'd told to whom. "She just had a fall."

"Oh no! Poor thing!" Ellie drawled.

"Drinks," Lucas said, glowering at me and BB until we sat down. "Please."

Ellie clicked her fingers at a passing waiter, and he came to take our order as we took our seats. Lucas didn't wait to hear our preferences and ordered some unpronounceable wine from the list before telling the waiter to hurry up. None of us dared to speak again until he returned. Once he'd finished his first sip, we put our food order in. Unluckily for us, Ellie was the first to break the silence, and she droned on for ten uninterrupted minutes about her recent brand deals, like any of us gave a toss, followed by a story about some reporter who wanted to run a feature on her about mindfulness in the inner city.

"It sounds amazing," I said, resting my chin on my hand.

"You're a bit quiet, lad," BB said to Lucas, bumping his shoulder. "Everything alright?"

"Hmm," he grunted without looking up from his glass.

"He's still a little upset about the big fundraiser," Ellie explained, rolling her eyes.

"I am not fucking upset, okay?" Lucas snapped.

"Tell your face," Ellie whispered.

"Fuck this. I'm going for a smoke."

BB and I watched as Lucas stormed off, almost toppling a waiter on his way out. When I turned back, Ellie wasn't even glancing in his direction. She was just swirling her wine and blowing her hair out of her face.

"What's eating him?" I asked.

"Daddy Blackthorn," she said, letting out a discontented sigh.

"What about him?"

"He usually wheels the whole family out every year for the photo ops on the estate, but he told Lucas he isn't welcome this year," she explained.

"That's awful," I said, glancing out of the window at Lucas below. "Why?"

"Probably because of what happened last year."

I leaned in. "What did he do?"

"Lucas? Nothing," she dismissed. "But his sister went missing a few weeks after. They ended up naming the foundation after her."

I paused. "Sofia?"

"Yep," she said, quite blue all of a sudden. "She was a really nice girl. Not like the rest of the family."

Sofia must've been quite the woman if Ellie described her as nice. She routinely used 'bitch' as a term of endearment, so hearing her pay someone an honest-to-God compliment hit the ear wrong. Maybe if I went missing, she'd be flattering about me, too.

"How are you two, anyway?" Ellie said, forcing a smile. "You seem like a good match."

I winced slightly when BB reached out for my hand, grinning. "I think so too."

"Ahh!" Ellie squealed. "Young love."

"Yeah, well," I began, delicately trying to shake his fingers loose. "It's early days yet."

"Have you fucked?" she asked, as dry as the wine.

I nearly choked. "Ellie!"

"What?" She lifted a shoulder. "We're all adults."

"No," BB explained awkwardly. "We're taking it slow, aren't we, Robyn?"

I didn't utter a word.

"If you want my advice, do it sooner rather than later. You don't want to find out later and get stuck with each other."

A touch of hidden bitterness there.

"Actually, I think true love waits," I announced.

Ellie sniggered. "Very funny."

"I'm being serious."

"What?" she gasped, sliding her glass away. "You mean you haven't—"

Thankfully, the food arrived before Ellie could continue her line of questioning. The server dumped a plate on my place setting, with a dollop of some green, foamy substance shaped into a little dome in the centre. It looked outright unappetising, but I was starving, so I picked up my knife and fork to tuck in. Before a single prong disturbed it, Ellie grabbed my wrist with one hand and whipped her phone out with the other to take a dozen pictures. She gave me the nod of approval once she was satisfied, so I flashed BB a look before scooping a polite measure on the end of my fork and placing it between my teeth. It didn't taste fancy. It just reminded me of mushy peas.

"Don't you just love it when your food is waiting for you when you come back?" Lucas chattered, throwing himself back down in his seat.

I scowled at him, then moved my gaze over to BB, who discreetly tapped his nose to explain Lucas' sudden change in mood. Ellie had perked up too, grinning like a maniac.

"Darling, this is delicious!" she exclaimed, spearing a speck of chicken doused in some yellow sauce and offering it to Lucas. "You must try it."

Lucas peered at Ellie's plate before quickly pushing the fork away. "Urgh. Do you want me to keel over or something?"

"Shit," she said, looking down. "Sorry."

BB looked left out and did the same, presenting me with a chunk of undercooked beef a few inches from my face. Before I had a chance to tell him how revolting it looked, my phone started ringing, so I waved my hand dismissively and reached into my pocket to take it out. A jolt of pins and needles raced up the back of my neck when I saw the number for the hospital flashing up on the display, so I wiped the corner of my mouth with a napkin and jumped out of my seat.

"Sorry, I have to take this," I uttered, unable to take my eyes from the screen.

"We're in the middle of lunch!" Ellie said with a scowl.

"It's Salford Royal," I said before turning on my heel.

I made for the washroom and entered a cubicle, pressing the phone against my ear after accepting the call.

"Hello?" I said.

"Is that Miss Fletcher?" a female voice asked.

"Speaking," I said, impatiently tapping my heels against the tile.

"I'm calling about your mum, Jada." She paused. "Are you free to talk?"

The back of my neck went tight. "What's happened?"

"Calm down, it's good news. The doctor has just informed me that she should be ready to be discharged tomorrow morning."

A tsunami of relief crashed over me. "Er—great."

"He'd like to go over her care before we arrange an ambulance to take her back, though. Can you nip into the ward at nine tomorrow morning?"

"Yes, of course," I uttered.

"Fantastic. We'll see you then," she said before hanging up.

Well, I guess my stint of freedom was over.

Don't get me wrong, I was happy that Mum was well enough to come home, but it also meant that I'd have to be with her twenty-four seven. I couldn't leave her alone again, not even for five minutes, especially if her so-called accident wasn't an accident at all. I pulled my knickers down with a groan, planning to take the opportunity to have a quick wee, but the sound of the bathroom door thudding made me pause. The stall next to mine creaked open, and I saw a tan *Berluti* poking from underneath. Then came the chopping sound, followed by a huge inhale.

Was he for real?

I pulled up my underwear and left the cubicle, making sure to slam the door behind me to announce my presence. Lucas emerged from the stall, squeezing his nostrils together and staggering from side to side, almost toppling over when he saw me standing there.

"You do realise this is the women's bogs, don't you?" I asked, washing my hands.

He shrugged with a crooked smile. "Who gives a toss?"

Just being this close to him made me feel sick, but considering we were alone, it was an opportunity I couldn't afford to waste.

"I've been meaning to get you on your own, actually," I announced.

"Oh?" he said with a flirtatious simper. "What for?"

"No." I raised my hand. "Not…that."

He looked disappointed. "Why, then?"

"I wanted to carry on our conversation from the other night. My mum, she—"

"Why are you always going on about your fucking mum?"

I bit my tongue, turning around to grab a paper towel. But, as I leaned over, I felt fingers snaking up the back of my dress. I spun around, my hand raised in the air to deliver a smack, but Lucas grabbed me by the wrist and wrenched it down, thrusting his body into mine.

"What the fuck are you doing?" I groaned, fighting against his grip. "Ellie will—"

"I don't care what she thinks," he rasped in my ear. "Don't tell me you don't want this."

"Seriously! Let go of me!" I said sternly. "Now!"

"Come on! She won't find out!" he said, undoing his belt. "She's too busy glugging wine and talking shite."

I started batting him with my free hand, and he shunted me forwards, pinning me against the counter with his hips as he dragged his hands down my body to lift my dress. I fought and I kicked, but he was too strong, a mad, glazed-over look in his eyes like he didn't even know what he was doing.

"Lucas!" I yelled. "I'm saying no!"

"I saw how you were looking at me in the club," he argued, tugging at my underwear with clumsy fingers. "Even Ellie saw it."

"Ellie!" I screamed, turning my head to the door. "Help!"

Before I could make another sound, he clasped one of his hands around my mouth.

"Relax, Robyn," he said softly. "You're going to enjoy this."

I went limp, but at the very last second, the creak of the door opening disturbed him. He pulled away, turning from the exit to buckle his belt back up, and I reached down and yanked up my underwear before Ellie appeared from around the corner.

"What the fuck are you two doing in here?" she barked.

I flicked my eyes over to Lucas, and he answered for us.

"Nothing, gorgeous!" He laughed, grinding his teeth. "We were just having a chat."

Ellie turned to me. "Robyn?"

I should've told her the truth, that her worthless, scumbag, druggie, waster of a boyfriend just tried raping me in the toilet when she was sitting twelve feet away, but I couldn't. She would've only blamed me, and she'd never let me anywhere near him ever again.

"Yeah," I uttered, my voice cracking. "It's true."

"But I heard you screaming. In fact, the whole restaurant heard you screaming."

Lucas clapped his hands. "She saw a rat! Isn't that right?"

"Yes," I murmured.

"Eww, a rat?" Ellie said, symbolically clutching her pearls. "Really?"

"The fucker was massive," Lucas said, scratching the back of his head. "To be honest, it was probably me you heard screaming."

"Where is it now?" Ellie asked, turning to me.

I pointed at the vent near the corner. "It scurried into there."

"That's absolutely disgusting! I'm going to speak to the manager right now!"

"Give 'em hell, babe!" Lucas cheered. "I'll be right out."

Ellie took one last look at me and left, leaving Lucas leaning in the doorway, making sure she was out of earshot before turning back to me.

"You good?" he asked.

I nodded.

Without another word, he almost skipped out of there, and I turned back around to face the mirrors. As soon as I saw my reflection, my bottom lip went, and I started sobbing into my hands. After a moment of blubbering, my fingers began trembling, and the anguish I felt hardened into pure rage.

He may not have had his comeuppance that day, but it was coming.

I'd make sure of it.

20

THE PANTRY

ROBYN

I didn't sleep a wink that night.

Every time I shut my eyes, I saw the ring glinting in the light on Mr Blackthorn's desk, exactly where I'd left it, dead centre so that he wouldn't miss it. Although it was stupid to leave it there, I didn't know what else to do. I mean, I couldn't put it back in the safe, could I? I didn't have the combination. So, I was living in the hope that he forgot he locked it in there in the first place, and that he'd simply return it in the morning.

After I planted the ring, I returned to Sofia's room, feeling like I was cleaning the scene of a murder. I wiped the tub, folded the towels exactly how Martha likes them, and smoothed out the bedcovers so it looked untouched. I even went as far as to use my phone torch to spot any stray hairs that had got embedded in the pillow when I had been on the bed. It was excessive, but I couldn't be too careful, not with everyone's eyes still on me.

I was back in my room by two, wired from anxiety and shaking like a leaf. After an hour of debating whether

I should make a run for it, I heard tyres on the gravel, Lucinda's heels, then Mr Blackthorn's voice, low and short. I was sure there'd be a knock on my door, but it never came. When I popped for a wee an hour later, the light was on in Martha's room; she was collapsed face-down on her bed with her borrowed dress still on and a half-drunk bottle of fizz on the floor. I was careful not to wake the beast from her slumber. I just pulled her door shut and crept back to bed.

By five, I gave up on the idea of sleep altogether and got ready in the dark for another day of work. I told myself that if I got to the kitchen extra early, maybe I could keep my head down, and I wouldn't be subjected to yet another cross-examination. The air was cold and damp on my ankles when I tottered over the courtyard, the peacocks lightly chittering as I cut through the side door and bolted into the warmth.

My appetite roared when I detected the smell of eggs and bacon drifting out of the kitchen, so I lingered in the doorway and checked the time on my phone to see if I had enough time to grab a bite before Martha got on my back again. Breakfast on the estate was usually more of a challenge than a break. Typically, it was ten stolen minutes between one demand and the next, ramming some cold toast down my throat like I was going for a *Guinness World Record*. In fact, I couldn't remember the last time I ate a meal there sitting down, let alone with a knife and fork.

With that in mind, I was pretty shocked when I walked into the kitchen and saw the other girls sitting at the table, with two mugs of coffee and a full English breakfast between them. Catherine had her wrist brace on, and Elena had her bad leg up on a chair with a hot-water bottle tucked under it. Even weirder, they looked up and grinned as soon as they spotted me entering, instead of the frosty reception I usually received.

"Bloody hell! You're keen, aren't you?" Catherine said. "It's just gone six."

"Couldn't sleep," I said, hovering. "What's all this?"

"Breakfast!" Elena said in broken English. "Join us."

"Won't Martha go apeshit if she catches us?"

"She's not awake, love." Catherine waved me in, pulling a chair out with her foot. "Besides, we've got to eat sometime, haven't we?"

Against my better judgment, I sat down as Elena poured me a coffee and took a sip. It was good, like the first breath of the day.

"How's the job treating you, anyway?" Catherine asked.

"Well, I'm still here, aren't I?" I remarked.

"That's the spirit," She smiled. "Keep your head down, don't make waves, and only cry if you're in the pantry."

"We should get that on T-shirts!" Elena added.

They both laughed, and I couldn't help but join them. The camaraderie in it surprised me. In my first week, I'd filed them under chilly and distant, but up close and out of Martha's shadow, they just looked tired and kind.

"Did either of you hear anyone in the house last night?" I asked, pinching a bit of toast.

"Like who?" Catherine asked.

"I don't know," I said quickly. "I was just making Lucinda's room up, and I swear I heard someone out in the hall."

"It was probably Lucas stumbling in after a heavy session or Penelope and one of her night terrors again," she explained.

"Yeah, of course," I said, dropping the corner of the crust back on the plate.

"Maybe it was ghost," Elena suggested, adding some ghoulish wails for effect.

"Speaking of the undead," Catherine began, glancing at me, "Martha was muttering something to Lucinda about you and a ring yesterday."

Something sank within me. "You heard about that?"

"Relax!" she snorted. "Lucinda misplaces something twice a month, and we all get frisked. Isn't that right, Elena?"

Elena lifted a shoulder, clutching her mug for comfort.

"Why, what happened?"

"Once, she made Elena empty her bra, right there in the pantry," Catherine said flatly. "Over a damned brooch. It turned up down the side of a chaise a week later."

"Did she apologise?" I asked.

Both of them giggled as if I'd made a joke, and Elena adopted a pose that I immediately recognised as Martha.

"Mrs Blackthorn is the lady of this house! She has no need to apologise!" she mocked.

Despite her accent, the accuracy of her impression was astounding, so I threw my head back in laughter before unashamedly plucking a lukewarm sausage from their shared plate.

"By the way, did a Jada ever work here?" I asked, taking another sip of coffee.

"Jada... no, I don't think so," Catherine said, shaking her head at Elena. "Then again, there's been plenty of faces coming and going over the years, and it's pretty difficult to keep track."

"Fair enough," I said, setting my mug down.

"Who was she to you?"

"No one," I lied quickly. "Just someone I used to work with."

"What did you do before, anyway?" Catherine asked. "Before you landed a job in paradise."

"Nothing much. I was in—" I began before stopping myself. "Er—sales."

"Why come here?" Elena asked, crinkling her forehead.

"I needed a job," I said, rolling my eyes. "But I needed a bed more."

They both exhaled through their noses as though that made perfect sense.

"Listen, love, this ring thing will blow over," Catherine said. "You'll be back to scrubbing toilets in no time."

"Can't wait," I said flatly.

Catherine reached for her mug with her braced hand before checking the clock. "Right, we'd better get going before *Mother Superior* rises."

"Mother—who?" I asked.

"It is what we call Martha," Elena explained, nudging me on the shoulder. "Do not use it to her face."

I smiled. "Wouldn't dream of it."

We begrudgingly got back on our feet and cleared the table. I washed the pots as Elena weighed flour and sang only to herself. Catherine measured butter by eye and cut it into cubes with quick, economical strokes. We'd only been at it a few minutes when the back door opened and Harris stumbled in, dropping his fresh kills on the table we'd just cleaned with a dull thud.

"*Gilipollas!*" Elena exclaimed.

"Bloody hell, Harris!" Catherine yelled across the kitchen. "Did you have to dump those there?"

"Sorry," he grumbled. "Mrs B wants them plucked for this evening."

She sighed as she walked over to inspect them and put her hands on her hips.

"And heads up, she's on the warpath," he added.

"When isn't she?" Elena muttered, smirking as she said it.

"Is Martha up yet?" he asked, straightening one of the pheasant's legs out.

"Not yet. I think she'll be a little worse for wear," Catherine replied.

He grunted and left, thumping the door shut behind him.

Elena shot Catherine a knowing look before we went back to it. Catherine sat at the table, ripping out chunks of pheasant feathers with her bare hands like she'd done it a thousand times before, and Elena started mixing bread dough together with a giant wooden spoon. I started drying the pots, trying to get rid of the evidence of our stolen breakfast before Martha returned from the dead.

"What's Lucinda doing up at this time, anyway?" I asked. "That's a bad omen if I've ever seen one."

"Well, it's the big dinner tonight, isn't it?" Catherine replied. "She's probably preening."

"Dinner?"

"Yeah—the big swinging dicks from the Sofia Blackthorn Foundation. She holds it every year."

"Huh. I must've missed the memo."

Catherine swivelled her head around, looking for something, then stormed out of the kitchen in a huff. As my eyes followed her, I suddenly felt Elena's hand grip my arm, and then she yanked me into the pantry. She half-closed the door with her hip and then leaned on the counter.

"Elena? What the hell?" I said, feeling my pulse spike.

"It is—" She paused to catch her breath. "It is not safe for you here."

A lump formed in my throat. "What? Why?"

"This family—they are bad."

"I've dealt with women like Lucinda before, okay? Her bark is worse than her bite," I scoffed. "And Lucas? He's basically a stroppy teenager."

"No, no. Not them," she said, peering around the door. "*Señor Blackthorn*."

I gripped my elbow. "What are you talking about?"

"Do not be alone with him, okay? If he asks, make excuse. Definitely do not go into his study."

"Listen, I can manage a handsy boss, alright?" I said, trying to push past her.

"It's not that," she said, raising a hand to stop me. "He misses his daughter."

"I know he does." I furrowed my brow. "Obviously."

"No, he misses her…" she began before struggling to find the words. "My English, it's—"

"Very much?" I suggested.

"No," she said, levelling her eyes with mine. "Wrong."

The room seemed a little colder. "He misses her—wrong?"

"This is what he does. He hires girls who look like her. Makes them feel special."

I chuckled nervously before making another attempt to leave. "I think you're just confused."

Elena blocked my path again. "The last one was from the village. She was pretty. Slim. Bronze skin. Red hair."

"Fine, I'll bite," I said, crossing my arms. "What happened to her?"

"One night, she was there. Next morning, gone. Room cleared."

"She couldn't take the heat and left. So what?" I argued.

"Not just her." Elena rubbed her bad leg. "When Sofia was here, I saw something."

I narrowed my eyes. "What?"

"*El señor*, he was creeping out of her room, doing his belt up. She was crying inside."

"You mean…"

Elena nodded expressively.

"You're mistaken," I dismissed feebly. "She was his daughter."

"Hija adoptiva."

"What?"

"Not real—adopted."

I wasn't sure if I flat-out didn't believe her, or if I just didn't want to. However, one thing I was certain of was that the whole idea that Mr Blackthorn was inappropriate with his daughter, adoptive or otherwise, made me feel sick to my stomach. Is that what he was trying to initiate in his study? Live out some kind of disgusting sexual fantasy? Is that the reason Sofia lost her life?

"If that's true, why didn't you tell someone?" I uttered.

She was taken aback. "No! I couldn't."

"Why not?" I asked.

Elena parted her lips to speak, but quickly buttoned them back up again. Instead, she looked down at her leg, and I followed her eyes as she slowly lifted up her tunic. I recoiled when I saw the state of her left thigh. The skin was discoloured, scarred, and covered in pockmarks, with a huge chunk missing from the muscle. It had long since healed, but it explained why she was so unsteady on her feet.

"This is what happens when you upset them, Robyn," she said.

"What happened to you?"

"Lucas, he—"

A door slammed, and footsteps passed by the door.

"Hey! Are you two slacking off in there?" Catherine called from the kitchen.

"Coming!" Elena shouted back, grabbing me by the shoulders. "Do not give *them* chances, Robyn. They do not need many."

"I—I won't," I stammered.

She searched my face, decided to believe me, and limped back through. When I walked back into the kitchen, Catherine was back at her station, and Martha had just rushed in, hair all over the place and still tying her tunic around her waist. She zeroed in on me with a scowl and stormed over, clearly in the mood for an argument.

"What were you two doing in there?" she demanded.

I glanced at Elena for direction, but she'd already moved her eyes to the ground. "I was just helping Elena with something."

"What?"

"Flour!" I announced, rubbing my neck. "We needed more flour."

She frowned, choosing to accept my lies as the truth. "Go and scrub the downstairs toilets. Mrs Blackthorn is entertaining tonight."

"Of course!" I said, but I didn't move.

"Well? What are you waiting for?"

I leaned forward, sucking in my bottom lip. "How was last night?"

A fleeting smile curled the corners of her mouth. "It was so much fun!"

"Really?" I asked, artificially widening my eyes.

"Yes! And you won't believe it, Mrs Blackthorn said I could keep the dress!"

I let out an exaggerated gasp. "You lucky cow!"

"I know!" she enthused, tucking some hair behind her ear.

Catherine shot me a dirty look while cleaving one of the birds with a dull thud.

"Anyway, I'll let you know when I've finished with the toilets. I bet there's loads to do for tonight."

Martha paused. "On second thoughts, don't bother with the toilets," she said, touching my arm lightly. "I'll get one of the other girls to do it."

"You sure?" I said, glancing over her shoulder.

"Do you know how to knead dough?"

"Er—yeah."

"Good. Swap with Elena."

I glanced over. "But what about her leg?"

"I'm sure she'll manage."

I watched Martha stride over to the cupboard to grab the cleaning caddy and then dump it in Elena's arms. Begrudgingly, she limped to the kitchen door, firing a rotten look my way as she hobbled through. In truth, I felt a little bad for manipulating Martha into turning her attention to the other girls, but that feeling quickly fizzled away when I remembered how badly I'd been treated. As far as I was concerned, I'd received more than my fair share of abuse, so I was happy for them to take the flak for a while.

What stuck with me was Elena's warning about the red-headed girl who vanished from the estate. I may have brushed it off, but the fear in her eyes told me it was true, or that she believed it wholeheartedly, at least. Was Mr Blackthorn collecting broken women like me, only to discard them when he'd had his fun? Did he do the same to Sofia? To Mum? Did Lucinda know?

"Robyn?" Martha prompted, clapping her hands. "Chop, chop!"

I rushed over to Elena's station and started kneading, Catherine's commandments repeating in my head.

Head down. Don't make waves. Only cry if you're in the pantry.

But rules were made to be broken.

21

THE HOMECOMING

ROBYN — BEFORE

After two weeks' respite, the hospital discharged Mum just before lunch, as promised. I was snapped back into reality when Dr Khan went through her new treatment plan: wound care, painkillers, follow-up scans and stitch removals. I was almost made dizzy by the time he'd finished, with a note on my phone longer than my arm just to keep track of it all, but Mum didn't seem to care. In fact, she hardly even acknowledged a single word coming out of the doctor's mouth.

More responsibility on my shoulders. Just what I needed.

In my opinion, she didn't look anywhere near ready to come home. The split near her temple had crusted over, held together by disposable stitches and left to dry in the open air. The bruise surrounding it was maturing into a deep purple, accented by dried blood and old dressing fibres. The nurses had done a terrible job of cleaning it up, and I spent the whole ambulance ride home wanting to clean her up with a wet sponge, but annoyingly, we hit the tail end of rush-hour traffic on the way back.

After forty-five minutes of being jostled from side to side and sitting in an uncomfortable silence, we eventually made it home. The paramedics were kind enough, even offering to push her up to our floor, but Mum shot me a look, so I declined and took over. She remained mute on the short walk across the courtyard, clutching the paper bag of tablets on her lap and shivering underneath the cardigan resting on her shoulders.

I had so much to say, and I'm sure she did too, but neither of us dared to, not in the cold light of day. I mean, how would I even bring it up? Welcome home, Mum! By the way, I was almost raped while you were in the hospital. Do you fancy a brew? No—I'd just have to keep it to myself. Besides, the last thing I needed was another lecture about her being right, ending in her telling me she told me so.

"You're quiet," she pointed out as I called the lift. "Is something the matter?"

"So are you," I replied, ignoring her question.

"I've still got a banging headache. The doctors said the pills would help, but so far, they haven't touched the sides."

The lift arrived, so I forced her through the doors, holding my nose to keep out the pong.

"It's good to be home, though," Mum remarked, waving her hand in front of her face.

"There's no place like it," I murmured, squeezing past one of the wheels.

"I'm just excited to get a proper, home-cooked meal down me," she said, patting her stomach. "The food at the hospital was a joke."

"Uh-huh," I grunted in agreement, pressing the button for our floor.

After a few clunks, the lift started whirring, and I kept my eyes locked on the display.

"Are you sure you're okay, love?" she asked, reaching out to touch my leg.

As soon as her fingers made contact with my thigh, it felt like a jolt of electricity shot through my body. It brought everything back: The Glasshouse, Lucas, the toilets, my knickers around my ankles and his hips pressed into mine. I flinched, recoiling into the most disgusting corner of the lift, pulling my jacket tight around me.

"Robyn? What's going—"

"Nothing," I jumped in.

"Has something—"

"No," I said firmly. "Just leave it."

The lift creaked to a stop, so I got back behind the chair and reversed her through the opening. Once we were inside our flat, I started the usual routine. I wheeled her into the lounge and whipped open the curtains, replaced the bag of pills on her lap with the TV remote, then headed to the kitchen. But on my way through, I spotted something in a heap on the bathroom floor that rooted me to the spot.

My dress.

Our old shower didn't get hot enough to scald away the memory of the last time I wore that dress—believe me, I tried. In fact, I spent over an hour trying to get myself clean in there the night before, scrubbing my skin until it was red raw, sitting beneath the showerhead in the hope that the running water would drown out Lucas' whispered words still ringing in my ears. After a cursory glance at Mum in the lounge, I scooped it up off the tiles and stuffed it into the bottom of the kitchen bin, then filled up the kettle to pop it on. Luckily, there were two clean mugs in the cupboard, so I got them out and dropped a teabag in each. Bubbles began to rise as the kettle started hissing steam, so I grabbed it to fill up the cups, but I wasn't paying attention and accidentally splashed the back of my hand.

"Ow!" I yelped, rushing over to the sink. "Bastard!"

"Are you alright in there?" Mum shouted from the lounge.

I sucked my teeth. "It's nothing."

Mum wheeled herself in a beat later, putting two and two together after glancing at the puddle of water on the floor.

"Let me look," she said, holding out her hand.

"I'm fine," I said, keeping my arm under the tap.

I heard Mum reverse a few feet and then let out a huge sigh. It was lecture time.

"Robyn, what's happened to us?" she asked.

"What do you mean?" I asked without looking back.

"We used to be inseparable, but lately, I feel like we're drifting apart."

I turned the tap off and turned around, shaking my hand dry as I leaned my back against the sink. "That's not true."

"All the sneaking around, the lies, the arguments—it *is* true."

My hand started smarting again. "What do you want me to tell you? Huh?"

"I want you to tell me what's going on," she explained. "You're all I've got, Robyn. I can't lose you."

With a cynical shake of the head, I walked over to the mugs to take the teabags out and then grabbed the milk from the fridge. After pouring a measure in each cup, I placed one on one side of the table, then plodded to the other side and sat down. Mum wheeled herself over and picked it up, clutching it with both hands.

"Just talk to me, love," she pleaded. "I can't stand all this."

"Do you really want the lies to stop?" I asked.

"Yes."

"Good," I said, flattening my palms on the table. "You first."

"Robyn, I—"

"Mum, just tell me, okay?"

"Okay," she uttered, shame in her eyes. "I didn't fall," she admitted.

I gritted my teeth. "Who did this to you, then?"

"I—I don't know," she mumbled.

"I thought we were cutting the bullshit."

"Fine, fine!" she spat, her eyes meeting mine. "The Blackthorns."

"Richard?" I suggested. "Lucas?"

"They don't do their own dirty work!" she scoffed. "One of their goons."

I dug my nails into my palm. "Just tell me what happened."

"Well, there was a knock at the door, so I unlocked it. A man forced his way in."

I clutched my chest. "Why did you open the door, Mum?"

"I thought it was you and you'd forgotten your key."

Great. Another thing to be guilty about.

"Then what happened?"

"He forced me into the bedroom and told me to get out of the chair. When I couldn't, he started waving a bat or something in my face."

I touched my cheeks and pulled my face down. "Why?"

"He told me I'd broken the terms of my agreement."

"What agreement?"

"I said I'd never get in touch with any of them again, and I called Richard, didn't I?"

I slumped back into my chair in shock.

"Why did you lie to me?"

Mum rubbed her eyes. "I was trying to protect you."

I tapped my nails on the table. "Some good it did."

She moved a little closer, narrowing her eyes. "What happened?"

"Nothing," I said out of reflex.

"No, no, no. You don't get to do that," she warned. "It's your turn to tell the truth."

"Mum, I—"

"Robyn! Tell me!"

I sighed and pushed my brew away, dipping my finger in the ring mark it left. "There was an incident."

"Incident?" she echoed. "What incident?"

"I went out with Ellie. Lucas was there, and he…" I trailed off.

"What?" she interrupted.

"Nothing happened," I said quickly. "Not really. He just cornered me in the toilets and—"

"Did he hurt you?" she asked, almost pushing herself out of her chair.

"No," I uttered, dropping my shoulders and my voice. "He got disturbed."

Mum gasped, dew forming in her eyes. Just the sight of her getting upset broke me, and before I knew it, I was blubbering into my hands. She rushed over, leaning over the chair to wrap her arms around me, and I lightly patted her arm as tears streamed down my face.

"Oh, Robyn. I'm so sorry," she sobbed.

"There's nothing to be sorry about, is there?" I shrugged, pulling away. "You warned me. I should've listened."

"Now you understand why I was so worried!" She grabbed my hand tightly. "He isn't even the worst of them!"

"I know," I muttered.

She pursed her lips. "Tell me you're done messing with them."

I nodded, wiping the tears from my cheeks and staring into space. "Yeah. I'm done."

"Good." Mum let out a long exhale. "I'll ring an estate agent in the morning. Let's see if we can sell this fleapit."

"Move?" I said, my jaw agape. "Mum, is that necessary?"

"Yes," she said quickly. "Trust me."

I opened my mouth to argue, but shut it immediately. "Okay. Do it."

Mum allowed a tentative smile to span her lips. "Besides, a change of scenery will do us some good, won't it?"

I smiled back. "It will."

She took the brake off her chair and started wheeling out of the kitchen, almost as if she was about to start packing, but there was one more thing I needed to tell her.

"Wait," I said after her. "I need to speak to Ellie."

"Weren't you listening to what I said?"

I took a long inhale. "She deserves to know the truth."

"She is not your responsibility!"

"She is. She's my friend."

"No, she's a girl who made her own choices and will have to unmake them!" she protested. "You don't owe these people anything!"

"I need to warn her, Mum. I wouldn't be able to live with myself if something happens."

Mum peered down, scowling into her lap. She knew I was right; she just couldn't bring herself to say it.

"After that, I'm finished," I insisted. "I swear."

"Fine. Call her and tell her over the phone."

"No. It has to be in person. She won't believe me otherwise."

"And what if Lucas shows up?"

"He won't."

"But what if he does?"

"I'll meet her somewhere public. There's no way he'll get me on my own again."

"Robyn, I don't know…"

"I have to do this, Mum. I have no other choice."

She stared at me for a while and gave the slightest nod. It wasn't agreement, it was resignation: a mother's compromise with the woman she raised.

"If you even see a glimmer of him, you turn around and come home, okay?" she instructed.

"I will."

"I'm serious. I don't care if you're halfway across Manchester with your shoes in your hand. You come home."

"I will, Mum. I promise," I said, picking up my phone.

Mum begrudgingly wheeled herself back into the lounge, and I retreated to the corner of the kitchen, dialling Ellie's number. She answered on the seventh ring like she'd been deciding whether to, the hum of traffic and vague amusement behind her voice.

"Oh, it's you," she said with a side of scorn. "What the hell happened to you after The Glasshouse?"

"Sorry, I had to run. Mum was getting discharged from the hospital."

She sighed. "Is she okay?"

"She's fine. Listen, I need to—"

"Poor BB looked like a lost puppy when you took off," she interrupted. "He was absolutely distraught."

"I don't care about him, El. I need to talk."

She paused for a beat, just long enough to prick the skin.

"What about?" she asked.

"Is Lucas with you?"

Another pause.

"No," she said with an upward inflexion. "Why?"

"Can we meet?"

"Sure. When?"

"Now if you can."

"I'd love to, but I'm just about to—"

"Whatever it is, it can wait. This is more important."

"Can't you just tell me now?" She laughed uneasily. "You know I hate surprises."

"No, I don't want to do this over the phone. Where are you?"

"Er—about to meet a friend."

"Ditch them and meet me somewhere."

She sighed. "Where?"

"I don't care. You pick."

"Fine!" she exclaimed. "Baker and Roberts on St Ann's Square. If I'm late, just go inside and do some shopping."

I already knew she was going to be late. She was *always* late.

"Perfect. I'll see you—"

She hung up without saying goodbye. That was new.

I grabbed my bag and then popped my head through the lounge door on my way out. The TV was on, but Mum wasn't even facing it. She was pointed towards the mantelpiece, staring at the photograph of the Blackthorns sitting on top of it.

"I'm heading over there now," I announced.

"Where are you meeting her?" she asked without turning.

"Some jewellery shop in town."

"Text me when you get there, okay?"

"Okay," I sang, rolling my eyes.

"And every half an hour until you leave."

"I will—Mum, relax! It's going to be fine."

Mum blew a puff of air out, blankly staring into space again.

"And Mum?" I said, lingering in the doorway.

"Yeah?"

"I love you," I said.

"I love you, too." She smiled. "Be careful, sweetheart."

"Always," I said before walking out of our flat.

I didn't know it at the time, but it was the last time I'd ever see her.

22

THE PARTY

ROBYN

It was all-hands-on-deck by lunchtime. The grounds had been flooded with unfamiliar faces, drafted in from some temp agency to give us a hand with the preparations for the big Sofia Blackthorn Foundation dinner. Every surface had to be dusted. Every tile scrubbed. Much to his disgust, even Harris was put to work, tasked with changing a few lightbulbs in the foyer that had become dim. Martha meandered through the staff like a general, unashamedly ticking off items from a clipboard and barking orders at anyone foolish enough to catch her eye.

    I felt like I'd been chained to one of the worktops in the kitchen, positioned in front of a mountain of onions which needed to be peeled and chopped. When I started, I could scarcely make out the edge of the knife through the tears, but after forty-five minutes of incessant slicing and dicing, I'd become immune to the effects. I was just finishing up the penultimate one when the pantry door banged shut, so I peeked over my shoulder and saw Catherine stumbling towards me, struggling with a sack of potatoes. I turned back just as she was about to pass, but she barged into me, almost making me cut the tip of my finger off with the blade.

"Hey! Watch it, will you?" I said before grabbing the last onion.

"*Fucking traitor*," she uttered under her breath as she continued trudging along.

One problem at a time.

"Robyn?" I heard Martha call behind me.

I turned around and saw her beckoning me over, so I wiped my hands on my tunic and rushed to her side.

"Did you need something?" I asked.

"Are all the vegetables for the starter prepped?"

"Just finishing the onions now, and then I'll start sautéing."

"Perfect," she said, ticking something from her list. "Are the pheasants in the ovens?"

"Crisping up as we speak."

"The silverware?"

"So shiny it's blinding."

Martha unearthed a contented smile and dropped the clipboard by her side. "I have to say, Robyn, you've really stepped up your game, and it's wonderful to see."

"Well, the *lady of the house* is entertaining tonight. Everything has to be flawless, doesn't it?"

Her grin widened. "It does."

"What's after the onions? I can always make a start on the white-wine sauce."

"No, Catherine can take care of that. You should get a shower and get changed into a fresh tunic."

"Really? Why?"

She moved forward slightly. "How do you feel about doing front of house with me tonight?"

I raised my eyebrows. "What does that entail?"

"Mostly topping up glasses and handing out canapés. It beats being stuck in the kitchen, believe me."

"Er—yeah, sure!" I exclaimed.

"Great, well make it snappy. The guests will be arriving shortly."

"Will do."

Martha scooted over to Catherine to check her work as I finished the last onion and then started transferring them into hot skillets. I dropped a few sticks of butter in each one and started them going before heading over to the sink to wash my hands. Catherine downed tools the instant Martha was out of the room and let out a huge sigh, shaking her head as she peered at the ceiling.

"Will you just come out with it?" I said, drying my hands.

"Don't think we can't see what you're doing," she remarked.

A chuckle leaked from my lips. "And what is that, exactly?"

"Sucking up to Mother Superior," she said, turning her back to continue peeling. "It won't work."

"That thing with Elena—it wasn't personal," I said, replacing the hand towel. "I'm just trying to survive."

She spun back around, lifting her peeler in the air like a weapon.

"Let me tell you something, I've been here a lot longer than you, and you won't last if you start fucking over your friends."

"*Friends?* We aren't friends!" I scoffed. "You're just pissed off that I'm not Martha's skivvy anymore."

"Oh, Robyn," she said, rocking her head. "You have a lot to learn."

"Whatever," I snapped back, removing my hairpin to let my hair drop. "Just keep an eye on those onions, will you? I don't want them to catch."

Catherine muttered something scathing as I breezed out of the room.

Given we were on a schedule, I unknotted the tie around my waist as I rushed over the courtyard to the servant's quarters. Once I was inside, I ducked into the communal shower to set it running, then headed over to my room to grab a clean towel. I was only halfway through the door when I pulled my uniform over my head to take it off, but to my horror, I realised that I wasn't alone.

It was Mr Blackthorn. Perched on the edge of my bed.

I recoiled, quickly gathering my tunic over my body until my back hit the wall.

"What—what are you doing in here?" I stammered.

"It's my house. I can go where I please." His icy gaze slid over me. "Besides, we need to have a chat."

"Okay," I said, sidestepping over to the wardrobe. "But can you just—"

"Of course," he interrupted, reluctantly averting his eyes. "Take your time."

I'd never got dressed so fast in my life. As soon as his head was turned, I jumped back into my tunic and tied it around my waist, keeping my hairpin behind my back, clutched in my fist.

"Okay, I'm decent," I announced. "What's all this about?"

He slowly turned his head and then rose to his feet, hands in pockets, stepping over before stopping so close that I could taste his lunch colliding with the back of my throat.

"I just wanted to apologise for how my wife behaved last night. It's been a difficult time."

I recoiled slightly with the intention of telling him it was okay, but at the last minute, I decided against it.

Fuck it.

"I think I'd like an apology from her," I said boldly.

He chortled heartily. "From Lucinda?"

I bobbed my head.

"I don't think that's going to happen," he said, wincing.

"She berated me for almost an hour and then spat in my face, Mr Blackthorn. It's the least she can do."

"The thing you need to understand about my wife is that she doesn't apologise. Not ever."

"Okay," I said, closing the gap between us even further. "Well, in that case, I think I deserve a raise."

A grin broke out on his face. "Wow—you're a dark horse, aren't you?"

He reached into his jacket pocket for his wallet, counted out some notes, then waved them in my face.

"Will three hundred do it?" he asked.

I wrinkled my nose. "I think I'd be more understanding if it were five."

"You drive a hard bargain," he sniggered as he added more notes. "Here."

I reached out to grab it, but to my horror, he dodged my hand and tugged the top of my tunic open with his free hand instead. He leaned forward to peer down it for a split second, then stuffed the wad of banknotes through the opening. I didn't dare move a muscle until he stepped back.

"It's a pleasure doing business with you, Miss Marsden," he said.

I fought the urge to gag. "Thank you," I uttered.

"Don't be silly," he said, shaking his head. "You earned it."

I pulled my ill-gotten gains out as I walked over to the bedside table and safely tucked them away at the back of the drawer, my pulse hammering in my neck.

"There is one thing I'm confused about," he mused.

I froze. "What?" I said over my shoulder.

"It's strange—the ring ended up back on my desk after I put it in the safe. You wouldn't know anything about that, would you?"

"No." I swallowed hard before turning back. "Maybe Mrs Blackthorn took it out of—"

"She doesn't know the combination," he interjected. "I'm the only one who does."

I opened my mouth to speak, but nothing came out.

"Were you aware that there's a camera in my study?" he asked.

My heart stopped. "No."

"Imagine my surprise when I checked the security system this morning and—"

"Mr Blackthorn, I—"

"Found it wiped," he continued.

My heart started beating again. "Wiped?"

"Totally clean. Poof. As if last night never happened."

"Right," I said, scratching the side of my head. "That's annoying."

"Quite. I guess we'll never know who was responsible, will we?"

"I guess not."

Mr Blackthorn stepped close to me again and lowered his head to my ear, his bushy moustache tickling my lobe.

"Don't worry," he whispered. "Your secret is safe with me."

With that, he gave me a firm smack on the arse, then walked out of the room, leaving me in bits. I tossed the hairpin on the bed. I should've stuck it in his neck.

* * *

After quite a bit of crying in the shower and a walk around the grounds, I finally regained my composure. It wasn't very smart to test Mr Blackthorn like that, and I should've known he would react if I backed him into a corner. I was praying that he didn't think he had some kind of ownership over me now, especially considering he was pretty sure it was me messing around in his office.

Still, I was five hundred quid better off, and it only cost me my dignity.

I reluctantly made my way back over to the main house. The driveway was lined with expensive motors, each more luxurious than the last, with a few straggling guests still making their way over the gravel. I jogged the last few metres and hurried into the kitchen, where Martha was running around like she was seconds away from a panic attack. Instead of giving me a bollocking for taking so long, she actually looked relieved to see me and grabbed two trays of canapés, placing one in each of my palms.

"Thank God you're here," she said, fanning herself with her hand. "Take those through to the foyer."

"Sorry that I'm late—I ran into Mr Blackthorn in the quarters," I explained.

Elena stopped stirring the soup and swivelled her head.

"It's okay, just move it, will you?" Martha asked. "We can't have the guests going hungry."

I could already hear the buzz in the foyer as I strode into the hallway. There were at least twenty or thirty visitors standing there, all holding a glass of champagne and mingling with each other, with Lucinda in the epicentre, schmoozing and chitchatting. She spotted me as soon as I set foot inside and clicked her fingers impatiently, gesturing for me to walk over. I dutifully complied, and the circle around her began picking one of the trays clean like a pack of vultures as her eyes burned into the side of my skull.

"Do be on your best behaviour tonight," she instructed in my ear.

"Always," I uttered through a forced grin.

"Tell me, have you seen my husband on your travels?"

"Nope," I said too quickly. "Not seen him."

She selected a smoked salmon crostini from the pile, bit into it, then discarded the other half back on my tray.

"What are you still doing here?" she snapped. "There are other guests to attend to."

"At once," I said, embarrassingly doing a little bow before meandering through the room.

The rest of the guests treated me like a piece of furniture, whipping food off my trays as I slid through them. I kept my head down, trying to avoid eye contact wherever possible, until I recognised the bracelet of one of the hands reaching for my tray. I looked up and saw Allisyn standing there with Kait, dolled up to the nines and sipping prosecco through a straw so as not to ruin their lipstick. Sydney arrived beside them a beat later, sucking on a disposable vape, jaw dropped as she ran her eyes over me.

"Robyn?" Sydney gasped. "What the hell are you doing here?"

"She works here now," Ellie announced as she materialised between them. "Isn't that right?"

I nodded, stacking the empty tray beneath the full one.

"Oh my God, that's tragic!" Kait remarked. "Look at her little tunic!"

"I think it suits her," Allisyn added. "In fact, it's the best dressed I've ever seen her."

"What happened to your top-secret 'job' in 'fashion?'" Kait asked.

I opened my mouth to speak, but she jumped back in before I got a single word out.

"Oh yeah, I forgot—you made the whole thing up."

"Come on, guys," Sydney meekly said, tugging at their arms. "Lay off her."

"No! This bitch *lied* to us," Kait said, shaking off her grasp.

"I know I did," I said, dropping my shoulders. "I'm sorry."

"Whatever." Allisyn rolled her eyes. "I always knew there was something fishy about you."

The sound of Lucinda tapping a crystal glass behind me silenced the room, and we all turned to face her.

"Please be seated in the dining room. Dinner will be served shortly," she announced.

"See you, Robyn," Kait uttered with disgust as she sauntered past me.

"Yeah, see you," Allisyn grunted, bashing into my shoulder and sending the tray plummeting to the floor, "*liar*."

Ellie didn't leap to my defence; she just followed them through to the dining room in silence, leaving only Sydney standing in front of me. I squatted down to pick up the ruined canapés off the floor, and to my surprise, she did the same.

"Ignore them," she said softly. "They're just angry."

I laughed despite myself. "They're right. I lied about everything."

"Not everyone was born with a silver spoon in their mouth."

"They're going to tell the family about me, aren't they? One whisper about prison and I'm done for."

"Don't worry," she whispered. "I'll make sure they keep quiet."

"Sydney?" Allisyn called from the hallway. "What the hell are you doing?"

"Sorry, Robyn," Sydney uttered before turning to her. "Coming!"

The last person left in the foyer was Lucinda, watching in delight as I scraped every morsel of food from the tiled floor with my bare hands. Once she left, I threw my head back to decompress before heading back to the kitchen to return the trays. It was utter madness when I stepped inside. All of the agency staff were running around like blue-arsed flies, with Catherine and Elena in the middle, busy plating up little pots of French Onion Soup and crusty bread. Martha was lurching her head around, wiping splatters of soup from the white porcelain with a cloth before signalling for the servers to take them. Without a word, I grabbed two completed dishes, but Martha placed her hand on my arm to stop me.

"Could you let Lucas know the guests have arrived?" she asked. "He's in his room."

"Certainly," I said, setting the plates back down.

I rushed into the hallway, stepping to one side to allow a few guests to pass me. Once it was clear, I hurried down the corridor and took the stairs two at a time, then bashed on Lucas's bedroom door. I thought about just walking inside when he didn't answer, but the thought of him lying in bed with his laptop and a box of tissues at the ready stopped me.

"You'd better come down," I shouted through the door. "Everyone's here."

He didn't reply.

I reached for the handle and turned it, holding my free hand over my brow to obscure my view of inside, but the wheezing noise he was making made me instantly drop it. I saw the bed first. As predicted, his laptop was there, but the lid was closed, with several lines of cocaine and a razor blade still sitting on top of it. His quilt was skew-whiff, so I followed it with my eyes and saw Lucas on the other side of the bed, on all fours, fighting for every breath and crawling towards his jacket on the back of his chair. I'd seen him in a state before, but he looked particularly terrible: shirt ripped open and sweat beading on his translucent skin.

"Lucas!" I said, dropping to his side. "What's the matter?"

"Jacket," he croaked, chest heaving. "Inside pocket."

I dashed over to his jacket and patted it down. There was an EpiPen in the pocket, so I pulled it out and rolled it over my hands.

"What do I do?" I asked.

Lucas spun onto his back, lips turning blue, clawing at his neck with one hand and slapping his thigh with the other.

"Shit," I muttered, reading the instructions.

"Now!" he rasped.

"I'm fucking trying! I've never done this before, have I?"

Lucas started violently shaking, so I ripped the blue cap off the top of the pen and held it above my head, but just as I was about to bring it down, I paused. Was I seriously about to save this worthless fucker's life? I could just leave, shut the door, and go back downstairs like nothing happened. It wouldn't get traced back to me—everyone would simply assume that he overdosed.

"Robyn!" he snarled.

I heard footsteps approaching outside, so I gritted my teeth and drove it into his leg, just below the hip. The wheezing stopped. The clawing ceased. His eyes closed, and his limbs went limp.

"Lucas?" I asked, leaning in.

At that very moment, Lucinda burst into the room, shunting me out of the way before wrapping one hand beneath Lucas's head and pawing at his face with the other.

"Lucas!" she shouted, distraught. "Just wake up, son!"

"Mrs Blackthorn! I just found him like this!"

"Come on! Just take a breath, baby! One breath, please!" Lucinda pleaded.

She started shaking him, so violently that the pen finally fell out of his thigh. She then gripped his wrist with two fingers, feeling for a pulse, but after a moment, she dropped back onto her shins, her trembling hands finding her face.

I swallowed. "Is he—"

The noise that Lucinda made next would stick with me until the day I died. It wasn't a scream, as such, or even a shout. It was more of a hissing roar, the kind that a wild animal would make if they were mortally injured, so loud that it rattled every wall in the house.

Then, she turned to me.

"What have *you* done?"

PART THREE

"BLOOD"

ONE WEEK LATER

23

THE LAKE

ROBYN

Fuck, he was actually gone.

The boating lake on the far side of the estate almost looked pretty if I ignored everything that I knew about the people standing around it. The harsh wind clipped at the surface, disturbing the reflection of the old, stone mausoleum on the other side. A slim willow leaned into the bank, leaves dipping into the murky water, cracking and creaking as if it were seconds from falling in. The sun's invite must've got lost in the post because the sky was as black as charcoal, and the spit of rain that had been threatening all morning began to ripple the skin of the lake.

The Blackthorn plot sat just beyond the path on the left-hand side, edged with rusted iron railings and clipped yews. The stones all boasted the same surname in different fonts; some were fat and smug with gilded letters, others were thin and crumbling, the names almost eroded away. The single rectangle of freshly dug earth stuck out like a sore thumb, slightly bulging on the surface and littered with damp bouquets. To be honest, it didn't suit Lucas. I was half expecting his funeral to be in some fancy nightclub in Manchester, complimentary glow-sticks and baggies on entry, champagne fountains and deafening club bangers inside. However, Lucinda was insistent that it should be a small affair, just immediate family and close friends present.

She was right about one thing, though: black *did* wash her out.

Although her dress was simple, the jewellery wasn't. She'd chosen pearls the size of gobstoppers, a pair of thick-rimmed sunglasses, and a hat that threw a shadow all the way to her chin. Mr Blackthorn stood beside her like a sentinel, decked out in a black suit and awkwardly resting his arm over his wife's shoulders, eyeballing the mausoleum over the lake like a hawk. Penelope shivered next to them in a fur coat, quietly sniffling and dabbing her eyes with a tissue. My old friends were huddled around Ellie like penguins, nestled beneath a black golf umbrella, somehow thinking it was appropriate to have their bare legs on show at a funeral. Ellie was the only one not crying. If anything, she looked annoyed to be there.

As for the help, we'd been instructed to keep to the edges. Heads down. Don't speak. Invisible unless summoned. Elena stood to my left with her weight pitched on her good leg, and Catherine was on my right, jaw clenched, hair scraped back so tight it looked painful. Harris was posted at the edge of the plot, dark tweed to the throat, lingering beside the graves like a warning to anyone who dared show up without an invite. Martha had wedged herself in front of us, hands behind her back, repeating Lucinda's whimpers back to her like a mockingbird as a show of support.

I'd be lying if I said I felt nothing.

Let's be honest, it was a hell of a nasty way to go, and the image of him lying lifeless on his bedroom floor as the paramedics tried to revive him would stay with me for a while. They couldn't even get the tube down his throat to get some air into his lungs because it was so swollen, and even after fifteen minutes of bashing on his chest, they still failed to restart his heart. Then again, I'd also be lying to myself if I said that I didn't think he had it coming. I mean, he was a vile, obnoxious and greedy piece of shit, totally devoid of empathy and with a level of narcissism that would put most serial killers to shame. He took drugs, he abused women, and he made everyone around him totally miserable, just for his own enjoyment.

Good riddance, if you ask me.

"Robyn! Keep your head down!" Martha ordered in my ear.

"Sorry," I mouthed back.

Lucinda turned her head. If looks could kill, I would've had a plot of my own.

The mourners stepped forward to the grave in turn, whispering their goodbyes into the soil. They didn't linger for much longer after that and started trundling down the path to the house, chins tucked into collars, eyes on the gravel. The help followed at a respectful distance, Harris leading the charge and picking at stray foliage as we passed.

There wasn't a single word uttered on the way back, primarily because there was nothing to say, but also because nobody wanted to put themselves in Lucinda's crosshairs. Harris raced ahead to open the doors when we arrived at the front steps, and Lucinda stood beside him, painted-on smile, waving everyone in. Mr Blackthorn was the first to enter, peeling his jacket off as he turned right to go up the stairs.

"We've prepared some nibbles in the library," she announced to the group. "Please go and help yourselves."

The kitchen gang were the last to go up the steps, but Lucinda stepped into the doorway, arms outstretched, to block any of us from entering.

"Not you four," she said, her voice like ice. "You're needed upstairs."

Harris leaned in. "Mrs Blackthorn, surely Martha doesn't need to—"

"Stand outside Richie's study and don't move a muscle," Lucinda ordered without acknowledging him. "All of you."

She didn't say why, but she didn't need to. In fact, I'm sure all of us had spent every day of the last seven wondering when this was going to happen. We trudged up the stairs without a word and lined up outside the study like we were queuing for our own executions. Lucinda had followed and ducked into her bedroom, only to return a moment later with a half-drunk bottle of gin.

She started swigging it, passing her eyes over the four of us, eyes like stones.

"Are you worried, Robyn?" Lucinda said, leaning against the frame. "You look a little peaky."

I shook my head without lifting it. "I'm fine."

"Why are you shaking so much, then?"

"Just cold," I mumbled, rubbing my elbows.

"Hmm. I don't think it's cold in here." Her eyes flitted between the other girls. "Do you, Elena?"

Elena looked terrified. "No."

"How about you, Catherine?" Lucinda turned her head. "Do you think it's cold in here?"

"No, Mrs Blackthorn," she responded.

"Hmm. I agree." Lucinda swallowed another mouthful. "If anything, it's a little stuffy, so I'll ask again. Why are you shaking so much?"

My eyes flicked from the floor, and she seemed to take it as an admission of guilt because she took one last drink from the bottle before launching it down the hallway in the direction of Sofia's room. We all winced when it shattered into pieces, and she was inches away from my face when I turned back, pressing a single digit into my shoulder.

"I *know* it was you!" she hissed.

I pulled a face. "He overdosed, Mrs Blackthorn, how could I have possibly—"

"My son didn't bloody overdose!" she jumped in. "He was poisoned!"

My pulse skittered. "*Poisoned?*"

The girls awkwardly shifted around next to me.

"How did you do it?" she said, violently bobbing her head.

"I didn't! I wasn't even—"

"You did. I *know* you did."

"Mrs Blackthorn, why would I want Lucas to die?"

"To punish me, of course!" she yelled, rocking on the spot. "Why else?"

I looked her dead in the eyes. "And why would I want to do that?"

The study door swung on its hinges, and Mr Blackthorn marched through it. The rest of the girls straightened their backs as he walked the line, stopping between Lucinda and me, softly grabbing the top of her arm to pull her to one side.

"I thought we agreed to question them in isolation?" he asked quietly in her ear.

"It was her! She all but admitted it," Lucinda responded.

I gasped. "I did no such—"

"Shut your mouth!" Mr Blackthorn boomed at me before turning back to his wife. "I will deal with her. Alone."

"Richie, she—"

"I've got it under control," he said, rotating her head to face him. "Why don't you go and entertain our guests?"

"No!" she shouted. "I need to be in there!"

"You're grieving, darling. Just go and have a rest, will you?"

"Fine, just don't believe a word that comes out of her mouth," she said through gritted teeth. "She's a pathological liar."

He patted her on the shoulder. "Listen, I'll summon you when we're done, okay?"

Begrudgingly, she left the hallway and stomped towards the staircase, growling something beneath her breath. Mr Blackthorn turned to me, gesturing for me to head into his office, so I glued my chin to my chest and hesitantly walked through the door. He closed it behind him, then walked over to the small bar in the corner of the room to pour himself a scotch. I felt like I was on the brink of a heart attack.

"Do you want one?" he asked over his shoulder.

I narrowed my eyes. "No, thank you."

"Suit yourself," he said, the bottle glugging into a glass.

"Mr Blackthorn, I had nothing to do with Lucas' death. Lucinda, she's—"

"I know you didn't."

I parted my lips to continue my arguments, but what he'd said had caught me off guard.

"Just sit down, will you?" he said, his voice a touch above a whisper.

I complied, landing on the edge of the seat. He sat down a second later, knocking back a mouthful of whisky before setting it on his desk and scraping the rain off the top of his head with both hands.

"I'm going to ask you some direct questions, and I expect direct responses," he announced. "I'm not in the mood for games."

I nodded fearfully.

"What happened?" he asked.

"I went to his room to summon him downstairs. He was on the floor."

"And then what?"

"He couldn't breathe—like he was choking. He told me to get his EpiPen."

"And did you give it to him?"

"Of course!"

"What next?"

"It didn't work. It was—" I paused. "It was too late."

Mr Blackthorn closed his eyes and exhaled slowly. "Oh, Lucas. You silly, silly boy."

"What is it?" I asked.

"You must've known about his... vices."

I straightened my face. "I'd heard rumours."

With a groan, Mr Blackthorn reached into his top drawer and slammed something heavy onto his desk. It took me a second to realise that it was the pestle and mortar from the kitchen, sealed in a large plastic bag, with some residual dust still inside from whatever was ground down in it. Just as I was about to ask him what the powder was, the following item he slapped on the table answered my question: a small baggie filled with peanuts.

"Are those—"

Mr Blackthorn snorted to himself. "Yes. Peanuts."

"Sorry." I cleared my throat. "Peanuts?"

"You see, Lucas has been fiercely allergic to them ever since he was a toddler. It was so bad that we forbade them from even being on the grounds."

"Are you saying someone did this to him on purpose?"

"Yes. Harris found the pestle and mortar stashed in the pantry this morning," he said before narrowing his eyes. "It was covered with fingerprints."

My lungs went tight. "Whose?"

He stared at me, almost like he was trying to see inside my head. "Elena's."

"No," I said, sitting back while rocking my head in disbelief. "Why would she do that?"

"Tell me, what do you know of her injury?" he asked.

The back of my neck started pricking. "Er—not much."

"She acquired it right here on the estate. There was an accident involving a shotgun some years ago."

"Right," I said, leaning forward. "I had no idea."

"Lucas was shooting at some targets, Elena got in the way and, well… I'm sure you can imagine the rest."

"Jesus," I said, barely audible.

"I can assure you that she was well looked after, but I always had a hunch that she never got over it. That's why I called my friend."

"Friend?" I uttered.

"He's the Chief Inspector of Greater Manchester Police. He tested it for me."

As if by magic, red and blue lights started dancing across the walls, so Mr Blackthorn walked over to his window to see what was happening. I followed him, and two police cars had stopped on the gravel, with two plain-clothes officers and two uniforms stepping out of them.

"What the hell are they doing here?" he asked.

"You didn't call them?"

"No," he grumbled, lowering his sleeves and putting on his jacket.

"Mr Blackthorn, what's going to happen to her?" I asked softly.

He didn't answer. He simply strode over to the study door to open it, and the two uniforms were already slapping the cuffs onto Elena in the hall. Catherine was clutching a tissue to her eyes. Lucinda had a fresh bottle and was drinking from it deeply, clearly debating whether she should smash it over Elena's skull.

"Elena Hernandez, you are under arrest for murder. You do not have to say anything, but it may harm your defence if you do not mention when questioned something which you later rely on in court. Anything you do say may be given in evidence," one of the officers recited.

"I—I did not do this," Elena uttered.

"Get her out of my fucking sight!" Lucinda spat.

Martha and the Blackthorns followed the officers escorting Elena outside, and I remained upstairs with Catherine, numbly watching as they dragged her down the stairs. Catherine pulled me back with her dodgy wrist and pushed me into the wall as soon as they'd disappeared.

"You can't let them take her," she said.

"I tried! I told Mr Blackthorn that Elena didn't have anything to do with it."

"No, you need to tell them the truth."

"*Truth*?" I raised an eyebrow. "What are you going on about?"

Her eyes flitted to the stairs, then back to me. "I know it was you."

"What? No, I was—"

"I *saw* you."

The malice in her eyes turned the air in my lungs to frost. If there was even a whisper of me being involved in this, I was done for. It wouldn't matter to Lucinda if there were any evidence. I'd be dragged out of there by my hair and handed over to the police. Or worse.

"Listen to me very carefully, Catherine," I said, stern but quiet. "You didn't see a damn thing because I didn't do anything."

"It was just before we started plating the starters up. I saw you sneaking out of his room."

I laughed incredulously. "I wasn't even in the house! I was in the quarters."

"Very convenient! The one place where no one can confirm your story."

"Actually, they can," I said before gauging her reaction. "Mr Blackthorn was with me."

"With you?" she echoed, releasing her grip. "In your room?"

"Yep."

"Alone?"

"Just the two of us."

"Why on earth would—"

"What are you two doing up there?" we heard Lucinda shout up the stairs.

Catherine pushed past me to head towards the stairs, but I was the one to hold her back this time.

"Don't breathe a word of this to anyone else, you hear? Keep your wild theories to yourself."

She exhaled sharply through her nose. "Or what?"

"Or I'll have to speak to Mr Blackthorn," I said, my voice hushed. "Maybe Elena had an accomplice."

The colour drained from Catherine's face.

"Get down here this instant!" Lucinda barked.

"After you," I said, gesturing for Catherine to walk ahead of me. "We're needed."

She took one last look at me as I stepped aside, and then I followed her down the winding stairs into the foyer. Mr Blackthorn was holding Lucinda, half-comforting and half-restraining her as Elena was being carted off on the driveway. He peered up at me as I started walking down the steps, so I shot him a crooked smile.

Nothing on that estate would ever look the same again.

24

THE RESIGNATION

ROBYN

Catherine had already fled before the peacocks woke up.

I'd always been an incredibly light sleeper since Mum's accident, even more so in prison, so I knew that she'd be gone by morning when I heard her door click shut in the dead of night. However, I still threw on my nightgown and stalked after her to confirm it. From the bushes, I watched her traipse down the gravel, suitcase dragged by her dodgy wrist, until she disappeared down the driveway and into the early-morning darkness. I didn't try to stop her—she'd made the right decision. It wasn't safe for her on the estate, not after Elena.

Catherine's abrupt departure had its advantages for me, too. For a start, she'd somehow got it in her head that she'd seen me have a hand in Lucas' death, and it was only a matter of time before she blabbed her harebrained ideas to somebody who'd actually listen to them. Given that my employment there was already dangling by a thread, I knew that even a whisper of my involvement would land me in cuffs at best, or dead in a ditch at worst. She left me a parting gift, though: her mantra. I kept repeating it in my head over and over.

Head down. Don't make waves. Only cry if you're in the pantry.

To that end, I was already in the kitchens by 6 am, firing up the stoves and poaching eggs. I knew it was utterly pointless because they'd be stone cold before the family that I was cooking them for would be awake, but I thought it best to keep up appearances. Besides, we'd lost two pairs of hands within twenty-four hours, and I knew that Martha would be in a tizzy when she chiselled herself out of bed.

Despite the sullen mood on the estate, I was feeling quite chirpy. Even after being woken by Catherine's moonlight flit, it was still one of the better nights' sleeps I'd enjoyed in that place. I assumed that I would've had the place to myself for at least a few hours before anybody showed up, so I had my earphones in, Eighties bangers on full blast, singing and bopping along with the music.

"Tell it to my heart! Tell me I'm the only one. Is it love, or just a game?" I belted out.

The chorus started to repeat, so I filled my lungs with air, but the buds were ripped from my ears before I could chant another word.

"What do you know about this?" Martha barked.

I kept my eyes locked on the boiling water before turning around. "Know about what?"

"This," she said, shoving a sheet of paper in my hand.

I stretched my eyes out and then narrowed them, holding the handwritten note at arm's length and reading it in a low murmur.

Martha,
I can't stand you and your pomposity any longer.
With Elena gone, there's nothing keeping me here, so treat this letter as my resignation.
Please don't contact me. I won't be coming back.

Yours,
Catherine

"Catherine's gone?" I asked, mouth agape.

"Apparently," she replied, snatching the note back. "This was shoved underneath my door last night. Can you believe it?"

"I can't!" I exclaimed. "Have you tried calling her?"

"About a dozen times. No answer."

The timer went off for the eggs, so I took them off the heat and started draining the water over the sink.

"How long had she worked here?" I asked over my shoulder.

"Over five years!"

"And she couldn't give you the dignity of telling you she was leaving face-to-face?" I asked, clicking my tongue. "Well, that's just rude."

"Extremely!" Martha cried. "We weren't exactly friends, but there was a mutual respect there, you know?"

Sure, Mother Superior.

"What are you going to do?" I asked, setting the pan down. "We were short-handed as it was."

"I have no idea," she admitted, leaning against the table. "First, Elena, now this."

"We'll manage." I gestured to the stove. "Look, I've already made a start on breakfast."

Martha sighed before locking her eyes with mine. "You aren't thinking of leaving, are you?"

"No, of course not!" I said quickly. "I need this job."

"That's a relief," she said softly.

"Besides, I quite like it here," I added without irony.

"Have you made a start on the coffee yet?" she asked.

"Not had a chance."

"Well, I'd better hop to it then."

I took my hand back and leaned against the counter opposite her. I wasn't sure if her eyes were red and puffy because she'd been crying after receiving the note or because of the emotion of the day before, but she was a shadow of her former self. She looked utterly broken—not a scrap of makeup on her face, her hair lank and greasy, and dressed in a tunic that appeared to be on its third wear.

"I can do it," I said, going over to place a hand on her arm. "Why don't you take a beat?"

"But there's so much to do…" She threw her hands in the air.

"No, you had a tough day yesterday, so you should take it easy."

"Easy?" she repeated. "How can I?"

I folded my arms across my chest and donned my most sympathetic face. "You must've known Lucas well."

"I did. Ever since he was two or three."

"I bet you're devastated by what happened. I mean, it was so sudden, wasn't it?"

Martha started sniffling. "It was. He had his problems, sure, but he had a heart of gold deep down."

I battled the yearning to take the piss. "I know he did," I managed with a straight face.

"More than anything, he just needed help. And poor Mrs Blackthorn—God only knows what she's going through right now."

"It's a tragedy, to say the least," I said, putting on my most sympathetic face.

"The worst cross to bear is that it happened on my watch. How could I have been so foolish?"

"Martha, you weren't responsible for Elena's actions," I insisted. "You must know that."

She lifted a shoulder, toying with her tunic.

"Listen, why don't you have a quick walk around the grounds? To clear your head if nothing else."

"No, I need to—"

"I can hold down the fort," I interrupted. "It's the least I can do."

Martha shrank slightly. "Are you sure?"

"Dead sure," I said, stepping forward to take Catherine's note from her grasp. "I'll give you a shout when the family wake up."

"Okay," she said, wandering towards the door before stopping. "Thank you, Robyn."

"Don't mention it," I gushed, but the smile nosedived off my face the instant her back was turned. In truth, I didn't care how she felt, and I was surprised she didn't sense it. I only wanted her out of my hair, and if I had to run the entire household to make that happen, then so be it.

After waiting a moment, I took Catherine's scrawled resignation to the hob and lit the corner. I shielded the fledgling flame as I walked across to the sink and dropped it inside. I let it burn for a few seconds before reaching into my tunic pocket to pull out the *real* note that Catherine had left, the one that exonerated Elena and flat-out accused me of murder, and then cast it into the fire.

Problem solved.

I couldn't allow her to share her speculations, could I? So, when I saw the envelope peeking out from beneath Martha's door the night before, I did what anybody would do. I read it, rewrote it, and replaced it before anyone else knew it existed. I didn't know why Catherine thought it necessary to drop a bombshell like that when she was already planning to leave, but it seemed needlessly malicious. I was just thankful I got to it first.

The timer for the bacon started chiming, so I ran over to the stove to pull the tray from the grill. It was a little overdone, but who cared? It was only going to dry up outside of the Blackthorn bedrooms uneaten, anyway.

***

The main house was eerily quiet. My battered work flats clacked against the marble floors as I dawdled over to the staircase, holding a huge tray with three identical breakfasts balancing on top of it. I actually made four by accident, and ended up eating Lucas's while the others were left to go cold. I left the first outside of Mr Blackthorn's study, tapping gently on the door before crossing the hall to Lucinda's chambers. I didn't bother knocking on her door; I just dropped the plate onto the carpet from a foot in the air, splitting the delicate yolk in two. The last was for Penelope, so I propped the tray against the wall and carried the remaining plate down the hall. To my surprise, I could hear what sounded like muffled music coming from her room.

"Miss Blackthorn? It's Robyn," I said into the timber. "Are you feeling up for a spot of breakfast?"

"Go away!" she shouted back.

I was taken aback. I didn't realise she'd taken her brother's death so badly.

"I'll just leave it outside, okay?" I suggested.

I waited a second for a reply, but when none came, I headed back towards the kitchen.

"Wait!" I heard Penelope yell.

"Yes, Miss Blackthorn?" I asked, turning on my heel.

She beckoned me over, so I reluctantly backtracked to her room. I picked up the plate with the intention of bringing it inside, but I quickly realised there wasn't anywhere to put it. The floor was littered with dirty clothes and used tissues on every surface. Empty wine bottles on the nightstand, sitting next to Lucas's order of service, scrunched up into a ball. Penelope didn't look any better. She was in her *Burberry* pyjamas, mascara staining her cheeks, a stuffy nose and oily hair.

"What the hell happened in here?" I asked, my jaw agape.

"What?" she snapped back, walking over to the Bluetooth speaker plugged into the wall to turn it down.

"Nothing," I said, sweeping some laundry with my foot. "It's just a little messy."

"Can't you see that I'm heartbroken? Must you add insult to injury with your snide comments?"

"Sorry," I said, the word squeezing out through pursed lips.

As a slow, romantic track continued playing on the speaker, Penelope started lifting each of the wine bottles in turn, searching for one with any amount pooled in the bottom. She finally found one with an inch still left and threw it down the hatch before, to my horror, discarding the open bottle on her bed. That was another thing to clean up later.

"Listen," I began, stepping closer. "Losing someone is the hardest thing you can imagine, but I promise you: it gets easier."

She scoffed bitterly. "And what does someone like *you* know about losing someone?"

"More than most," I stated.

She lifted her chin dismissively and then plonked herself on the edge of the bed. I didn't make eye contact with her. I was too busy fixating on the trickle of red wine seeping into her once-white bedcovers.

"It's just not fair!" she wept, throwing her hands in the air. "He had everything, and he threw it away!"

"I know he did," I muttered.

"I thought he was going to be around forever, you know? And just like that," she began, clicking her fingers, "he's gone."

"He wouldn't want you to be upset about it, though, would he?"

She ignored me entirely. "I could've stopped it. I should've said something."

"It wasn't your fault, Miss Blackthorn, alright? You can't blame yourself."

She started blubbering, so I reached over to put a hand on her shoulder, but instantly had second thoughts when the track changed to the next one on the speaker. It was almost an exact replica of the song preceding it, but slightly more upbeat.

"Oh, God!" Penelope wailed, placing a palm on her chest.

"What is it?"

"This was his favourite song!"

I winced. "Really?"

"Yes!" she shouted. "He simply adored it. Knowing him, he probably insisted on it for their first dance."

I yanked my neck back, wondering if I'd misheard her. "Lucas?"

Penelope's jaw dropped. "I'm not talking about my damned brother!" she roared. "I'm talking about the love of my life!"

I rewound the conversation in my head, debating whether I felt more embarrassed because of what I'd said, or more ashamed that she'd accepted it.

"He had the audacity to tie the knot with that whore Camilla on the day of my brother's funeral," she blubbered. "Seven years of my life wasted!"

"What can I say?" I cringed. "Men are pigs."

"Just look at this!" she exclaimed, holding her phone to my face. "How could he pick her over me?"

A picture was displayed on her phone of the happy couple, confetti floating through the air behind them, each with a beaming grin on their faces. It was only when I saw the tattoos beneath the groom's rolled-up sleeves that I whipped the phone out of her grasp and zoomed in.

"What's his name?" I asked, flicking my eyes to her.

"Aubrey! He was supposed to be *mine*!"

Oh, BB. I thought you were different.

"That lying sack of shit!" I roared.

Penelope matched my energy. "I know!" she shrieked. "How could he?"

"I don't believe it—he was engaged to some tart the entire time?"

"Yes! He promised he was going to leave her!"

A wicked thought crossed my mind, instantly cooling my temper.

"You should tell her," I suggested.

She smiled uneasily. "What?"

"Call her. Tell her what a lying scumbag her husband is."

She shook her head dismissively. "No, I couldn't possibly. It's far too embarrassing."

"Only for him! He was two-timing you!"

Her face went stony. "Maybe I should."

"Definitely!" I goaded. "Make that fucker's life hell!"

"You know what, I will!" she exclaimed, perking up. "Thank you, Robyn!"

"You're welcome. And give him a swift kick to the bollocks from me if you see him, okay?"

She chortled. "How colourful!"

"Do you need anything else, Miss—"

"No," she cut in. "You've been quite helpful. Thank you."

I seized the opportunity and left, and I couldn't help but chuckle and shake my head at the sheer ridiculousness of that whole exchange.

For a start, not only was the so-called love of her life engaged to one of her friends, but the scumbag was also messing around with me just before I went to prison, too. Even worse, her brother had just died in horrific circumstances. Yet, instead of grieving that loss, she was more cut up about some random gym rat who had used her for an occasional fuck before he got married. How can someone with so much be so wrapped up in jealousy? It boggled the mind.

"This fucking family…" I uttered as I climbed down the stairs.

Martha was stumbling through the front doors when I got back into the foyer. My suggested walk hadn't done her any good because her hair was all over the place, and she had a new ladder in her tights, exposing her pale thigh beneath. She stopped dead when she saw me and quickly turned around to fix her hair in the reflection of the window, so I slowly made my way over, narrowing my eyes.

"Where have you been?" I asked.

"Hmm?" she said over her shoulder. "I did what you suggested. I went for a walk."

I laughed despite myself. "Where? Up a bloody mountain?"

"It's windy out," she shot back.

"Is it?" I asked, peering out of the open doors.

"Never mind me," she said with a sternness I hadn't heard in a while. "Has breakfast been served?"

"Left outside their doors."

"Splendid," she said flatly. "We'd better make a start on lunch, then. Idle hands are the devil's playthings, aren't they?"

"That they are," I remarked, shaking my head.

She sauntered in the direction of the kitchen, but I remained stationary, peering through the doors for some clue as to what she'd been doing.

"Robyn?" she called from down the corridor.

"Coming," I uttered back.

What was she up to?

25

THE BREAK

ROBYN

The fortnight after Catherine left was nothing but a blur.

The well-oiled machine that The Blackthorn Estate once was had fallen to pieces. Floors were left dirty. Pots unwashed. Windows smeared. Even the pantry was starting to look depleted because nobody had a spare minute to make an order with the wholesalers. To make matters worse, Martha went into meltdown almost hourly, flapping about like a maniac as she tried and failed to hold everything together. I wasn't immune to the workload and did what I could to take the pressure off, sometimes working into the night just to tick items off her list, but somehow, it only ever seemed to get longer.

How could one family create so much mess, anyway? Considering we were two staff members short, I assumed that the family would've helped out. Nothing much, maybe just pick up their own dirty underwear or feed themselves once in a while, but that was just wishful thinking. To tell the truth, it was less like serving three, fully-grown adults, and more like operating a crèche. In fact, they were so useless at looking after themselves that I was adamant they would've died of starvation within the week if Martha and I weren't around.

There was only one woman who was a worse cook than I, and that was Martha, so the responsibility of head chef automatically fell to me. I didn't mind particularly, and it certainly beat being on my hands and knees with a scrubbing brush. However, it was safe to say that I was a little lacking in the inspiration department because lunch became the same four flavours of soup on rotation. Not only was it the quickest thing to make, but I could batch cook it and even freeze some for a later date. No one seemed to grumble about it. They just shovelled it into their heads every afternoon before trudging back to their respective rooms to do God knows what.

I was just seasoning the latest vat of brown fluid when Martha stumbled in and floundered over to the table, sitting down to remove her shoes. To be honest, it turned my stomach a bit when she started massaging her feet so close to the food I was preparing.

"Robyn, I don't know how much more of this I can take," she remarked, digging her thumbs in. "I'm absolutely exhausted."

"Me too," I said over my shoulder. "Has Mr Blackthorn not interviewed anybody yet?"

"Not that I've heard. Then again, no one tells me anything these days."

"Can't you call that temp agency? They could lend us a few warm bodies."

"Mrs Blackthorn won't have them back after what happened."

"What? Why?"

"She doesn't want any unknown faces on the estate, so we're on our own."

I puffed out my cheeks. "Great."

"Are you almost finished there?"

"Almost," I said, turning up the heat. "It needs something else. I just can't figure out what."

"Could you do me a massive favour?" she asked.

"What?"

"Mr Blackthorn asked me for some lemonade, but he's out on the lawn and I think I'll keel over if I take one more step."

I smiled, wiping my hands on a dish towel. "Sure. Just keep an eye on my soup."

"I will do. You're a lifesaver, Robyn."

I walked over to the fridge and grabbed the jug, then placed a fresh glass on the counter. I filled it three-quarters full, topped the rest up with ice, and carried it through the service entrance. I very nearly dropped the bloody thing when there was an almighty bang coming from the direction of the lawn, and it was only when I saw a little clay disc flying in the air that I realised what was happening. After a few more steps, I saw Harris behind the trap, resting on a stool far too small for his frame and sending the discs airborne whenever Mr Blackthorn dipped his head.

"Ahh, Miss Marsden! Aren't you a sight for sore eyes?" Mr Blackthorn boomed, lowering his ear defenders when he spotted me.

"I've brought you your lemonade, Mr Blackthorn," I said.

"Thank you, thank you," he said, tossing the shotgun over his shoulder and taking the glass.

"Will that be all?" I asked.

He chuckled. "Why the rush?"

"We're just preparing lunch and—"

"Come on! It's a lovely day, and I'm sure you'd rather be out here than stuck in that blasted kitchen."

I crossed my hands over my front. "I can spare a couple of minutes."

"Marvellous!" he cheered before his face dropped and he turned to Harris. "Leave us."

Harris lifted himself off the stool with a groan, sending a strange look my way before he disappeared in the direction of the kitchens. Mr Blackthorn set his glass down in the gamekeeper's place, then loaded the shotgun with two fresh shells, leaving it broken over his forearm as he returned to me.

"Tell me, have you fired one of these puppies before?" he asked.

"A gun?" I gasped. "No, never."

"Then you must try it."

"Mr Blackthorn, I—"

Before I could protest further, he closed the barrel, shoved it into my grip, and hung his ear defenders from my neck.

"Let's see your form," he instructed.

"My... what?"

"Can you see that cloud over there? The one that vaguely looks like a giraffe on its side?"

I peered up and spotted it. "I think so."

"Aim at it."

With quite a bit of sighing, I did as he asked. It was far heavier than I anticipated, and the sights were shaking from side to side. He let out a hearty laugh and then got behind me, making sure to press his groin into my backside as he took the weight for me.

"Keep the stock tight against the shoulder," he whispered in my ear.

I pulled it in, and the aim steadied slightly.

"Tighter," he muttered.

I submitted, and he tucked the usual curl of hair over my birthmark behind my ear, running a single finger down my neck when he'd finished.

"Close your left eye, and rest your cheek on the stock," he said.

"Okay, done," I replied.

"You see the eye of the giraffe?"

"Maybe," I uttered. "Yeah."

"Bring the barrel slightly to the left," he said before stepping back. "Now, pull the trigger."

I inhaled deeply. I had no idea what to expect when I eventually pulled that trigger, so I closed my eyes tightly and then gave it a squeeze.

Click.

"What the—"

"Now let's try it for real, shall we?" Mr Blackthorn said.

He reached over to turn the safety off and pulled the defenders over my ears. Then, he walked over to the trap and rested his hand on the lever, waiting for my signal. I tipped my head, and he pulled it. The clay soared through the air, arcing over the treeline before hovering just above the giraffe's eye for a split second. I jammed my finger on the trigger, and it went off with an almighty bang. My shoulder shunted backwards, failing to bury the recoil, and a blink later, the clay had shattered into atoms.

"Oh my God!" I exclaimed. "I hit it!"

"Beginner's luck, I suspect!" He chortled. "Again?"

I brought the barrel back up and nodded. The second clay flew at a slightly different angle, which I wasn't expecting, so I rotated my hips slightly and pinched the trigger. To my glee, it instantly became dust in the air, showering tiny shards onto the immaculate grass.

"Remarkable!" Mr Blackthorn yelled. "Are you sure you haven't done this before?"

"No! Not even once!" I cheered, pulling the ear defenders down. "It's a lot easier than I imagined."

Mr Blackthorn scoffed through his nose. "Not for everyone."

He took the shotgun back off me, broke it in two, and rested it on the stool.

"Sofia was one hell of a shot, too," he said over his shoulder before turning back around. "Far better than I."

I glanced over my shoulder before turning back. "What was she like?"

"Well, she was perfect, wasn't she? Intelligent, witty, thoughtful, caring—all of which she clearly didn't inherit from me."

"She was adopted, though, wasn't she?" I asked innocently.

"Yes," he uttered, the question taking him back. "Forgive me, but who told you that?"

"Not sure." I rubbed my jaw. "People talk."

"Hmm," he hummed, choosing to accept what I'd said. "They certainly do."

"You sound like you're very proud of her."

"I am."

"I'm just sorry we couldn't have met."

"Yeah—me too. You'd have got on like a house on fire."

Mr Blackthorn stared into my eyes before something caught his eye behind me. I swivelled my head to follow his gaze and saw Lucinda standing at the doors of the library, gin and tonic in one hand and a book in the other.

"Fantastic. It's the *fun police*," he uttered.

"Richie, what on earth are you doing?" she yelled, storming over.

"Just shooting the shit, dear," he responded.

"And you," she spat, turning to me. "Don't you have toilets to scrub?"

I removed the ear defenders from my neck and handed them back to Mr Blackthorn, then pivoted back to Lucinda.

"Can I get you anything, Mrs Blackthorn? A refreshing glass of lemonade, perhaps?"

"No. Just get out of my sight this instant."

"At once," I said, giving a little bow and turning on my heel.

I looked over my shoulder as I started ambling back to the kitchen, smirking at Mr Blackthorn as he received a scolding from his wife. He was compelled to grin back, and Lucinda must've noticed because she spun her head around, but I was already facing away before she made eye contact.

Stop messing with him, Robyn. It won't end well.

I straightened my face as I turned the corner and pushed through the service entrance door. To my horror, the soup that I'd left simmering was boiling over, so I sprinted over to the hob to turn the ring off. I grabbed the spoon to stir it, but the bottom had caught, welded onto the pan in a black and charred slurry. It was totally ruined.

"For fuck's sake!" I grumbled.

Just at that moment, I heard something in the pantry. It was like a dull, rhythmic sound, like someone trying to hammer in a nail, interspersed by the laboured grunting of whoever was doing it. On instinct, I grabbed the knife I'd used to chop the vegetables earlier and held it upside down behind my back, slowly making my way over to the door. It was almost closed, allowing just a sliver of a view inside. My stomach started doing flips when I saw Martha's face through the crack, seemingly in agony, fighting someone off.

I sucked in a deep breath and burst through the door.

Oh boy, did I wish I hadn't.

Martha was lying on the stainless-steel table, gripping opposite edges with her hands, tunic wrenched up to her collarbones. Harris was sandwiched between her bare legs, tweed trousers around his ankles, his hands pinning her arms to the surface. Martha was the first to notice me and started trying to push him off, but he managed a few more hip thrusts before finally spotting me himself.

I wanted to bleach my eyeballs.

"Holy shit!" I screamed, running back into the kitchen with my hand clasped over my mouth.

"Robyn!" Martha shouted from the pantry. "It's not what it looks like!"

"Is it not? Because it looks like you're being railed by the gamekeeper where we store all the food!" I barked through the giggles.

She emerged a second later, cheeks redder than a baboon's backside, still adjusting her tights and flattening her tunic.

"He was just helping me with something," she explained.

"Oh?" I snorted. "What, exactly?"

Martha scrunched her face up. She couldn't offer a single plausible alternative. "Er—"

"I saw you both, okay?" I said to put her out of her misery. "I wish I hadn't, but I did."

She clutched her elbow. "You aren't going to tell anyone, are you?"

I paused to think. It was the opportunity I'd been waiting for. She was supposedly a proud woman, diligent in her duties and faithful to the family she served, so what would that family think when I told them she was making the beast with two backs when she should've been working? I could almost see Lucinda's face when I told her in my head. She'd hit the fucking roof.

"I don't know," I answered after a while. "What's my silence worth to you?"

Her skin went even paler. "What do you—"

"I mean, the way I see it, you'd owe me one hell of a favour if I keep quiet about this."

"A favour?" she said, stepping closer. "What favour?"

I shrugged. "Haven't decided yet."

Martha's expression softened. "Come on, Robyn. I honestly thought we were becoming friends."

I tried to tone down my first thought, but I ended up saying it unaltered. "Martha, I will *never* be your fucking friend."

She gasped. "Why?"

"You've made my life a misery since the day I started here, and now you want me to forget all that?" I explained. "You're beyond belief."

"I know I was tough on you, and I'm sorry, but look at you now! You're basically running this kitchen!"

Harris stepped out of the pantry, still knotting his tie as he went to Martha's side.

"Is this under control?" he grunted.

"Yes, love," she said, placing a hand on his chest. "It's all taken care of."

"Good," he groaned, leaving the kitchen with a frown.

"What a catch," I remarked, as dry as a bone.

"Can I count on your discretion or not?" she asked.

I took my sweet time to answer. "For now."

She closed her eyes in relief. "Thank you."

"Can you remake the soup?"

She glanced at the hob. "Remake?"

"Yes. It was out here burning while you were on your back in the pantry."

"Oh," she uttered.

"I'm going to go and put my feet up in my room."

Her face hardened. "Now, Robyn, do you truly expect—"

"What's the matter, Martha? Do you have a problem with that?"

She withered again. "No, no, no. Forget I said anything."

"I thought so," I said triumphantly. "Let me know when you're finished, will you?"

"I will."

"And please, wash your hands first."

With those biting final words, I slid the hairpin from my hair and started walking out of the kitchen, grabbing a fresh apple from one of the baskets on my way past. To be honest, the glum expression on Martha's face would've been worth it alone, but knowing that she was now indebted to me was the icing on the cake. Best of all, never again would I have to take any shit from her, and that prideful little tart had been put well and truly in her place.

Things were going to change around the Blackthorn Estate.

Martha's submission was only the beginning.

26

THE PAINTING

ROBYN

Oh, how the tables had turned. The weekend had come and gone since I found out about Martha's filthy liaisons, and working on the Blackthorn Estate had become an absolute delight. She was scared shitless of me, so much so that I started rocking up in the kitchen just after eight to give her enough time to do breakfast on her own. By Monday, she looked like she was on the verge of a mental breakdown, still washing the pots from the day before as multiple timers went off for the pans bubbling over on the stove. I was sitting at the table, feet up and earbuds in, diligently supervising.

"Martha, you're boiling over," I said, pointing to the hob as I killed the music.

"I can see that," she said, rushing over to turn down the heat.

"By the way, did you finish the dining room floor?"

"Yes," she snapped. "At five this morning."

"And did you polish the table?"

"Yes," she said, clenching her jaw.

"And what about Mrs Blackthorn's breakfast?"

She paused to check the time. "I was just about to—"

"For God's sake, Martha!" I said. "What are you playing at?"

She saw red and threw the dish sponge into the sink as hard as she could in frustration, and the resulting splash showered her in dirty water from head to toe. I felt a pang of guilt, so I stood up and grabbed a cloth so she could dry herself off. She snatched it from my grip as soon as I offered it, and I went over to the stove to turn the timer off.

"Robyn, how long are you going to keep this up?" she asked.

"Until you've learned your lesson."

"Oh, but I have!" she exclaimed, tugging at my tunic. "I treated you very badly, and I'm sorry, okay?"

I squirmed out of her grasp. "It's been three days, Martha. You treated me like this for weeks on end."

"I know I did! But—"

"But what?" I interrupted.

She lowered her chin to her chest.

"I thought so. Now go and take Lucinda her breakfast. We can't have the 'lady of the house' going hungry, can we?"

"Right away," she uttered.

She went to grab the plate, but I put my hand in front of hers to whip a piece of crispy bacon off it before she managed it.

"Ooh! Lovely!" I remarked, crunching it with my teeth.

She took Lucinda's breakfast and walked out of the room, leaving me to my own devices. I sat back down at the table, pulled another chair out and rested my feet on it, sipping the cold coffee that Martha had made me twenty minutes before. I hit play on my phone and put my earbuds in. Ironically, 'Blue Monday' by New Order started playing, one of my favourites, so I leaned back, making the decision to rest my eyes for a minute.

"This is the life…" I mused.

Okay, going for a snooze on that rickety wooden chair wasn't the best idea. I was jolted awake when I felt myself tumbling to the ground, with not enough time to brace for impact. I cracked the back of my head on the stone floor, so I turned to one side to check for blood with my hand. By the time I flipped back over, I realised that I wasn't alone.

"Ellie? What the fuck?" I asked, wincing in pain.

"Working hard, I see," she remarked.

"I must've dozed off," I said as I got back on my feet. "What are you doing here?"

"I left some things in Lucas's room. I've just come to collect them," she said, walking over to the fridge. "Is there any booze in here?"

"Er—yeah, sure. Check the pantry, there's always a few bottles stashed away in there."

Ellie flashed me a withering look before heading into the pantry. She returned a few moments later with a dusty bottle of red she'd found, inspecting the label as she went over to the cupboard to get a glass. She looked dreadful—eyes red and puffy from crying, wearing a baggy black sweatsuit, hair scraped back with at least two inches of dark roots showing through the blonde.

"Do you want one?" she asked.

"Can't," I replied, picking the chair up off the floor. "I'm on the clock."

Ellie sat down at the table and brimmed her glass, then knocked it back before I could even blink.

"How are you holding up, anyway?" I asked. "I didn't get a chance to speak to you at the funeral."

"Not sure, to tell you the truth." She sighed. "I don't think it's hit me yet."

I tried my best to look sympathetic. "Yeah, I bet."

"Sorry," she said, steadying herself. "How are you getting on?"

"So-so. Good days and bad."

Ellie reached for the bottle again, so I moved it away before she could get a hold of it and sat down across from her.

"Listen, I just wanted to tell you how sorry I am about Lucas. We didn't exactly get on, but—"

"What are you sorry for? It's not like you're the one who poisoned him."

"No," I said, picking at the grain of the table with my fingernail. "But I know how important he was to you."

"Come off it," she scoffed, snatching the bottle from my grasp. "He was a piece of shit."

I raised an eyebrow. "I thought that—"

"Don't look so surprised, Robyn. You said it yourself."

"You loved him, though, right?"

She looked at me like I'd taken leave of my senses. "Loved is a bit strong, don't you think?"

"Why did you stay with him, then?"

"Seriously?"

I let the silence do the answering for me.

"I mean, look at this place." She rubbed her neck. "This all could've been mine someday."

"So, you're just some gold digger?"

"Guilty as charged." She raised her glass. "He didn't love me either, by the way. I was just a possession to him."

"Sorry," I murmured.

"It's fine. We both knew we were using each other."

I exhaled sharply through my nose. It wasn't exactly a shock admission, but there was something in her eyes that told me it was all bravado, and she was more affected by his death than she was letting on. Despite their tumultuous relationship, they were together for years, so there must've been at least some feelings involved.

"Anyway, I have packing to do," she announced.

"You're moving?"

"There's nothing here to stay for, is there?" she said, shaking her head. "Besides, Lucas was paying my rent, and I doubt his dad is going to take over."

"Shit," I mumbled.

"Yep," she said flippantly.

She looked as though she was about to stand up and leave, so I reached out for her hand and grabbed it.

"Look, I need to tell you something before you go," I began, hands trembling. "It isn't easy."

"What?"

"That afternoon at The Glasshouse. You walked in on me and Lucas in the toilets, remember?"

Ellie crossed her legs over. "Vaguely."

I paused to gather my words. "Lucas tried to—"

"I know," she interrupted.

"He told you?" I said, taking my hand back.

She poured another measure. "He didn't have to. I'm not fucking blind, am I?"

"Why didn't you say something?"

"He would've only denied it."

I grabbed the glass and took a sip. It took everything I had not to smash it against the wall.

"That's what you were going to tell me that day you asked to meet, wasn't it?" she asked.

"Yeah, but I never got the chance."

"Babe, you weren't the first, and you definitely weren't the last," she said, swigging from the bottle.

Neither of us spoke for a minute until she'd finished her second glass and reached out for my hand.

"For the record, I'm not playing down what happened to you, okay? He was a degenerate, just like the rest of his family."

"I know," I uttered.

"That's why you can't stay here."

"What?" I gasped.

"It isn't safe, and it's only going to get worse, trust me."

I leaned back, folding my arms. "You're the one who sent me here in the first place."

"I know I did, but it was a mistake. Lucas was bad, but he was fucking harmless compared to the rest of these bastards."

"I can look after myself, okay?" I snapped, pushing myself off the table to my feet and heading to the door.

"Has he tried it on with you yet?" she called after me.

A shiver ran through me, and I stopped dead. "Who?"

"Richard—Mr Blackthorn."

"No," I said firmly, swivelling back.

She arched an eyebrow. "Genuinely?"

I licked my bottom lip, then bit it. "I mean—he's been a bit touchy-feely, but nothing I can't handle."

Ellie snorted bitterly. "You have no idea, do you?"

"What about?"

"Come on." She lifted herself off the chair and grabbed the bottle. "I need to show you something."

Ellie led me out of the kitchen, back into the hallway, stopping at one of the storage cupboard doors. She slowly opened it, twisting her head as she checked for anybody behind it. Once she'd decided it was clear, she beckoned me inside and shut the door behind me, handing me the bottle before pushing the various washing baskets out of the way.

"What the hell are you doing?" I asked.

She squatted down and peeled back the corner of the rug. "Just give us a hand, will you?"

I set the bottle down and complied, and we peeled back the carpeting to expose a large hatch cut out of the floorboards. Ellie struggled to release the ring-pull from the timber with her false nails, so I took over, and we lifted it open. I peered down at the dark, stone steps as she got her phone out to illuminate them, then she stepped down the first few before turning back to me.

"You coming?" she asked.

I nodded and followed her down.

The staircase went down about twelve feet before it flattened out, exposing the catacombs built beneath the Blackthorn manor. Passageways splintered off in all directions, but Ellie seemed to know where she was going, swiftly negotiating the corners like she'd done it a thousand times before.

"What is this place?" I asked, my voice echoing back at me.

"Tunnels. They lead all over the estate."

"How did you know about them?"

"Let's just say Lucinda wasn't too thrilled when her precious son started dating me. He used to sneak me through them at least twice a week in the early days."

I walked through a cobweb and started spitting the remnants out of my mouth. "It's grim down here."

"The things we do for love, eh?" she retorted. "It's not much further."

We took a left, then another, continuing on for a minute before turning right. The stone hallway widened out, but the passage at the end was blocked off. There was a door, carved out of oak, embellished with the Blackthorn seal and fitted with at least six bolt locks on the outside, all left open.

"This is what you wanted to show me?" I asked.

"Yeah."

"What's in there?"

"Go in and see," she instructed.

I put my hand on the door to push it open, but instantly thought better of it.

"What if you lock me in there?"

"Fucking hell, Robyn," she said before pushing past me and walking inside.

I reluctantly followed her in and got my own phone torch out, but it was made entirely redundant when Ellie flicked a light switch, and a single, bare bulb glowed to life. If I hadn't just walked through some dank tunnels to get there, I would've assumed this place was a bedroom. A stripped bed was in the corner, a small cupboard that was open and only had a few empty hangers inside, and a wooden chest in the corner, with a cobweb spanning the opening. Although the floor was carpeted, it was thin and worn, and I could feel every imperfection in the stone below, even through my shoes. The walls were roughly plastered, crumbling at the bottom where the damp had got to them, and covered in deep cracks and scratches.

"Did someone… live here?" I asked.

"Uh-huh," Ellie grunted, plonking herself down on the edge of the damp bed. "Sofia."

I laughed, wondering how strong that wine was. "You're kidding, right?"

"Nope," she said, delicately wiping her hand on the mattress.

"But her room is upstairs," I protested. "It's full of her things."

"She stayed there in the later years, sure. But this is where she grew up."

I flicked my eyes to the ceiling and sneered. "Pull the other one, El. It's got bells on it."

"I'm being serious. I used to visit her here sometimes."

I narrowed my gaze. "You were friends?"

"Yes. Mostly because of our shared hatred for her brother."

I swallowed. "Did he kill her?"

A strange smile broke her scowl as she returned to her feet and walked over to the wardrobe. "Give me a hand, will you?"

Ellie started trying to drag the wardrobe to one side, so I rushed over to help. It made a jarring screech when it began to move, and after a few feet, Ellie let go to bat the dust off her hands as she walked around the other side. I followed her around, and what it had been hiding made my toes curl. Whoever had repainted the room didn't have the foresight or the inclination to move the wardrobe out of the way, so there was a seven-by-four-foot rectangle left untouched where it had once been, filled with child-like artwork, some in crayon and others in acrylic paint.

"Did Sofia do this?" I asked, running my hand across it.

"Yep. She was quite the artist."

The left-hand side depicted the Blackthorn mansion, half-painted over by whoever redecorated. To the right of it were a number of figures which, on closer inspection, I realised were the Blackthorn family, with each of their names scrawled underneath.

First was Lucas. He was illustrated with a massive bar of chocolate in his hands, and his face was covered in it. Although her skin had a strange green tinge to it, the likeness of Penelope next to him was a little more accurate, and the artist had even managed to capture her trademark scowl. Martha was next. The years had not been good to her because it was the kindest version of her I'd seen. Harris was next in line, sitting on a lawn chair, shotgun a little wonky, but the cartoonist had nailed the tweed. Then, Lucinda. Her hair was jet-black with thick streaks of grey, clearly before she discovered bleach, and she was posed with her hands over her eyes in a ruffled, black dress. The last figure didn't even look human, and the illustrator had only used two colours: black and red, portrayed almost in silhouette, with two red dots in place of his eyes and no label.

"Is this—"

"Mr Blackthorn," she interrupted. "It's a good likeness, isn't it?"

I sucked in a breath. "It's fucking terrifying."

Ellie leaned over my shoulder and batted the dust off the wall, and the last two paintings were visible. The little girl standing next to Mr Blackthorn, with his shadowy arm extended around her, could've easily been a self-portrait of me. She was smaller than the rest of them, with caramel skin, chestnut hair, and green dots for eyes. The final depiction was the most detailed of all, with a painstakingly painted tunic, dark skin, and hair tucked away beneath a brightly-coloured durag. The name was obscured by crumbling plaster, so I wiped it away with my hand.

"Jada," I said, running my fingers over the name. "That's my mum."

"Mr Blackthorn locked his own daughter down here," Ellie explained. "Lucas didn't even know he had another sister until he was almost ten and they finally let her upstairs."

"Why would they do that to her?"

"I don't know." A peculiar bitterness sparked behind her eyes. "But trust me, you don't want to stick around to find out."

27

THE SWAN

ROBYN

My mind was racing after what Ellie had shown me. I couldn't eat. I couldn't sleep. In fact, just the knowledge of its existence was enough to put me into a frenzy for the entire week after. Since Martha had stopped breathing down my neck at every opportunity, I used that time to search the estate for anything that would explain why Sofia was kept down there. I scoured every room. Searched every crevice. I turned over rooms that nobody had set foot into for years, but I didn't find a damned thing.

There were only three rooms left to investigate: Penelope's room, Lucinda's room, and Mr Blackthorn's study.

I was pretty convinced that I'd find nothing of note in Penelope's room, and considering she was still feeling sorry for herself and barely left the place, it made having five minutes alone in there pretty much hopeless anyway. Lucinda's was difficult, but not impossible. Although she usually spent hours at a time in the library every day with a drink in one hand and some smut in the other, her schedule was erratic, and there was a very real possibility that she'd catch me red-handed. Mr Blackthorn's study seemed the most likely candidate, but also the most secure because he rarely left it unattended and always locked the door if he went out.

Thank God for *YouTube*.

I went down a rabbit hole of lock-picking tutorials the night before, practising on my own bedroom door into the early hours. By the time morning came, I was pretty confident that I could gain entry into his study in two minutes flat, so armed with my hairpin and the cleaning caddy for cover, I took the stairs two at a time the instant I heard Mr Blackthorn's Jaguar speeding down the gravel. I'd delegated a long list of tasks to Martha that would keep her in the kitchens until the early evening, and Lucinda was nowhere to be seen, so I knew I wouldn't get another chance like it.

I dropped the cleaning caddy by his door and fell to my knees. The lock was ancient, far older than me, so I jammed the hairpin in the chamber and started rattling it about. Even though I felt a little deflated when I didn't nail it on the first try, I kept repeating the voice of the American locksmith in my head, diligently trying to feel for any movement within. A moment later, I started panicking, sweat dripping from my forehead. Why wouldn't the bloody thing budge? My frustration got the better of me, and dread climbed up my throat when I felt the hairpin snap in my hands, sending the pieces to the floor.

"Fuck!" I shouted.

"Robyn?" I heard Lucinda's voice behind me. "What are you doing, exactly?"

Shit.

"Mrs Blackthorn!" I announced, scuttling to my feet. "You startled me."

"Evidently," she said, peering down at the caddy at my feet. "I asked you a question."

I paused to place my foot over the broken hairpin. "Did you?"

"Yes! Are you deaf?" she cried. "I asked you what you were doing!"

"Er—cleaning!" I said abruptly. "Just trying to keep on top of everything."

Her eyes narrowed. "*What* are you cleaning?"

"The study door?" I suggested. "The door handle was looking a little grubby."

"The whole estate is going to wreck and ruin, and you choose to do that, above all else?"

"It needed doing."

Lucinda seemed to accept my half-baked explanation and let out an exasperated sigh.

"Anyway, I'm finished here, so I'd better head back," I said, bending over to subtly conceal the broken hairpin in the caddy.

"Tell me, did I dismiss you?" she asked, her tone menacing.

"No," I said, returning to my feet. "You didn't."

She stepped closer. "I need some help with something."

"Great. What can I do for—"

"No, no. Not you," she cut in, almost offended. "Where is Martha?"

"Last I saw, she was in the kitchen."

"Urgh," she muttered, looking me up and down. "I suppose you'll have to do."

I puffed out my cheeks slightly. "What can I do for you, Mrs Blackthorn?"

"I just need someone to carry something."

"I can certainly help with—"

"Even someone as dim-witted as you couldn't possibly cock that up, could you?"

"No," I said, biting my tongue. "What am I carrying?"

"Flowers. I need to replace the spoiled ones at my son's grave."

"Oh," I said, making a sympathetic face. "I'd be honoured."

I thought what I'd said came off as heartfelt, but she seemed to see straight through my act. After a moment of staring, she flitted her eyes to the ceiling and sauntered down the hallway towards the stairs, and I unwillingly followed, leaving the caddy in the hall. She led me outside, stepping out of the front door and gesturing down at the two buckets beside one of the pillars. They were packed tightly with bouquets of bright white flowers, swaying lightly in the breeze. I went over and picked up what seemed like the heavier of the two, thinking that Lucinda would grab the other, but she was already halfway down the steps before I got a chance to ask her.

"Come on!" she barked. "I haven't got all day."

I groaned and picked up the other bucket, then rushed to catch her up.

"These are beautiful flowers, Mrs Blackthorn," I remarked, slightly breathless from the short jog.

"As they should be," she said without turning her head. "Only the best for my son."

I chose my words carefully. "How are you coping with it all? It must be difficult."

"Dreadful," she muttered. "But I'll feel better when the vile maid who did it to him finally faces justice."

"Is there no word about her yet? It's been weeks."

"They've released her pending investigation, if you can believe it."

"Why would they do that?"

"Lack of evidence, apparently."

"You're kidding," I said flatly. "They had Elena banged to rights!"

She stopped abruptly. "Why are you so interested?"

"She poisoned your son, Mrs Blackthorn!" I rubbed my neck. "She deserves to pay for what she's done."

Lucinda raised an eyebrow in agreement before continuing down the path. "And she will when we get our hands on her."

Jesus Christ, those buckets were heavy. I didn't know whose bright idea it was to brim them with water, but the blood was already cut off from my fingers. Lucinda put some distance between us as I set them down to readjust my grip, but they'd barely touched the floor before she came bounding back to reprimand me for it.

"Are you some kind of weakling or something?" she hissed.

"I'm sorry, Mrs Blackthorn. They were cutting into my hands."

"You really are pathetic, aren't you?"

"No, it's just—"

"Some maid you are! You can't even carry two damned buckets!"

I kept my eyes on the ground, scraping together a little courage before I raised them to hers. "Can I ask you something?"

She shrugged her shoulders combatively.

"What have I ever done to you?"

"Excuse me?" she said, tilting her head.

"I've done nothing but serve your family to the best of my ability, and you've been absolutely horrible to me at every turn."

"Don't be absurd."

"It's true. First, it was Sofia's robe. Then you accused me of stealing that ring. You even blamed me for Lucas' death, for Christ's sake."

Lucinda folded her arms across her chest. She was obviously trying to conjure some plausible justification for how awfully she'd treated me out of thin air, but we both already knew she was going to come up short.

"I just don't like the cut of your jib," she managed after a while.

"The cut of my jib?" I echoed, laughing.

"Yes, and besides, I know your type."

I arched my eyebrow. "What type?"

"You see all this and think you can take a piece of it. That's why you keep sniffing around my husband."

"I do not 'sniff' around your husband!" I argued. "If anything, I avoid him."

"A smirk here, a wink there. You couldn't be more obvious."

I stood back up, leaving the buckets on the ground. "You're wrong."

"I've seen you!"

I folded my arms across my chest, sniggering. "I've been in Sofia's room."

A fresh fury ignited behind her eyes. "I told you to never set foot in—"

"Not that one," I interrupted. "The *other* one."

Lucinda waved her hand dismissively and began walking down the path again.

"Why did he keep her down there, Mrs Blackthorn?" I shouted after her.

"I don't know what you're talking about," she said over her shoulder.

"I saw the artwork she did," I announced. "The entire family, right there on the wall."

She stopped dead, pausing to reset before returning, only to pick up one of the buckets herself.

"Come on," she said, strangely soft all of a sudden. "We're losing light."

Lucinda started down the path again, so I picked up the remaining flowers and followed her. We didn't utter a word to each other on the short walk over, but her small act of kindness in picking up the bucket spoke volumes.

Whatever happened to Sofia down in the catacombs, she knew about it, maybe even had a hand in it. The only things that were still in question were why she was down there in the first place and whether I'd eventually meet the same fate.

I went ahead of Lucinda and opened the gate to the Blackthorn plot for her, then set the bucket next to hers beside Lucas' headstone. The old flowers were brown and wilted, scattered in all directions by the wind. I set about picking the dead ones up, which is when I spotted the next grave over. I hadn't noticed at the funeral, but the stone next to his had Sofia's name etched into the granite. The only thing missing was the dates.

"Go and wait by the water," Lucinda instructed. "I can do this part on my own."

I didn't say anything through fear of antagonising her further. I simply wandered back through the gates, leaving the dead flowers I'd picked up by the rusted fence. I paused to peer over at Lucinda as she dropped to her knees and began diligently arranging the new ones over the mound of earth that was already sprouting grass. That image of her, hunched over her son's grave, made me forget how she'd treated me for an instant, and I actually felt bad for her.

Before she spotted me gawking, I turned my back on her and pottered over to the lake. The dying light was shimmering on the surface, the water delicately swelling in the slight but persistent breeze. There was a small wooden pier to the left-hand side, housing tiny boats that hadn't been taken out for years, so I approached it and walked to the end, hugging my chest to keep out the cold. As I scanned the water, I witnessed something floating beneath the willow. It looked like a large bird, belly up, drifting backwards and forwards even on the almost still water.

"Mrs Blackthorn?" I called out without looking away.

"What is it now?" Lucinda barked back.

"I think there's something out there. In the water."

I could still hear her sigh in spite of the wind. "What?"

"I don't know," I said, craning my neck left and right. "It looks like a dead swan."

"Harris will take care of it," she dismissed. "Don't disturb me again."

The breeze picked up, so I turned back around to find cover between the trees. However, in the corner of my eye, I noticed that the swan had begun to escape the shadow of the old willow, so I spun my head for one last look. It was then that I realised it wasn't a swan at all.

It was a body.

Burberry pyjamas. Face down. Completely still.

"Er—Mrs Blackthorn?" I yelled, my voice shaking.

"Did you not hear me?" she bellowed back.

"I think it's Penelope!"

In no rush whatsoever, Lucinda pushed herself up and came to the gate. It took her a second or two to confirm what I'd said, and then she started screaming at the top of her lungs.

"What are you waiting for?" she howled. "Get in and save her!"

I took one look at the water, kicked off my shoes, and placed my phone onto the pier. Then, without thinking too much about it, I dived in. The cold spread through my body instantly, snatching all the air from out of my lungs. I surfaced a beat later, scarcely able to hear Lucinda's shrieking over the icy water rushing over my ears. Once I'd got my bearings, I started thrashing towards Penelope and got close enough to grab her a few strokes later, wrapping my fingers around her collar as I started paddling back to the shore. Lucinda ran around to meet us when it became shallow enough to wade in, and I dragged Penelope onto dry ground, then collapsed in exhaustion beside her.

"Do the thing!" Lucinda screeched, miming resuscitation.

I filled my lungs with air and crawled over to Penelope to turn her on her back. Her skin was grey, her lips blue, and she'd undoubtedly been in the water for hours before we found her. I looked at Lucinda for guidance, and she shot me a look of thunder. So, as futile as it was, I got on my knees and started delivering chest compressions as she'd instructed.

"Harder!" she snapped.

"I'm trying!"

"Harder! Now!"

I did a dozen more before giving up and leaning back on my ankles. "It's no use, Mrs Blackthorn! She's gone."

"Oh, get out of my damned way!" she ordered, pushing me aside.

I picked myself up, spluttering water and shivering from head to toe. As Lucinda began to thump her daughter's chest, I peered back out onto the water to where Penelope had been floating, and then beyond it to the mausoleum on the other side. Just as my eyes locked on it, I noticed movement.

A figure. Head to toe in black, face mask to match.

They were stepping out of the shadows, cast in silhouette. After they made it to the shoreline, they didn't move for a second. Then, they raised a single finger to their throat and dragged it across before disappearing into the woodland.

"Don't just stand there!" Lucinda yelled, still pumping away. "Go and get help!"

"At once," I said on autopilot.

/

28

THE ROSE

ROBYN

I'd never been so cold in all my life. It was trapped in my bones.

The fire in the library did little to help. No matter how close I got to it or how many blankets I wrapped around myself, I still couldn't stop shaking. My hair was still wet from the water of the lake, clinging to my face and dripping onto the carpet. My tunic was soaked through too, smelling of dirt and damp, but I was convinced that I'd transform into a block of ice if I strayed even a few steps away from the hearth to change it.

Nobody stopped to check on me after I stumbled back into the house like a drowned rat, begging for help. Harris and Mr Blackthorn just sprinted past me towards the boating lake, following Lucinda's desperate screams that carried across the grounds. I already knew where the blame would land for Penelope's passing, even though there wasn't a shred of evidence that I had anything to do with it. The fact that she witnessed me dive into ice-cold water to save her daughter wouldn't exonerate me either—she'd still find a way to twist what she saw to hold me accountable. Besides, the Blackthorns were dropping like flies, and there was only one person left to point the finger at other than me: the masked figure.

My next thought was Elena.

It was pretty plausible. She was back on the streets, supposedly released under investigation after being accused of Lucas' murder. Maybe she came back to finish the rest of the family off. Perhaps I was next. Dicky leg or not, it wouldn't have been too difficult to drag Penelope into the water, especially considering she had at least half a bottle of wine in her system at all times since her darling Aubrey chucked her. Perhaps it was Aubrey himself. It can't be easy having your phone blown up by your psycho ex-mistress at all hours of the night, especially when your new wife starts asking questions.

"How are you feeling?" I heard Martha ask from the doorway.

I laughed, swivelling my head to her. "What do you care?"

"Come on now, Robyn. We can put our little spat to one side for one night, can't we?" she said, coming over. "A young woman just lost her life."

I sighed, turning back around to hold my hands out to the fire. "I suppose."

"Have you warmed up yet?"

"Not a bit," I uttered, my jaw trembling.

"Here," she said, holding out a steaming cup of cocoa. "I made you this."

I raised my eyebrows, hesitantly bringing it to my lips for a taste.

"It's not poisoned, if that's what you're worried about," she added.

I set it down on the coffee table. "See, it's comments like that which make me think it *is* poisoned."

Martha pulled a chair closer to the fire and sat down on it. "Poor Mrs Blackthorn…" she mused.

"You should've seen her. She was beside herself."

"Who wouldn't be?" she remarked. "She's lost all of her children."

Although it was obvious, it hadn't occurred to me—poor woman.

"Have they made it back yet?" I asked.

"About ten minutes ago. They've taken Penelope up to her room to await the ambulance."

"They shouldn't have moved her. The police are—"

"I know," she interrupted. "But Lucinda insisted on it."

Ignoring my instincts, I grabbed the cup of cocoa and took a sip. Tainted or not, it was needed.

"They're going to blame me for this," I announced. "I just know it."

"I doubt it. I've caught her many times sleepwalking by the water."

"You think she just walked in there?"

"Maybe. Either that, or it was just guilt."

I swallowed another measure. "About what?"

"You haven't heard? Some woman called the house earlier, saying she found out her husband was having an affair with Miss Blackthorn."

"Camilla…something-something?"

"Cavendish-Bowes?" she suggested.

"That's the one," I announced, taking another nip.

"Well, it's Cholmondeley, now," she corrected. "You knew?"

"I knew about the affair. I didn't hear about the phone call."

"Well, perhaps Miss Blackthorn took the news hard and went out to the lake to… you know."

I clicked my tongue. "Right."

"Such a damned shame. She had so much to live for."

We were disturbed by Lucinda howling in the hallway. With a groan, I pushed myself off the chair and walked out of the library and into the foyer, still clutching the blankets around me. An hour after being called, the paramedics finally arrived, clearly in no rush as they carefully carried Penelope's body down the stairs. Lucinda was almost fighting with them, like she didn't want them to take her daughter, but Mr Blackthorn raced down the stairs and held her back, pulling her in close.

"I need to go with her!" she announced.

He tightened his grasp. "Lucinda, you can't possibly—"

"I *need* to!"

She didn't give Mr Blackthorn another opportunity to argue. She wrestled herself free and rushed after the paramedics, aiming a dirty look in my direction on her way out. Martha ran after her like the faithful lapdog she was, leaving me alone in the foyer with Mr Blackthorn. He dried a tear from his cheek and then placed his hands in his pockets, kicking at the ground as he approached me. I rested my chin on my chest. I didn't want to look him in the eye.

"Here she is: the hero of the hour," he announced.

"I'm no hero, Mr Blackthorn. I couldn't save her."

"No, but you tried. Not everyone would've jumped into that lake like you did."

"I suppose," I groaned, raising my gaze slightly.

"Speaking of which, maybe we should get the paramedics to give you the once over before they leave."

"That's not necessary."

"Nonsense!" he exclaimed, taking a single step towards the door before I held his arm back.

"Seriously. I'm good," I insisted. "Just let them take Penelope."

He grunted in agreement before pivoting back. "Well, at least allow me to get you a drink."

"I have some cocoa in the other—"

"I mean a proper drink," he corrected with a smile. "Come on, I fancy playing barman anyway."

I was utterly confused on the way back through to the library. I didn't know whether it was classic British stoicism or shock, but he seemed largely unbothered by the death of his daughter. If it were me, I'd be at my wife's side in the ambulance, clutching her hand and demanding answers, not offering to make the maid a stiff drink.

He patted the back of the chair beside the fire as he walked past it towards the small bar in the corner, then got two whisky glasses out. After pouring two fingers in each, he carried them over while humming a tune and placed one in my hand before taking Martha's former seat. I took a taste. It was like drinking liquid fire.

"Jesus Christ," I croaked, spluttering into my free hand.

"It's got a wee bite to it, hasn't it?" he remarked in a bad Scottish accent.

"I'll say," I replied, going for another drop.

"Enjoy it," he said, staring into the fireplace. "It's almost older than me."

"Wow, that is old."

"Hey!" He slapped my thigh lightly. "How old do you think I am?"

I took another mouthful, tilting my head as I thought about my answer. "Mid-sixties?"

"Now, now, Miss Marsden!" he jested. "Don't be cruel."

I downed the last puddle left in the glass. "Higher or lower?"

He did the same and then grabbed my glass as he made his way back over to the bar. "I'm not going to dignify that with a response."

I smirked into the flames until another chill took me, so I scooted the chair a little closer and rubbed my shoulders.

"Why do you think she did it?" I asked.

"Penelope?"

I looked over and juddered my head up and down.

He shrugged, bringing two fresh drinks and the bottle over. "To tell you the truth, I blame myself."

"What? Why?"

"If I hadn't given her everything on a silver platter, maybe she wouldn't have been so wrapped up in jealousy when she finally discovered something she couldn't have."

"It wasn't your fault, Mr Blackthorn."

"I've outlived all of my children, Robyn. As a father, you have to take a hard look at yourself."

I didn't have a response to that. How could I possibly even begin to relate to what he'd been through?

"Anyway," I began, lifting myself off the seat. "I'll leave you to your—"

"Please don't go," he interrupted. "We don't have to talk. I just don't want to be alone."

His words tugged at my heartstrings, so I dropped back down. "Okay, Mr Blackthorn."

"Besides, I need someone to help me polish this fine single malt off, don't I?"

* * *

Okay, trying to go toe-to-toe with an ex-Navy officer who routinely drank Scotch through the day was a dire mistake. We spent over an hour getting ourselves into a drunken stupor as Mr Blackthorn regaled me with tales of other times he got himself into a drunken stupor. I was elated when we eventually finished the bottle, thinking that it was my opportunity to stumble back to the quarters to get my head down. However, it was short-lived when I watched in horror as he simply returned to the bar for another.

"I think I've had enough," I said as he scoured the drinks cabinet. "It's almost midnight."

"Come on, Robyn!" he boomed. "Drowning your sorrows is a Blackthorn ritual."

I winced at the use of drowning. "I'm not a Blackthorn."

"You are tonight," he said, raising a glass from behind the bar.

"Is puking up on the carpet a tradition, too?"

"You'd be surprised," he mumbled, rattling the bottles around.

I counted to three in my head and leapt to my feet. I misjudged it slightly and almost went headfirst into the fireplace until I used the chair to steady me. The sudden rush of blood to my head sent the room spinning, so I shut one eye as I carefully began making my way to the door. Mr Blackthorn only noticed I was trying to make a quiet exit when I'd made it halfway across the library. He quickly rushed to my side, placing his hand in the small of my back.

"I need to go," I said, swaying on the spot. "I feel like I'm going to pass out."

"One for the road?" he said, forcing a glass into my hand.

Even the way that the amber liquid was moving tipped my stomach. "Honestly, I can't."

"Now, now, Robyn! Wasting a fine whisky like this is punishable by death in this house," he said, grinning. "Anyway, I only poured you a half-measure."

I knew he wasn't going to let up, so I knocked it back without further complaint. "Happy now?"

"Very. Come on, I'll walk you back to your quarters."

"No." I placed my hand on his chest. "I can make it."

"Are you sure?"

"Yes," I said, removing my hand. "Good night, Mr Blackthorn."

I turned around and took another few steps towards the door, but I rolled my ankle and ended up crashing to the floor. Faster than I could process, Mr Blackthorn lifted me up with his forearms underneath my armpits and then propped me up by his hip.

"Mr Blackthorn, I'm fine!" I slurred. "I just tripped."

"I'm not taking no for an answer," he said, leading me to the door.

Once we were in the hallway, Mr Blackthorn turned right instead of left, towards the foyer. I didn't think much of it because only the staff used the service entrance, and he was probably walking me around the perimeter of the house. It was only when he started walking me towards the stairs that my pulse began to pound.

"Where are you taking me?" I asked, burrowing my head in his shoulder.

"You'll stay in the house tonight, where I can keep an eye on you," he said without even turning.

"No—can't. Need to get changed."

"Don't worry about that."

I began to feel odd, almost as if my vision was closing in. The lights of the foyer were blinding, so I tried to pull one of the blankets over my face to cover my eyes, but they all fell to the floor in a damp heap. Mr Blackthorn swept them away with his foot, then stopped abruptly by the stairs, only to place one arm behind my knees and lift me into his arms against my will.

"No, put me down," I murmured, rocking my head to the side.

"You're going to be okay. Let me help you."

"Where are you taking me?"

"To bed."

"No. I don't feel right," I muttered, my eyes uncontrollably twitching.

He stopped halfway up the stairs and stared me dead in the eyes.

"Just relax," he said softly. "I'll look after you, Sofia."

Panic gripped me.

I intended to flail my arms, claw at his neck, kick my legs—anything to stop him taking me upstairs. But I could see my limbs, and they didn't move a single inch.

Something *very* wrong was happening to me.

I was a dead weight by the time we reached Sofia's room. My arms were drooping by my side, my legs totally unresponsive. He shifted me in his grasp and reached down to turn the key, then shouldered the door open. Before I knew it, I was tossed onto the bed, totally unable to move, squinting at Mr Blackthorn in the corner while he rummaged through the wardrobe.

"What are you doing?" I asked, my words coming out slow.

"What's your colour? Black? White?"

"Mr Blackthorn, please, I—"

"Definitely black," he said to himself, taking out a dress at arm's length. It was the same dress Sofia modelled in her portrait.

He flung it on the bed and then went into the bathroom, splashing some cold water on his face and unbuckling his belt whilst peering into the mirror. By the time he dropped it to the floor and returned to the bed, I didn't even feel like I was in my own body. I was hovering above it, watching him climb on top of me, his knees pressed against my calves as he lifted my sodden tunic over my head. Once it was off, he peered down at me for a second or two, then he carefully placed one hand behind my head and sat me up, struggling to pull Sofia's dress over my shoulders as I swayed on the spot. He kept me propped up and rotated around me to zip it up, then allowed me to fall back onto the pillows, flattening a thick strand of hair over my birthmark.

"I've missed you so much, Sofia," he said, tucking an artificial black rose behind my ear.

"Please," I whispered, managing to raise my head. "I'm not—"

"Shush," he said, leaning forward to put a finger on my lips. "Don't ruin it."

The room was spiralling out of control at that point, so I used my last scrap of energy to throw my head back on the bed. The ceiling had a crack in it, about a quarter of an inch wide, with a yellow stain surrounding it. I stared at it. Focused on it. It began to widen into a black maw, spitting spiders and cockroaches until I blinked and it went back to normal. Mr Blackthorn's hands were tracing the rose on my hip, fumbling with my underwear.

I closed my eyes and my gut twisted. I was utterly helpless.

Smash.

"What in the blazes?" Mr Blackthorn exclaimed, stumbling off the bed.

I allowed my head to drop to one side. There was a brick on the floor, surrounded by shards of glass. I strained my eyes up the wall and saw the gaping hole in the window. Mr Blackthorn placed his hands on either side of the frame, trousers undone, leaning through the opening to see who'd thrown it. After a second of searching, his face dropped and he leapt backwards.

Bang.

Mr Blackthorn clutched a gash in his cheek, blood spewing out between his fingers. Harris and Martha burst into the room a moment later, shouting something my state wouldn't allow me to make sense of. Their eyes flicked onto me on the bed, then to the window, and Harris rushed out of the room, shotgun in hand. Martha ran to my side, running a hand down my face.

The room folded in on itself. I slipped unconscious.

29

THE SWING

ROBYN

I opened my eyes. I was back in my quarters, sheet tucked in so tightly around me that I could barely move a muscle. I wriggled free and sat up, slapping my lips together in thirst as I peered at the clock for the time. It was almost seven, so I got out of bed with a whimper and stumbled over to the sink. My legs ached the instant I put my feet on the floor, as if I'd gone on a long run in my sleep or I was coming down with something. I thought nothing of it and rinsed my mouth out before spitting it back into the sink.

The water. The lake.

My memory came back in patches: the cold eating away at my skin, the weight of Penelope as I dragged her to the shore, and Lucinda's cries when she couldn't bring her back. I shook my head and almost felt the warmth of the open fire on my skin afterwards. Martha's cocoa. Mr Blackthorn's whisky. The tales of his misspent youth, the banter and the laughter. I couldn't recall a single detail of what happened after, but it was sitting in the pit of my gut like a lead weight.

"Urgh," I muttered. "What the fuck was I thinking?"

I wanted to crawl back into bed and die, but duty called. I spotted my damp tunic left to go rigid on the tiles near the door, and as I was bending down to pick it up, I noticed that my right ankle was swollen and struggling to hold my weight, as though I'd twisted it. I stumbled back on the bed and dragged my hands through my hair, gathering it up with the intention of tying it back. However, on the first scrape, I felt something tangled up in there. I carefully freed it, unwrapping the strands of hair that had coiled around it in my sleep and held it in my hands, peering down at it as the back of my neck started sweating.

A black rose.

Just the sight of it filled in the gaps. It forced me to relive Mr Blackthorn carrying me up the stairs and throwing me on the bed to strip me. The dress pulled over my head. His fingers running down my thighs. The smirk on his face. Sofia's name whispered in my ear. The smashed window and the gunshot.

Heat shot through me, and my fingers clenched, crushing the delicate flower in my grip.

That *fucking* bastard.

I dropped my uniform and raced back to the sink, retching up the last of the priceless single malt he'd plied me with the night before. What the hell was in that final glass he gave me? Did he *spike* me? What with? I rinsed my mouth out again and washed my face before stepping over the bed to open the window and let some air in the room. That's when I realised that it wasn't seven in the morning at all, but in the evening, so whatever he gave me must've knocked me out clean for almost nineteen hours. Why the hell didn't Martha come and get me? Why was I even still alive? I wasn't going to get the answers to those questions standing next to my bed, so I threw on some casual clothes and trainers before storming out of my room, the rose scrunched up in my hoodie pouch.

I was utterly blinded by fury by the time I stepped out onto the courtyard. About halfway to the service entrance, I heard an unusual creaking noise coming from the lawn, so I tilted my head around and spotted the back of Lucinda's head. She was sitting on an old swinging bench, reflectively peering off into the distance, fag in hand. I began thundering over, and she must've heard me coming because she craned her neck back, taking a few pulls of her cigarette before shaking her head and returning to her earlier position.

"Robyn, can't you see that I'm grieving?" she commented, bringing the cigarette to her lips for another puff. "Leave me alone."

I was *done* with the games.

"Mr Blackthorn tried to rape me last night," I blurted out.

She froze, took a deep drag, and then leaned on the armrest of the bench as she turned to face me. "Go away. I'm not in the mood for your insipid nonsense."

"It's not nonsense!" I yelled, stepping closer. "He drugged me."

A bitter chuckle escaped her. "Farcical."

"Then he carried me up to Sofia's room, half-unconscious," I continued.

She scowled at me, full of fury. "Tell me, must you make everything about you, today of all days?"

My jaw dropped. "Excuse me?"

"My daughter lost her life yesterday!"

"I know, but—"

"And now you're trying to do what, exactly? Making up stories to drive a wedge between me and my husband?"

"They aren't stories!" I spat. "I'm telling you the truth!"

She didn't reply, not verbally at least, but the way her face dropped told me that a small part of her wasn't surprised. I stumbled around the bench to sit next to her, and she used the last embers of her spent cigarette to light another, eyes locked on the horizon.

"How much?" she asked without turning.

"How... much?" I parroted.

"To leave this estate and never come back."

"I don't want your hush money!" I uttered in disbelief.

She arched an eyebrow. "Then what do you want?"

"Justice!" I shouted.

"You can't be serious!"

"Oh, I'm serious. He's going to pay for what he tried to do, one way or another."

She turned to face me. "Robyn, you've been a thorn in my side since you set foot on this estate. If it weren't for Richie, you'd have been out on your arse on your first night."

I let out a sardonic laugh. "Well, we know why he was keeping me around now, don't we?"

"My husband is a pillar of the community. He wouldn't risk all that for someone like *you*."

I exhaled through my nose. "So, you don't believe me?"

"No. And neither will anyone else."

I leaned in. "He's done it before, hasn't he?"

She swivelled her head back but tipped it slightly, freeing a trapped tear from her eyelashes. "No," she said firmly.

"How many times?"

Lucinda brought the cigarette to her lips, but her hands were shaking so violently that she could hardly take a puff on it. "I don't know what you're talking—"

"Sofia, too?" I added.

She dragged her lip across her bottom teeth. "No."

"That twisted bastard—" I began, pausing to fight the urge to gag. "He fucking dressed me up like her, you know?"

She widened her eyes, dithering as she tugged her cardigan around herself. "You're lying."

I threw my arms down in desperation. "I am not lying!"

"If they didn't disturb him, then he would've—"

"Who?" she said, turning her head.

"I don't know, but they took a potshot at him."

She chortled incredulously. "Nice try. He cut himself shaving."

"Wake up, Lucinda!" I reached into my pouch and tossed the crumpled rose in her lap. "You can't cover for him anymore."

She was done listening.

Lucinda shot off the bench, grabbed me by the back of my hoodie, and started frogmarching me towards the house. I was more or less on my hands and knees by the time we made it to the foyer, but she continued to drag me up the stairs, finally releasing me in front of Sofia's room. She gripped the handle and rattled it violently, but it wouldn't budge.

"What the devil is going on out here?" Mr Blackthorn yelled, appearing at the study door.

Every part of me wanted to pounce on him, gouge his eyes out with my fingernails, beat him bloody or wrap my hands around his neck. But I did none of those things. I just remained paralysed at the end of the hall, staring at the plaster on his left cheekbone and the few spots of blood soaking through it.

"I need to get into Sofia's room," Lucinda barked at him down the hallway.

He sauntered over with his hands in his pockets. "I'm just in the middle of a call, dear," he said to her, shooting a glance my way. "Can it wait?"

"No," she grunted. "Now."

Mr Blackthorn's eyes flashed upwards before he took his hands out of his pockets, along with a set of keys.

Lucinda whipped them from his grasp before opening it, and we all bundled inside.

There wasn't a single shred of evidence that anything happened there at all, apart from the faint smell of solvents and lemon-scented bleach. The window had been replaced, but it didn't look new. It had water staining on it, as if someone had taken it from another room in the house. Even the bedspread had been laundered and ironed. The whole room looked like it hadn't been touched in years.

"As you can see, everything is as expected," Mr Blackthorn said, holding his arms aloft. "Now, if you don't mind, I'm rather busy and—"

"How can you just stand there and pretend nothing happened?" I roared.

He didn't respond to me directly; he only looked at Lucinda for her reaction, who took a few tentative steps towards him.

"Robyn has made some… allegations," she explained in his ear.

"Allegations?" he asked, flicking his eyes to me. "What allegations?"

"She claims you were inappropriate with her last night."

"Utter claptrap!" Mr Blackthorn threw his hands up in surrender. "Robyn had a little too much to drink, so I walked her to her quarters. I didn't even go inside."

"You drugged me and tried to rape me!" I spat.

He ignored me and kept his eyes on Lucinda. "We may have got a little carried away with drowning our sorrows, but I assure you, nothing untoward happened."

"Liar!" I cried.

Lucinda inhaled deeply and released it, turning her gaze to me. "You said something about a smashed window?"

Mr Blackthorn looked shocked. "Where?"

"In this room," she replied, walking over to run her finger over the sill. "Supposedly."

"It happened! Someone threw a bloody brick through the window and then followed it up with a bullet!"

"You can't be serious!" He threw his head back in laughter. "Who would even do such a thing?"

"I don't know! But they stopped you dead in your tracks, didn't they?"

Lucinda and Mr Blackthorn exchanged a look before he reached out to put his hand on my arm. I immediately recoiled, so he put his hands back in his pockets and closed the gap again.

"Listen to me very carefully, Robyn. You went through a lot yesterday, we all did," he said softly.

"No, I—"

"But you can't be making baseless accusations like this," he continued. "It makes you look quite mad."

"You got Harris to fix the window, didn't you?" I demanded.

He chuckled. "Now you're claiming that our gamekeeper, as talented as he is, managed to replace a window without anyone noticing?"

"Yes!" I shouted. "And you got Martha to scrub the room clean."

"Not a soul has set foot in this room for weeks!" He turned to Lucinda. "Darling? You aren't buying this, are you?"

She took the crumpled-up rose out of her pocket and delicately placed it in his hand. "She had this."

The colour drained from his face. "Well, there's a perfectly reasonable explanation for that, isn't there?"

Lucinda cleared her throat. "What, Richie?"

"She must've taken it from this room!"

"No, you tucked it behind my ear," I interjected. "Right after you called me Sofia."

He paced forward. "I've tried being sensitive with you, Robyn, but you're starting to get on my nerves now."

I met his stare until my eyes slid down him, and I noticed his trousers were riding a little low.

The belt.

"We haven't checked the bathroom!" I announced, reversing towards the door.

"Robyn? I'm about to lose my patience," he threatened.

"Come on, Mr B! It will take all of thirty seconds!" I said, resting my fingers on the handle. "What are you so afraid of?"

"Nothing." He shrugged.

"Like you said, no one has been in here for weeks, so there shouldn't be anything amiss, should there?"

He touched his waistband and flicked his eyes to Lucinda. "No."

"Then you won't mind if we check it, will you?"

Before he could stop me, I turned around and opened the door, and lo and behold, there was his belt.

However, it wasn't coiled up on the floor like I expected. It was wrapped around one of the old exposed beams. And on the other end, around Martha's neck.

"Oh my God!" I gasped, stumbling backwards and falling onto the bed.

Starting at the top of her head, my eyes slowly raked downwards. She was wearing thick mascara, half-running down her cheeks. Her lips were painted red, smudged on either side. She wasn't wearing anything on her top half, and her bare chest was covered in cuts and scratches. She had a pair of black knickers on and a black garter, which was holding up a set of fishnet stockings that were torn at the knees. Her feet weren't touching the floor; they were suspended twelve inches above it, lightly swinging in the breeze from the wide-open window, muddy footprints all over the sill.

Lucinda was the first to rush over to see what had spooked me, clutching her chest in the doorway. Mr Blackthorn walked over last, calmly reaching up to release Martha's neck before he sent her hurtling towards the floor with a dull thud. Written on the mirror in the same shade of lipstick she was wearing were her final words, jagged like she'd scrawled them in a hurry.

"I couldn't live with the shame," Lucinda read out loud, turning to Mr Blackthorn. "What does it mean?"

"I have no earthly idea," he uttered.

Her eyes turned to me. "Did you know about this?"

"No!" I said, my voice quivering. "Of course not!"

She pivoted back to Mr Blackthorn. "What are we going to do about her?"

"Well, Harris can collect the body and—"

"Not Martha," she corrected. "*Her*."

"I don't know."

"Two bodies in two days?" She approached him, leaning into his ear. "If this gets out, we're finished."

With a single nod, he calmly strode over to the door and locked it. Every muscle in my body seized.

"What are you doing?" I asked, my voice faltering.

He put his hands back in his pockets. "We can't let you leave, Robyn. You've seen too much."

I swivelled my head to Lucinda, who'd suddenly become fascinated by her fingernails.

"No, I won't tell a soul!" I pleaded, my stare darting between them. "I swear it!"

Mr Blackthorn lurched over, squatting in front of me. "We can't take the risk, unfortunately."

"So, you're just going to kill me? Like all the other girls?" I paused for a beat. "Like Sofia?"

He remained silent.

My eyes pinged to Lucinda before I made a run for it. I crashed into the door at full tilt, desperately trying to twist the handle that I knew was locked. Mr Blackthorn appeared behind me a moment later, tenderly placing a hand on my shoulder to turn me back around. Without any other option and nowhere to go, I spat directly in his face. He recoiled, immediately taking out a handkerchief to wipe it.

He let out a sinister chuckle. "You know, you're just like your mother."

The room closed in on me. "My mother?"

"Jada Fletcher," he announced, tossing his hankie to the ground. "You thought I didn't know?"

My heart hammered. "But you—"

"I recognised you the instant you walked into my study," he interrupted. "How could I not?"

My lips curled into a manic smile. "Just let me go, okay? You don't have to do this!"

"Oh, Robyn," he said softly. "You aren't going anywhere."

30

THE DIG

ROBYN

I could almost feel every stroke of the brush against the hard tiles grating up my spine. I'd never cleaned in Sofia's chambers before, but considering the Blackthorn skivvy club had been reduced to a membership of one, the responsibility automatically fell onto me. I wasn't doing it willingly, of course. Lucinda was balancing on the edge of the bath a few feet behind me, observing my every move as she ran the blunt side of a brass letter opener over her dress. I couldn't help but laugh. The Blackthorns had the brass-necked cheek to squeeze a few more hours of work out of me before they were going to dispose of me for good.

"Where did Harris take her?" I asked over my shoulder.

"Who? Martha?" Lucinda asked.

"Yes," I said sharply, scrubbing harder.

"Well, I suspect he's getting rid of her body somewhere."

"How long did she work her fingers to the bone for you, eh? Almost three decades?"

She slanted her head left and right. "Sounds about right."

"And you're just going to toss her into a ditch like she was nothing?" I dipped the brush in the bucket. "*Un-be-fucking-lievable.*"

"We can't exactly risk bringing the police back here, can we? They'll think something amiss is going on!"

"Amiss?" I snorted.

"Just keep scrubbing," she ordered.

"I mean, in the last twenty-four hours alone, your daughter drowned, I nearly got raped, and a woman just hanged herself," I listed on my fingers. "And here I am, being forced to destroy the evidence."

"Martha *chose* to end her life. Why should we be held accountable for it?"

I didn't know why I was bothering. Lucinda didn't have a single empathetic bone in her body, and she'd rather watch the bodies pile up rather than accept for one minute that she might be in the wrong. I threw down the scrubbing brush and leaned back into a squat, turning to her.

"You're going to kill me, aren't you?" I asked.

"In this outfit?" she replied, chuckling. "Only if you force me."

I sighed. "Just let me go, okay? I haven't done anything wrong."

"Stop talking and pick up the brush," she ordered softly.

"You'll never see me again," I pleaded, clasping my hands together in prayer. "I promise."

She slammed the handle of the letter opener against the tub. "You aren't stupid, are you?"

I remained silent, glowering at her.

"Are you?" she prompted.

"No," I replied through gritted teeth.

"Then you'll know we're way past letting you go," she explained before tipping her head towards the brush. "Now, pick it up."

"How many girls have been in this same position, huh? Five? Ten? Twenty?" I asked, feeling my throat tighten.

Her eyes became slits. "What girls?"

"The girls who looked like me! The ones who looked like Sofia."

She blew some hair out of her face. "This has got nothing to do with her."

"It has *everything* to do with Sofia!" I shouted.

"Enough," she said sternly. "I can't stand any more of your twaddle."

"He was abusing her, you know?"

A vein in her neck popped. "Quiet."

"Elena saw it and told me."

"Richie loved his daughter! She wanted for nothing!"

"What about her childhood room in the basement, huh? Did she *want* that?"

"Shut up this instant!" she snapped.

"Your whole family—it's fucked. If you knew what he was doing to her, then you're just as bad as he is."

I could see that I had got on Lucinda's last nerve. She jumped to her feet, stepping so close that I could barely crane my neck back to look her in the eyes.

"Pick. Up. The *fucking* brush!" she bellowed, spitting every vowel. "This instant!"

I shook my head defiantly. "Go fuck yourself."

She lifted the back of her hand and cracked it across my face, sending me crashing into the tile. The ring on her finger had split my cheek open just below my birthmark, so after holding it for a second, I struggled to my feet, and the sharp end of the letter opener was inches away from my neck. We remained frozen like that for a split second until something caught Lucinda's attention behind me.

"It's time," I heard Harris grunt from the doorway.

"Well, it looks like this is where we part ways, Robyn," Lucinda said triumphantly.

I steadied the tremor in my chest and then leapt to my feet in an attempt to get past him, but I didn't get far. I was greeted by the business end of a shotgun pointed directly at my face, his finger hovering over the trigger.

"Now, now. Don't make Harris here undo all your frankly average work by blasting your brains out over the tiles," Lucinda warned.

"That'd teach you, wouldn't it? It's almost worth it knowing you'd have to clean it up," I remarked.

"I didn't get to where I am by being on my hands and knees."

I couldn't help but snigger. "I'm sure Mr Blackthorn would disagree."

"Get her out of my sight," she hissed at Harris.

"Shouldn't we ask Mr Blackthorn first?" he asked, sights still trained between my eyes. "He might have plans for her."

"I am the lady of this house!" she bellowed. "I don't need my husband's permission to take out the trash."

Harris tipped his head once, and I felt Lucinda's bad breath landing on my ear.

"Goodbye, Robyn," she uttered.

Harris cocked his head back, signalling me to walk ahead of him out of the bathroom, so I begrudgingly complied. Lucinda followed us out, stopping at Mr Blackthorn's study door. I flitted my eyes between them as Harris forced me down the stairs, muzzle pressed into my spine, grunting on every footfall. The lights in the foyer were turned off, so he guided me through the darkness and out of the front door, down the stone steps and onto the gravel below.

"You don't have to do this, you know?" I said.

"Hmm," he grunted.

"These people—they're sick in the head. It's only a matter of time before they decide it's time to get rid of you, too."

"Walk," he uttered.

"You loved Martha, right?" I asked.

I felt the muzzle slide down my back a few inches, but he didn't reply.

"She loved you—I could tell. Do you think she deserved to be tossed aside like that?"

"Keep moving," he murmured.

I stopped dead, raising my hands in surrender as I slowly turned around.

"Just let me go," I said with a lopsided smile. "They won't even know that you didn't go through with it."

"They'll know," he said, using the barrel to point behind me. "Now, move."

He led me down the path towards the lake, and around the shoreline to the mausoleum on the other side. We continued for another five minutes or so until we reached the treeline at the edge of the estate, and I saw a small, battery-powered lamp sitting beside a hole in the ground, with a shovel piercing the earth next to it. I stopped about ten metres shy of it, and he pushed me the rest of the way. I peered into the hollow. Martha was lying about four feet down in the soil, dressed in her tunic, arms folded over her chest, and the makeup wiped from her face. She looked strangely peaceful.

"Kneel," he instructed.

I tried turning around for one last plea, but dropped to the ground when his boot pushed into the back of my knee.

"Please," I begged, shutting my eyes.

The safety clicked.

"I—I don't want to die," I mouthed.

Bang.

The crows sitting in the trees exploded into the sky, cawing and flapping their wings for dear life. The wind howled, swaying the treeline in unison as the shotgun blast echoed over the grassland, slowly fading until there was nothing but silence and the sound of ringing in my ears. I looked down, expecting to see blood, expecting to feel pain.

But there was nothing.

All of a sudden, Harris groaned behind me, punctuated by a wet thud. I spun around and ran over. The garbled sound he made when I arrived didn't even resemble a word. He just writhed on the spot in agony, coughing blood and trying to roll over. I helped him on his side, and there was a gaping hole beneath his shoulder blade, the wound ragged.

"*Martha...*" he snarled.

His eyes were glazed over when I allowed him to return to his back.

Then, there was a shrill whistle.

I looked up and saw a silhouetted figure walking towards me: head-to-toe in black, face mask to match. They were holding a shotgun of their own, smoke curling from the barrel. On instinct alone, I grabbed Harris's firearm and crab walked away as they approached, my arms trembling as I tried to keep it trained on them.

"Who are you?" I said, my voice shaking.

They put their weapon down beside Harris and grabbed both of his ankles, attempting to drag him towards the grave without a word.

"Hey! Did you hear me?" I asked. "I'll fucking shoot."

They stopped briefly before continuing. "Please. You couldn't hit the broad side of a barn."

Her muffled voice gave me the chills. I was sure I'd heard it before, but I just couldn't place where. I tried looking at the small opening between her mask and her hood, but the light was too low to make out even a sliver of her face.

"What are you doing?" I asked, lowering my aim.

"What does it look like?" she grumbled.

I paused. "Are you Sofia?"

She sniggered. "Just help me, will you? This fucker is heavy, and I don't want to be here when the Blackthorns come looking."

I didn't hesitate. I grabbed Harris's arms and helped drag him towards the crater, and she pulled him inside. I peered down at him and Martha, breathless, before she grabbed a shovel and started filling in the hole.

"Run to the gamekeeper's cottage," she ordered. "They won't come looking there."

"Fuck that!" I exclaimed. "I'm leaving here and never coming back."

"No," she said sharply. "We aren't done."

"But I—"

"If you want answers, you'll go and wait for me. Everything you need to know is inside those walls."

"Okay, well I'll—"

"Go!" she bellowed.

I strode over to Harris's shotgun and picked it up off the floor before fleetingly staring back at the strange woman. It would've been so easy to point it at her again and demand answers, but there was something in her voice that made me trust her. So, I did as she instructed. I started jogging towards Harris's cottage.

***

I didn't have a clue what I was doing. I was in bits by the time the cottage was in view, eyes swimming in tears, heart pounding through my throat, legs about to give up the ghost. I was so close to spending eternity rotting in that hole, face-to-face with Martha, buried in an unmarked grave where nobody would even think to look. I owed that stranger my life, but as I tried breaking my way into the cabin, she was the one I feared most.

I stopped a few metres shy of Harris's abode. It was a small building: single-storey with an outbuilding tacked on the side. Ivy climbed the walls and mostly obscured all the windows, which were dimly illuminated from within. I stepped through the gate and tried the door, but it was stiff, so I barged it with my shoulder until it gave way. I had never set foot in there before, and it was a lot cosier than I imagined. There was an open fire, two old leather couches, but various animal skulls displayed on the walls, which were totally killing the rustic vibe.

"*Creepy*," I sang as I took a seat.

I placed Harris's shotgun on the table and noticed a small, leather-bound diary sitting on the top. I went for it and turned it over in my hands. It was pretty battered and obviously quite old, with most of the pages ripped out, and a fragile strap clasping it shut. I carefully unbuttoned it and peered at the first page, and a tingle shot from the top of my head right down to my toes.

"Sofia Blackthorn's diary," I read out loud. "Lucas—if you're reading this, you're dead."

PART FOUR

"PAIN"

SIX YEARS BEFORE

31

THE ACCIDENT

SOFIA — BEFORE

Lucas was such an insufferable prick. That was hardly a revelation—I had known it since we were kids. However, as we both grew up, my older brother's once playful shenanigans became more and more dangerous. Case in point: I was standing at my bedroom window, observing him wave Harris's shotgun around like a toy, ordering the terrified staff to set up empty bottles as targets in the gardens below.

Although that was hazardous enough, what made it immeasurably worse was that I knew he'd spent the morning gorging himself with alcohol and then tried to perk himself up by snorting a few lines of blow afterwards. I knew that it was only a matter of time before an innocent took a face full of shrapnel, so I pushed open my window and leaned out to put a stop to it. He was lining up his latest shot, parked on a deckchair, swinging the barrel with one eye closed. There was an almighty bang and a puff of smoke, but to his disappointment, he'd missed by a country mile.

I started slow-clapping, and a moment later, he stumbled out of his chair and aimed his weapon directly at my window, swaying left and right like his legs were made of jelly. His usually perfectly preened hair was sticking out in all directions, and he looked like he hadn't had a shave for days because I could see the shadow on his jaw from the first floor. Embarrassingly, his shirt buttons were misaligned, leaving a gaping hole near his midriff, with half of it tucked into his trousers and the other flapping around in the wind.

"You always were a terrible shot!" I shouted down to him.

"I don't know, little sister, I think I might be able to pick you off from down here," he yelled back. "For a start, you're a big enough target."

"Just put it down, will you? Someone's going to get hurt."

"I'm the one who's hurt!" he bellowed back. "Ellie left, so I'm just trying to have a little fun to take my mind off it. Do you truly begrudge me that?"

Judging by his sorry state, Ellie must have realised that he was a vapid, spoilt brat like the long line of women before her and dumped him for good. He was punching above his weight with her anyway, and it was only a matter of time before a nice girl like her finally came to her senses. Still, he wouldn't be sore about it for long. He would already be onto the next victim by the weekend.

Knowing that I was going to get precisely nowhere trying to reason with him and also that there was a slim but very real chance he could pull the trigger and somehow hit me, I retreated from the window and stormed out of my room for backup. Despite Dad paying no heed to most of his antics, I was pretty sure that he wouldn't be okay with Lucas firing shells in the gardens under the influence of drugs and booze. Unfortunately, I found Lucinda first, lounging in the library with her nose buried in some smutty romance novel and her fingers clasped around a gin and tonic.

She sighed deeply, momentarily looking up. "What do you want now?"

"Lucas has got the bloody gun again," I announced. "And he's one drink away from passing out."

"I can hear the shots, Sofia," she explained, turning the page. "What do you want me to do about it?"

"Er—stop him?" I suggested, folding my arms over my midriff.

"He's an adult. Let him blow off some steam."

"Adult!" I scoffed. "He's three sheets to the wind, and he's got half of the staff setting up bloody targets for him."

"Didn't you hear? He's going through a breakup."

"It was a long time coming. He treated her like shit."

"Now, now, Sofia—put those claws away, will you?" she said, chuckling softly. "Hopefully, Elizabeth will take him back, and we won't have to endure his undignified pouting for much longer."

"Ellie," I corrected. "Her name is Ellie."

"The trashy blonde?"

I scowled at her before nodding my head.

"Hmm," she said, widening her eyes. "Good riddance to bad rubbish, then."

I was compelled to go into a spur-of-the-moment rant about how she was way too good for him, but I knew it would fall on deaf ears. Instead, I kept shtum, waiting almost a minute for her to speak again or get off her behind. She did neither.

"Are you seriously not going to do anything about it?" I asked.

"Oh, Sofia…" she started, lowering her book. "Why do you insist on sticking your beak where it isn't wanted?"

"Fine," I said, already turning for the door. "I just thought you should know what's going on in your own family."

She snapped her book closed and placed it on the table. "Wait a minute, will you?"

I pivoted back. "Why?"

"Sit down," she instructed, patting the seat next to her.

Reluctantly, I stepped over and plonked myself on the chair. I already knew that I was going to be in the wrong.

"I never wanted you, you know?" she announced.

Although it was a hell of an opener, it didn't come as much of a shock. "I know."

"But ever since Richard first laid eyes on you, he was utterly besotted. It took me a while, but I accepted you and welcomed you into the family."

"Resentfully," I added.

"And because of that," she continued, slightly louder. "We gave you the single most important thing you'll ever own."

I raised an eyebrow. "What?"

"Your name," she said, leaning in. "The *Blackthorn* name."

I lifted a shoulder. "I never asked for it."

"No, but we gave it to you regardless. Would it really pain you to show some gratitude for that every once in a while?"

I bit my tongue. "Where are you going with this, exactly?"

"For better or for worse, you're one of us," she said, reaching for her drink. "Act like it."

Another blast came from outside. Silence. Then, a scream.

Lucinda's eyes widened as we both realised what must have happened, so she leapt out of her seat and shadowed me as I sprinted out of the library doors and onto the lawn. By the time we made it to Lucas's makeshift shooting range, the shotgun was discarded on the grass, smoke still swirling from the muzzle. Lucas was pacing in circles around it, head in hands and blubbering like a child. Unbelievably, Lucinda went straight over to my brother to console him, rather than Elena, who was wailing like a banshee on the ground.

"The stupid bitch got in the way!" Lucas screamed like a petulant toddler.

"Elena? Are you with me?" I asked, dropping to my knees beside her.

"He shot me!" she moaned. "He shot my leg!"

"It was *her* fucking fault!" Lucas barked. "Tell them it was your fault! Now!"

"Has anyone rung for an ambulance?" I yelled, turning to Martha, who was standing there like a spare part. "Go and get Jada, she'll know what to do."

"No one is to call bloody 999, do you hear?" Lucinda hissed from behind me.

"What? She's really hurt!" I argued.

"For crying out loud," she chastised, pulling out her phone to make a call. "Must I do everything around here?"

"Who are you ringing?" I demanded.

"Brian—Doctor Finnegan."

"No—she needs to go to a bloody hospital!"

Lucinda strode over and peered down at Elena with the phone pressed to her ear, shaking her head with disdain.

"Brian, it's Mrs Blackthorn. We have a situation here down at the estate involving a shotgun," she said down the line. "No—it's only a flesh wound."

"You're going to be okay," I whispered to Elena. "Stay with me, alright?"

***

The next twenty minutes were spent perched on a stone step in the kitchen, watching Mum's dodgy doctor pull pellet after pellet out of Elena's leg and drop them into a stainless-steel tray. By that point, her intermittent screams had turned into lethargic whimpers, yet I still winced every time she let out a sound. She'd been to hell and back, operated on without a scrap of anaesthetic because her suffering was preferable to Lucas being held accountable for his actions.

As he plucked the last ball of lead out of her thigh, I could feel the smears of her blood drying on my face, so I walked over to the sink to clean myself up. When the water began to run clear over my hands, I turned back around in time to see Dad striding into the room, pipe secured between his teeth, counting out banknotes. Without a word, he brazenly tossed the stack of cash next to Elena, then ambled towards me, pulling a pitying face like it was the most normal thing in the world.

I knew that *Daddy dearest* would clear up Lucas's mess. He always did.

"Sofia! Are you okay?" he asked, putting a hand on my shoulder. "You aren't hurt yourself, are you?"

"No," I dismissed, sliding out of his grip. "Where's Lucas? He should be here."

"Up in his room, I think," Dad replied. "The poor boy—he's rather shaken up by the whole affair."

"Shook up?" I echoed. "He's the one who did it!"

He shrugged. "Accidents happen."

"It wasn't an accident—he was under the influence of God knows what."

"Nevertheless, it's not like he aimed the blasted thing at her."

"But he can't keep getting away with shit like this, Dad! He could've killed her."

He sighed. "I'll have a word with him."

"A word isn't going to cut it. He's totally out of control."

I looked over Dad's shoulder and noticed that Doctor Finnegan was finishing his medieval-style procedure. He doused the wound in something that made Elena howl, then dressed the leg in some bandages. After he tied them up, he tugged his nitrile gloves off before discarding them on the tray along with the removed shrapnel. I would be lying if I said that this was the bloodiest thing that had ever happened in that kitchen. Truth be told, our family got embroiled in situations like that one on a near-weekly basis.

"Are you sure you're okay, sweetheart?" he asked softly.

"Nope," I said firmly. "Not even remotely."

"Why don't you come and get a drink? You don't need to see this."

I blinked.

"Sofia…" he began, trying to grab my hand. "Come on now."

"Get off me!" I snapped. "Seriously."

Dad was taken aback by my outburst, and I used the opportunity to push past him and take my leave. Elena was sitting upright on the table when I blew past her, diligently counting the money she'd received in exchange for a pound of flesh. The house was suffocating, the rich metallic smell of blood coating my airways, so I darted down the dark corridors towards the front door, where all the old paintings of Blackthorns gone by stared down at me in disappointment.

Back when it actually meant something, the Blackthorn name used to command respect. It was a symbol of all things British: integrity, family virtues and impeccable quality. However, we were the new generation now. My siblings couldn't spell integrity, family values were measured in pounds and pence, and quality was dependent on which sweatshop we used to produce our wares. We were nothing more than an obnoxious band of unfathomably wealthy psychopaths who didn't give a solitary fuck about who we hurt or whose lives we destroyed, as long as we could still enjoy our affluence afterwards.

I wasn't proud to be a Blackthorn. I was fucking ashamed of it.

"Did she pull through?" I heard Lucas ask as soon as I stepped into the fresh air.

He was lounging on the steps, blowing smoke rings into the sky without a care in the world. Unlike me, he didn't have a single spot of blood anywhere on his person because he didn't lift a single finger to help after he maimed one of the staff. Rather than answer his question, I decided to respond by storming over and giving him a swift kick to the ribs, with the intention of rolling him down the mansion's steps. I managed to get two or three solid hits in before he got back onto his feet.

"Sofia! What the hell is wrong with you?" he shouted.

"Wrong with me? *Wrong with me?*" I screamed. "You stupid bastard!"

"Shit, chill out, Sis! Everything's fine now!"

"You could've fucking killed her!"

He scoffed dismissively. "It was just a flesh wound."

"It wasn't! A few inches to the left, and she would've bled out right there on the lawn!"

"Fuck," he uttered, taking a drag of his cigarette. "Is Dad pissed off?"

I rocked my head in disbelief. "That's all you care about?"

He flourished a wry grin. It boiled my blood.

"No wonder Ellie dumped you! You're a joke."

"She'll come crawling back," he said triumphantly. "Even with you whispering in her ear all the time."

"What's that supposed to mean?"

"I've seen you fawning all over her. It's pathetic, and she thinks it too."

"Piss off!" I spat, taking a few steps towards the driveway. "I hate this whole fucking family."

"Oh, please!" he cried after me. "We all know that you're the favourite child!"

I stopped and turned around. "That isn't true."

"Yes, it is! Dad barely even glances at me or Penelope, and when he does, it's usually only to tell us how much of a disappointment we are."

"Shouldn't that tell you both something?"

"Pfft," he dismissed, the smirk fading from his lips. "What about your 'secret meetings?"

The hairs on the back of my neck stood on end.

"You don't know what you're talking about," I dismissed, continuing my descent.

"He's going to hand the business over to you when he retires, isn't he?" he said, following me down the steps.

"What?" I said over my shoulder. "No."

"I'm next in line, Sofia! Me! Hell, you aren't even a real Blackthorn!"

"I couldn't give a toss about the business," I said flatly. "It's not like that."

"What is it like, then? Huh?"

I would've done anything to wipe the egotistical, self-possessed grin off his face right there and then with the truth. However, he was precisely the last person on earth that I would share that part of my life with, so I turned on my heel instead and began racing down the remainder of the steps.

"That's right!" he hollered. "Fuck off back to the basement where you belong!"

"Oh, drop dead!" I yelled over my shoulder.

32

THE PUNISHMENT

SOFIA – BEFORE

As much as I hated proving Lucas right, I did always feel more at home in my old room in the catacombs, and I found myself down there much more often in the weeks after what he did to Elena. It was ironic—I had spent my entire life convinced that I was beneath my adoptive family, but the only place I ever felt truly safe was under their feet. Besides, those tunnels were my playground when I was younger, and I knew every square inch like the back of my hand. They led to every corner of the estate, and I would often go walking down there to clear my head, be myself, and stay shielded from prying eyes.

They weren't always like that, though. Initially, they were a prison.

For the first years of my life, I didn't even know the world outside that big, wooden door existed. As far as I was concerned, Earth had a population of three: me, Dad, and Martha, who I was convinced was my mother. Although she was cold and hardly said a word to me, she prepared and brought all of my meals, brushed my hair and even bathed me. As for Dad, I would get so excited when I heard his shoes clacking against the stone. He would visit every evening without fail to spend a few hours with me and tell me a story before bed. Once I had a firm grasp on reading myself, I begged him for new books almost daily, and he would traipse into my room, arms filled with dusty tomes from the library, and plonk them on my nightstand for me to devour the next day.

That was the mistake—it sparked my curiosity.

I remember the first time I stepped out of that room like it was yesterday. I was about six or seven years old when Dad had accidentally left the door unlocked after one of his nightly visits. It was my first chance to see the rest of the house, so I prepared to set off exploring, even packing a little bag like I was embarking on some long expedition into the vast unknown. I was only in the corridor for a matter of minutes when he discovered me. He was furious and took me back down to my room immediately, explaining that it wasn't safe for me to be up there and that I shouldn't ever return.

Although I believed him implicitly, the cat was out of the bag, and it was the beginning of a long line of escape attempts. I was an inquisitive child, so I took every opportunity I could to get out of there, if only for a few minutes. After a hell of a lot of practice, I became surprisingly skilled at squeezing through the opening and pushing past them whenever either of them came to visit me.

It didn't take long to run headfirst into Lucinda.

After she discovered that I existed, everything changed. Suddenly, I was a fully-fledged Blackthorn and even given my own room in the house, but it was still a prison. In fact, every time that I wanted to leave the estate or even walk around the grounds, I had to be escorted by one of the family, but never Lucinda. To be honest, I couldn't get my head around why she hated me so much, yet deep down, I knew she was the reason why I was condemned to the basement in the first place. Even though Dad always argued that he did it to protect me, who or what he was protecting me from remained a mystery.

I nearly jumped out of my skin when there was a knock at my door. Before I answered it, I stuffed the book I was reading underneath my pillow and then perched on the edge of the bed, hands folded in my lap.

"Come in!" I shouted.

I was put at ease when the door creaked open and Jada walked in, holding a plate in her left hand. Out of all the staff in the Blackthorn employ, she was pretty much the only one I liked. For a start, she always had time for me, and if I were being brutally honest, she was more of a mother to me than Lucinda or Martha ever was. Jada didn't live on the estate because she had a daughter of her own, Robyn, who was just finishing up her time in sixth form. I always envied her for having such a lovely mum.

"I thought I'd find you down here," she said. "What are you doing?"

"Just reading." I smiled. "It's the only place I get any peace and quiet."

"I'll bet," she replied, sitting down on the bed beside me. "Anyway, I thought you'd be hungry."

"No, not really."

"But I made your favourite! BLT, minus the T."

"I shouldn't," I said, patting my stomach with the novel.

"Don't pay attention to what that dreadful Lucinda says to you," she said, dropping it on my lap. "You're perfect the way you are."

I grinned in spite of myself. It looked good, so I reached over and picked it up, squeezing it together to take a bite.

"How's Elena getting on?" I asked between chews.

"Don't worry about her, love. I have Martha waiting on her hand and foot."

I let out a chuckle. "I bet Martha loves that."

"She doesn't have a choice, does she?" she jested. "I'm the boss around here, and what I say goes."

"God, Jada—you're such a tyrant," I drawled.

She put her hand on my knee and gave it a light squeeze. "How are you, anyway? We haven't had a chance to talk about it."

"What's there to talk about?" I said with a mouthful. "There's no justice in the world."

"I'm sure Mr Blackthorn is cooking something up."

I rolled my eyes and returned the sandwich to the plate. "Sometimes, I think I should just run away and never come back."

She paused. "What's stopping you?"

"Are you kidding? Dad would have half of Manchester out looking for me before the day was out."

Jada raised her eyebrows in agreement before nicking a corner of my sandwich from the plate.

"Besides, the whole place would fall apart the second I left," I continued.

She smirked. "Amen to that."

"Have you ever thought about leaving?" I asked. "Getting another job, I mean."

"Me? God, no!" she said, fishing out a stray bit of bacon from her teeth with a fingernail. "I'd miss you all too much."

I leaned over to put my head on Jada's shoulder, and she pulled me in for warmth before returning to her feet a few seconds later.

"By the way, Mr Blackthorn's been looking for you outside. Shall I give it ten minutes before I let him know where you are?"

"No, I'd better head up," I groaned. "He doesn't know I still come down here."

With a weary smile, Jada held out her hand and pulled me up, grabbing the crumb-laden plate from me before we traipsed through the dim passageways and into the main house. She gripped my hand before we parted ways, then tottered off to the kitchens down the corridor. I followed the hallway out onto the driveway, and I saw Lucas standing by his obnoxious Range Rover, observing Dad leaning in the passenger side door, inexplicably throwing random items over his shoulders onto the gravel.

"What's going on?" I asked Lucas on my way over.

"No, no, no! Not you!" he barked after swivelling his head. "Go back in the house!"

"What the hell is your problem?" I asked.

"This doesn't concern you. Just return to your fucking books or whatever it is that you do all day."

"Ahh, Sofia!" Dad announced, reversing out of the vehicle. "I was hoping you'd join us."

Lucas started pacing, pushing his hair back.

"What's all this? Are you having a clear-out?"

"Something like that," he said, tossing me the keys. "It's yours."

"What?" I gasped.

"No! Dad! You can't do that! It's mine!" Lucas pleaded.

"This car isn't a right, son. It's a privilege, and it rubs me the wrong way to allow you to continue having access to it when you're quite clearly running amok."

"It was a fucking accident! The maid got in the damned way!"

"Her name is Elena," I interjected.

"That notwithstanding, there needs to be an appropriate response," he said, slamming the door. "This is it."

"But you're just going to give it to *her*?" he asked, gesturing at me. "She can't even bloody drive!"

"Well, she'll learn!" Dad said, turning to me. "Won't you, darling?"

"Er—yeah!" I squealed with excitement before Lucas dropped to his knees.

"Do you want me to beg? Is that it?" Lucas asked, clasping his hands together. "Dad, please don't take my car from me. I beg you."

"Lucas, get up this instant!" he hissed, glancing over his shoulder. "You're making a complete fool of yourself!"

Begrudgingly, Lucas returned to his feet, chin on chest and batting the dust from his shins.

"Also, I don't want you at the fundraiser this year," Dad announced.

"You've got to be joking!" Lucas argued. "I promised Ellie we were going! It's the only reason she took me back!"

Dad paced forward. "Then you'll have to un-promise her, won't you?"

"I don't believe this," Lucas grumbled.

"Now," Dad spat, getting in Lucas's grill. "Get out of my sight."

"You'll pay for this, *Sis*," Lucas whispered in my ear as he trudged back towards the house.

"Are you sure about this, Dad?" I asked, jangling the keys.

He nodded. "Dead sure."

"Won't Lucinda—Mum—throw a fit?"

"It's not up to her."

I looked beyond him to what I had just been given. Although a considerable part of me wanted to jump up and down for joy, it didn't sit right with me that Elena had almost lost her leg, and the only thing the guilty party lost was his gas guzzler.

"Do you want to take her for a spin?" Dad asked.

"What, now?" I laughed. "Are you being serious?"

"Why ever not?"

"I don't even know how to."

"It's easy!" he boomed, opening the driver's side door for me. "Hop in."

I jumped inside, and Dad took the passenger seat before hitting the start engine button. It roared to life as I lightly ran my hands over the leather steering wheel. Even though I had driven Dad's Jaguar a few times, I only made it as far as the end of the driveway, and we had to swap places at the gates to turn around. The Range Rover was much bigger, and I felt like I was sitting in a tank rather than a car.

"Seatbelt," he prompted, clicking his own shut.

"Okay," I said shakily as I drew it across my chest.

"Now, put your foot on the brake and move it into drive."

I did as he said. "Now what?"

"Slowly bring your foot off the brake and tickle the accelerator."

It started moving, so I began turning the wheel until we were pointed towards the exit.

"Go on, Sofia. Open her up a little bit."

I tapped the pedal, and the whole vehicle jolted forward, so I eased off at once. I remained at a leisurely pace until we were within spitting distance of the gates, then jumped on the brakes, bringing the car to a jarring halt.

"Are we turning back around?" I asked.

"No, edge out onto the road and take a left."

I started sweating in an instant. "Really?"

"Yes, really!" he said, placing his hand on my thigh as Harris opened the gates.

"But I don't think I'm ready for this."

"Codswallop!" he exclaimed. "We'll take it slow."

The way was open, so as instructed, I trundled through the gates, breathing in like it made any difference to the breadth of the vehicle. I stopped just shy of the junction, then inched forward to check it was clear. With Dad's go-ahead, I put my foot down and the tyres spat gravel at the gates behind us before they finally gained traction and we moved onto the road.

* * *

Despite Dad stating otherwise, my first so-called driving lesson was an absolute disaster. I nearly crashed almost a dozen times, ran a handful of red lights, and caused a massive pileup when it took me nearly ten minutes to make a right-hand turn. That being said, it was one of the most exhilarating things I had ever done in my life, and I already couldn't wait for the next one. It wasn't the driving, as such. It was more the freedom that it brought, and the hope that one day I might actually be able to go out on my own.

"Go on then! How was it for you?" Dad asked as I came to a grinding halt.

"Terrifying," I uttered, my hands still trembling. "I think my blood pressure is through the roof."

"Well, I think you did brilliantly!" he boomed. "I'm a very proud father right now."

I couldn't help but grin, yet Dad's fingertips making little circles on my thigh soured it before I even noticed it happening.

"Can I ask you something?" I said, staring down at my leg.

"Of course," he said, pausing for a beat. "What is it?"

I drew a lungful of air and held it. "Why did you lock me down there?"

His face dropped as he snatched his hand back.

"We've been over this," he said, swivelling his head away. "Don't make me repeat myself, Sofia."

"*You did it to protect me*," I quoted before leaning in. "But who were you trying to protect me from?"

"You aren't stupid, Sofia." He looked me dead in the eyes. "You already know."

"Lucinda?" I suggested.

He tipped his head.

"Why, though?" I asked.

He didn't speak for almost a full minute, looking at the house while he tapped his fingers on the dashboard.

"Listen to me, Sofia," he began, choosing his words carefully. "I love my wife, but there's one thing you need to understand about her: she's at her most dangerous when she doesn't get her own way."

"Trust me, I—"

"No, Sofia, you don't," he cut in. "I don't think she's ever made a secret of the fact that she didn't want you here."

"Uh-huh," I sang sarcastically. "She reminds me almost daily."

"Well, back when we were discussing taking you in, she refused to come around to my way of thinking. She said two children were enough."

"So, you did it anyway and kept me hidden in the basement? You do realise how weird that is, right?"

"I had no other choice!" he said, his voice snapping like a whip.

"Why?"

"I knew from the moment I held you in my arms that you were destined to be a Blackthorn. What was I meant to do? Let you go to some random family? You deserved far better than that."

"But I missed out on so much: friends, school—"

"You've been handed everything you ever wanted!" he interrupted.

"What about my freedom, Dad?"

I could physically see his anger rising to a fever-pitch until it slowly fell again. He clutched the door handle and pulled it, but didn't allow the door to swing open.

"You'll get it," he uttered. "Soon."

My eyes lowered. He seemed to read my mind about the next thing I was going to bring up because he pushed the door open with the intention of making a getaway.

"What about our meetings?" I asked.

He didn't turn back to face me. "What about them?"

"Lucas and Penelope—they know," I announced.

He clicked the door shut. "You told them?"

"Of course not," I said quickly. "But they suspect."

He paused for a beat. "They haven't spoken to Lucinda about them, have they?"

"No," I said softly. "I don't think so."

"Then there's nothing to worry about, is there?" he said, pushing the door open again.

"Wait," I said, grabbing him by the shoulder. "One more thing."

"What?"

I suddenly felt hollow. "I want them to stop."

He didn't reply, just like always. He simply stepped out of the vehicle and slammed the door behind him.

On the face of it, most people would kill for a father like him. He did give me everything, after all. I had a roof above my head, expensive clothes, extravagant jewellery—literally anything I asked for. However, that lifestyle had a price tag attached. It cost me things that most would take for granted. Freedom. Independence. Love. I was never going to get any of that whilst I was confined to the estate. He would make sure of it.

After watching him stride over to the house and head inside, I broke down at the wheel, gripping it so tightly that my knuckles were bleached white. I was plagued with so many questions, so much bitterness, but one question screamed louder than the rest.

If Dad was protecting me from Lucinda, who would protect me from Dad?

33

THE SHAME

SOFIA – BEFORE

The boating lake was simply magnificent in the early morning.

There was a family of swans sleeping beneath the leaning sycamore, necks tucked in on themselves, delicately drifting by the water's edge. The sun had only just risen behind the old mausoleum, casting a reddish glow over the perfectly still surface. It was pretty cold, but I liked the cool breeze against my skin and the fresh air in my lungs. I approached the shoreline, squatted down, and peered at my own reflection in the water.

I looked terrible, like I hadn't slept in weeks. In reality, that wasn't too far from the truth.

Even by our standards, the family had been avoiding me like the plague since my supposed heart-to-heart with Dad. Lucas was either out pestering Ellie to take him back for the umpteenth time or still pouting about the car in his room. Penelope went out shopping almost daily, spending Dad's cash as a poor substitute for actually feeling something. Dad and Lucinda were pretty busy themselves, having to delegate twice as hard with the Blackthorn Foundation dinner looming, leaving Jada and Martha with a seemingly endless list of tasks to work through.

So, I was alone, with only my thoughts for company. It was torturous.

A particularly pleasing pebble beside my foot caught my eye, so I picked it up and rubbed my thumb over the smooth surface. After a moment of inspecting it, I lifted my head and hurled it as close to the old sycamore as I could. It landed with a huge splash, startling the swans awake and sending them into flight in all directions. I tracked one of the bigger ones as it soared into the sky, quickly making it past the treeline before disappearing behind it. They had no idea how lucky they were.

"Sofia? What are you doing here alone?" I heard Martha bark behind me.

Shit.

I picked up one more stone and plonked it in the middle of my reflection, then rose to my feet to face her. She had her arms locked over her chest, looking me up and down like she'd caught me in the middle of something grievous.

"I was just clearing my head," I explained. "It's a beautiful morning and—"

"You aren't meant to leave the house without a chaperone!"

"Right," I said, smiling. "Everyone was busy, though."

"Then you must wait!" she said, closing the gap between us. "Return, at once!"

"I was finished anyway," I remarked, sidestepping to the path. "I'll head back now."

"It goes without saying that the lady of the house will be hearing about this!"

She always carried on like that, her head so far up Lucinda's arse that it would require a team of surgeons if she ever had cause to remove it. Although she kept my existence a secret from Lucinda for almost a decade, Martha had shown unwavering loyalty to her ever since, which made her nothing short of incredibly annoying. Maybe she felt some variety of twisted guilt for betraying her in the first place, or she was just angling for a promotion. Either way, her constant brown-nosing made me feel queasy.

"Fine by me," I announced. "You'll have to explain why you were out here, though."

She shrugged. "I'm not the one breaking the rules, am I?"

My gaze raked over her. Her hair was all over the place, and I was pretty sure she was wearing yesterday's mascara. Despite her tunic not being dirty as such, it didn't look fresh on her, and if I didn't know any better, I would say that she'd been wearing it for two days in a row. Little did she know that I had seen her take that same walk of shame almost twice a week since I was let into the main house.

"Where have you been, anyway?" I asked.

"That's none of your—"

"Up to the gamekeeper's cottage, perhaps?"

Her cheeks flushed. "I had to drop my—"

"Knickers?" I chuckled.

Martha's jaw dropped before she snapped it shut, teeth gritted. "Listen to me very carefully, Sofia—"

"It's Miss Blackthorn to you," I corrected. "And I'm done listening. If you go snitching to Lucinda, I'll be forced to tell her about all the times I've seen you wandering up to Harris's lodgings and then staggering back after you'd received a good seeing to."

She gasped, bringing her hands to her mouth. "That is entirely untrue!"

"Look, Martha. How you spend your time is none of my business," I explained. "And the reverse goes for you."

"I practically raised you, and this is how you treat me?" she exclaimed.

I leaned in. "You didn't fucking raise me."

"Yes, I did! I cooked your meals, I cleaned your clothes—"

"Maybe," I cut in. "But you were nothing more than a jailer to me."

She parted her lips to speak, but instantly stopped herself.

"You knew it was wrong what they were doing to me, and you didn't lift a finger to stop it," I explained. "You're no better than *them*."

She buried her chin in her chest. "I was just doing as I was told."

The silence was telling.

"Let's just keep this chance meeting to ourselves then, shall we?"

She nodded reluctantly. "Okay."

"Is breakfast prepared?" I asked.

She kicked at the pebbles. "I was just about to start it."

"Then you'd better hop to it, hadn't you? I wouldn't want to see you on the receiving end of a bollocking from Jada."

With her tail firmly between her pasty legs, Martha started trudging back towards the house, looking over her shoulder every few feet or so to check if I was still there. I waited until she disappeared from view before I moved a muscle. She was right about one thing: I shouldn't be out there, and if I did get caught, my so-called life wouldn't be worth living.

Through fear of being discovered out there by someone else, I opted to skip breakfast and take the passageway beside the mausoleum to the main house and hide in my childhood room for a few hours. I had pretty much read every book in the library twice over, so at that point, I was making my way through the dusty encyclopaedias that no one ever touched since they were purchased. Did you know that sloths are incapable of shivering? I didn't either.

Jada was obviously too busy upstairs to drop one of her famous sandwiches down for me, so I headed up to the main house to grab a bite to eat once lunchtime hit. The kitchen seemed to have its own microclimate when I walked inside, sticky and humid, with four huge stock pots simmering away on the stove. Jada was diverting her attention between them, tasting the contents with a little spoon and adding a touch of seasoning here and there. She looked truly at home in that kitchen and clearly loved her job, whistling a merry tune and swaying her hips.

"What are you making?" I asked, taking a seat at the table.

She glanced over her shoulder. "Why? You hungry?"

I smirked. "I could eat."

"You can be my guinea pig, then," she said, beckoning me over. "I've gone taste-blind at this point."

I got back on my feet and sauntered over, trying to get a look at the pots. My only knowledge of cooking came from books, but even with my untrained eye, it appeared as though Jada was preparing some kind of seafood bisque. It was bright red, creamy, and lightly bubbling with a bit of saffron floating on the surface. She grabbed a clean spoon and scooped some up, blowing on it before offering it to me. My taste buds started dancing when I took a polite sip. It was delicious.

"Wow, that's amazing!" I cheered, taking the spoon off her for another try.

"You like it?"

I widened my eyes. "It's incredible!"

"I didn't go overboard with the chilli?"

"No, no, not at all! It's perfect, honestly."

She breathed a sigh of relief. "Good."

"Where did you even learn to cook like this?" I asked, setting the spoon down on the counter.

"My muma back on Jamrock," she said with a measure of pride. "There was nothing about cooking that lady didn't know."

I laughed in spite of myself. "The only thing Lucinda ever taught me was how to pair a necklace with a dress."

I moved out of the way and returned to the table, plonking myself down on one of the old wooden chairs.

"Do you miss it?" I asked. "Jamaica, I mean."

"I don't remember much," she explained over her shoulder. "I was only a little girl when we moved over here."

"Right," I said, picking at the grain of the table. "Of course."

"I've visited a few times, though," she added brightly, stirring the pot. "Back when I was around your age."

"What's it like?"

She tapped a wooden spoon on the rim of the pan. "Beautiful. It's a totally different way of life over there."

"I wish I could go."

"You should! It beats rainy Manchester every day of the week."

"I'll need a guide—maybe you can come with me?" I jested.

She chortled. "I'd love to."

"When I'm finally allowed to leave the grounds, that is," I continued. "Maybe one day, eh?"

"Sure, love," she said, walking over to the sink to wash her hands. "One day."

The kitchen door swung open, and I turned around to see Penelope breeze in through the gap. Despite it being in the middle of the day, she was wearing nothing but a silk robe, black hair tied up in a high pony and sparkly slippers. I gave her a razor-thin smile, but she hardly even registered mine or Jada's presence as she flounced over to the fridge to browse inside. She clicked her tongue loudly when she didn't find anything that appealed to her and slammed it shut before leaning her back against it.

"Oh, Sofia," she began wistfully. "Have you ever been in love?"

"Well, I—"

"No. Of course you haven't," she dismissed. "Let me tell you, there's no better feeling."

I would've loved to wipe the smirk off her face with the truth, but it could only end in tears.

"Are you still seeing the bloke with the tattoos, then?" I asked.

She scrunched up her face. "How do you know about him?"

"I've seen him coming out of your room a few times," I explained. "What's his name?"

"Aubrey Cholmondeley," she swooned. "He's an absolute delight."

The snigger escaped me before I could stop it. His name was more of a mouthful than Jada's bisque.

"Is something funny to you?" she said, voice sharp and arms folded across her chest.

"No!" I said, flicking my eyes to Jada, who was struggling to hold it together. "Not at all."

"You can take the mickey out of my relationship when you have one of your own."

I scratched my jaw. "I don't think there's any danger of that happening anytime soon," I remarked.

"Me either," she retorted.

We were plunged into an awkward silence, but Penelope seemed to be exempt from it. She began happily rifling through the pantry for a snack whilst Jada and I exchanged uneasy looks with each other.

"Anyway, I've been thinking about Lucas's car," she yelled from the other room.

I twisted my head. "What about it?"

"I think I'd like to have it," she said, returning to the kitchen. "Aubrey and I are thinking of taking a romantic trip to The Lakes."

My forehead creased. "But Dad gave it to me."

"What use is it to have a car like that when you can't even bloody drive?"

"He's been teaching me," I answered. "In fact, he says I'm quite good at it."

"It's not like he'll let you go off the estate alone, though," she countered. "Give it to me."

I folded my arms across my ribs. "Don't you have your own bloody car?"

"That yellow piece of shit? It's almost twelve months old!" she exclaimed as though my suggestion was an insult.

"How is that my problem? Speak to Dad."

"I did, and he told me he gave the Range Rover to you."

"Well, there's your answer, isn't it?"

She thundered over, leaning on the table with one hand and holding the other out expectantly.

"Where are the keys?" she demanded. "Do you have them on you, or are they up in your room?"

"Pick one," I grunted. "It doesn't matter to you either way."

She straightened her back, looming over me. "I'll tell Mum."

"The fuck if I care!" I exclaimed. "She isn't going to give a shit about some spat with a car."

"Not about the car," she said quietly. "About you and Dad."

My throat closed up. "You wouldn't."

"Oh, but I would. I'm sure she'd be very interested in what you two have been getting up to in the middle of the night."

I gripped the table. "You don't know what the hell you're talking about."

"Don't I?" She chortled. "Maybe I wouldn't if you didn't spend so long crying about it afterwards."

I clenched my jaw. "Fuck you."

Jada must have seen how upset I was getting because she bounded over, delicately placing her hand on Penelope's forearm.

"Come on now, Miss Blackthorn. I'm sure you can settle this amicably."

"How *dare* you touch me!" Penelope yelled, batting Jada's hand away. "Who the hell do you think you are?"

"Look, you can *borrow* the damn car, okay?" I interjected. "When do you need it?"

She smirked triumphantly. "This weekend."

"It's the foundation dinner. There's no way Dad will let you go."

"Urgh," she grunted. "The weekend after, then."

"Fine by me. Just calm down, okay?"

Without even uttering a word of thanks, she headed over to the stove, wafting some steam in her face from the pots. Jada gripped my arm, silently asking if I was okay, but I simply shook my head and pointed at Penelope. I didn't plan on saying anything else until she left again.

"What even is this?" she asked Jada. "Is it edible?"

"Er—a seafood bisque," Jada explained, stepping closer. "I don't think it will be to your taste."

"I'll be the judge of that, won't I?" she said, lifting my used spoon from the counter.

She dipped it inside, blew on the contents, then took a taste. Her eyes widened within seconds, and she spat it back into the pot before racing over to the sink to rinse her mouth out. I nearly burst out laughing, but the expression on Jada's face stopped me. She looked furious that her meal had been ruined, so she stormed over to peer into the top of the pan with disgust.

"What the hell did you put in it?" Penelope gasped, panting through a wide-open jaw.

"Too much chilli?" I asked, grinning.

"Very much so!" she scolded. "Jada, must you make that foreign muck in our kitchens?"

The smile plummeted from my face, leaving Penelope's repulsive comment hanging in the air for at least thirty seconds. Jada appeared as if she was fantasising about dumping the whole vat of it over Penelope's head, so I stood up and went over to her, tugging at her tunic in support.

"I'm sorry, Miss Blackthorn," she murmured, clenching her fist.

"Dispose of it this instant," she ordered, turning to me. "And you—drop the keys off in my room."

My knuckles cracked. "Sure thing, Sis."

Overly satisfied that she'd got what she wanted, Penelope glided out of the room, banging the kitchen door shut behind her. Jada stomped over to the stove, grabbed the pot with both handles, and poured it straight down the plughole.

"Shit, I'm sorry, Jada," I said, going over to place a comforting hand on her shoulder.

"What was she talking about?" she asked, batting away my grip.

"What do you mean?"

"Something about you and Mr Blackthorn in the evenings."

I stumbled backwards a few paces, rocking my head. "Nothing."

She narrowed her eyes. "What's going on, Sofia?"

"Nothing!" I insisted. "She's just making stuff up."

Jada didn't look convinced.

"Sofia," she said softly. "Look at me."

I didn't. I stared at the orange streaks circling the plughole.

"Did he hurt you?"

"No," I said too fast.

"Is he asking you to do things you don't want to do?"

"Jada, drop it."

She cursed in patois, grabbed a fresh cloth and started pointlessly wiping the already spotless counter, like scrubbing hard enough would erase what she suspected. I didn't say anything else. I just slipped out of the kitchen while her back was turned. By the time I reached the cool stone of the passageway, the shame was back: thick, hot and crawling up my throat.

No one else needed to know what was happening to me.

It was my cross to bear, and mine alone.

34

THE FUNDRAISER

SOFIA – BEFORE

The Blackthorn Foundation's annual fundraiser dinner was a very prestigious affair. In fact, it was a veritable who's who of Manchester, and business leaders, local celebrities, and socialites alike would happily trade one of their kidneys for an invite. For me, it wasn't all that it was cracked up to be. I was mostly just wheeled out for a few photographs after all the festivities were over, and then kept on a short leash for the rest of the night while the rest of the family drank themselves senseless on donor-sponsored fizz.

Then again, it was an excuse to dress up, and it was nice to see so many fresh faces on the estate. I was waiting at the top of the stairs, looking down at them in the foyer. It was a sea of plump donors, cash burning holes in their pockets, with Lucinda circling them like a shark, ready to pounce on them when they least expected it. Penelope was clearly several drinks deep in the corner with her ghastly friend Camilla, pointing and bitching at some of the other guests' wilder outfit choices. Much to my delight, Lucas was nowhere to be seen after being forbidden from attending, but it would've been nice to see Ellie. Still, at least he was one less thing to worry about.

I spotted Jada making her way through the crowd, and we locked eyes, so she wormed her way through and trudged up the stairs, a tray of champagne flutes balanced on one hand. It had been a few days since the row with Penelope in the kitchen, and I hadn't spoken with either of them since, mostly because I was terrified Jada would drag the truth out of me and make my situation even worse.

"Hey, stranger," she said, standing by my side. "Have you been avoiding me?"

I shook my head firmly. "Of course not. Just busy."

She didn't look satisfied with my lie. "Do you want one?" she asked, offering me a drink.

"Can't," I said quickly. "About to throw up."

"Why, love?"

"Lucas isn't here, so Dad wants me to make a toast. I'm shitting myself."

"You'll do fine, sweetheart!" she assured, stroking my forearm. "Just speak from the heart."

"No can do," I said, raising some notes in the air. "Lucinda gave me a script."

She let out a flat laugh. "Then what's there to worry about?"

"There are just so many people, and they're all going to be staring at me."

"I'll be in the room, so keep your eyes fixed on me and pretend everyone else isn't there."

"Oh, yeah. That'll help," I said sarcastically.

"If all else fails," she began, forcing a glass into my grip, "there's always a little Dutch courage."

I didn't need any more convincing and knocked it back without a further thought. By the time the glass was empty, Lucinda was standing on the bottom step, tapping a glass of her own with a small, silver spoon.

"Friends, please be seated in the dining room," she announced. "Dinner will be served shortly."

"Knock them dead, honey!" Jada gushed, patting me on the shoulder.

She took my glass from me and started walking downstairs, and I followed a few steps behind her. The dining room was bursting at the seams by the time I made it inside, and Dad was at the head of the table, gesturing for me to sit beside him. With a smile, I snaked through the guests and walked over to him, balancing on the edge of my seat as I took one last look at my notes.

"Have you learned your lines yet?" he asked, bumping his shoulder into mine.

"Not even remotely," I said, getting flustered. "You do know I'm going to fuck this up, don't you?"

"No, you aren't," he said, gripping my thigh under the tablecloth. "I wouldn't have asked you otherwise."

I sighed deeply. "Can't Penelope do it?"

We both turned to her and saw that she had one eye closed, swaying violently in her chair.

"Okay," I added. "Maybe not."

"Listen, you're a remarkable young woman, and you're going to blow their bloody socks off."

Lucinda touched Dad's shoulder as she sat on the other side of him, so he waited for the rest of the guests to be seated and then rose out of his chair. He didn't need to tap a glass to get their attention because all of their eyes were on him within seconds. The room was so quiet that I could have heard a pin drop.

"Friends! Welcome!" he boomed, clapping his hands together. "I appreciate you all for coming to what will be the eighteenth annual Blackthorn Foundation dinner!"

The room erupted into chaos, some of the guests even going as far as to bash the table with their fists. Dad waited for them to calm down before speaking again.

"I don't need to tell you how important this charity is to the people of Manchester and beyond. Our pioneering outreach programmes are now in full swing, working with young offenders in prisons across the UK. Furthermore, we continue to help thousands of broken children every year to rebuild their lives with their forever families, and we're only able to do all of that because of the generous donations you all provide." He clutched his chest. "From the very bottom of my heart, thank you."

Raucous applause followed, but quickly fell silent when Dad picked up his glass, taking a slow mouthful before placing it down again.

"It's funny: I never set out to create this charity. I was content just running my business, making a name for our family, and continuing a legacy that would last for generations to come." He turned to me with a peculiar grin on his face. "But one special little girl changed that."

All of the air left my lungs.

"This amazing young woman sitting right here is living proof of the good work that the Blackthorn Foundation carries out. Our no-expenses-spared group homes have saved the lives of hundreds of children like her from a life of poverty and anguish, and they will keep doing so long after I'm gone."

The room broke out into spontaneous clapping again, and the pitying faces gawping back at me made me want to sprint for the nearest exit. Dad seemed to notice me squirming and put his hand on my shoulder to comfort me. It only made me feel worse.

"We love our daughter like our own, and that love is the lifeblood of the Blackthorn Foundation. If anyone is to be thanked for all the fantastic work we've done over the years, it's her. She changed our lives the day we met her, and since then, she's changed the lives of countless families, all over the country."

A few of the more emotional guests started dabbing at their eyes with a tissue, which is when Dad turned to me, holding out his hand.

"Come on, Sofia!" he whispered to me. "Stand up."

I allowed him to pull me up and then squeezed my hands together to stop them shaking.

"So, without further ado, I hand you over to my beautiful daughter: Sofia Blackthorn."

The room suddenly felt half the size. I slowly lifted my notes up, my hands rattling like they were about to drop off my wrists.

"Good evening, everyone," I said, as quiet as a mouse. "My name is Sofia, and—"

"Speak up!" Dad reminded me.

"Sorry," I uttered to the room, raising my voice. "Tonight, I want to talk to you about gratitude."

I paused, trying to read any of the words on the page through the shakes.

"Mum and Dad," I began with one eye still on the page. "Firstly, I want to thank you for inviting me into your home all those years ago. I know it wasn't easy at first, but you've both given me a life that wouldn't have been possible without your kindness and generosity."

The woman next to Lucinda gripped her arm and pulled her in, almost as if she was congratulating her.

"Through circumstance, I was born to parents who couldn't look after me. I could've easily been swallowed up by the system, thrown in an underfunded group home or worse, but Mum and Dad couldn't let that happen. They *refused* to let that happen."

I looked out into the room at the scattered applause, but when I looked back at my script, I had lost my place.

"Er—sorry," I said, tracing the lines with my finger.

The kitchen door swung open, and Jada quietly snuck in to stand with the rest of the staff at the back of the room, shooting a disarming grin my way. I smiled back as she tapped her chest with one hand, then gestured for me to speak again. To Lucinda's horror, I tossed the useless notes onto the table and cleared my throat.

Fuck it.

"I'm supposed to stand here and subtly tug at your heartstrings for the next five minutes. By the time I've finished, you'll all feel so guilty that you'll have no option but to dig deep and donate." I paused to glance at Dad. "That was the plan, anyway."

The donors all started mumbling to each other. Lucinda was already halfway out of her chair, but Dad raised his hand to prevent her from stopping me.

"When I came into this world, I had nothing. Not even bloody parents. But the Blackthorns changed that and welcomed me into their home. They fed me. They clothed me. They raised me and treated me like one of their own, and I don't need some script to tell me how thankful I am for that."

Lucinda relaxed slightly, returned to her seat, and hid behind her wine glass. I followed her lead and leaned down, grabbed a random glass from the table, and took a swig.

"It's not my place to tell you how you should spend your money. You can buy some piece of art you'll never give a fuck about, some fancy dress that you'll only wear once, or another car that you'll never drive if that's what you want. Go ahead. But what I will tell you is that you have the power to transform a child's life, to give them hope, to give them love—so why would you spend it any other way?"

I turned to Lucinda and Dad, raising my glass.

"The truth is, I was lucky. I know that. I never had to experience what so many kids have to go through because I've never known any other life. You guys—you opened your home and your heart to me, and I'll be forever grateful for that."

The room exploded in celebration as Dad stood up and hugged me, giving me a kiss on the cheek before getting his glass.

"Everyone, please charge your glasses to join me in a toast," he began, lifting his glass aloft. "To love!"

"To love!" everyone repeated.

"Jada and the girls in the kitchen have laid out quite a feast for you all, so I do hope you've brought an appetite," he announced.

"And your chequebooks!" Lucinda added, provoking spontaneous laughter.

"How could I forget?" Dad said with a chuckle before turning to me to whisper in my ear. "Bravo, Sofia. Bravo."

* * *

Dinner passed, guests scattered, and I could finally breathe again. I was the star of the show and had my ears chewed off for hours by the donors who were desperate to hear more of my heavily redacted story. I was wiped by the time taxis started pulling up the drive to ferry them home, so I took the opportunity to take myself off to bed as the foyer emptied. The dress that Lucinda had picked out for me was about two sizes too small and had been cutting into my ribs all evening, and I was already fantasising about peeling it off as I climbed the stairs up to my room.

Dad was in his study, probably totting up all the donations we had solicited, but I didn't bother him. I just crept down the hall and closed my bedroom door behind me. After unzipping the back of my dress, I threw myself onto the bed and stayed face down, kicking off my heels and sending them clattering to the floor. I heard my door open a moment later, so I quickly sat up in bed and saw Dad slowly stepping towards me, arms behind his back.

"Go on then, what are the scores on the doors?" I asked.

"Incredible," he said, perching on the end of the bed. "We raised more tonight than we did in the last two."

"Wow!" I gasped. "That's amazing!"

"Quite, and we have you to thank for that, don't we? Your speech—it was inspired."

I flashed him a coy smile. "It was nothing."

"It was not nothing!" he exclaimed. "You're doing that every year from now on."

"Won't Lucas throw a hissy fit?"

"It isn't his decision, is it? Are you up for it?"

My grin went wider. "Yeah. I'd love to."

"Good!" he cheered. "By the way, I have something for you."

"Really? What?"

"I was saving it for your birthday, but I want to give it to you now."

"What is—"

"Close your eyes," he instructed.

I did as he asked, and he slipped a ring onto my finger. When I opened them again, I saw it in all its glory, diamond shimmering in the light.

"Oh my God," I gasped.

"It was my mother's ring. It's been in our family for generations."

"I—I can't take this."

"You certainly can!" he said. "Besides, she would've wanted you to have it."

I looked up from the ring and into his eyes. "Okay. Thank you."

"You've earned it."

Although it was beautiful in its own right, it was much more than just a piece of jewellery to me. In my eyes, it made me a true Blackthorn. All those years of feeling lesser and beneath them fizzled away because I had a reminder that I was one of them, firmly surrounding my digit. I flashed Dad a wilting smile as a yawn escaped my lips, and he patted the bed before getting back to his feet and walking to the door to leave. I rolled back onto my front, rotating my hand around to catch the glimmers again, but I stopped dead when I felt something.

His hand was running up the back of my calf.

I spun back around, an uneasy smile on my face, backing up into the headboard.

"Dad, not tonight, okay?" I asked, my voice shaking. "Please."

"Quiet," he grunted, running his palms up my bare shins.

"I'm tired, you're tired," I said quickly. "Can't we leave it?"

"Shush," he said sharply, bringing a finger to my lips.

I giggled uneasily. "There are still people downstairs."

He ignored what I had said and yanked me down the bed, parting my legs with a single finger.

"Dad, please! Please don't ruin a nice evening," I pleaded.

I knew my pleas would be ignored. They always were.

It would be much, much worse if I resisted, so I rested my head on the pillow and stared at the crack in the ceiling. I heard his belt click open, and he lunged forward, the usual sting making me wince. I looked beyond his mass to the door, and the last thing I saw before I closed my eyes was Lucinda standing there, tears streaming down her cheeks, but pure rage at *me* in her eyes.

"Just relax," he said softly in my ear. "I'll look after you, Sofia."

35

THE BARGAIN

SOFIA – BEFORE

I woke up. I say that, but I don't think I truly ever went to sleep in the first place. Every breath hurt, probably because of the uncomfortable dress digging into me all night that I didn't dare take off—a dull ache that had spread all the way from my ribcage to the back of my neck. I had no earthly idea what time it was, so I swung my legs onto the floor and stumbled towards the bathroom. Last night's mascara had streamed down my cheeks and had since dried, and my eyes were puffed up beyond recognition, so I lifted my hand to touch them when I saw what was still surrounding my finger.

The ring. It sat there like a nail.

The diamond threw a shard of light onto the wall as I tried to yank it from my finger. It was jammed on there pretty good, so I ran it under the cold tap to try to loosen it, but it still wouldn't budge. It rested there, mocking me like a brand, telling everyone who saw it that I was property of Richard Blackthorn. I pulled on it harder, gritting my teeth as my knuckles cracked, and it finally gave way.

His abuse started on the evening of my eighteenth birthday. I was wearing white that night, gifted to me an hour before the party by Lucinda, who was insistent that it would be slimming. Just like the fundraiser, it started with speeches and food and ended with everyone drinking too much, so I retired just after midnight. Before I drifted off to sleep, there was a polite knock at the door, and suddenly, my so-called father was standing there, holding an artificial black rose that he'd plucked from a bouquet in the foyer on his way up to my room. I didn't know what he wanted at first; he only mumbled about one last present he wanted to give me. I laughed and invited him in.

The first time was quick and clumsy, full of whispered apologies that I barely heard. Not that it mattered because they weren't for me, were they? They were for himself, a way to bury the shame of what he'd done and a lie to help him sleep at night. I told myself that it was a one-off, and if I tried hard enough, I could forget that it ever happened at all. He didn't say sorry the second time. Or the third. In fact, he'd got it down to a fine art by the fourth visit, creeping into my room in the middle of the night, stinking of scotch and tobacco, and he was back in his study before the rest of the family even stirred from their sleep.

There was a tap at my bedroom door, so I threw some water on my face to wash away the mascara runs, dropped the dress to my feet and put on my robe. No one had entered my room in the time it took, but I waited for the second knock before speaking.

"Come in," I muttered.

Lucinda swept in like it was any other Saturday morning, blonde hair set in a well-ordered bob, pearls dangling from her ears and a dusky pink cardigan. As cold as she was, I was expecting a hug or even a few tears from her eyes, but she sauntered straight over to my wardrobe and started plucking out clothes and throwing them on the bed, seemingly at random.

"Get dressed," she said, dropping her bag on the chair. "We're going out."

I blinked. "Where?"

"Manchester. I've a bracelet to collect." She looked at me properly for the first time and then looked away. "And you could do with some fresh air."

I tugged the gown tighter around me. "No. I'm not going anywhere."

She ignored me and strode over to the window to throw open the curtains. I winced when the sunlight hit my eyes and backed into the corner. "I assume you'll need a shower. Hop in, and I'll pick out a suitable outfit."

"Lucinda—"

She turned, smile tight. "I wasn't asking."

We stood there for a while in silence as I waited for her to say it, but she didn't.

"Are we not going to discuss last night?" I asked.

She flicked her gaze back to the wardrobe and started casually rooting through it again. "It was quite the night, wasn't it? You had me worried with your speech for a minute, but everything turned out well."

"You know what I'm talking about," I said, stepping closer. "What happened after."

Her expression hardened, and she brought a single finger to her lips. "Not here."

I stumbled back a few paces, separating my lips to argue but thinking better of it.

"Downstairs in twenty minutes," she said, nodding towards the bathroom. "Wear the black one, okay? It's slimming."

★ ★ ★

My thighs were aching as I hobbled down the stairs. I was wearing the black dress that Lucinda had tossed on my bed, my hair still wet from the shower, ring back on for appearances' sake. Martha was in the foyer, car keys looped around her finger, rocking on her heels and humming a merry tune. Lucinda emerged from the hallway as I reached the bottom step, donning a pair of oversized sunglasses and her cardigan tied around her shoulders.

"Are you ready?" she asked.

"As I'll ever be," I said, glancing at Martha.

"Good morning, Miss Blackthorn," she said to the floor. "The car is parked out front."

"Morning," I said flatly. "Where's Harris?"

"He's… busy," she replied as she held the door open for me.

I gave her a knowing look as Lucinda raced ahead of me through the open door. She was the first to get into the car, scooting over and patting the seat next to her. Begrudgingly, I sat next to her and closed the door as Martha got behind the wheel. She started the engine like she was defusing a bomb, and we began rolling down the drive. The gates were wide open, so we squeezed through and hit the road.

"About last night," Lucinda began, pushing her sunglasses over her hair. "We can keep that unpleasantness between us, can't we?"

I pointed at Martha in the driver's seat, but Lucinda waved her hand dismissively in the air, giving me the go-ahead to speak.

"Are you joking?" I asked, my voice soft. "You saw what was happening, right?"

"I did."

"And that's all you have to say?"

She turned to the window, letting out a sigh, then turned back, her expression blank. "He was drunk. It was a mistake."

I literally had no words. I just let my jaw hang in the air until she spoke again.

"Just let it go, Sofia. No good can come of this."

I leaned in. "Your husband, my father—"

"He isn't your biological father," she pointed out.

"And that makes it acceptable?" I countered.

"Lower your voice," she scolded, glancing at the back of Martha's head.

"You're unbelievable," I uttered, slowly rocking my head. "You haven't even stopped to ask me if I'm okay."

Lucinda reached over and patted my knee, but took her hand away when I flinched.

"Look," she began, fixing her glove. "We have a good life. A *remarkable* life. If you make this into something bigger than it is, everything that we've worked so hard to build could disappear in the blink of an eye."

"So, let me get this straight," I started, swallowing the lump in my throat. "You're okay with this, as long as it doesn't interfere with your perfect little life?"

"Of course not!" she spat. "But I have no choice but to accept it, and neither do you."

"What?" I gasped. "So, you're just going to allow it to carry on?"

"If I have to! That's what it means to protect this family."

I blinked in amazement. "You're just as bad as him."

"Don't be ridiculous!" she scoffed, folding her arms. "What do you know, anyway? You're just a silly little girl."

"Excuse me?"

"We welcomed you into our home, gave you everything, and this is how you repay us? By threatening to destroy us?"

I was stunned. "You can't be suggesting this is my fault!"

"No," she said, tilting her head back. "But it will be if our family gets obliterated because of it."

I turned away, my chest shallow. "I can't believe you're taking his side."

"Do you think it's been easy for me? To hear him creeping into your room at all hours of the night? When I'm only down the hall?"

The penny dropped. "You knew all along, didn't you?"

"Please!" she dismissed, flicking her wrist. "It's my house. Of course I bloody knew."

"Why didn't you stop it?"

"It wasn't my place."

I paused. "What kind of a mother are you?"

Her face dropped as if I had said the worst thing imaginable.

"Stop the car!" Lucinda barked at Martha.

She pulled in at the next opportunity and put the handbrake on, stepping out of the car and shutting the door behind her without a word. When I turned back to Lucinda, she looked like she wanted to grab me by the throat and squeeze the life out of me.

"Listen to me very carefully, you ungrateful, wretched brat," she hissed. "I am *not* your mother."

"Shock, horror," I remarked.

"If it were up to me, you'd have been shipped off to one of those ghastly group homes the moment you were born."

My nostrils flared. "Why didn't you, then?"

"He hid you in the basement!" she bellowed. "In fact, I didn't even know you existed until I saw you prancing around the house in your bloody pyjamas!"

I huffed, crossing my arms as she released a strange noise before scouring her bag for her cigarettes.

"Look, you do what you need to do, okay?" she explained. "But let me warn you: not a soul will believe you."

"They will when—"

"*Not a soul*," she repeated. "They'll say you're mad. They'll say you did it for attention. They'll say you wanted it. In fact, they'll say anything to convince themselves that it was your fault because that's easier to stomach than the truth."

"What truth?" I spat.

"That Richard Blackthorn, famous philanthropist and loving father, ever put a single foot wrong."

My heart started thumping at the back of my throat. "I'll go to the police."

"Sure. I'll be certain to take it up with the Chief Inspector's wife when I play bridge with her on Thursday."

"I'll talk to the papers."

"Which ones? Hmm? Most of the owners were stuffing their faces in our dining room last night."

"Then I'll run away."

"He'll find you."

We were plunged into an awkward silence for a few moments after I ran out of ideas. Lucinda broke it by tapping on the window, and Martha got back inside and began driving again. Lucinda opened the window an inch and lit her cigarette, blowing out the smoke through pursed lips as though the previous conversation had never happened.

My chest rose then fell again. "I just want it to stop."

"So do I," she said, replacing her shades. "But even Blackthorns don't always get what they want."

* * *

Martha pulled up on the double-yellow lines outside of St Ann's Church and let us out of the car before disappearing down the road to park. Lucinda stood outside of Baker and Roberts, peering into the windows with glee at the jewels displayed within. She beckoned me over, so I trudged over from the kerbside to stand next to her, and she tapped my arm to bring my attention to one of the more expensive pieces.

"Tell me, what do you think of that one?" she asked. "It's simply gorgeous, isn't it?"

"Mmm," I murmured, lifting my shoulders.

"Come on, let's just forget all the upset, shall we? I'm sure a nice lunch will perk you up."

I scoffed. "Not hungry."

"Rubbish!" She chortled, prodding my tummy. "I've never known you to pass up food."

I remained silent.

"Fine, well, let's see if there's something in here for you. My treat!"

She swaggered through the double doors, removing her glasses again to greet the doorman as we entered. The manager, Michael, spotted her from across the room and dropped the customer he was with like they were a dead weight. He sprinted over, his arms outstretched to offer a hug, and Lucinda politely patted him on the back before pulling away.

"Mrs Blackthorn, as I live and breathe!" he announced.

"Michael, how the devil are you?" she drawled.

"Really good, really good," he said before turning to me. "And I see you've brought Sofia along with you! To what do I owe the pleasure?"

"I ordered something with Suzanne, didn't I?"

"Sally," he corrected.

"Yes, she said it would be here today, so I'm just picking it up."

"Wonderful!" he cheered, turning over his shoulder. "Sally!" he howled. "Come and assist Mrs Blackthorn!"

Sally dutifully came over and took Lucinda by the hand, leading her to some cabinets at the back.

"Would you like to look at anything, Miss Blackthorn?" Michael asked.

"No," I said, trying my best to smile. "Not today."

Michael peered down at my hands and gasped. "That's a beautiful piece. Where did you get it?"

I raised my hand with a furrowed brow. "The ring?"

"Yes! It's gorgeous—may I?"

I shrugged. "Sure."

I eased it off my finger and placed it in his grasp. He held it out to the light, and his eyes widened.

"I knew it! It's a Kozlov!"

"A what now?"

"He was a Russian designer from the late 1800s," he explained. "He placed a tiny ruby inside the band of every ring he made. They're almost impossible to come by."

I made an uninterested face until a thought crossed my mind. "Is it worth much?"

"A ring like this? It's absolutely priceless."

"What would you give me for it?"

Michael looked like all his Christmases had come at once. "You're looking to sell?"

"If the price is right."

He took a loupe out of his pocket and started inspecting the diamond before letting out an exasperated sigh. "How much?"

I looked over his shoulder at Lucinda standing on the other side of the shop. "I don't think I could let it go for less than four grand."

"Four?" he exclaimed. "Unfortunately, the best I can do is two."

"I thought you said it was priceless?" I asked. "Four."

"Miss Blackthorn, you're killing me here!" He chortled. "The very most I can go to is three."

"Three and a half, and keep your voice down, will you?"

He paused to contemplate, then outstretched his hand. "Deal."

I shook it quickly. "The other thing—no one can find out about this, okay?"

"I assure you, we're very discreet."

"And I need it in cash."

His jaw dropped. "Cash?"

"Yes. Now, preferably."

He laughed as if I had made a joke. "Miss Blackthorn, we aren't some back street pawn shop."

"Forget it, then," I dismissed.

"Wait!" he exclaimed. "We don't have that kind of funds on hand, but I can arrange it for tomorrow, though?"

"Okay," I said, nodding. "Tomorrow morning."

He went to hand me the ring back, but I held my hand up.

"You keep a hold of it. I'll be back," I said, leaning in. "And mum's the word, okay?"

He gave a shallow nod before Lucinda materialised behind him, clutching a Baker and Roberts bag in her grip.

"I've got it!" she sang from behind him. "Have you reconsidered lunch?"

I grinned back at her, baring my teeth. "Sure! Let's eat."

I didn't know what I was going to do. I just knew I needed money to do it. I was going to disappear, somewhere far, far away where even the Blackthorns wouldn't be able to find me.

If I stayed, he would only carry on.

36

THE GOODBYES

SOFIA – BEFORE

By the time Martha got us back, it was early evening. I ran straight to my room, locking the door behind me so I could pack some essentials. I limited myself to one rucksack, with as many clothes as I could cram into it, my unstamped passport, and a few keepsakes that I couldn't leave behind. Anything else that I needed would have to be bought once I picked up the cash for the ring I had sold.

A knock at the door. *Fuck.*

I stuffed my worldly belongings underneath my bed before unlocking the door and blocking the doorway.

"What are you doing in here?" Dad asked, trying to see past me. "I heard clattering."

"Nothing, nothing," I dismissed, glancing over my shoulder. "I'm having a quick tidy up."

"Why? Get one of the maids to do it."

"No, I prefer to do it myself," I said, drumming my fingers on the doorframe.

He narrowed his eyes. "Is something the matter?"

"Of course not!" I exclaimed half-heartedly. "Just tired."

"Come on now, Sofia. I know you," he said gently. "Did something happen on your shopping trip?"

I shook my head.

"Are you sure?"

"Yes!" I cheered as convincingly as I could. "Against all odds, we actually had a nice lunch."

"Oh, lovely," he remarked blandly. "Well, I wish I could've been there."

"Accompanying two women on a shopping trip is your idea of hell, isn't it?"

He chuckled. "Quite, quite."

There was an awkward silence for a few moments as his laughter petered out.

"Anyway, can you come downstairs when you're finished?" he asked. "I have an announcement to make."

"Er—yeah." I smiled. "Sure."

"Splendid!" he said, clapping his hands together. "See you down there."

I waited until he was out of sight before shutting the door and putting my weight against it. I knew that the logistics of disappearing were going to be difficult, but I had totally forgotten about the emotional implications. What I said in my speech at the fundraiser was true—I did owe them everything. Despite suffering for years at their hands, I still had a weird sense of obligation that I just couldn't shake. I mean, God only knows what would've happened to me if they hadn't taken me under their wing.

No, Sofia. Stay strong.

That was the point where I reminded myself that literally anything would be better than being locked away on this estate, patiently waiting for the next bout of abuse and being treated like utter shit by the rest of my supposed family members. I had spent years focusing on the bad, trivialising the pain I was going through by imagining that it could have been worse, but what if it could have been better? I could have had a loving family, friends, freedom, a life beyond reading in my room and living in constant fear.

I took one last look at the rucksack beneath my bed and then started making my way downstairs.

The atmosphere was strange when I walked into the dining room. The entire family was there, huddled around some weird stand with a sheet thrown over it in the corner of the room. Lucas and Penelope gave me the stink eye as I approached, and Lucinda forced a flute of champagne into my hand. They appeared as though they had been celebrating something, but I knew better. Whatever was concealed beneath that thin cotton wasn't good.

"What's all this?" I asked.

"Your mother and I have come to a decision, and I think you're going to love it," Dad announced.

I looked at Lucinda for direction. "What?"

She didn't say anything. She just swallowed mouthfuls of champagne like it was the only thing keeping her upright.

"Perhaps it would be easier if I showed you…" Dad began, whipping off the sheet.

I almost dropped my glass when I saw what was hidden below. It was the Blackthorn Foundation logo, but not as I remembered it. One word had been added: Sofia.

"*The Sofia Blackthorn Foundation*," Dad declared. "It has quite the ring to it, doesn't it?"

My eyes flicked over to my siblings, utter contempt staring back at me. "I don't understand."

"It's obvious, isn't it?" Lucinda drawled. "We're renaming the foundation in your honour, and we want you to be the face of it."

I turned to Dad. "That's… fantastic."

"It will mean much more responsibility, of course: speeches, dinners, benefits…" he listed.

"And there's the other thing, Richie," Lucinda prompted.

"Ahh, yes!" Dad said with excitement. "We want to take it international."

The glass nearly cracked in my hand. "International?"

"Just think of all the good we could do if we set up Sofia Blackthorn Foundation group homes in other countries! Starting with Europe, and then, who knows?"

I choked up. "Yeah," I uttered. "That's amazing."

"We can start looking at new sites in the next few weeks. How does spending a few months travelling across Europe alone with your old man sound?"

No. Fuck no. Over my dead body.

"It sounds great," I remarked, my hand vibrating.

"Perfect!" he enthused, raising his glass. "To new beginnings!"

"To new beginnings," everyone but me repeated.

I sipped a bit of champagne for appearances' sake, but Dad leaned forward and tipped the glass, so I ended up downing the whole thing. He grabbed the bottle to top me up, but there was no more than a drop left inside.

"I'll just grab another bottle," he said, moving towards the door before stopping. "Where is it kept again?"

"Richie, you really are useless, aren't you?" Lucinda jested as she linked his arm and escorted him out.

Lucas and Penelope dropped the charade as soon as they left the room, exchanging a look before placing their empty glasses down on the dining table.

"It looks like you're getting everything you want," Lucas remarked, getting in my face. "Well fucking done."

"You think I *want* to do it?" I laughed cynically. "I can't think of anything worse!"

"Bullshit," Penelope spat. "Was it his idea, or yours?"

"His!" I exclaimed, stepping back. "I didn't even know about it until just then."

"Tell him you aren't doing it," Lucas instructed. "Make up some excuse."

"You think I have a say in it? Or anything, for that matter?"

"I don't give a fuck, okay? Just turn it down."

"I—I can't," I admitted. "He won't let me."

Penelope scoffed, pacing around on the spot before turning to Lucas. "She shouldn't even have our last name, and now they're naming a fucking foundation after her? It's beyond a joke."

"I didn't ask for this," I insisted.

Penelope narrowed her eyes. "You do know the *real* reason they adopted you, right?"

I didn't answer.

"Your fucking skin colour." She chuckled. "You're nothing but the diversity hire!"

"Fuck you," I hissed.

"It's true! You're just someone they can dust off at these fancy dinners to make sure we don't look like massive racists. It's the same reason they picked Jada for the kitchens."

Rage piled up inside me, begging to be released.

"While we're spitting home truths," I began, stepping forward, "do you know why they picked me over you?"

Lucas and Penelope glanced at each other before shrugging in unison.

"Because you're a jealous, pissed-up slapper who can barely string a sentence together."

"How *dare* you stand there and—"

"And Aubrey?" I interrupted. "You do realise he's spoken for, yeah?"

She pressed her lips into a thin line.

"I wonder what Camilla would think if she knew her bestie was fucking her boyfriend?"

"Alright, sis!" Lucas remarked. "No need to get personal!"

"And you!" I shouted. "You're just a coked-up man-child who thinks more with his dick than his head."

"It's certainly big enough," he remarked, making Penelope and me gag slightly.

"I've heard you and Ellie, you know? Going at it."

He frowned, sniggering. "So, what?"

"I've had farts that have lasted longer."

He chortled. "These are bloody brilliant! Did you prepare them beforehand?"

"Just telling it how I see it."

The door swung open again, and Dad strode back in with Lucinda, popping the cork of a fresh bottle, but I couldn't face them again. I pushed past them, muttering that I needed the toilet, and headed straight for the kitchen. Jada was inside, lifting some trays out of the oven and whistling a merry song. I thumped the door shut behind me and fell into it, giving her a fright.

"Sofia!" she gasped. "I nearly jumped out of my bloody skin!"

I didn't reply. I just took a few steps forward, staring into space.

"What's the matter, Sofia?" she asked.

"I need to get out of here," I announced.

Her brow dropped, and she threw the trays she was carrying onto the table before rushing over.

"What on earth are you talking about?" she asked.

"Dad—Mr Blackthorn—he wants me to take over the foundation."

"That's good news, isn't it?"

"No," I said, trembling. "I lied to you."

Her shoulders slumped. "About what?"

"He *does* hurt me," I admitted. "He *does* make me do things I don't want to do."

"Like what?" she whispered.

My bottom lip started quivering, so she reached out and clutched my arm. "He—"

"What did he do?" she interrupted.

"He—he's been," I stopped to take a breath. "He comes into my room at night and—"

I didn't get a chance to finish. She wrapped her arms around me and pulled me in tight.

"Whatever happened, it wasn't your fault, okay, sweetheart?" she said, rocking me softly.

"I—I just want it to stop!" I blubbered.

Without warning, she instantly turned on her heel, raced over to the knife block, and selected the biggest one.

"Jada, no!" I pleaded, running over to hold her back.

"I'll kill him!" she bellowed.

"No," I said, my voice coming out calmer than expected. "I just need to leave. I'm not dragging anyone else into this mess."

She tentatively lowered the blade, her arm pulsing. "When?"

"Now. I've come to say goodbye."

"Do they know?"

"No," I said quickly. "And it needs to stay that way."

"Where are you going?"

"Don't know, don't care," I said, leaning on the table. "I just need to be gone."

She pulled out a locket from underneath her tunic and spun it around to unclip it, then hung it over my neck.

"What's this?" I asked, holding it up.

"Take it. For luck."

She grabbed my face with both hands to give me a kiss on the forehead and then ran over to the hob. She put an empty frying pan on each ring before splitting a whole bottle of oil between them, then put it on full heat before untying her tunic at the waist.

"What are you doing?" I asked.

"You'll need a distraction, won't you?" she said without turning around.

My chest rattled. "Jada—thank you."

"Why are you still here? Go!"

I did as she asked. I raced over to the door leading into the hall, stopping for a moment to watch Jada fly through the service entrance. The oil was already lightly smoking when I left for the hallway, so I sprinted up the stairs and to my room, my knees skidding on the carpet as I dived to grab my bag. I leapt back to my feet, plucked Lucas's keys from the dressing table, put them in my pocket, and burst out of my bedroom door. But I immediately ploughed into something.

Mr Blackthorn's chest.

"Where the hell do you think you're going?" he asked, his eyes locked on my rucksack.

"Nowhere," I blurted out, breathless.

"Then what's with the bag?"

"This?" I said, lifting it slightly. "I, er, I don't—"

"Hand it over."

I offered it out, my arm trembling. He took it from my grasp and started pulling items of clothing out at random.

"Are you *leaving* us?"

The veins were throbbing in my neck. I thought about lying, but I would rather have died than spend another moment in that house.

"Yes," I said firmly.

Pure wrath ignited like petrol in his eyes. "Why?"

"Because, Dad," I began, squaring my shoulders, "you're a rapist."

He dropped the bag, clutching his chest as if I had caused him great offence. "Sofia, I have never—"

"Don't," I interrupted. "Don't do that."

His arm fell by his side. "Listen to me! I have given you *everything*. Everything! You are mine to do with as I please."

"No," I said, gritting my teeth. "Not anymore."

"You have an obligation to this family! To me!" he threw his hands in the air. "You can't just run away whenever the mood suits you!"

"I'm getting out of here tonight," I said, stepping forward. "And you can't stop me."

He scowled and grabbed me by the arm. "I think you should spend some time back in your old room."

I tried fighting against his grip, but he tightened it and started dragging me down the hall.

"Let go of me!" I wailed.

"No!" he shouted, yanking me forward. "Never!"

We reached the top of the stairs, and I held onto the bannister for dear life. He struggled to pull me any further until he managed to pry my grip from the handrail. I screamed as he forced me down a few steps. If he succeeded in getting me down there, I would never see daylight again. It would just be me and him. Forever. That thought gave me strength, and I managed to break free, but he grabbed me by the hair a second later, yanking me down one step at a time.

"Look what you're making me do!" he bellowed. "Do you think I enjoy this?"

"You're hurting me!" I shrieked.

I heard Lucas's keys jangling in my pocket, so I reached into it, put a key between each of my fingers, then swiped at him. The first strike missed entirely. So did the second. But the third left a slash across his cheekbone, and he finally released me. He lost his footing in the commotion and started waving his hands around to keep his balance. His right foot slid off the step, so I helped him down the rest, shoving him with all my strength. He tumbled down the marble steps into the foyer below, cracking his head on the hard tile.

"Shit," I said, racing after him.

I dropped by his side, placing my hand on his chest. It was still moving, barely, but I didn't have time to do anything, one way or the other. The smoke alarm from the kitchen began blaring. I checked down the hall and saw smoke billowing out of the kitchen door. Lucinda stepped out to see what the disturbance was, and we locked eyes.

"Sofia?" she mouthed.

Run.

I sprinted for the front door, already pressing the car key to open Lucas's Range Rover. It chirped as I stepped outside, and I looked over my shoulder to see my siblings crowded around Dad on the tiles. Lucinda and Harris were making a beeline for me, so I dashed over to the car and hopped inside. I just about got the doors locked before Lucinda started bashing on the glass.

"How could you?" she screeched.

I mashed the pad of my thumb onto the start engine button and welded my foot to the floor, spitting gravel at Harris and Lucinda as I sped down the driveway. Harris was aiming his shotgun directly at me, and I kept my eyes locked on him in the rearview mirror as they gave chase on foot. I had never driven the car in the dark before, so I faced the road, hitting random buttons to try to get the lights on. Before I managed it, a massive bang at the front of the vehicle startled me, so I slammed on the brakes.

I opened the door to poke my head out, and my heart was in my throat when I saw her.

Jada. On the ground. Bloodied and completely still.

I didn't take a breath until she did. I jumped out and took a single step towards her, but she lifted her palm up to stop me. Lucinda and Harris were gaining on us, yelling something I couldn't quite hear over the ringing in my ears. Jada tapped her heart and pointed to the gates she'd just opened for me, letting her arm flop down by her side as her eyes shut.

I tapped mine back, got in the car, and gunned it through the open gates.

I was finally free, but at what cost?

PART FIVE

"COST"

37

THE STRANGER

ROBYN

I dropped Sofia's diary to the floor. It was her. She was the one who turned my life upside down.

The overriding feeling was fury: an unfathomable rage that could only be quelled by wrapping my fingers around Sofia's throat and not letting go. She took my mother's legs from her. She took my future from me. She traded our lives for her own and did so without even a second thought before riding off into the sunset. I mean, she just *left* her there, totally at the mercy of that disgusting family. It was a miracle they didn't finish her off there and then.

But my anger was misdirected.

Physically, there was no question that Sofia set off the chain of events that devastated my existence. That being said, what choice did she have? She was just trying to escape the suffering they inflicted on her. Besides, it's not like she set out to hurt Mum. If her diary was to be trusted, it seemed like she loved Mum just as much as I did. What was really getting to me was that Mum gave literally everything to make sure that Sofia got away that night, but in all the years of struggle and misery that followed, she never once uttered Sofia's name. Maybe Mum did it to protect her. She tried protecting me, too, but I was too pig-headed to listen and ended up in the exact same mess.

I picked up Harris's shotgun and broke the barrel open. There were two shells in the chamber: one for each of the surviving Blackthorns. I snapped it back shut and made for the cottage door, but it creaked open as soon as my hand touched it. The masked stranger was standing there, with a shotgun of her own, her black clothes now covered in soil and dirt. She held out her hand for my weapon, but I clutched it tighter and refused to give it up.

"Hand it over," she instructed.

"Nope," I said, squaring my shoulders. "I'm going to finish this."

"Not until we've had a chat."

"I'm done talking, *Sofia*."

She let out a muffled chuckle, pushing past me to drop her own firearm on the top of the coffee table. She plonked herself down on one of the sofas with a groan, then began to remove her muddied gloves and boots. My pulse ticked when she dropped her hood, but instead of Sofia's red hair like I was expecting, it was bleached blonde. The shotgun slid out of my grip, and the butt slammed into my shoe when she took off her mask.

"Ellie?" I gasped, propping Harris's gun up in the corner. "What the actual fuck?"

"*Surprise…*" she sang, scraping her hair back.

My face was straight, calm even, but inside, I was freaking out.

"Look, I'm sure you have questions—"

"More than a few, yeah," I interrupted, jaw still agape.

She groaned, bending over to pick up Sofia's diary from the table. "Did you read it?"

I nodded once, unable to avert my gaze.

"This diary—it's all I've got left of her," Ellie admitted.

I stood and peered at her for a moment without speaking. The look on her face wasn't one of someone who'd lost an acquaintance, a friend, or even a potential sister-in-law. It was far deeper than that.

"Who was she to you?" I asked.

She shrugged indifferently. "A friend."

"Bollocks!" I exclaimed, laughing. "You wouldn't do all of this for just a 'friend.'"

Her eyes flicked to me before they went back to the diary. "I would, and I did."

"No, it's more than that." I inched closer. "You were in *love* with her, weren't you?"

She took a beat to answer. "Yes."

"That's why you stayed with Lucas, wasn't it? You were waiting for her to come back."

She lifted a shoulder.

"Where did she go?" I asked.

"That's why I'm here. To find out."

"She got away, though, didn't she? The diary said so."

"Apparently."

"So, you've not heard from her since?"

"Once," she said, placing the diary beside her. "One lousy phone call about six years ago, totally out of the blue."

"What happened to her, then?" I asked, taking the seat across from her.

"She went on the run."

"Yeah—where?"

She looked annoyed. "Does it matter?"

"It does to me," I shot back.

"Why?"

I hesitated, trying to centre myself. "I just want to know that Mum didn't sacrifice everything for nothing."

Ellie let loose a long sigh, staring into space as she began fiddling with her hoodie drawstrings.

"I don't know the specifics, but Sofia's face was plastered on the front of every newspaper, so she hid," she explained. "For the first year or so, she slept in shop doorways, underneath bus-stop canopies, anywhere she could find. She begged and stole just to feed herself and get as far away from Manchester as she could."

"So, the rich girl had to rough it for a while?" I mocked. "Boo-hoo."

Ellie didn't seem to take offence. "It was better than her staying another second in that house."

I crossed my arms. "She can't have survived on the streets all that time."

"No. She met a nice family and worked on their farm for a while: picking fruit and mucking out stables."

"Why did she leave?"

"The Blackthorns," she said, rolling her eyes. "The farmers discovered Sofia's true identity and saw the reward money, so she had to move on. That's why she returned to Manchester."

"She came back for you?"

Ellie nodded gravely. "She planned to pick up the cash from the ring, use it for a couple of fake passports, and disappear."

"Did you say yes?"

"Of course, I did." She closed her fists. "She told me to meet her in St Ann's Square."

The realisation hit me like a smack in the face.

"I don't believe it," I muttered.

"What?"

"It was you!" I laughed despite myself. "*You* robbed Baker and Roberts!"

"Not me," she admitted, unable to meet my gaze. "Sofia."

"Why?" I barked.

"She tried collecting what they owed her, but that dickhead manager refused to cough it up. He threatened to go to Lucinda and blow the lid on—"

"So, she came back a few hours later and just robbed the place? Who the fuck does that?"

"She was desperate," she grumbled. "The Blackthorns were closing in, and she had to get the hell out."

I closed my eyes and tilted my head back. "I spent six years in fucking prison for what she did."

Ellie stopped what she was doing and squatted in front of me, trying to grab my hands. I didn't let her.

"I'm sorry," she murmured.

"Why the hell did you tell me to go to that damn jewellery shop in the first place?" I yelled. "You could've picked anywhere else."

"I didn't know what she was going to do, did I? We arranged to meet there and then run away."

"But you dragged me into your fucking mess! You could've just taken off!"

"You twisted my arm, and I wanted to say goodbye."

"You could've done that at the hearing, Ellie. You could've cleared my name."

"No, I couldn't," she said firmly. "If Sofia were still alive, I would've led the Blackthorns right to her. Besides, if they found out about me and her, they'd have killed us both."

"So, you never saw her again?"

"No," she said bitterly. "She just vanished off the face of the earth."

"Well, it looks like she fucked both of us over, doesn't it?"

"Something must've happened to her, Robyn. She wouldn't have left without letting me know where she was going."

"She *ruined* my life, El!"

"I know she did."

"She got me put in prison, and she—" I paused to get my breath back. "And she crippled my mum."

She dropped back with a sigh. "I know, and I'm so sorry, Robyn, but Sofia never meant to hurt her."

I leaned forward, glaring at the ground in defeat. "I know she didn't."

"Jada saved her life that night. If she hadn't opened the gates, Harris and Lucinda would've caught up with Sofia and—"

"I know," I whispered.

"Sofia loved your mum," she mused. "She was the only one who made living in that house bearable."

"That's Mum," I sang, unable to hide the sorrow. "Always putting others before herself."

Her eyes lifted to the ceiling. "I should've been there that night. Maybe I could've helped."

"We all have regrets."

We didn't speak for almost five minutes. I just glowered at Harris's macabre skull collection until a thought popped into my head that was impossible to ignore.

"The night we met at that cocktail bar, you knew who I was, didn't you?" I asked.

She took too long to answer. "No."

"Bullshit! You knew what happened to my mum! You must've made the connection."

"Okay, fine," she conceded. "I knew who you were."

"So, what the fuck was that then? You were just using me for information?"

"Oh, please!" she dismissed. "You were doing the exact same to me. Don't tell me you weren't planning to get close to us so you could find out what happened to Jada yourself."

She was right, but it didn't mean I had to like it.

"You know what?" I said in total disbelief. "You're both just as bad as *them*."

She inhaled through her nose. "Please, don't say that, Robyn."

"You are. Either you or Sofia could've come forward and fixed everything, but you were both too busy saving your own hides."

"How can you even say that?"

I scoffed. "It's the truth!"

She jumped to her feet. "Do you not think I felt guilty? Huh?"

"You can't have done. You wouldn't have let me rot or sent me right into the Blackthorns' arms if you did."

She clutched her elbow, looking me up and down. "I needed an ally. If you were on the inside, maybe you'd find out what happened to her, and I'd get answers too."

"Fuck me, how could I have been so stupid?" I asked, rubbing my temples. "You planted the ring in my pocket that night you dropped me off."

She pinched the bridge of her nose. "When I hugged you. I thought it would pique your curiosity and you'd start digging."

"Well, it worked a treat. I nearly got myself killed over it."

"I was watching you pretty much the entire time, okay? I wouldn't have let that happen."

"They're total maniacs, El! It's a wonder I'm still alive!"

Her face hardened. "Don't make out like you're totally innocent in this."

I arched an eyebrow. "What's that supposed to mean?"

"I know about Lucas, alright?" she said.

My blood ran cold. "What about him?"

"An overdose, eh? Nasty way to go."

"He was poisoned, remember?" I corrected. "Elena did it."

"No, she didn't." She smirked, pointing at me. "You did."

I blinked.

"Peanuts in his cocaine?" She chortled. "I'm not mad. It was inspired."

"You don't know what—"

"Save it," she interrupted. "I saw you."

I narrowed my eyes. "You were in the kitchen?"

"Only because I had the same idea. I had to do something to rattle them, but you beat me to the punch, didn't you?"

I pressed my tongue into my cheek. "What did you see?"

"I saw you grinding a big old bag of nuts up with a rolling pin in the pantry," she explained. "There are just a few things I'm confused about, though."

"What?" I mouthed.

"Firstly, why did you sprinkle some in the pestle and mortar?"

I touched my face. "Elena used that every day, so I knew it would be filled with her prints. I needed to get her off the estate. They'd have killed her otherwise."

"So you rang the police to cart her off?"

"Uh-huh."

"Secondly, how did you get it in his drugs?"

"You're kidding, right?" I laughed. "That degenerate left it out in his room for all to see."

"Lastly," she began, moving closer, "why did you kill him? Because he tried raping you?"

"No, actually," I said, my eyes going cold. "He was just a piece of shit."

Ellie smirked. "So was Penelope."

"That was you?" I gasped.

"She came out by the lake, pissed as a fart and crying about some bloke. It was an opportunity too perfect to miss."

"So, what, you just *drowned* her?"

Her face was scarily composed. "Trust me, that bitch had it coming."

"Why?"

"She made Sofia's entire childhood a fucking misery. She was an ungrateful, spiteful, little witch."

"Funny, Penelope said the same thing about Sofia, word for word."

"Then, Mr Blackthorn. He chose the night Penelope died, of all nights, to finally start doing to you what he'd been doing to Sofia."

I put two and two together. "You stopped him."

She raised her finger and thumb in the air. "I missed the fucker by about three inches."

"Harris and Martha covered it up, you know."

"Of course they did—it's what they do," she said, spitting on the floor. "That's why they had to go next."

I wasn't even surprised anymore. "How did you do it?"

"Straight-up strangled Martha," she admitted. "She watched Sofia grow up in a fucking prison and didn't lift a finger to stop it. She deserved what she got, through and through."

I simply raised my eyebrows in agreement.

"You already know what happened to Harris. If I hadn't pulled the trigger when I did—"

"Then I'd be buried alongside Martha."

"I've been protecting you the whole time. You just didn't know it."

I didn't know what to do. I was so angry with Ellie for all that she'd done, but at the same time, I owed her my life. If she hadn't taken me under her wing all those years ago, I probably still would've found a way to worm my way into the Blackthorn family, so I couldn't completely blame her for that, either. As for Sofia, I still couldn't imagine the true horror of what she'd been through, even though I'd just read about it. She did what she had to, and like I always said, I was just in the wrong place at the wrong time.

"Anyway, if you want to march back into that house on your own, fine, but I have something for you first," she said, reaching into the back of her hoodie to undo a chain around her neck.

"What is it?"

"See for yourself," she said, balling it up in her hand before tossing it at me.

"Mum's locket," I muttered.

"It was in Mr Blackthorn's safe, along with the diary and the ring."

"You don't think she's still alive, do you?"

"I don't know." She peered down. "Maybe, but probably not."

I remembered the locket from when I was a kid, but after her accident, I never saw her wear it again, assuming that it had just got lost or she'd stopped bothering to put it on. I opened the tiny clasp, and the picture of Mum holding me on the day I was born was still inside.

"She gave it to Sofia for luck, remember?" she said. "You should have it."

"Why did my mum give it to her?"

"Take out the picture."

I did as she asked and started picking at the corner of the tiny photograph with my fingernail. After a few moments, I managed to release it, but I still didn't understand what she was getting at.

"Turn it over," she instructed.

I did as she suggested and, to my surprise, three letters were written on the back in my mum's handwriting: J, R, and S.

"J: Jada. R: Robyn. S—"

"Sofia," Ellie butted in. "I think Jada was her mother, too."

38

THE TUNNELS

ROBYN

The locket became a lead weight in my hand, my head absolutely banging as I desperately tried to make sense of everything that I'd learned. I had answers to questions that had plagued me for weeks, and others for years, but in truth, I felt even more clueless than when I started. If Sofia was indeed my sister, why the hell didn't Mum tell me about her? More confusing than that, on what planet would she allow the Blackthorns, of all people, to lock her up like some kind of pet? The only two people who knew the full truth were holed up in their mansion, probably waiting for me to be stupid enough to come asking for it.

"I don't understand," I uttered. "Why would Mum keep this from me?"

"To protect you," Ellie said firmly. "To protect both of you."

"From what?"

"The truth."

I took a moment to collect my thoughts. "He must've had something over Mum. There's no other explanation."

"Maybe," she said, tossing a rucksack onto Ethelbert's grave and rifling through it.

I craned my neck, trying to peer into the bag. "What are you planning exactly?"

She grabbed a few shotgun shells out of her bag, counted them, and put them back in. "I'm going to make them tell us the truth."

I swallowed. "And then what?"

"I'm going to kill them," she said matter-of-factly before pivoting to me with an odd expression. "Bitch, I thought that was obvious."

Between us, four people had already lost their lives, however justified any of it might have felt. Did systematically killing the Blackthorns make us just as bad as them? We were either murderers or heroes, but I couldn't decide which. I had no doubt in my mind that Lucas earned his death. Just from Ellie's reaction to Penelope, I was pretty sure she deserved it too. But Martha? Harris? They were just following orders.

Sofia suffered so much at the hands of the Blackthorns, but so did I. Not just the months that I had been working there, but for years before and after what they put their so-called daughter through. Ellie had endured her fair share of hardship too, forced to cosy up to Lucas for years on the off chance his sister would show up. Then there were the other girls, the ones I didn't know the names of, who Mr Blackthorn had recruited to play his wicked games with. They deserved some form of justice, too—we all did.

I placed my hand on her arm. "We weren't alone, you know."

Ellie froze. "What do you mean?"

"Elena told me before she got arrested. Mr Blackthorn has been recruiting girls who look like me and Sofia for years."

She pulled a face. "Why?"

"I think he was trying to replace her." I shrugged. "I was next, clearly."

"Even more reason he needs to die, then." Ellie carried on sorting through her rucksack. "They aren't going to stop unless we stop them."

I rushed over to grab Harris's shotgun, but there was a niggling voice in the back of my head telling me to drop it and run, and it sounded like Mum.

"What about the police?" I suggested.

She sniggered. "What about them?"

"We could tell them everything. They'd arrest them both."

"And what about you? Are you honestly that eager to go back to prison?"

"No, but they deserve to pay for what they did."

Ellie stopped what she was doing and swivelled her head to me, folding her arms across her chest.

"Honey, you do realise they'd never see the inside of a jail cell, right?" she asked.

"But there must be so much evidence and—"

"What does that matter?" she rejected. "They know *everyone.* They've spent their lives collecting important people and gathering dirt on them. One phone call, and all that so-called evidence vanishes in a puff of smoke."

"No—there has to be some other way."

"I've spent the best part of a decade trying to think of one. Trust me, there isn't."

"Believe me, I want them dead just as much as you do."

She sneered. "I highly doubt that."

"You know what they did to me, El," I reminded.

"The tip of the iceberg…" she remarked, barely listening.

"Oh, God, just stop, will you?" I shouted.

Ellie zipped her bag up and threw it over her shoulder, pressing her lips together.

"Can we just *try* to do the right thing?" I asked. "For once."

She juddered her head. "It isn't going to work."

I puffed out my cheeks. "It might not, but we should at least attempt it, shouldn't we?"

She sniggered, eyeballing the shotgun with desire. "My way is cleaner."

"We're still going in there armed to the teeth, but we can do this without shedding any more blood."

"Not possible."

I widened my eyes. "Do you think Sofia would want you going back in there?"

Ellie shot me a dangerous look. "Listen, babe," she began, shuffling forward. "I saved your life. That makes us even."

"So, what?" I argued.

"You can't just show up at the last minute and start barking orders at me. This is my show."

"They aren't worth throwing the rest of your life away for, though! You must see that."

"Robyn," she began, her eyes cold. "It's too late."

"Why?" I challenged, putting my hand on the shotgun before she could pick it up.

"Lucas, Penelope, Martha, Harris—they're already dead."

"We did what we had to, but we can put a stop to it right now. It's what Sofia would've wanted."

Ellie paused to think for a minute as she put her gloves back on. "Fine," she grunted.

I breathed a sigh of relief. "Thank—"

"But if shit goes sideways, I'm going to start blasting, deal?"

I gave her a thin smile. "Deal."

"Well then, *killer*. What's the big plan, huh? Stroll in the front door and wave a gun in each of their faces?"

I bit my bottom lip, slightly mortified that I couldn't think of anything better. "Something like that."

"You'd be dead before you make it up the steps."

I shrank slightly. "What are we going to do then?"

"Well, for a start, we won't be going in through the front door," she remarked.

Leaving me confused, Ellie walked over to the corner of the room and lifted a small hatch built into the floor. I walked over to inspect it and saw a thin, stone shaft, only lit by the candles in the cottage, with a dozen or so steel rungs fitted into the wall, rusted and disappearing into the darkness. As I squatted down to get a closer look, Ellie dropped her rucksack into the opening and tossed the shotgun over her shoulder before climbing a few steps down.

"You coming?" she asked.

I paused before grabbing Harris's shooter from the corner. "Lead the way."

She continued her descent, and I followed. I'd been down in the tunnels before when she showed me Sofia's old room, but much closer to the house. This far out, there wasn't any lighting, and the old stone tunnels were leaking from the ceiling, pouring water onto the porous ground below. Before I could ask, Ellie produced a flashlight from her bag and illuminated the passageway, slowly walking down it as I trailed a few feet behind her. To my horror, a rat scurried past, and I embarrassingly let out a little squeal as it disappeared in an opening between two bricks.

"You get used to those," she remarked over her shoulder.

"What else is in your bag of tricks, anyway?" I asked.

"Stuff," she grunted, lifting her shoulders.

"Do you fancy being any more specific?"

"Shells, a flick-knife, rope, some lighter fluid and matches," she listed, stopping to turn to me. "Is that specific enough for you?"

"You're going to torch the place?"

She exhaled through her nose. "I haven't decided yet."

"I thought we were just going to get answers and then ring the police?"

"It doesn't hurt to be prepared, does it?" she asked, already walking off before hearing the answer.

"I suppose."

"If you're dead set on playing *Nancy Drew,* we'd better check Mr Blackthorn's study. He keeps everything in the safe."

"You have the combination?"

"1807," she recited.

"Hey, that's my birthday!" I babbled.

She stopped again, waiting for the penny to drop.

"Oh yeah," I said, wrinkling my nose. "Fuck—that's going to take some getting used to."

We continued for at least ten minutes, dodging falling water and more rodents. Once we made it underneath the main house and turned a corner, Ellie turned her flashlight off as the dim sconces lit the rest of the way. She stopped outside the hatch leading to the laundry cupboard, which is when the gravity of the situation finally hit me. What the hell was going to happen when we poked our heads upstairs? Were we really going to do this?

"You aren't getting cold feet, are you?" she asked.

"No," I said quickly before allowing the shotgun strap to slide down my arm. "Maybe a little," I admitted.

"Listen, I'm sorry about before, okay? The truth is, I need you. There are two of them, and two of us."

"I just don't know whether—"

"We need answers." She grabbed my hand. "And we'll get them together."

"Okay."

"Whatever happens, we stick together, alright?"

I closed my eyes and tipped my head.

She placed a single finger to her lips and took the shotgun off her shoulder, using the muzzle to push the hatch open. The room above was pitch-black, and she helped me through the opening before peeking through the tiny crack in the door and into the corridor. After she was satisfied the coast was clear, she slowly made her way through, the shotgun aloft, and beckoned me to follow. I kept my gun low, trailing a few metres behind. I could hear the front door smacking against the façade in the wind, letting in a draught so cold it made me shiver. The doors to the Blackthorn library stood half-open, the softest glow seeping out into the corridor like the room itself was alive. Ellie hovered beside me, finger trembling at the trigger, but neither of us spoke. We didn't need to. The silence said everything.

I pushed first.

The only light source was the roaring fire, casting long, distorted shadows across the thousands of books lining the walls. Lucinda was sitting beside the fire, slouched in one of those ridiculous wingback chairs like she belonged on the cover of some glossy magazine, except she wasn't immaculate anymore.

She was caked in blood.

Not splattered, either; soaked. Her dress, her forearms, even the delicate chain resting on her collarbones. Her usually perfect hair hung limp and matted against one cheek. She glanced over her shoulder at us with eyes that had seen something unspeakable and hadn't fully returned from it, then turned back to the fire, glugging directly from a bottle with tears ripe in her eyes.

"Lucinda? What have you done?" I uttered in total disbelief.

She sniggered. "Something I should've done a long, *long* time ago."

39

THE NIGHTCAP

ROBYN

Lucinda lifted herself out of the chair and casually walked over to the bar to start making herself a drink whilst Ellie and I gawped at her in shock. In all my time on the estate, I'd barely seen the lady of the house with a single hair out of place, yet there she was, looking fresh from the slaughterhouse and not bothered in the slightest. Ellie kept her gun trained on her, delicately dropping her rucksack to the floor as Lucinda grabbed three glasses. She wrapped her crimson-stained fingers around the largest and poured herself a healthy measure of gin before hovering the neck of the bottle above the others.

"Can I interest you ladies in a nightcap?" she drawled.

"No," I uttered in disbelief. "No, thank you."

"Elizabeth? How about you?"

"It's Ellie," she corrected. "And no. I'm good."

"Suit yourselves," Lucinda said, adding another dash to hers.

I let my shotgun fall and set it down beside the mantelpiece, but I didn't stray too far from it. Lucinda had blatantly lost her last marble.

"Well? Where is he?" I asked.

Her lips twitched. "Which *he* would that be, Robyn?"

"You know damn well," I said, my teeth gritting.

Lucinda inhaled slowly, letting it sit in her lungs like poison before releasing it. "I'm afraid Mr Blackthorn won't be joining us."

"Is he—"

"Oh yes," she interrupted, taking a drink. "As a doornail."

Ellie took a half-step back, but I held my ground, jaw agape. "You killed him."

"I had no choice," she said, wincing after she took a sip. "Wow! That has a real bite to it."

"What—what did you do?" I stammered.

"I drove this through his chest." She casually lifted a blood-tainted letter opener from the bar and waved it in the air. "Or what was left of it."

"You murdered him because of what he tried doing to me?"

"You think a lot about yourself, don't you?" she exclaimed, almost chuckling.

"Did you?" I demanded.

"Please! Do you seriously think I'd ruin a perfectly good outfit on your account?"

"Why, then?" I shouted.

"He attacked me," she began with an air of nonchalance. "I was only defending myself."

"Why would he—"

"Let's say he took umbrage at my last order to Harris and leave it at that," she cut in, baring her teeth after the next nip of gin.

My gut clenched. "What order?"

Her eyes glimmered with something between pride and shame. "To have you killed, dear."

I blew my fringe out of my face, rocking my head from side to side.

"Oh, don't look so sore about it, Robyn," she drawled. "It wasn't personal. Not for me, at least."

"Not personal?" I barked. "You ordered my death!"

"And I paid the price for it," she snapped. "Richie came at me in the study like a rabid dog, ranting about loyalty and insubordination. I'd only just finished my drink when he had me by the throat." Her hand drifted to her neck, fingers brushing an invisible bruise. "So, I improvised."

"Because he found out you went behind his back?" I pressed.

"Yes," she said, swirling her drink.

"Well, that was clearly a mistake, wasn't it?" I remarked.

"Quite." She raised her brow in agreement. "I assume your friend here dealt with Harris before he could complete his duties?"

"I did," Ellie replied.

"A crying shame," she said, almost sullen. "He was an exemplary gamekeeper."

"Hey! Focus!" I said, clicking my fingers in her face. "Why would Mr Blackthorn attack *you* because of *me*?"

A muscle in her jaw ticked. "Richie never liked decisions being made without his say-so. Especially decisions regarding his projects."

A cold shiver crept up my spine. "Projects?"

Her gaze swept over me with disdain. "You."

"I don't understand."

"Of course you don't," she sighed. "He planned to lock you downstairs until your attitude adjusted."

A lump grew in my throat. "What for?"

"He wished to replace *her* with you, if you can believe it. Obviously, I couldn't allow that to happen."

"Replace who?" Ellie whispered, although we both knew.

"Sofia," Lucinda said plainly.

I exhaled through my nose in frustration, but Ellie's patience had already worn away.

"Enough of your bloody games!" she ordered. "We're here for answers!"

Lucinda looked confused. "What about?"

"Sofia!" she spat.

Lucinda took a minute for the penny to drop and suddenly started smirking. "You and Sofia?"

Ellie's grip on the shotgun wavered slightly as she bobbed her head.

"Well, that is a surprise," Lucinda remarked before her face turned. "Disgusting, but a surprise nonetheless."

Ellie clicked the safety off, so I touched her arm and shot her a stern look. It was apparent that our plan was already derailed, so I reconsidered my earlier position and walked over to the bar, perching myself on a stool.

"On second thoughts, Mrs Blackthorn," I began, leaning in, "I think I will take that drink."

Lucinda raised her brow and set the letter opener down to pour me a drink. I swilled it back without a second thought. She was right: it did have a hell of a kick to it.

"So," I started, setting the glass down with a tiny clack. "Did you do to Sofia what you tried doing to me? Have her killed?"

A thin crack formed in her composure. "I have no idea what you're—"

"We know about the abuse, Lucinda," I interjected. "And we also know you covered it up."

She gritted her teeth, ogling the letter opener. I slid it down the end of the bar with the back of my hand before she got any bright ideas.

"Why must everything be about that wretched child?" she hissed.

"Because you *made* it all about her," I spat. "Your husband's obsession, your greed—you both brought all this on yourselves."

She tittered. "I didn't want anything to do with her."

"Then why did you keep her here? Huh?" I probed, gripping the bar. "Caged up like a fucking animal?"

"I was protecting the family!" she snarled, taking a swig. "If word got out about what Richie was up to—"

"Then you'd lose everything."

She gave a weak nod. "I hated what he was doing, but what other choice did I have?"

"For a start, you could've come clean and done the right thing for once in your miserable life."

"And watch the life I'd built for myself burn to ashes? For the sake of a pathetic runt like her?" She chortled. "Don't be so fatuous."

"You could've protected her! Put a stop to it!"

Her face turned. "I tried, but she was too stubborn to listen."

I shook my head in doubt. "How, exactly?"

"I thought if I could keep her close and make her loyal to the family, then I could shield her from the worst parts of him." She stared down into her glass. "Keep her quiet and him contained."

"You were grooming her," I said. "You were fucking grooming her and enabling him."

"Do you seriously blame me for my husband's proclivities?"

"Proclivities?" I echoed. "He raped her, Lucinda. Repeatedly."

Lucinda clicked her tongue, shaking her head as though using the word rape was an insult. She leaned on the bar too, spreading her arms at a shoulder's width before looking me dead in the eyes.

"It wasn't rape," she announced. "She practically begged for it."

Ellie swiped the glasses off the bar with her shotgun, and Lucinda barely blinked when they smashed on the floor.

"You'd better start explaining yourself, or I'll fucking redecorate this room with the contents of your head," Ellie demanded.

"Ever since she was old enough to talk, she fawned over him. Manipulated him. It was utterly perverse."

"She was a child! He was her father!" I protested.

"Sofia knew what she was doing," Lucinda explained, hands in the air. "She wanted all this for herself. That's why she had to go."

The room fell silent for a few seconds.

"Did—did you kill her?" Ellie stuttered.

Lucinda's eyes darted to the floor. When she looked back, all her bravado had evaporated. "No."

"Liar!" Ellie barked.

Lucinda blew out a puff of air. "If you must know, she returned some years ago, full of demands and threats to blackmail us."

"She'd never come back here!"

"Well, she did. She ran out of money, you see, like we all knew she would. She tried to intimidate us into giving her a payout so she could abscond."

My throat tightened. "And did you?"

"God, no," she said, dragging some of her matted hair back. "She was dealt with appropriately."

"Where is she?" Ellie asked, voice breaking.

Lucinda paused. "In the mausoleum by the lake."

"Alive?" I mouthed.

She sniggered. "What do you think?"

Ellie had heard enough. She swung the shotgun, slamming the butt into the bridge of Lucinda's nose. She went down like a sack of spuds, landing palms-down in the broken glassware. After a brief moment, she tried to get up, but Ellie already had the muzzle pressed against Lucinda's temple.

"Ellie, no!" I begged, hovering my hand above her forearm. "Not yet."

"She needs to die!" Ellie yelled, jaw clenched. "It's her fault! All of it."

"I need to know about Mum," I said quickly.

Lucinda's eyes lit up through the blood, like a shark scenting an opportunity.

"There it is," she croaked. "The leverage."

Ellie pressed the muzzle harder into her skull. "You don't have leverage. The best you can hope for is a quick death."

"El!" I tightened my grip on her arm. "If we shoot her now, I'll never get answers."

"She said Sofia's dead," Ellie said, tears shimmering in her eyes. "They put her in a fucking tomb, Robyn."

"And what about my mum?" I asked. "You want me to live the rest of my life never knowing what truly happened to her?"

Ellie wavered, chest heaving. "No."

Lucinda gave her a bloodied grin. "Listen to your friend, darling. She's making sense."

"Shut up," I said. "You're going to talk, or I'll let her pull that trigger, and we can find someone else who knows where the bodies are buried."

Lucinda gave a small, bitter laugh. "Trust me, there isn't anyone else. We made sure of it."

She winced as she pushed herself up onto one elbow. Ellie reluctantly loosened her hold, but kept the shotgun trained on her.

"You want to know why your mother risked everything to save Sofia?" Lucinda asked.

I swallowed. "Yes."

"You want to know why your sister ended up in a tomb by the water?"

I flinched at the word sister but nodded.

"And you want to know why a girl who looked just like Sofia Blackthorn ended up working here instead of living the life she always wanted?"

My heart stopped. "Yes."

"Oh?" she droned. "Tough shit. Neither of you has the guts to pull that trigger, so why don't you just leave me in peace before there are two more bodies?"

Ellie raised her shotgun again, intent in her eyes, but I pushed the barrel down with my hand. I stepped around the bar and held out my hand, and Lucinda reluctantly accepted it, allowing me to get her back onto her feet. My palm was coated in a putrid concoction of Blackthorn blood, so I wiped it on a clean patch on her shoulder before returning to the other side of the bar and sliding the bottle of gin over to her.

"I poisoned Lucas," I admitted.

Her jaw fell. "You did what?"

I cocked my head at Ellie. "She drowned Penelope."

Lucinda swivelled her head to Ellie, closing her fist.

"Don't forget Martha," Ellie added.

"Oh yeah!" I said with mock surprise. "Thanks for reminding me."

Lucinda bit down so hard I thought her teeth were going to shatter. "I'm going to kill you! Both of you!" she screeched.

"Not today," I uttered, nudging Ellie's shoulder as I walked away. "Pull the fucking trigger. I was wrong—she isn't going to talk."

"With pleasure," Ellie said, bringing the sight to her eye.

"Wait!" Lucinda pleaded, hands raised in surrender. "I'll tell you everything! Just let me live!"

I swivelled my head. "Everything?"

"Everything! I won't leave out a single detail!"

I chuckled, running my tongue over my top teeth. "You had your chance."

"Jada had you and Sofia right here in the library."

I narrowed my eyes and returned to the bar. "Mr Blackthorn took Sofia for himself, didn't he?"

The library door creaked open.

Before any of us could react, Mr Blackthorn staggered into the room, one hand clutched to a spreading red stain below his left shoulder. In his other hand, he held an old service revolver, pointed directly at his wife.

"Lucinda," he rasped.

She turned towards him like a puppet on strings, all the bluster draining away, leaving only pure terror in its place.

"Richie?" she gulped.

The gunshot cracked through the library, shattering the silence. Lucinda jerked back, eyes wide, as fresh blood bloomed across the old on the front of her dress. She fell onto the ground a second later as Mr Blackthorn took a single step into the room, gun now trained on Ellie.

"Lose the shotgun," he snarled. "We need to have a discussion."

40

THE TRUTH

ROBYN

Ellie didn't drop the shotgun at first. My ears were still ringing from the gunshot, my brain playing catch-up with what had just happened. Lucinda was splayed across the carpet in front of the fireplace, eyes wide and glassy, the front of her dress blossoming with fresh red. The smell of ignited gunpowder hung in the air, hot and metallic, fighting with the stench of spilt gin and blood.

"Now!" Mr Blackthorn roared, coughing after it.

The pistol was aimed straight at Ellie's chest. His hand was shaking, but not enough to comfort either of us. Blood seeped between his fingers where he clutched his shoulder, soaking through his shirt in a dark, expanding patch.

"It's fine," I uttered to Ellie, trying to keep my voice steady. "Just do it."

She swallowed hard and let the shotgun slip from her grip. It landed on the rug with a heavy thud.

"Kick it over here," he ordered.

She nudged it towards him with the toe of her shoe. He didn't look away from us as he shuffled forward, wincing, and hooked the barrel with his foot, sending it sliding behind him near the door. The look in his eyes was ferocious, but there was something chillingly lucid behind them, like a predator that'd been wounded but had decided he wasn't finished.

"Hands," he instructed.

I slowly lifted mine to shoulder height. Ellie mirrored me, tears still glistening under her lashes.

He drew in a ragged breath. "Now, both of you, over there," he said, jerking the gun towards the pair of armchairs by the fire. "Sit."

It was automatic, and my legs carried me before my brain had time to object. Ellie stumbled beside me, nearly tripping over Lucinda's outstretched arm. We took our seats like we'd been summoned for afternoon tea, and the absurdity of that thought made bile creep up my throat.

Mr Blackthorn stayed behind us and returned to the door for a long moment, pressing his shoulder to the wood like he needed it to stay upright. Sweat beaded on his forehead, plastering strands of hair to his skin. He looked older and smaller than I'd ever seen him, yet somehow, he still managed to fill the room with his commanding presence.

"We can take him," Ellie whispered to me. "He's wounded."

Uneven footsteps clacked behind us. "I wouldn't advise that."

Her mouth snapped shut.

He carefully hauled himself towards the bar and propped himself up on it, swiping the broken glass away with his feet. His aim never strayed from us, though his arm dipped slightly as his wound complained. He glanced down at the smear of blood and glass where Lucinda had stood earlier, then at her form on the floor.

"Oh, Lucinda," he droned. "You never knew the way to my heart, did you?"

No one dared to reply. The fact that he was cracking jokes turned the contents of my stomach to concrete.

He reached underneath the bar to grab a bottle of single malt with his free hand, grimacing as the motion tugged his shoulder. The first swig was taken by mouth, but the next he dashed directly into his wound, slamming the bottle down so hard afterwards I thought it might smash. He let out an agonising groan, inhaling deeply through his nose as the alcohol burned into the opening.

I sat forward a fraction. "Why don't I call you an ambulance, Mr Blackthorn?"

"Nice try," he grunted, taking another swill.

"You're going to bleed out."

"Well, let's hope I don't," he replied. "We've got a lot to cover."

His eyes flickered to Lucinda again. For a split second, something that resembled grief brushed his face, but it had vanished after the next swig.

"She always overreacted, you know?" he announced, still peering down at her. "I always told her it would be her downfall."

"You just shot your own wife," Ellie muttered, stunned.

He shrugged, as much as his injury would allow. "She tried to kill me. What did she expect? Flowers?"

"She tried to stop you." The words left my mouth before I could catch them. "From locking me downstairs. From replacing Sofia with me."

"Did she now?" He stared at me. "Because from where I'm standing, she didn't change a damned thing."

I turned back to the fire, fixating on the crackle of the logs. "She told us everything."

"Not everything," he corrected, walking around the bar to lean against it.

"What are you going to do to us?" I asked.

He didn't answer straight away. Instead, he bent with a pained grunt, picked up the letter opener from the floor, and tossed it into the bin like it offended him.

"You two have caused an awful lot of trouble," he said finally. "Breaking into things. Snooping. Killing my family."

Ellie stiffened. "We didn't—"

"Don't insult me," he cut in. "I heard every word of your confession."

The silence thickened.

"I told Lucinda years ago that our family are an extension of us: our arms and legs. If you cut them off, well, the whole body suffers."

Goosebumps broke out across my arms. "Mr Blackthorn, I—"

"And you've hacked off most of mine," he added.

"Why don't you call the police, then?" I said, heart hammering. "Tell them everything. Tell them how Lucas tried to rape me, and how you tried to do the same. Tell them how you forced a child to grow up in a basement while you abused her. See how far your creepy analogies take you then."

His jaw tightened. "Careful, Robyn."

"You think we're scared of you?" I barked. "We've got nothing left to lose."

He stared at me for a long time, something weighing up behind his eyes. "Stand up."

I stayed glued to the cushion. "Why?"

"So that I can see you properly."

Ellie shot me a warning glance, but I reluctantly pushed myself to my feet. He took me in from head to toe, almost like he'd never really looked at me before, a sickly-sweet smirk slithering across his lips.

"You honestly do look like Sofia," he murmured. "It's uncanny."

I stiffened. "What do you expect? She was my sister."

He snorted, but it quickly developed into a vicious cough. He struggled to keep the gun on me, so I stepped forward, but he adjusted his aim before I got close enough to attempt anything.

"Lucinda had a big mouth," he spluttered.

"Not your wife," I corrected. "Sofia."

His eyes became saucers. "You spoke with her?"

"Her diary," Ellie cut in. "She recorded every vile thing you did to her."

He chuckled as if it were a joke. "I never touched her."

Ellie jumped out of her seat, so Mr Blackthorn immediately unloaded a shot into the fireplace, showering us in embers. She retreated back to my side, lifting her hands in submission.

"Do you honestly want to know what happened to Sofia?" he asked.

Ellie and I nodded in unison.

"Fine," he said. "Let's go for a walk."

He pushed himself off the bar, stumbling a little as his feet tried to remember how to work. The pistol jolted back up towards us, a reminder he was still very much in charge, no matter how much blood he was leaking.

"Move," he grunted, waving the gun towards the door.

We moved as one, Ellie and I staring at the shotgun lying useless near the rug as we were ushered out of the library doors and onto the lawn. It was freezing outside, the wind was howling, and a fine, needling rain beat down, soaking through my hoodie in an instant. Even the peacocks were avoiding the weather, chittering beneath a hawthorn for shelter in a neat huddle. Ellie walked in front, arms rigid by her sides. I stayed beside her, so close that our sleeves brushed and I could feel her trembling through the fabric. Behind us, Mr Blackthorn's footsteps were heavy and uneven, each one accompanied by a light whimper.

"If he stumbles, leg it," Ellie mouthed.

"He'll fucking shoot," I mouthed back.

"Then we take our chances."

He cleared his throat. "I can hear you, you know?"

We both flinched.

"And I've survived worse than this," he added. "Trust me."

"Where are you taking us?" I asked over my shoulder.

"The lake," he grunted.

"Is that where you're going to dump us?" Ellie cut in.

"I haven't decided yet. It depends on how our chat goes."

The rest of the walk felt like we were being marched to the gallows. It was the second time I trekked over to that side of the estate that night, but this time, there would be no stranger there to save my life. My saviour was trudging beside me, sobbing so desperately that she could barely walk in a straight line.

Once we reached the lake, any beauty that it once held was long gone. The wind had battered all the leaves off the trees, leaving only skeletons in its wake, with a few crows spectating from the withered branches. The water was as black as a Blackthorn's soul, reflecting the moonlight so brightly it burned my eyes as he guided us to the pier. He stopped about halfway down, leaning on a post to catch his breath, but ordered us to continue to the end.

"I used to love it down here when I was a young lad," he announced. "Mucking about in the water, climbing the trees."

"What a lovely story," Ellie remarked, as flat as a pancake.

"I didn't have any siblings, so my childhood was pretty lonely. I always resented my parents for that."

"My heart bleeds," I added.

"Your mother used to love it here, too," Mr Blackthorn mused. "I'd often catch Jada out here, peering over the water."

My fist clenched, and Ellie grabbed it.

"Don't you dare say her name," I threatened.

"I really enjoyed her company, but she was a little troublemaker, just like you."

"What did you have over her?"

Mr Blackthorn looked flustered. "What could you possibly mean?"

"There's no way she would've willingly handed her daughter over to you. There must've been something."

"Tell me, what was your childhood like?" he asked, ignoring my question.

"Perfect," I said, stepping a little closer. "Until you."

"I very much doubt that, Robyn," he said. "You struggled—you both did. Living in that squalid little flat in Salford, scarcely able to make ends meet. I gave Sofia a life that you could only dream of."

"We were doing fine until she was crippled."

He dipped his head. "That was an unfortunate accident. Nothing more."

"Sofia did it, trying to get away from *you*," I spat. "It wouldn't have ever happened if you weren't abusing her."

"It wasn't abuse!" he exclaimed. "I *loved* her."

"You don't know the meaning of love," I said, locking my eyes with his. "You're some sick fuck who can't keep his hands to himself."

"Maybe," he said before holding his shoulder in agony. "But I was always kind to your mother."

"You strongarmed her into an agreement to keep quiet and then let us rot in that shoddy flat while you and your family lived the life of Riley," I explained. "How is that kind?"

"I never knew what became of her. She stayed away after Sofia until—"

"She called you and you sent one of your thugs to go and beat her half to death," I interrupted.

"I regret that, I do," he admitted. "But there's nothing I won't do to protect my family and our interests. Surely you're aware of that by now."

I wasn't sure who was going to keel over first: Mr Blackthorn succumbing to his wound, or me from a bullshit overdose. I rolled my eyes and turned on my heel, facing out to the water, not giving a toss whether he pulled the trigger or not. He was going to do it anyway.

"What are you doing?" he demanded. "I haven't finished speaking yet!"

"I'm done listening to your pathetic ramblings, so do what you've got to do."

He sniggered. "I was there when you were born, you know."

I spun back around. "What?"

"Actually, I was one of the first to hold you."

"Bollocks," I dismissed.

"Sofia, too."

I stood in quiet contemplation to steady myself.

"If you want me to end it, fine, but don't you want to know what happened?" he asked.

"Okay," I said, wrapping my arms around my chest. "Enlighten me."

41

THE SCREAMING

RICHARD – BEFORE

Jada's sporadic screams carried across the estate like a hacksaw biting into wet timber. Despite my best efforts to avoid the gory part, I could still hear them all the way up in my study, even with her confined to the library. Another particularly agonising shriek filled the air, so I strode over to my door to shut out the ungodly racket, checking my pocket watch as I did. By my estimation, she had been in labour for almost twelve hours.

The poor thing.

It was a particularly thrilling evening for me because there hadn't been a child born on the Blackthorn estate for generations. Penelope was delivered at Salford Royal Hospital, a last-minute decision made out of necessity rather than choice. In fact, she almost took her first breath out in the car park because we had left it so close to the bone. We were a little more prepared when Lucas was due. Given the sheer bedlam that the birth of our first child brought, Lucinda insisted on going private, surrounded by blasted machines and a team of highly paid doctors by her side. Nevertheless, there was something truly magical about knowing it was happening just downstairs. It was exhilarating.

I always wanted a big family, so once I had completed my stint in the Navy, I set about starting one. I married relatively young, meeting Lucinda through a mutual acquaintance and tying the knot less than a year later. She seemed like an appropriate match: rather aspirational, but easy to control when needed. If it were up to me, each and every room in our home would have had a young Blackthorn bedding down at night, but my darling wife disagreed. She was adamant that two was enough and refused to entertain the idea of any more.

My pipe began to taste bitter, so I set it down with the intention of replacing it with a celebratory glass of scotch instead. I had barely brought it to my lips when there was a polite tap at the study door.

"Enter," I shouted.

Dr Brian Finnegan walked in, an old Navy chum of mine, dressed in blue scrubs and nitrile gloves to match. Brian was the resident sawbones on our shore base and certainly one of the more valuable connections I had made over the years. I had called him when Jada started showing early signs of labour, and he dropped everything to come and help deliver her child. He was good like that.

"How's it going down there, old chap?" I asked. "I've not heard screaming like that since the Falklands."

"It's all over bar the shouting," he announced, wiping his brow with his forearm. "We're just waiting for the afterbirth to—"

"Come on, Doc! Spare me the gritty details, will you?" I interrupted, taking a mouthful. "I haven't had my supper yet!"

"Sorry, Rich." He laughed. "I forgot you had such a weak stomach."

With a grin, I gestured for him to take a seat, and he removed his gloves as I poured him a stiff drink. I slid it across my desk, and he reached over to grab it, taking a sip as he sank into the chair.

"I can't tell you how much I needed that," he groaned, swilling his glass.

"Come on then, lad! Girl or boy?"

"Girl," he announced, sucking his teeth.

"Were there any complications?"

He cleared his throat. "None to report."

"And how is the child getting on? Strong?"

"As an ox," he remarked. "Mother is doing well, too."

"Splendid!" I boomed, clinking his glass.

"Where's Lucinda? She'll be thrilled there's another child on the estate."

"On the contrary, she has made herself intentionally unavailable," I said, leaning in to whisper. "Couldn't abide the noise."

He raised his eyebrows in agreement. "I don't blame her."

I grabbed a box of cigars from my desk drawer and offered them to him. He craned his neck, fingers poised to select one. However, before he could pick one, there was a particularly harrowing cry coming from downstairs, and he immediately dropped his hand.

"I thought you said she was finished?" I pointed out, brow furrowed.

"I did," he said gravely. "I'd better get back down there."

I set my glass down. "I'll join you."

Brian strode out of the room, leaving me lagging a few steps behind. The screams grew much louder once we arrived in the foyer, so we followed them through to the library. Jada was writhing around on her back in front of the fire, legs akimbo, sweating profusely and shrieking in pain. One of our newest hires, Martha, was on the floor beside her, plumping up the patient's pillows and dabbing her forehead with a damp cloth.

One of the other girls from the kitchen was rocking the newborn gently in the corner of the room, so I went over and plucked the babe from her arms. The child was much lighter than I expected and frightfully delicate, like she would break if I held her too tightly. She had caramel skin and a head of thick, black hair, with a heart-shaped birthmark beneath her right cheekbone.

"Tell me, what has Jada called her?" I asked.

"Robyn, I think," the maid replied.

"Pretty," I remarked.

"I think something's wrong, doctor!" Martha cried. "The contractions—I think they're even stronger than before."

"Fuck! It hurts so much!" Jada wailed, neck contorted.

The doctor sprinted over to his bag and grabbed some fresh gloves, then began examining Jada. After a few ums and ahs, he rocked back onto his ankles, face as white as a sheet.

He wiped his brow with his forearm. "Martha's right. She's still getting contractions."

"That's normal, isn't it?" I asked.

"Not this strong."

Jada yelped again, involuntarily kicking her legs so violently that she nearly caught Brian square in the face.

"What's going on?" I asked, handing Robyn back to the maid.

"I don't know, do I?" he barked back. "I told you: I'm not a damned midwife."

"Well, do something, man! She's in pain!"

His eyes flitted over to the chair. "I need my bag."

I glanced at Martha, and she retrieved his bag for him, dropping it by his side. He selected a vial and drew up the contents into a syringe before stabbing it directly into Jada's thigh, pushing the plunger down with his thumb.

"What have you just given her?" I demanded, trying to see the label.

"Morphine," he uttered.

"*Morphine*?" I echoed. "Have you gone mad?"

"It's all I had in the bag!" he explained. "If we had taken her to the hospital like I suggested—"

"Yes, fine, fine, fine," I interrupted.

Jada let out a horrifying howl, followed by another, her face warping into expressions I never thought possible. Yet, a few minutes and a couple of contractions later, she seemed to relax, slumping down onto the bed of blankets, almost groggy.

"Well, that seems to have done the trick," I mused.

"Can I have a word, Rich?" he asked me before flicking his eyes to Martha and the maid. "In private."

I nodded and walked out into the hallway, closing the door behind Brian, who was still holding his bloodied hands away from his clothes. The expression plastered on his face told me everything I needed to know before he even spoke.

"We need to ring an ambulance," he announced. "Now."

I leaned in. "Is that necessary? She seems calmer."

"Yes. She's already lost a hell of a lot of blood, and it's showing no signs of stopping. I can't stitch her up while she's still getting contractions."

"Can't you stop them?"

"No," he grunted. "Not here."

"What's happening to her?"

"It could be any number of things, but I don't have the expertise or the equipment to find out why."

I grunted. "Is there a chance she won't survive?"

He tipped his head, so I took a few seconds to ponder my response. If the worst happened and Jada died in labour, we'd be obliged to take the child in. I'd get what I wanted: another Blackthorn, and Lucinda wouldn't be able to say a damned thing about it.

"Make her comfortable," I answered after a while.

"Rich, she needs expert medical attention. You can't expect me to—"

"Just make her comfortable," I repeated. "Let nature take its course."

His eyes flitted back to the library. "What about her daughter?"

"She'll be well looked after here on the estate."

His jaw slackened. "Richie, old pal, I'm not sure about this."

"Please!" I dismissed. "You've been involved in your fair share of morally grey dealings on this estate. Don't tell me you've suddenly sprouted a conscience."

"Yes, but she's—"

"You'll be compensated," I cut in. "Handsomely."

He considered my offer before shoving the library door open with his shoulder and walking back inside. To our surprise, Martha was between Jada's knees, holding out her hands as though she were poised to catch something.

"Doctor!" she exclaimed. "There's another one!"

"What?" I gasped.

Martha scrambled aside, and the doctor took her place, his eyes widening.

"Why didn't you tell me she was having twins?" he barked.

"I didn't bloody know, that's why!" I shouted.

Jada was almost half-asleep at this point, only snapping out of it when her body convulsed against her will. That happened maybe six or seven more times until she dialled up a few notches. She gritted her teeth, yanked her head back and roared, every muscle in her body tensing. She released to take a breath and then repeated, letting out a thunderous bellow. Brian's eyes lit up as Jada's cries of agony turned to whimpers, and he emerged from her legs a beat later, inexplicably holding another baby girl.

"It's a miracle!" Martha proclaimed, running over with a fresh towel to take the baby.

Without a word, the doctor started rifling through his bag, producing a small pair of shears and some kind of plastic peg.

"Hold her still," he instructed Martha, trying to clamp the cord and cut it.

"I'd like to do the honours, if it's all the same to you," I interjected.

He turned to me, panting. "She isn't breathing."

I threw my hands up. "Well! Do something, damn it!" I ordered.

He eventually managed to sever the cord, then rushed out of the room, bursting into the kitchen with Martha and me in tow. He laid the child down on the table, pressing on her tiny chest with both thumbs, pausing every ten seconds or so to force air into her mouth. I observed this for at least a whole minute before I decided I didn't want to see what happened next. With a heavy sigh, I made for the exit to leave the kitchen, but the sound of the baby finally crying behind me rooted me to the spot.

"She's breathing, Mr Blackthorn!" Martha exclaimed.

I turned around, and Martha was already wrapping the baby back up in the towels before she was handed over to me. She was the spitting image of her sister: caramel skin and a head of jet-black hair, but no birthmark. For a fleeting moment, she opened her eyes and stopped crying, her lips almost curling into a smile.

"She's... perfect," I mumbled.

"I'll let Jada know!" Martha said dutifully before rushing to the door, but I placed one hand on her shoulder to stop her.

"Is something the matter, Mr Blackthorn?" she asked.

"Take her upstairs to one of the guest rooms," I uttered without taking my eyes off the babe-in-arms. "Don't come out until I get you."

Her forehead tightened. "Okay, Mr Blackthorn," she said, taking the child from me.

"Richard? What the devil are you doing?" Brian asked.

"It's a shame, isn't it?" I asked, nodding in the direction of the library.

"What is?" he asked.

"Two sisters, and only one survived."

Brian's face dropped. "I—"

"Not a word when we go back in there," I warned. "She's been through enough."

He gave me a shallow nod, and we made our way back inside. Jada was sitting up in her nest of blankets at this point, gently rocking Robyn with one eye closed. She looked at me in anticipation, so I shook my head gravely, and she immediately began blubbering.

"I'm so sorry, dear Jada," I said, squatting down to grip her forearm. "We did everything we could."

She held Robyn tight, smiling through the tears at her. "Where is she?"

"With Martha," I whispered.

She lifted up slightly. "I need to see her."

"No," I said, holding Jada back. "You need to rest. Let us take care of her."

She slumped back down, her face cracking in grief.

"Did you have a name in mind?"

"Sofia," she uttered.

"Sofia?" I smiled. "That's beautiful."

42

THE PIER

ROBYN

No one uttered a word for a long time after Mr Blackthorn had finished talking.

The wind howled across the lake, whipping my hair into my face, stinging my cheeks with icy rain. The boards of the pier beneath our feet creaked and groaned like they were sick of holding us. Somewhere in the trees, a bird shrieked once, then fell silent. His skin was almost translucent at this point, either because of the perilous cold or the blood he'd lost. The pistol was dangling by his side, loose, but not loose enough.

"So," he groaned. "Now you know."

It hit me all at once. Everything.

The library. Mum screaming. The second baby dragged out of her. Him telling the doctor to "make her comfortable" instead of calling an ambulance. The indignity of it. The lie: two sisters, and only one survived. Except we both had, we all did, and that's what angered me the most.

"You piece of shit!" I screamed.

In a sudden burst of rage, I tore down the boards at full tilt. He scarcely had the energy left to raise the pistol in the air as I ran over, but he managed it just in the nick of time, pressing it into my ribs. I pushed my weight against the barrel, daring him to press the trigger. He flicked his eyes over to Ellie, and she came over to drag me back towards the end of the pier.

"You just took her!" I yelled, fighting Ellie's grip. "You stole Sofia from Mum and told her she was dead!"

He didn't look at me. He watched the water instead, eyes tracking the ripples without a flicker of remorse.

"I corrected a mistake," he said eventually. "I gave Sofia a life she never would've had otherwise."

"Yeah, a life of abuse in a fucking basement!" Ellie snapped.

"I made mistakes too, but I gave her so much more in exchange." He shrugged with his good shoulder. "More than most people with her start could ever dream of."

Rain hammered the lake, making it shimmer like a sheet of broken glass. My head buzzed, trying to cram his entire confession into some sort of order. Ellie decided to let me go once we were back beside the water, keeping one hand hovering above my forearm in case I tried charging him again.

"Did Mum find out?" I barked.

"Yes," he replied before coughing violently. "When young Sofia happened across the main house."

"Bullshit!" I cried. "She wouldn't have allowed her to spend one more second on the estate."

"Oh, Robyn," he chuckled hoarsely. "Jada was many things, but she wasn't stupid. I gave her a choice."

My eyes narrowed. "What choice?"

"She could stay here, continue her duties and watch her daughter grow up. Or she could tell Sofia the truth and watch me slit her daughter's throat in front of her."

"It wasn't much of a choice, was it?"

"No, but she did the right thing. She stayed, kept her mouth shut, and put her own daughter's life over the truth," he explained. "To be honest, I admire her for that."

By condemning Sofia to that revolting family, Mum thought she was saving her, but what she didn't know was that the truth would ruin us all, regardless. All those agonising years of keeping me and Sofia in the dark ended in the exact way that she'd sacrificed so much to avoid. Utter devastation for everyone involved.

"You're fucking disgusting," I hissed.

He finally turned his head towards me, his face carved out of stone.

"You've made me out to be a villain in your head," he said. "That's understandable. People like you need villains. Whatever helps you sleep at night."

"You *are* a villain," Ellie insisted.

"No," he corrected calmly. "I am a man who does what's necessary to protect what's his. My land. My name. My legacy."

"Your legacy is dead," I shot back. "Lucas. Penelope. Lucinda. Sofia. They're all gone."

He looked faintly amused at that. "You're right. I failed, didn't I?"

"Yes," I said. "And it was all your doing."

He shifted his weight, wincing, and for a second, I thought he was going to slump straight down onto the pier. He caught himself, knuckles whitening around the rotting post as he stared beyond us, eyes locked on the mausoleum over the water.

"I think it's your turn to explain something," he grunted, straining his shoulders.

"What?"

"What did you hope to achieve by coming here?" he asked. "Avenge your mother?"

I took a while to answer. "Yes."

He smiled at that. It made my skin crawl.

"Then you, Robyn, are no better than me," he explained. "Perhaps I selected the wrong infant that night."

He nearly chose me for the basement. He nearly gave Sofia the tower-block life. He played God with us like we were interchangeable parts, and he wasn't bearing a scrap of shame for any of it.

"Why *did* you pick her?" I asked.

He snorted, bashing the middle of his chest with the heel of his hand. "Honestly?"

I jerked my head.

"Your birthmark," he announced. "You were defective."

I tried to pounce on him again, but Ellie saw it coming from a mile off and grabbed me with both hands. She loosened her grip slightly when Mr Blackthorn slid down the post he was leaning on and spread his legs across the pier, eyes still fixed on the vault over the lake. I glanced at her over my shoulder, but she shook her head, signalling me to wait.

"You aren't looking so good, Mr Blackthorn," Ellie remarked. "Are you sure you don't want that ambulance?"

"Quiet," he whispered.

"Do you not feel guilty for any of it?" I asked.

"Not one bit," he said, voice barely audible.

"You're about to meet your maker, and you're telling us you regret nothing?"

A peculiar smile cracked his scowl. "I did remarkable things in my life—amazing things: the foundation, the business, my family's success…"

"No one will remember," I muttered. "In fact, the only thing people will remember about the late, great Richard Blackthorn is that he was a vile, loathsome rapist. I'll make sure of it."

My words seemed to hurt more than his wound. He tried to get back onto his feet and failed. "History is written by the victors."

"I know it is," I mumbled.

Lightning flickered somewhere behind the clouds as I took a single step towards him. When he didn't react, I took another. The third let out a jarring creak, and he swivelled his head, trying to lift his arm to keep the pistol on us, but it was too heavy for his weakened state, and it didn't leave the pier. Ellie was the first to arrive at his side, relieving him of the revolver and aiming it directly at his face. He didn't put up a fight. He was using too much energy just to keep his eyes propped open.

"It looks like it's time, Mr Blackthorn," I announced.

"Quite." He chuckled softly. "I think I will take that ambulance, after all."

I snorted. "You're kidding, right?"

He allowed his head to drop back. "It was worth a try."

"Babe, it wasn't," Ellie insisted.

"It is a shame, though," he croaked, struggling to get the words out. "You'll never find out who your father was."

"No," I uttered, my skin prickling. "You mean—"

He donned a sickening smirk, moistening his lips as he parted them to answer.

Bang.

He plunged into the water, already drifting to the centre of the lake, eyes as wide as saucers, with a fresh hole in his forehead that was barely bleeding. With my jaw on the floor, I turned to Ellie, who had a thousand-yard stare in her eyes, smoke spiralling from the revolver with the sights still trained on him. It should've been me to pull the trigger, not her. She had no right to take my question away.

"Ellie?" I shouted. "Why the fuck did you—"

"You didn't want to know," she interrupted. "Trust me."

Part of me wanted to drag his body out of the water and shake the answer out of him. The other part had heard enough of his version of the facts to last a lifetime. Deep down, I knew the truth already, but I just didn't want to face it. On balance, it was the kindest thing that Ellie had ever done in her life by stopping him from confirming it. Just hearing the words leave his mouth would've been immeasurably more devastating than anything he'd done before.

I squatted down, squeezing some of the rainwater out of my hair. "What now?"

"Police, I suppose," she said. "I've got one last thing to do first."

"What?" I asked, already knowing the answer.

She turned her gaze to the mausoleum, so I pushed myself onto my feet and grabbed her hand, then we slowly began making our way around to it. I kept my eyes glued to Mr Blackthorn in the water, half-expecting him to rattle back into life to stop us, but he didn't. He looked so small in the water, so frail, like a bitter old man who had lost everything he'd ever worked for.

The Blackthorn tomb was even more domineering up close. It was built from stone, about five metres wide and deep, with the Blackthorn name engraved above the doorway in ornate lettering. The door itself was carved out of oak, not too dissimilar to the one in Sofia's old room, but there was a clunky, rusted padlock barring us from entry. Without a word, Ellie started searching for something in the undergrowth and produced a rock, smashing it into the padlock as hard as she could. It eventually broke to pieces, and she pushed the door open.

There was a grand, marble box in the centre of the room, illuminated by a thin column of moonlight made colourful by the stained-glass window at the rear. There was a granite bench on either side, but they weren't empty. There was a thin sleeping bag on the left, creased up beside a few essentials as if Mr Blackthorn had camped there. On the right, there was a makeshift kitchen of sorts: a small gas stove, some empty tins, and scattered wrappers from protein bars and snacks. I stepped over to the crypt in the centre and cleaned the gold plaque with my sleeve so I could read the inscription.

Ethelbert Blackthorn.

My brow wrinkled. "El, I don't think this is—"

"Ellie?" a voice came from behind us.

We both turned around in unison, and there she was: red hair, caramel skin, and emerald-green eyes.

Ellie broke. "Sofia?" she gasped.

They met in the middle of the tomb, frantically wrapping their arms around each other and crying into each other's necks. I stood there like a third wheel, tearing up myself but unable to hide the grin spanning from ear to ear. Sofia noticed me standing there after a few seconds, pulled away from Ellie and approached me, hugging herself for warmth.

"You must be Robyn," she announced.

I gave a small wave. "Guilty as charged."

She ploughed into me, squeezing me tightly before grabbing me by the cheeks to plant a kiss on my forehead. Up close, though, she was a wreck: too thin, lips cracked, hair tangled and greasy, but her eyes were still sharp. It was almost like I could see every single day of what she'd endured in them.

Every abuse. Every indignity. Every trauma.

But she survived them all. We both did.

EIGHT WEEKS LATER

EPILOGUE

ROBYN

If there was one thing you could count on Manchester for, it was the weather. It was absolutely bucketing it down outside, the rain beating off the pavement so violently that I was left wondering if I'd need a dinghy to get back to the car after I'd finished my session at the tattoo parlour. *Needles To Say* was one of those places with a waiting list longer than my arm, specialising in something they called body modification. I wasn't too sure what that entailed when I booked it, but after taking one look at Lee, who was doing the work I requested, it quickly became apparent.

There was barely an inch on his skin that wasn't covered in some kind of art. His left arm was coloured in black like he'd dipped it in a vat of ink, and his right was made up of intricate illustrations that he'd done himself out of boredom between clients. That was impressive enough, but it was his nose and forehead I was fixated on. He had a gaping hole above each nostril, inlaid with a neon-green plastic ring, and a pair of prosthetic horns sitting just underneath his skin. I'd been in the chair for over an hour, and I'd spent that time speculating about how he would blow his nose if he ever caught a cold.

Behind me, the machine kept droning: a high-pitched buzzing noise that was somewhere between a dentist's drill and a pissed-off wasp. The room stank to high heaven of antiseptic and hot skin, apart from the odd whiff of black coffee keeping the artists awake. A radio blared in the corner, heavy metal that was more anger than melody, only just audible over the sound of my jaw clenching when Lee started going over a sensitive patch of skin.

"Ow, fuck!" I exclaimed. "I thought you said this wouldn't hurt?"

Lee chuckled. "I didn't say any such thing. In fact, I distinctly remember telling you in the last session to spread it over a few weeks *because* it would hurt so much."

I squeezed my fist together. "Are you nearly done?"

"Almost. There's just this stubborn bit left near your wrist," he said before leaning back. "Do you want to take a break?"

I peered down at my battered skin, nodding my head but mouthing, "No."

To take my mind off it, I turned my head and concentrated on my other wrist, where the bracelet that Ellie had once given me sat, inscription down, glinting in the lights.

They didn't stick around for long after we'd rescued Sofia from captivity. We all sat and listened to Sofia's story about how she returned to the estate in desperation after robbing Baker and Roberts, planning to clear out Mr Blackthorn's safe, but she was discovered. She'd been confined to that mausoleum ever since, the only building without access to the network of tunnels. She didn't offer any more detail than that, and we didn't press her. I knew all too well what a long, unearned stint in captivity does to someone.

After that, we all ran up to the house so they could empty the safe. Ellie stuffed her rucksack with as much of Lucinda's jewellery as would fit into it, and they said their goodbyes before disappearing into the night. Even though they all but begged me to go with them, I was done having my life decided for me, so I chose to stay. Besides, I'd miss Manchester too much, and it still felt like I had unfinished business there. They promised they'd stay in touch.

The buzzing stopped, and cool gel was slicked over my arm. The song faded out on the radio, and a presenter took its place, harping on about a pile-up on the M60 like it was the worst thing to ever happen to Manchester.

"Go on then," Lee said, batting my shoulder to get my attention. "How much do you hate me right now? On a scale of one to ten?"

"Twelve," I grunted, inspecting his handiwork.

He laughed. "Do you fancy a brew?"

"No, ta. My friend should be back any minute."

"No worries," he said, cracking his back after standing up. "Keep your mucky mitts off your arm until I have a bandage on it."

"I'm not promising anything," I remarked as he headed for the kettle, turning down the radio when the news came on.

"Breaking news from Manchester, the inquest into the deaths at the Blackthorn estate concluded today that businessman and philanthropist Richard Blackthorn was responsible for what police have described as 'a sustained campaign of abuse and controlling behaviour' spanning over several decades," the presenter announced.

"Hey, can you turn that up?" I shouted.

Lee gave me a thumbs up and turned the dial.

"The coroner found that Mr Blackthorn unlawfully killed his two children and wife, as well as two members of staff, before taking his own life in the grounds of the family home eight weeks ago," the presenter continued. "The only surviving member of the family was Sofia Blackthorn, who had been confined to a tomb for years before she made her daring escape."

My throat constricted when I saw one of the other artists approach Lee and whisper something in his ear while pointing to me. After a few words were exchanged, they both started tapping away on their phones, flicking their eyes between me and their screens.

"Further investigations are ongoing into historic offences linked to the Sofia Blackthorn Foundation, which has been suspended pending a full review of its finances and safeguarding practices," the newsreader said before a jingle played, and the weather started.

Lee reached up and switched the station before he came back over, brew in hand, taking a sip before he perched on the stool again.

"How's your arm feeling?" he asked.

"It still stings."

He started wrapping it in clear plastic before he got about halfway up my forearm and stopped.

"That thing on the radio, you weren't involved in that, were you?"

I gave a shallow nod, and he carried on mummifying my arm.

"Shit," he mumbled. "That Blackthorn bloke sounds like a right nutjob."

"Honestly, you don't know the half of it."

The bell over the door chimed, and air rushed in, carrying the smell of cold rain and hot coffee. Elena pushed her way inside, muttering apologies as she hobbled through the other technicians to my chair at the back. Her left arm was in a crutch, and her right was carrying a cardboard tray with two cups slotted into it.

"So sorry, but I think I messed up your order," she announced, setting a cup beside me.

"As long as it's hot and vaguely caffeinated, it'll do." I giggled, taking a sip.

"I do not know about that, but it is green."

"Jesus Christ!" I exclaimed, almost spraying Lee in the process. "What the hell even is that?"

"Looks like a matcha latte to me," he pointed out.

"Take it," I instructed, holding it out to him. "Take it very far away from me, please."

Lee took a sip himself, looking rather contented.

"By the way, I had a phone call from the police earlier," Elena chimed in.

I smiled. "Have they dropped the charges?"

"Yes! I am finally free, and I have you to thank for that," she said, putting her hand on my good arm. "If you hadn't exposed Mr Blackthorn then—"

"Don't mention it," I cut in, placing my hand on top of hers and squeezing.

Elena wasn't aware that the whole reason she got into hot water with the law in the first place was that I planted the evidence, but she didn't need to know. As far as I was concerned, it was a white lie designed only to get her off the estate before the bodies started piling up. That being said, it was a little difficult to keep the secret when she was so obviously grateful for my intervention.

"I thought you were getting a tattoo?" Elena asked, pointing at my wrapped arm. "This doesn't look like anything."

"I wasn't getting a new tattoo." I chortled. "I was having them removed."

She looked puzzled. "Why?"

"Well, Mum always hated them, and after everything that's happened, I hated them too."

Elena shrugged like I was talking nonsense. I more or less agreed with her.

"Besides," I continued, "I'm sick of hiding them in case there's a camera about."

"All done," Lee announced, taping the last piece of plastic down. "Keep it clean and don't even think about taking the bandage off."

It was already itching. "Wouldn't dream of it."

"Hit me up when it's healed. You might need another session."

My arm started smarting again. "Can't wait."

"Pay at the counter on your way out, will you? I don't fancy chasing you down the street in the rain."

I chuckled. "Will do."

I stood up slowly, cradling my forearm. The skin was an angry pink, blotched and raw, but the meaningless tattoos that once sat there were now ghosts, faded and pale. I headed over to the counter to pay my bill, then we rushed outside, jackets pulled over our heads. We'd left Mr Blackthorn's old Jaguar parked on the side street, and a bright-yellow ticket had been placed on the windscreen, so I whipped it off before hopping in the passenger seat. Elena got behind the wheel and fastened her seatbelt before I did the same.

"Where are we going?" she asked.

"Take us home."

* * *

The rain had subsided by the time we arrived back at the Blackthorn estate, the sun threatening to come out behind the grey clouds. I sprang out of the car to open the gates, and Elena drove through, waiting on the other side for me to get back in. Instead, I walked over to her window and beckoned her to roll it down.

"I think I'll walk," I said. "I just need to make a stop first."

She smiled. "Mum?"

I nodded and patted the roof of the car, and she began trundling down the driveway.

Although I had hardly seen him lift a finger, the grounds had been left to go to ruin since Harris's untimely passing. The grass leading up to the house was patchy with long tyre marks from the police and forensics vans that had visited daily for weeks on end. Remnants of police tape were still tied around trees, flapping about in the wind. I walked over to the boating lake and made my way around to the mausoleum, where the Blackthorn name had been chiselled off above the door, and Jada was engraved in its place.

Inside, it looked entirely different from when it had been Ethelbert's final resting place. It turned out that he wasn't even buried there at all, and it was just some obnoxious monument that he commissioned years before his death because he was petrified that he'd be forgotten. Mum wasn't buried there either, but she deserved that place more than him, and I wanted somewhere to go when I needed to talk to her. Instead of the drab, marble interior, it was filled from floor to ceiling with flowers, pictures and keepsakes, and the gold plate on his crypt had been changed to my mother's name instead: Jada Fletcher.

If Mum could see me now, she'd probably have a fit, but I would do anything, and I do mean *anything,* to bring her back, even if it were only for one day. I'd push her chair to the local supermarket without complaint, happily make her a brew every ten minutes, and even endure an entire season of *Taggart* just to see her smile one last time. Looking back, those things weren't a burden at all, but a privilege, and it was one of my biggest regrets that I didn't savour every moment. She sacrificed so much for me and never asked for anything back. That was her all over: forever putting others before herself.

Sofia owed her everything, too. Our mum gave her legs so her daughters could fly, and the only way we could repay her for that was to live our lives like she always wanted: out from under the thumb of tyrannical men and free from danger. Mum's locket sat just under my collarbones, and I'd never take it off. It served as a constant reminder of what she did for her daughters, how love always triumphs over evil, but also the cost that comes with it.

"Hi, Mum," I casually announced as if I'd returned for dinner.

She didn't reply, but I still waited for it.

"So, I got my tattoos removed," I said, hopping onto the crypt. "What do you think?"

I paused for a heartbeat.

"I prefer it too," I said before lowering my voice. "It hurt like a bastard, though."

I noticed some flowers had fallen since I last visited, so I jumped back down to fix them.

"Sofia's doing well," I said over my shoulder. "Last I heard, she and Ellie were making their way into Belgium."

I stood up and polished her new plaque with my sleeve before resting both of my hands on the crypt.

"I know I've said it before, but I just want to thank you again for everything you did," I said, kissing my fingers and pressing them onto the plaque. "I love you, Mum."

My cute moment was interrupted by a vehicle beeping outside, so I rushed out of the mausoleum and shut the door behind me. From the lake, I could just see a van parked up by the gates, so I jogged over, breathless by the time I got halfway there. A courier was standing by the gates waving a box over it, and I walked the rest of the way, desperate not to look perilously unfit when I arrived.

"Fuck me, we really need a new gamekeeper," I muttered to myself.

"Are you Sofia Blackthorn?" he asked.

My blood turned to ice.

"Yes. That's me," I announced.

"Parcel for you."

I received the box over the gate and then scribbled my new signature on his tablet before he got in his van and drove off. I ripped open the box on the way back to the house, and there was a selection box of Belgian chocolate inside, with a postcard tucked under the bow.

"Wish you were here, bitch," I read out loud, sniggering.

I opened the box, but one of the truffles was missing. Instead, there was a thin, gold band, slightly misshapen, with a giant diamond attached to it and a tiny ruby embedded inside.

It was Sofia's ring.

Sorry, *my* ring.

THE END

Dear thrill seeker!

Thank you so much for choosing to read *The Silent Daughter*. I genuinely hope the twists and turns kept you up way past your bedtime.

As a self-published author still finding his feet, every single reader matters to me more than I can say. If you enjoyed the story, there are a few small (but mighty!) ways you can help support my writing—none of which cost a penny:

- **Download a <u>free</u> psychological thriller** from my website: philipanthonysmith.com/free-book/

- **Leave a quick review on Amazon.** Even a few words mean more than you could know!

- **Follow me on Amazon** to stay in the loop for future releases.

You can get in touch with me directly by sending me an email to twist@philipanthonysmith.com. I personally reply to every message and I love having a chinwag with a fellow thriller enthusiast!

From the bottom of my heart, thank you for reading. Your support means the world to me and my little family cheering me on from the sidelines!

Until we meet again,

Phil

ACKNOWLEDGEMENTS

Ten books in and somehow you still let me hang around—thank you for that. Truly, your support is the fuel that keeps me writing.

And to the Bookstagram legends who devoured early copies and fired off posts like pros: you helped send this book into the world with a flourish. I adore your spirit, your honesty, and your hustle.

Alexandra N - @maxi.mumbooks
Alyssa A - @Alyreadit
Amy B - @the_blonde_chapter
April N - @chapter30_april
Brittany H - @booked.by.brittany
Brooke W - @brookesbooks88
Carrie B - @booksbookscoffeecoffee
Chelsey P - @book_dragon_bel
Claire R - @readwithgzxklair
Denise L – Domestic Thriller Readers Bookclub
Emma M - @emma_bookaholic
Gemma I - @gemsbookloverlife
Haley C - @bookish.thrills
Holly - @_fortheloveofbooksx
Karen B - @Lovetoread2023
Kim M - @kimmymcb_readwithme
Lauren S - @drlaurensbookreviews
Lou W - @Lollysbooknook
Michelle M - @bookedbymiddleton
Sally S - @sally_stone63

Sam T - @sams.book.space
Vanessa K - @vdkeck_busy_reading
Zoe E - @northyorkshirereader
Jo W

Copyright © Philip Anthony Smith, 2025.

Philip Anthony Smith has asserted his right to be identified as the author of this work.

All rights reserved. No part of this publication may be reproduced, stored in any retrieval system, or transmitted, in any form or by any means, electronic, mechanical, photocopying, recording or otherwise, without the prior written permission from the author.

This book is a work of fiction. Names, characters, businesses, organisations, places and events other than those clearly in the public domain, are either the product of the author's imagination or are used fictitiously. Any resemblance to actual persons, living or dead, events or locales is entirely coincidental.

Printed in Dunstable, United Kingdom